A VINEYARD MORNING

JEAN STONE

KENSINGTON
PUBLISHING CORP.

www.kensingtonbooks.com

KENSINGTON BOOKS are published by

Kensington Publishing Corp.
119 West 40th Street
New York, NY 10018

All Kensington titles, imprints, and distributed lines are available at special quantity discounts for bulk purchases for sales promotion, premiums, fund-raising, educational, or institutional use.

Special book excerpts or customized printings can also be created to fit specific needs. For details, write or phone the office of the Kensington Sales Manager: Kensington Publishing Corp., 119 West 40th Street, New York, NY 10018. Attn. Sales Department. Phone: 1-800-221-2647.

The K logo is a trademark of Kensington Publishing Corp.

ISBN-13: 978-1-4967-2884-5 (ebook)
ISBN-10: 1-4967-2884-X (ebook)

ISBN-13: 978-1-4967-2883-8
ISBN-10: 1-4967-2883-1
First Kensington Trade Paperback Printing: February 2021

10 9 8 7 6 5 4 3 2 1

Printed in the United States of America

To Richard and Marcia Fenn,
my wonderful Vineyard friends
who are off to write the next chapter of their lives.
With big hugs, good wishes, and buckets filled with love.

Acknowledgments

Thanks to the many people, both on island and off, who contributed their expertise that made this book come to life.

Special thanks to Edgartown Police Detective Daycee Moore and Massachusetts State Police Sergeant Jeffrey Stone, for filling in many essential details; to island hairstylist extraordinaire Patti Linn, for introducing me to people and places I otherwise would not have known; to the Trustees of Reservations, for their wonderful properties on the Vineyard and their accessible, abundant information; to my friends at the island bookstores, newspapers, and libraries who are always ready to find answers to my often ludicrous questions; to my fabulous editor, Wendy McCurdy, and my awesome agent, Loretta Fidel, for continuing to keep the faith; and to my Western Massachusetts old friends Matt and Jane Villamaino, for our unexpected discovery on Chappaquiddick that, yes, made it into this story.

And, of course, biggest thanks to the two all-important, off-island tall boys for their patience and support and for continuing to bring so much good stuff to my life.

Books by Jean Stone

A Vineyard Morning
A Vineyard Summer
A Vineyard Christmas
Vineyard Magic
Four Steps to the Altar
Three Times a Charm
Twice Upon a Wedding
Once Upon a Bride
Beach Roses
Trust Fund Babies
Off Season
The Summer House
Tides of the Heart
Birthday Girls
Places by the Sea
Ivy Secrets
First Loves
Sins of Innocence

Books writing as Abby Drake
Good Little Wives
Perfect Little Ladies
The Secrets Sisters Keep

Chapter 1

"The pinkletinks are back!"

Cheers erupted through the West Tisbury Grange Hall as if it were sunset on the beach at Menemsha in summer. It wasn't summer yet, but it was finally spring, as the pinkletinks—the tiny paperclip-sized, toad-like peepers—announced every year with their long-awaited chorus.

The news was happy music to the group in the hall, who had just wrapped up plans for the upcoming season of artisan festivals. The planning, like the pinkletinks, was a sure sign that tourists would soon arrive on Martha's Vineyard.

Annie Sutton leaned against the doorway, savoring the April sunlight that seeped through the cracks of the historic, gray-shingled building. She watched as the organizers collected posters of floor plans and booth assignments while the refreshment committee scooped up remnants of coffee and cookies. Her fellow artists were abuzz, laughing and chattering, as they trickled toward the exits.

"Check out the sunshine."

"We deserve it."

"Yes, we do!"

It had been a blustery winter, though they'd been spared

the nasty nor'easters of the year before. But Annie didn't mind harsh off-season weather; after all, she was a native New Englander. Which she knew was why, in part, she'd picked there and not a tropical island when she'd left Boston to start over.

She glanced at her watch: 4:00 p.m. Time to head out to the cemetery as she'd promised Lucy, who was nowhere in sight.

"*Teenagers*," Annie muttered. She was, however, delighted that the girl had come with her, even though the primary incentive had been the promise of a side trip to a graveyard for Lucy's genealogy project. Despite the fact that Annie was a full-time bestselling mystery author, part-time soap maker, and soon-to-be innkeeper, she loved spending time with Lucy, the fourteen-year-old daughter of John Lyons—the kind, generous, and massively good-looking Edgartown police sergeant whom Annie had been dating for over a year.

"Annie!" Winnie Lathrop cried out in a jolly voice. "Did you hear? The pinkletinks are back!" Winnie was a Wampanoag woman who lived up island in Aquinnah and had taught Annie how to forage for herbs and wildflowers then craft them into boutique soaps to sell at the festivals.

Plunking down her cotton tote bag, Annie stepped into her friend's warm hug. "Earl says they're late this year because it was too damn cold."

Winnie laughed. "Earl Lyons knows everything about this island. I swear he welcomed Thomas Mayhew when he landed on the beach." Earl maintained that Mayhew had brought "the first boatload of tourists" in 1642, thereby creating the Vineyard's first English settlement. A much-beloved property caretaker on Chappaquiddick, Earl also was the father of the massively good-looking police sergeant, and, ergo, Lucy's grandfather. "Speaking of that old crow . . ." Winnie added, "how's the Inn? Will you open on time?"

The Inn was a new venture for Earl and Kevin, Annie's

half-brother. Earl had said they should call it *The Vineyard Inn* because the name was easy to remember, and would make a "perfect hashtag for Instagram." He'd winked when he said the last part, because Annie was well aware that the seventy-five-year-old curmudgeon would not know Instagram from instant coffee. Kevin was forty-three, nine years younger than Annie. He'd come last summer for a visit and wound up staying, working alongside Earl. The venture—(or, "*adventure*," as Kevin called it)—had been their harebrained idea, conceived "out of necessity" (Earl again), because at the time, Annie had little money and nowhere to live. She'd accused the men of being old-fashioned and wanting to rescue a damsel in distress. They'd all had a good laugh over that, because Annie was quite capable of taking care of herself. Though she wasn't always sure of that, their support helped her stay positive.

"I'm trying to be optimistic," she said to Winnie now. "Earl and Kevin insist construction is 'coming along,' but it's pretty hectic. Our first guests arrive Memorial Day weekend, so . . ." She shrugged. She didn't add that they were over budget, out of cash, and short on labor, or that suppliers were slow to deliver to Chappaquiddick, the Vineyard's easternmost arm that was a bit out of the way.

"And the first festival is that weekend," Winnie said.

"Right. Crazy times. But how's your family? How are you?" Annie didn't want to talk about the Inn: its rising problems and onrushing deadline made her stomach hurt. "Have you made lots of fabulous pottery?" Winnie was renowned for her exquisite bowls and mugs, and silver and wampum jewelry. She'd once told Annie that she made jewelry in summer when the natural sunlight helped her shape tiny details; she crafted pottery in winter when the thousand-degree kiln helped her stay warm. Winnie was as practical as she was loving to all people, all creatures, and the earth.

"The clan is well," she replied. "Me included. And I have a healthy stash of wares ready to sell. How about you? Have you had time to cook up more soap?"

Annie sighed. "I started writing a new book, which is always a challenge. But I managed to make a few cases with the help of my assistant, who right now has disappeared." She hoisted her bag back up on one shoulder, grateful it weighed less now that she had passed out samples of her latest soap. She reached in, dug out a bar, and handed it to Winnie.

Winnie held it to her nose, inhaling the fragrance. "Snowdrops. Light. Fresh. Nice work, Annie Sutton."

"Thanks. It was a whim. Lucy was a big help." Annie glanced around the hall again. "Right now, however, I suspect she's looking for another job."

Winnie laughed. "As I recall, her father was off in a million directions when he was a boy. Overall, he turned out okay." Winnie's deep brown eyes—the color of sassafras root, as John had once commented—sparkled with amusement and lit up her copper skin.

Annie smiled and hoped she wasn't blushing. John was a native islander; his family and Winnie's had been friends for generations. "Yes," she said, averting her eyes from Winnie's gaze, "you might say he's okay." She didn't want to explain, even to Winnie, that though she and John had agreed they were "officially dating," Annie wasn't ready to get serious, and John was still reassembling his life after his divorce.

At that moment, Lucy came skittering around the corner, just in time to hear the last bit of their conversation.

"Who's okay?" she asked as she stepped into the conversation.

"Your father," Winnie said.

"Gross." Lucy wrinkled her nose and dropped her iPad and a three-ring binder into Annie's bag. "Can we go now?"

"Where are you off to?" Winnie asked.

"Christiantown," Lucy said. "The burial ground. I'm trying to figure out if I have ancestors there."

"Wampanoags?"

The burial ground was one of the few known resting places for Vineyard Native Americans. But with eyes as pearl-gray as her dad's, and skin tones nearly as fair as the spring day, Lucy hardly looked like she had Wampanoag heritage. And it didn't help that she'd braided her hair into a long, single plait the way that Winnie did, because Lucy's hair was caramel-colored.

"My great-grandparents are buried at the sacred ground on Chappy," Lucy replied, though that was hardly proof, as several Caucasians also had been laid to rest there. "I used the money Annie paid me for helping her with her soaps for a DNA test. Turns out, I'm two-percent Native American. I'm hoping to find my people."

"If they were Chappaquiddick Wampanoags, they won't be up here in Christiantown. Those graves are only from the Aquinnah tribe."

"I know. It's crazy that there was more than one tribe here. But that's how it was even before Mayhew coughed up forty measly pounds and a couple of beaver hats to buy the Vineyard."

"And don't forget that his princely sum included Nantucket and the Elizabeth Islands," Winnie said with a wink.

Annie checked her watch again. Though daylight savings had begun, and the sun didn't set until seven-o'clock-ish, she wanted to get home in time to see Kevin and John, who'd gone fishing somewhere up island and camped out overnight. John had said Kevin needed a break before the final crunch to get the Inn done, and that he needed one to help him brace for summer chaos.

"I read online that there aren't any names on the stones at Christiantown," Lucy was saying. "Except Mary Spencer's.

She's been there since 1847, so who knows if she really was a Wampanoag."

Winnie nodded. "So what's your plan?"

"I'll take pictures of the stones—I read that they're just fieldstones—then I'll look for similarities with the ones on Chappy."

"That sounds great. But tread lightly. There's probably a thick blanket of wet leaves keeping the earth warm. The space was designated for the Christian 'Praying Indians,' but if you ask me, Moshup is the one who protects them in winter." A legendary god-like giant, Moshup had watched over the Wampanoags for centuries, but disappeared the day that the British stepped ashore. Then Winnie patted Lucy's shoulder. "Good luck, dear. And remember that if we don't know our past, we cannot guide our future."

The three of them hugged good-bye and moved toward the door. Then Lucy raced ahead, her braid happily bouncing, her life too new for her to have any angst over deadlines, finances, or the impending onslaught of summer vacationers.

Winnie had been right about Moshup's blanket: a weave of birch and oak leaves in weathered shades of terra-cotta covered the ground. Lucy announced that the site encompassed less than a single acre, was officially the "Christiantown Woods Preserve and Indian Burial Ground," and remained under tribal ownership.

Annie parked the Jeep off the narrow dirt road, grateful that she'd traded in her Lexus for something better suited to the terrain. When she'd first moved to the island, she'd replaced her Jimmy Choos with walking boots from L.L.Bean, and her Ann Taylor suits with flannel shirts. She hoped that eventually her former life would slide so far back in time that she'd no longer feel its sour breath on her neck.

She dropped her phone into her jeans pocket—a ritual she stuck to, especially when exploring off a beaten path, or in this case, off an ancient way.

Once outside, Annie noticed the quiet. It reminded her of when she'd been young, of when her small family had vacationed on the island, and she and her dad had explored the remote Menemsha Hills. They'd hiked alone; her mother had preferred the summer sounds of crashing surf and romping kids at South Beach in Edgartown. Annie's dad, like Annie, preferred silence. She hadn't, however, inherited the trait from him, as the Suttons—Bob and Ellen—had adopted her.

"There's the chapel," Lucy whispered, pointing to a small, ramshackle building. They treaded softly toward it, as if not wanting to disturb shadows of long-dead souls. Lucy unlatched a shuttered window, and they peeked inside.

"Thomas Mayhew Jr. gave this land back to the Wampanoags in the seventeenth century," she said. "But it was only for the ones who converted to Christianity—which is why they called them 'Praying Indians.'" Her tone remained hushed, her eyes wide. She pressed her face against the dusty glass. "This is a replica of the original chapel that burned down; the tribe replaced it in 1829. It only has a few pews and a small altar."

After closing the shutter, she turned and started across the road. "The cemetery is at the top of the hill. No one's allowed up there unless he or she is a tribal member."

Annie followed. "We should have asked Winnie to come with us."

They came to an opening in a split-rail fence. A large boulder sat there. A metal plaque with a moss-green patina was attached; an embossed message identified the spot as the head of the path to the "burying ground."

"Lucy? Are you sure it's okay to go up?" Annie did not like breaking rules, let alone on consecrated land.

"Nobody's around. Besides, I'm two-percent Native American, remember?"

In Annie's previous life, she'd been a third-grade teacher who'd maintained control of her class. But Lucy was fourteen, not nine, and not one of Annie's students. "Okay then, but I'll wait here. I'll check in with Kevin to see if he and your father survived their camping trip."

"Whatever." Lucy tromped up an embankment of dirt stairs that were framed by tree roots; her iPad was fixed in one hand, her three-ring binder in the other. Then she disappeared—again—this time into a stand of tall, newly budding oaks. She clearly was an island kid who knew where she was most of the time, and if she didn't, she wasn't afraid. After all, she hadn't been raised in the city as Annie had.

"This is so cool!" Lucy's voice called down from the hill-top. "Every stone has something on top!"

Annie cupped her mouth. "Like what?"

"A scallop shell. A piece of wampum. A couple have coins."

"Take pictures!"

"I am!"

Annie smiled with appreciation for the girl's enthusiasm. Then she leaned against the boulder and scanned the rustic forest, wondering if the trees were as old as the sacred site. She closed her eyes and listened to the stillness until her mind quieted and her shoulders relaxed, the stressors of her things-to-do list beginning to disintegrate like fine white sand be-neath an outgoing tide. She stood, trance-like, for several minutes until a brisk rustle of leaves warned her she was not alone. Maybe it was someone who had passed that way before.

Yup, it's the dead guys.

Annie's eyes flipped open, her body jerked, she nearly buckled to the ground. Quickly righting herself, she let her gaze skim the area. Of course, there was no one. Except Murphy, her old college pal who'd died nearly two years earlier from a rare, swift-moving cancer, but whose spirit tended to show up when Annie needed sage advice or a good laugh.

"Murphy!" Annie cried, shaking a playful fist up toward the sky. "Stop scaring me!"

Poltergeist-like laughter was swiftly muffled by the ding of Annie's phone. She checked the screen: it was Kevin.

PARTY'S OVER, her brother texted. GET YOUR BUTT BACK TO CHAPPY. WE'VE GOT AN INN TO FINISH. AND—SURPRISE!— MOM IS COMING SATURDAY. SIX DAYS FROM NOW. MINUS A FEW HOURS.

"Nooo!" Annie cried. Her birth mother was coming to the island? Donna MacNeish—the woman who'd raised Kevin but hadn't raised her? The woman Annie had only seen three times in her life?

Yes, my friend, Murphy whispered. *Her.*

Annie's things-to-do list blinked into sharp focus again— that time with an added entry: *Donna.* She braced herself, inhaled deeply, then sprinted up the embankment, traversing the tree roots, determined to help Lucy finish her research, while hoping that the souls of the Praying Indians would forgive her for tramping on their hallowed ground.

Chapter 2

She had no business longing for it. But it sat in the window of a small secondhand shop on Newbury Street, and she passed it every morning on her way from the T to her job. There was something about it that called to her: the supple, timeworn leather, the meticulous detail, the era in which it had been fashioned. It was a classic trunk, perhaps at home in a first-class sleeping coach aboard the Orient Express—Paris to Istanbul—in the early twentieth century. It made Donna wonder about the hundreds, or thousands, of stories stored within.

If she'd listened to Aunt Elizabeth, the trunk might have been hers. "Don't marry that man," Elizabeth had said. "Instead, find one with money so your life will be more interesting." She also had advised that if Donna only owned one sweater, she should make sure it was cashmere.

Years earlier, Donna had made the mistake of believing in true love, so she should have known to listen to her aunt. But though Jack was only a salesman of home cleaning products, he had proposed. At the time, he'd said he didn't mind that Donna had once lived in a home for unwed mothers, then given up her baby for adoption. He'd said he didn't mind, but after they were married and had a child of their own, he apparently felt otherwise. He left Donna with very little money and with Kevin, who by then was four. The pittance of child support that Jack provided trickled off after a while, though Donna didn't let Kevin know that. She took a job as a receptionist at a radio station where the pay was low, but her boss had suggested that one day she might be made office manager.

Aside from keeping Kevin healthy, the promotion became her only wish. That, and to own the Louis Vuitton trunk, which Donna knew had been made in Paris. After all, she'd paid close attention during countless hours of browsing for antiques with Aunt Elizabeth, until Alzheimer's had shoplifted her aunt's mind. At the store on Newbury Street, the tag read $400, so it was doubtful the storeowner knew the trunk's worth. Still, the price was equivalent to a month's rent. Out of Donna's league. Unless she found a way.

Then, on an ordinary Tuesday morning when she passed the shop, the Louis Vuitton was gone. She tried to tell herself it was just one more loss. And that, like other losses she'd endured, it must not have been meant for her.

After dropping Lucy off at John's town house in Edgartown, promising to join them for dinner the next night, then sharing a quick kiss with him before he left for the night shift, Annie headed home. Though she was always sorry when their schedules left them little time to be together, the spark of anticipation kept the embers glowing. This time, however, as she drove the mere two blocks to the Chappy ferry, the glow gave way to trepidation about her birth mother's impending visit.

Annie hadn't seen Donna since the fall when she'd arrived on the island after a months-long world cruise. The timing had been wrong: renovations to the waterfront mansion had begun; bedlam had enveloped them. And when Donna had offered a few design suggestions—art deco chairs, hand-knotted Mondrian rugs, a few pieces of enchanting art in the storytelling style of Hugo Mayer—Annie had politely (she'd hoped) rejected them due to (she'd said) budget constraints.

And though she could not dispute that Donna had terrific taste, Annie knew her choices weren't right for the Vineyard. Donna had left the next day, albeit with a smile. Annie had been too busy to be upset. She had, after all, only seen Donna twice on the Vineyard and once in Boston when Annie had gone there on her birthday. But unlike their jubilant first meeting, the last visits had felt strained. And despite monthly phone calls filled with pleasant anecdotes, Annie didn't know what Donna wanted from her—or what she wanted from Donna.

It hadn't been that way with Kevin. Their first meeting had only lasted as long as it had taken him to devour a Reuben and a beer at Annie's birthday lunch—yet from the instant she had seen him, she'd been comfortable. Then, when he showed up on the island and didn't leave, getting to know him had been seamless, natural, fun. Having been raised as the Suttons' only child, Annie liked having a sibling. And now, as she drove onto the inimitable ferry, she realized it was even easier to build a relationship with John's daughter than with her own birth mother. If Murphy were still alive, she'd have a heyday with that.

As the ferry chugged its ninety-second chug across the channel, Annie supposed she should try harder to get to know Donna—if only she knew how. Her adoptive parents had been great . . . well, mostly great. And though Annie had always known she'd been adopted, she'd never felt the kind of loss that she'd read many others did; she'd never been curious about her birth parents.

Lifting her eyes toward the sky, she said, "A little help would be appreciated." Murphy, however, didn't reply. Some things, Annie supposed, her old friend knew she had to figure out herself.

In a few short minutes, Annie was home—*the Inn*, as she now liked to think of it. She parked next to Kevin's pickup and wandered down the sloping lawn to the cottage that Earl and Kevin had custom designed for her and where Kevin was sitting on the porch in an Adirondack chair. He was gazing at the harbor, smiling.

"I love it here," he said, without glancing at her.

"Yeah, me too." She sat down beside him and followed his gaze. The water was calm, as if waiting for the boats to start their summer procession. "The Inn is going be spectacular."

"And you can't beat the view."

The cottage was down the hill toward the water and, as Earl said, "within shoutin' distance" of the Inn—the old Little-field house that was being restored, updated, and transformed for the twenty-first century. Adhering to the same top-quality workmanship that they were putting into the main house, the brand-new cottage had wide-plank floors in the small, but sunny living/kitchen combination; a porcelain-tiled, pristine bath; a cozy bedroom shaded by a multi-armed, thick-trunked scrub oak that stood outside the window; and, best of all, a writing room with space for Annie's laptop and her books and her imagination. The writing room also had two big windows that faced the harbor and the lighthouse and were designed to catch the eastward summer breezes. Originally, she'd wanted to have an apartment attached to the Inn. But she'd traded that idea for solitude. The cottage felt more like a real home, especially since she'd decorated it with a few childhood trea-sures: her grandmother Sutton's braided rug; the special quilt her mother had made; her mother's rocking chair. Her mother *Ellen's* things, not Donna's.

Annie wondered if she could hide there during Donna's visit. Then she cleared her throat and, as her dad would have said, she "came back down to earth." She tapped Kevin's arm. "Donna's going to be wicked impressed with everything you and Earl have done."

Kevin ran a hand through his dark hair. A shade lighter

than Annie's, unlike hers, it only showed a few strands of silver; he'd joked that as the younger sibling, he had plenty of time to catch up. "But it's the worst possible time," he said. "We don't even have a decent bedroom for her."

Annie felt a pressing sensation on her chest, followed by a flash of hope that he'd tell their mother not to come. Then she felt guilty about wanting that. "How long will she stay?"

"She didn't say. If things were normal, it would be fun for us to be together, but I don't have time to entertain her. Neither do you. You're writing a new book, you must have more soap to make, and you have to start pulling things together to decorate the rooms and common areas. There isn't time for Mom. But she doesn't take the word 'no' very well." His brow furrowed; his eyes squinted as if he were in pain.

Annie remembered that Kevin's life had not been perfect. After his father left, aside from Donna and her parents (who'd died when he still was young), Kevin had had no family. Not like Annie, who'd had her adoptive parents, two aunts, one uncle, and four grandparents. They were all gone now—had been gone for some time—but she'd never felt alone during her growing-up years.

"You're right," she said. "I'm busy, too." She didn't dare say she'd forgotten about choosing the touches of art and decorative items for the Inn. When she'd agreed to do it last fall, the deadline had seemed far into the future. After hesitating a moment, she added, "But my book's not due for months, Kevin. And I'm only going to do a couple of the festivals this summer. I'll need to make more soap for those, but maybe I can enlist Donna to help."

"Our mother? Making soap? Wow. You really don't know her, do you?"

An unexpected needle pierced Annie's heart.

Kevin's cheeks turned ivory, the color of the natural stone

that Annie had selected for her kitchen counters. "Oh, God," he groaned. "I'm sorry. I am the stupidest person in the world."

Annie knew he hadn't meant to hurt her. He'd become important in her life, and she knew the feeling was mutual. So she laughed. "You're right! I hardly know her!" She stopped herself from reminding him that it was partly her own fault, because when Donna had first contacted her, Annie hadn't responded. It had taken years for her to be ready.

"Well, now you know her son's an ass."

"I've known that for a while." Annie got up, bent down, and gave him a hug. "But you're the only brother I have, and I won't trade you for anyone. Now," she added, standing up and squeezing his shoulders, "let's talk about dinner. Did you come back with outstanding fish from your camping adventure?"

His shoulders drooped. "Nope. Turns out I'm a crappy fisherman, too. Freshwater ponds are open. But nobody told the fish. Or maybe somebody did, so they swam away. Squibnocket maybe. Or Ice House Pond. Anyway, we spent most of our time wrapped in our sleeping blankets in front of the campfire drinking beer."

Annie laughed again, mostly because Kevin seemed to have taken on Earl's gift of over-gab. "And John has a twelve-hour shift ahead of him. Well, I hope you had your fill of beer because I don't have any. And how does frozen pizza sound?"

"Terrible. But I hate to keep mooching off Earl and Claire, so, no offense, but pizza's better than nothing." Kevin had been sleeping on the sofa in the elder Lyons's house since he and Earl had purchased the former Littlefield place. With Kevin's background in construction and Earl's jack-of-all-trades talents, they'd been rehabbing and reconfiguring it into the Inn one hammer, one nail at a time. Their crew was competent, but small; many tradespeople didn't stay on the island off season, mostly due to a lack of housing that they could afford. So far, the only habitable place on the grounds of The Vineyard Inn was Annie's cottage. The workshop with her soap-making studio was close enough to being finished that she could use it, but Kevin's upstairs apartment hadn't yet been started.

Right then, however, all they could do was have dinner. So Annie got up from the chair, and he followed her inside.

"Okay," Annie asked as she preheated the oven, "what will we do with Mother?"

Kevin plunked down in the rocker. "I'll pick her up Saturday. She's coming in on the noon boat." He no longer called the big boat the "ferry," a sure sign that he was settled there.

"After that? Like, where's she going to sleep?"

"I have no clue," he replied. "You?"

"I guess she won't want to wrap up in a sleeping bag and sit in front of a campfire drinking beer."

"Not unless retirement has dramatically changed her lifestyle. We could always play it safe and book her at the Kelley House."

"No," Annie said. "She's our mother. We can't stuff her in a hotel like she's a visitor from out of town. Besides, if I ever want to get to know her better, it's only going to happen if we spend time together. Face-to-face." She took the pizza from the freezer.

Kevin looked around the room. "We can always shove your furniture against the wall and blow up an air bed for her."

Given the compact seven-hundred-square-feet of total space that Annie had wanted for the cottage, she knew that her queen-size air bed would be a tight fit. "How far along are the bedrooms?"

"We're Sheetrocking now."

"Is one close to being finished?"

"Maybe the one at the top of the stairs. The bathroom's ready because we've been using it as a template for the others. So the workers can see what goes where."

"Can you get that room done by the end of the week?"

"I'll have to ask Earl. He's in charge of the schedule. . . ."

"Tell him we need it. I'll bunk there, and Donna can have my place. She'll probably only be here a couple of nights. Especially once she hears the incessant noise that you guys make all day."

"Okay," Kevin said, then glanced around again. "This place might pass her inspection."

"Good grief. How fussy is she?" Annie knew that before Donna had retired, she'd owned a high-end antiques shop in Boston's sought-after Back Bay neighborhood.

"She knows what she likes in life. Her clothes. Her material stuff. You know?"

The first time Annie had met Donna, the woman had been stylishly dressed, as if she were in Manhattan and not on Chappaquiddick off season. Sliding the pizza into the oven, Annie wondered if getting to know her birth mother better was going to be, in reality, such a great idea after all.

Bang. Bang. Whirr. Whirr.

Annie woke up the next morning to sounds of construction puncturing her ears, and a headache squeezing her temples. She closed her eyes again. How would Donna deal with the commotion? Annie supposed it depended on exactly how fussy the woman was. Just because Annie looked like her birth mother—the same long-legged body, the same careful stride, identical hazel eyes (same as Kevin's)—didn't mean they'd actually *be* anything like each other. "Nurture over nature," her dad had often joked whenever Annie mimicked something he had done. But which had shaped her more?

She surveyed her bedroom. Aside from the construction

dust that she hadn't yet had time to clean, the room gave her the same warm feeling that she'd had in her little childhood nest in Bob and Ellen Sutton's modest home, the room they'd chosen just for her, the way she'd been chosen for them. But would Donna be comfortable there? If Annie had still lived in Boston she'd run out and buy new pillows, linens, everything. But, of course, there was no Bed, Bath & Beyond on Martha's Vineyard. No chain stores except two supermarkets, a convenience store, a few gas stations. And the Edgartown Dairy Queen, though that was only open in season.

What about the rest of the cottage? Would Donna be shocked that her daughter hand-washed dishes, stoked a woodstove for heat, and had a braided rug on the living room floor? In her antiques business, Donna had no doubt dealt with items from places like Sotheby's and Christie's, not dug out of an attic. Perhaps the women would have been more compatible if they'd met when Annie was still married to Mark, back when she'd pretended that pretty things could compensate for what her life was lacking, the kind of love she'd shared with her first husband, Brian, until his life was cut short by a drunk driver.

And then there was the Jeep. Would Donna be appalled that Annie no longer drove a Lexus but a Wrangler? The hard top seemed to offer better protection against winter winds than canvas—would Donna at least laud her for being smart about that? Or would she be disappointed . . . and disapproving?

And why on earth did Annie care?

Rabbit hole! You know better than to go down there!

Murphy's voice was followed by three quick raps on the door—Earl's special knock. Annie kicked off the covers, pulled on her fleece robe, and stepped into her slippers, grateful that Earl, like Murphy, had become one of Annie's saviors from herself.

Chapter 3

"I heard your mother's coming."

Annie set the coffeepot on the woodstove and wrapped her robe closer around her. The morning had brought a spiteful April chill. "Looks that way." Rubbing her hands together, she stared at the classic eight-cup pot as if that would help it percolate. Donna no doubt owned a Keurig. Or one of those fancy Italian things.

"Hello?" Earl asked. "Are you awake?"

Annie tucked her hair behind her ears. "Sorry. I didn't sleep well. Too much on my mind."

He pulled out a chair and sat at the small wood table. "If you wanted less to think about, you should have stayed in Boston and been content to write your books."

"My dad used to say I had a perpetual game of ping-pong going on inside my brain," she said as she grabbed two mugs from a natural hickory cabinet. She was glad she'd nixed her original idea for trendy, high-gloss acrylic that wouldn't have belonged in the cottage, though it looked great at the Inn. Cozy and home-like for her; sleek and fashionable for guests.

Annie had to admit that once they'd figured out a plan, they'd done a great job—especially when revamping the house. An architect had showed them how to use the original footprint and preserve the vintage details from the 1940s, while designing the contemporary kitchen and baths. They were also adding new flooring and a massive Vineyard stone fireplace in the great room. The seven bedrooms, the great room, the reading room, and the media room would be true to the look and feel of the island. After all, the Inn would not merely be a getaway for tourists—it also would have affordable rooms for islanders off season, with three reserved for year-round residents. In short, The Vineyard Inn—or #TheVineyardInn—would offer something for everyone.

Which reminded Annie, once again, about her overlooked task. "Damn," she blurted out as she plunked a cinnamon roll on a small plate and set it in front of Earl in what once had been their morning routine before building the Inn had interrupted. She sat down across from him. "I keep forgetting I have to decorate the rooms."

"What? Get a few tchotchkes? Piece of cake. The wall colors are all picked out. What's hard about finding a few ceramic cats, some glass candy dishes, and a basket or two for magazines? Then you'll only need a bunch of paintings for the walls. The kind of stuff that looks like the island."

"It's not as easy as it sounds, but . . ." and right then an idea popped into her head. "You're brilliant, Earl. But let's not just make it *look* like the island . . . Let's make it *be* the island." She jumped up, dashed into her bedroom, then returned with the tote bag she'd brought to the festival meeting. Fumbling through the contents, she found the sheet of paper she wanted.

Earl watched her as he chewed on the roll.

"Twelve," she said with a broad smile.

His spikey gray eyebrows elevated. "Care to elaborate?"

"Artists. Twelve artists are registered for this year's artisan festivals. Maybe they'll be willing to donate a couple of their favorite pieces to the Inn. We could offer them for sale, and rotate them around the guest rooms and the common areas. We'll be promoting the Vineyard and hopefully generating business for the artists, while we get to adorn our walls with authentic island creations. In our ads and on social media we can say the Inn is decorated in 'Vineyard natural.'" As she said the last words, she raised her arms and stretched them apart in elongated air quotes. "What do you think?"

"I think your game of ping-pong has a winner."

"It will save us lots of money, Earl. We'll be able to cut a good chunk out of the decorating budget."

"Now you're talking. Because Lord knows, we're pretty much out of cash."

She wondered how bad the finances had become, then she chose to trust that Earl and Kevin knew what they were doing. After all, she'd only ever been an elementary school teacher. What did she know about the cost of building? "Maybe Donna would like to help."

"Donna?"

"My mother. Birth mother."

Earl nodded. "Right. I keep forgetting her name. Kevin always calls her 'Mom.'"

"That's understandable."

Earl scratched his day-old beard. "Do you think you ever will? Call her 'Mom'?"

Annie laughed because she didn't know what to say. Then she leaped out of the chair, cried "Coffee!" and scooted to the stove where the pot had finished its dutiful, old-school percolating.

Of course, finding the right tchotchkes, as Earl called them, would be important. Especially since she didn't want the Inn to look like a souvenir shop. After he left, Annie took a quick shower, dressed, and headed to the *On Time* ferry in her Jeep, grateful that because it wasn't summer yet there would be room in the parking lot. Tradespeople often parked their trucks on either side and shared ferry ticket costs for vehicles; many of the workers were those who Earl and Kevin said were few and far between now, though Annie wondered if they simply lacked the funds to hire them. At least her new idea might free up a small part of the budget.

As she waited for the "little ferry," as her friend Francine liked to call it, Annie thought about how much she missed Francine and baby Bella. But Francine had reconnected with her aunt and uncle who lived in the Midwest. They had offered Francine and Bella free room and board, and, "Get this!" Francine had cried to Annie one day late last summer. "They want to pay for me to go to college! I can major in hospitality. Maybe I can come back to the island for the season if you'll have me—if you'll have *us*, Bella and me. By the time I have my degree, The Vineyard Inn will be in demand, and I can run the whole place if you want!" Annie hoped that Francine and Bella would be able to make it at some point over the summer. A room had already been earmarked for them, no matter if they made it that year or the next. After all, Francine and Bella were special to their small island family; they would always have a home at the Inn, whether or not money was tight.

The *On Time* arrived; an SUV and a dump truck drove off; the captain signaled Annie to walk on. She sat on one of the long benches and closed her eyes, a jumble of have-to-do's and want-to-do's spinning in her mind like a child's kaleidoscope. By the time they reached the other side, she'd resolved one thing: she'd wait to contact the artists until Donna was there. That way mother and daughter could share something more genteel than making soap.

Seconds later, Annie walked off the ferry and went up Daggett Street to North Water, then turned left for the short distance to Winter Street . . . where she promptly stepped into a place that teemed with whirring power saws and hammering carpenters, and emitted a pungent aroma of new paint—as if she didn't have enough of all that at home. She mused about how springtime often seemed like the noisiest season on the island; as much as Annie loved the accelerated pace when the Vineyard first woke up, sometimes even the birds chirped more loudly than seemed necessary. She wondered if the beloved up-island pinkletinks could get annoying, too.

Trying to stay focused on her mission, she walked directly to the thrift shop on North Summer. Her goal was simple: find secondhand, decorative pieces leftover from estate sales. She'd learned that people who sold their summer homes often didn't want the bother or the cost of shipping their household goods over to the mainland. With any luck, Annie might find tchotchkes that had been island-made.

"Hi, Annie!" The cheerful voice behind the counter belonged to a woman whose name Annie couldn't remember but whose face was recognizable as that of a clerk at the Edgartown post office. It continued to amaze her that if islanders weren't at their paying jobs (there were often two or three of those), they tended to volunteer. "What brings you here on this beautiful, chilly day?"

Annie had been so preoccupied she'd barely noticed the weather, though she had put on a corduroy jacket instead of a lightweight windbreaker. She also hadn't noticed whether the trip across the channel had been choppy or smooth. The little ferry had become such a way of life, it was hard to remember when she'd first moved there and had prayed she wouldn't be the first one to board, and wind up with only the canvas-covered chain separating the front bumper of her car from the deep blue sea as they bobbed and lurched toward the other side. Now, she felt that the motion was nicely soothing.

She smiled at the clerk. "Tchotchkes for the Inn. Decorative pieces for shelves or on top of bureaus or end tables. Earl suggested ceramic cats, glass candy dishes, and a few magazine baskets. But I'd like things that are special. Unique. And locally made, if possible. We're saving money for the big things like nice furniture and quality linens, so our budget for the 'extras' is a little tight." Her explanation sounded more positive than saying she'd come to the thrift shop because they were nearly broke.

The postal clerk frowned. "We had a lot of those here last fall after the typical spike in house sales. I'm not sure what's left. But poke around—you never know."

Annie thanked her, then wove around the shop, past clothing and kitchenware and trinkets from other people's lives. She browsed through old books of Vineyard photography; she found a pair of candlesticks decorated with small plastic fish, a couple of nautical maps, a pair of signs that read THIS WAY TO THE BEACH and CALL US WHEN YOU GET TO THE BOAT. But nothing evoked the authentic island feeling she wanted for the Inn.

Annie wondered if Donna had ever thought about the people who'd owned the antiques that had filled her shop. Had she considered what the family had been like, whether they'd been happy or riddled with misfortune? Annie stopped in front of a sofa with white fabric that featured navy blue illustrations of sailboats and anchors. Had the family who owned it been part of the annual regatta? Or had they simply thought that an island house had to convey a water theme? Then Annie remembered when she and her dad had taken long walks after supper; he'd called them his "constitutionals." Standing on the sidewalks, they'd tried to peer in windows when the lights were on but the drapes hadn't yet been closed. Once they saw a father with a little girl. They were sitting on a sofa—brown plaid had been in vogue. Annie's dad had made up a story: the girl's father no doubt worked at the Necco plant in Cambridge, making sugary, pastel wafers.

Annie had added that the daughter must be a Girl Scout like she was, and that the mother baked lots of yummy cakes or bought them at Star Market and pretended they were hers. On those walks, Annie and her dad had laughed a lot.

She wondered if Donna had baked cookies for Kevin or if she'd bought them at Star Market. Then Annie wondered why, with all she had to do, she was standing in the middle of the thrift shop, thinking about her birth mother. She supposed she'd get to know her sooner or later. Or not.

"Find anything?" The clerk was standing next to Annie.

She blinked, startled from her silly pondering. "Not really. I was reminiscing."

"We get a lot of that in here."

"I'm sure you do. But, no, I haven't seen anything."

"We have more plaques in the corner. 'Home is where the Beach is,' 'Vineyard Magic,' that sort of thing."

Annie shook her head. "I don't think so. We want to make a statement without saying it."

The clerk nodded as if that made sense to her.

"Thanks, though. Maybe if I go to one of the gift shops I'll get a better idea of what I want. Then I'll be back."

As she headed toward the door, she noticed several clumps of scallop shells glued onto a mirror frame. The effect was amateurish, almost as if it had been made in an elementary school art class, but the sight of it triggered a thought: scallop shells. Lucy had said the rocks that marked the graves at the burial ground had single items on top—a scallop shell on one, a piece of wampum on another. She'd also said that it was "cool."

"Perfect!" Annie said out loud. As the front door closed behind her, more thoughts started to gel. She could collect the things herself! On the beach. Right on Chappaquiddick. How much more local could she get? Maybe she'd find sea glass. Driftwood. White oyster shells that were intriguing for their gentle shapes and the rows of salt—layered by time—often sculpted on them.

She was so excited she wanted to run back to the ferry. If Donna didn't want to get her feet dirty in the sand, maybe Annie could coax Lucy into helping collect the artifacts. Annie could even pay her enough to cover the application fee for the Mayflower Society if one of Lucy's ancestors had come over on *that* boat, four hundred years ago.

With ideas still churning, Annie reached the wharf just as the *On Time* pulled in. And Kevin's pickup was driving off.

"Hey!" Annie called.

He put his window down, pulled over onto Dock Street, and stopped.

"Where you headed?"

"Hardware store!" His cheeks were bright, his freckles dancing on them. He gave her two thumbs-up. "Two!" he cried. "We got two!"

"How wonderful! Two what?"

"I have no idea how much help they'll be, but we hired two more workers this morning, thanks to your generous offer to ditch the decorating budget."

Annie laughed. "Two workers?"

"Yup. They're both good painters, and they can do cleanup stuff. What they don't know, we'll teach 'em. And they came cheap."

"Where'd you find them?"

Kevin laughed. "Right on Chappy. Taylor. And her son, Jonas. Remember him?"

As far as Annie knew Kevin was still dating Taylor, though he'd been quiet about the extent of the relationship now that Jonas had moved into the garage apartment at Taylor's house. And though Annie had come close to actually liking the quirky woman (for Kevin's sake), having her around every day for the next several weeks might be a challenge. Still . . .

She quieted her concern. "That's great news, Kevin. Keep it in the Chappy family, right?"

He nodded. "Yup. Nepotism all the way. Dinner tonight?"

"Sorry. I'll be at John's."

"Later then." Kevin gave her a quick salute, then pulled away, heading up the hill toward town, leaving the image of his smile resting on her heart.

Chapter 4

It was good to be back in John's kitchen, sitting at the table, slowly sipping wine, watching as he quietly stirred the pot of scallop chowder he'd made that afternoon. Cheerful daffodils—compliments of Lucy—stood in a glass canning jar that probably came from the collection that Lucy and her grandmother Claire used for their strawberry, elderberry, and beach plum jellies and jams. Lucy had also filled the house with a welcoming aroma of freshly baked bread—in addition to genealogy, baking had become a hobby. Annie wondered if the girl would like to earn some money by supplying the Inn with home-baked muffins packed with island berries.

But she supposed she was getting ahead of things.

Having left her Jeep on the Chappy side, Annie had walked up the hill to John's. She was tired; she hadn't been sure if she'd be hungry, but being in his kitchen had recharged her appetite. Lucy was upstairs doing homework; their recently acquired puppy—a mix of this and that with thick black-and-white fur and jumbo paws that were growing faster than the rest of him—still didn't have a name. Despite a number of random ideas (Rover? Spot? Lucas, after one of their ancestors who might have been Wampanoag if Lucy had her way?),

John and Lucy simply had not been able to agree. The name-less pup was nestled on his soft bed in the corner, surveying every move his master made. Since late last summer, when Lucy had left her mom's in Plymouth and moved back to the island to her dad's, John and Annie hadn't had much time alone, and less time for romance, let alone for sex.

They'd tried in the beginning. When John worked the four-to-midnight or midnight-to-eight shift, Lucy stayed with Earl and Claire, who had more space now that Francine was in college and she and Bella were away. When John was done at midnight, he often found a Chappy ferry captain will-ing to take him across to Annie's; when he worked midnight to eight, Annie sometimes went to Edgartown and greeted him when he got home. But all that changed over Christ-mas vacation when Lucy turned fourteen and announced that though she loved her grandparents, she was tired of schlep-ping back and forth from Chappy to Edgartown to go to school or to meet up with her friends. "I'm old enough to stay alone, Dad," she'd said. "The police station is two blocks from our house. I'm not going to do anything you won't find out about." John had tried to argue that he didn't like the thought of her being alone, not because he didn't trust her, but because he was concerned that something bad might happen. Lucy had laughed. "We're on the Vineyard, Dad."

Which, of course, was a solid argument, because nothing of much consequence happened in Edgartown, especially off season.

And though Lucy wasn't stupid, John and Annie had agreed not to sleep together when his daughter was in the next room. "Call me old-fashioned," Annie had said, to which he'd replied, "I'd rather call you wonderful."

So they sneaked around like teenagers, savoring the an-ticipation.

"It's so peaceful here," Annie said to him now. "It's so

crazy—and so *loud*—at my place. Everyone is hustling to meet the deadline. Speaking of which, I need to run something by you. I was wondering if I could borrow Lucy."

John nodded but kept his eyes fixed on the chowder. It might be the last batch of scallops until fall—as it was, Edgartown selectmen had voted to extend the season when small patches of the sweet shellfish had been found in the outer harbor. "Is it going to cost me anything?"

She laughed. "Not a dime. I'll even pay her."

He groaned. "Great. I wonder what she'll do with it this time."

"Winnie said you were off in a million directions when you were a boy, and that your apple hasn't fallen too far from you."

"Touché." He stretched his wide, well-muscled shoulders. ("Dad has *coply* shoulders," Lucy had once said, having "borrowed" the word from *Blue Bloods*, one of her favorite TV shows.) "So what's up? More soap-making?" He reached into an upper cabinet and retrieved three chowder crocks.

"No. Much more fun. And definitely cleaner. I want to decorate the Inn with things we can collect on island beaches. Sea glass, wampum, shells. Natural things, nothing all decked out like souvenirs."

"Sounds good." He pulled a ladle from a drawer and began to transfer the chowder to the crocks. "And you want her to . . . ?"

"Go beachcombing with me. Help me find unique things. Special things."

"Uh-huh. I see."

"So? Is it all right with you if I ask her?"

"No," he said.

Just then Lucy trundled down the stairs and whirled into the kitchen, her intuitive radar always seeming to know it was okay to interrupt. "Hi, Annie. When's dinner? I'm *starving*."

Annie knew she should have smiled and let the subject shift to Lucy, ask how her day had gone, and if she'd had a chance to work on her genealogy project. She wouldn't ask Lucy to help hunt for decorating treasure, though Annie was still stunned by John's negative reaction.

So she only said hello, then got up from the table, walked four feet to him, and looked him squarely in the face. It is a handsome face, she thought. *It is, indeed,* Murphy agreed.

Trying not to acknowledge Murphy's impromptu presence, Annie said, "No?" She wasn't sure if she should pursue the conversation with Lucy in the room.

John said nothing.

Lucy said, "Jeez, are you guys fighting?"

Then John started to laugh. "No."

Annie remained baffled.

He picked up two crocks, navigated around Annie, and walked them to the table where he set them down. "Annie wants to know if you'd like to help her look for stuff on the beaches to decorate the Inn. I said no."

"No?"

"No. But I didn't get a chance to add that you can go if you want—but only after you've done something else."

"What?"

"Help me think of a decent name for this dog."

The puppy was at John's feet, tail wagging, voice whimpering. He'd jumped up and raced over as soon as he'd heard the word "dog," as if that's what John had been calling the poor thing.

"How about Restless?" Annie asked. "He'd fit in with both of you that way."

"Restless" was agreed upon. As was an hourly rate for Lucy to help comb the beach.

The rest of the evening was pretty close to perfect. It was too bad that Annie knew perfection rarely lasted.

★ ★ ★

The next day, the warm sun returned. Annie wrote for a few hours, and she barely heard the thudding, banging sounds emitting from the Inn. She was blissfully immersed in the land of make-believe where her characters lived and breathed and laughed and cried.

But at 12:30, there was a loud knock on her door.

She sighed. She shut down her laptop, reminding herself to be grateful for the quiet time she'd had. Then she went to the door. Lucy was on the other side. "Hey, kiddo," Annie said as she let her in. "I didn't think you'd be here this early."

"It's almost low tide, the best time to look for stuff. So I skipped study period. I also skipped English class. I figured I'd be with a famous author so I should get a pass." She slung her backpack onto the rocking chair and smiled a bogus smile.

"Your father won't be happy."

"My father won't know. Will he?"

"Lucy . . ."

"I know. I shouldn't put you in the middle. My mom says I always do that with her and Dad. I've gotten good at it. Sorry."

Annie wasn't sure what to say; she was neither prepared nor had been asked to act as a stepmother. "Egg salad sandwich for lunch? I made them for the crew, with extra ones in case you were hungry."

"Sure. And you won't tell Dad?"

Dropping a couple of sandwiches, two small bags of Cape Cod potato chips, and two apples in a paper bag, she replied, "Not this time. But let's not do it again, okay?"

"Deal. But so you know, tomorrow is Wednesday. I have study periods all afternoon, so I can come then, too."

"Okay, you win. And as for today, we'll have a walking picnic while we hunt for treasures. Do you have water?"

Lucy grabbed a stainless bottle from her backpack. "I

could use a refill." Few year-round islanders used plastic water bottles anymore. The Vineyard had seen more than its share of plastic trash along the shoreline and beached sea life tangled in the debris. She went to the sink, turned on the tap, and filled her bottle. "Is Gramps up at the house?"

"I expect he is."

"After you left last night, I made him cookies. Peanut butter. His favorites."

Annie was surprised; she'd thought that chocolate chip were Earl's favorites, which was why she made them so often.

Lucy unzipped her backpack, dropped in the lunch bag, and pulled out a covered tin container. "Can we deliver the cookies first?"

"Absolutely." Then, armed with optimism and two cloth tote bags for stashing their treasures, Annie followed Lucy out the door.

As they went up the hill toward the house, Annie noticed a young man striding toward the dumpster, balancing a sheet of drywall high over his head. It took her a few seconds to realize it was Jonas.

"Hey, Annie," he called to her. "Man, this place is going to be outstanding."

"Yes, it is."

Lucy stepped forward and introduced herself before Annie had a chance. "Earl's my grandfather," she added. "We're bringing him my homemade cookies; if you're nice, maybe he'll share." She smiled sweetly, and . . . did she bat her eyelashes a little?

Stepping back, Annie wondered if Lucy thought Jonas was cute. A hunk. Whatever they called it these days. He had filled out in the past year; he seemed more muscular, more mature; his once ginger hair had lightened to almost strawberry-blond; his blue eyes were framed by long, dark lashes—the kind of lashes girls longed for, but that often went to boys. Annie figured he was at least eight years older than Lucy. Far too old for a fourteen-year-old girl. Well, she thought, maybe Lucy wasn't smitten. Maybe she was only being friendly. *Dream on*, Annie thought she heard Murphy whisper.

"Cookies," he said as he heaved the drywall into the dumpster. "Cool. I'll be right there."

Annie tapped Lucy's shoulder. "Come on, honey. We have work to do."

"He's gorgeous," Lucy said, after they'd delivered the cookies to a very grateful Gramps and walked down to the beach.

"You never met Jonas before?" Annie asked, trying to keep the conversation light. "He's Taylor's son."

"We don't exactly travel in the same circles." As if there were more than one big circle on the Vineyard. "What's the real story behind him? I know he hasn't been here forever."

"Long story. I'll tell you about it when we aren't on a more important mission."

"Does he have a girlfriend?"

"I have no idea. But he's a lot older than you, honey. He graduated from college last year."

Lucy made no further comment, but Annie supposed the conversation might resume at a later point. The girl was far too stubborn—like her dad—to let it go.

They trundled off to the low, soft dunes and found a path through slender stalks of beach grass that waved in easy synchronization, the way swimmers sometimes did.

Then Lucy asked, "How are you going to control beach access so your guests don't trample everything?"

Yes, Annie thought, for the hundredth time, John's daughter was definitely an island girl. "Good question. But Kevin and your grandfather have met with the environmental people several times. I expect it's been discussed."

Lucy unwrapped her sandwich and dove into it while they

walked. "It's very important to help prevent erosion wherever possible. I'll talk to Gramps to make sure it's been considered." Sometimes she seemed older, wiser than her years.

They kicked off their sneakers and stepped onto the beach that stretched below the Inn and proved its description as waterfront property. Like the burial ground at Christiantown, the beach looked as if no one had been there since the previous autumn; it seemed untouched by man or even the gentle beasts of Chappy—rabbits, chipmunks, deer. But nature had done its wild bidding, thanks to the icy winds of winter: quahog, scallop, and other shells were scattered across the sand; small stones of multicolor variations were gathered in a ribbon at the tide line; clumps of seaweed were wound around debris—a remnant of a fish net, a barnacled conch shell, charred remnants of a log. John had told Annie that charred wood on the beach was often from a campfire, but sometimes had been petrified after a fire on a wooden boat and had washed ashore. She had told him she'd rather think it was the result of a group of happy people who'd been together on a summer night, toasting marshmallows, telling tales, and studying the champagne bubbles of stars painted on the night sky.

"All I see is lots of crap," Lucy said. Perhaps she wasn't as much of a romantic as Annie. "But check out the driftwood." She pointed to a row of logs strung along the base of the dunes, as if the previous owners of the property had attempted to build a wall to protect the sand. "They'd have been better off to plant more beach grass. The more plugs in the sand, the stronger the hold."

The only experience Annie had with beaches was from when her family had rented a small cottage on the Vineyard for two weeks every summer. Back then few people were concerned about erosion—at least she didn't remember it being talked about at their dinner table.

Just then a ray of sunlight sparkled off a piece of something bluish that was tucked among the stones.

Sea glass?

Annie bent to check it out. She pushed away a clump of seaweed and grasped what looked like a disk from the bottom of a bottle; she pulled out an orb of aqua glass, about two inches in diameter, smooth and frosted by the tides.

"Lucy! Look! We have a winner!" She held it up to the sunlight, in awe of the work done by the sea.

Lucy scrambled over and held open a bag. "Nice going. Drop it in before you lose it."

Annie set it carefully in the bag, as if, despite its being tumbled who knew how many times on the seafloor, dropping it into a cloth bag would cause it to break.

"Years ago Gramps taught me to use my feet to pull apart the seaweed. He said that's where the good stuff is."

"Looks like he was right," Annie replied.

"He usually is." Lucy looked in the opposite direction from where they had been walking. "If we split up," she said, "we'll find more stuff. I'll go south. You go north." She handed Annie the bag and took the empty one.

Annie deferred to her; she doubted this was the first time Lucy had gone beachcombing.

So they split up, and Annie meandered to the right, strolling with her head bent to the sand, aware that this was far more fun than dwelling on her troubles. She collected several small, pretty stones, a few pieces of wampum, all with possibilities for a nice "Vineyard natural" décor. She thought it might be fun to challenge guests to add to the Inn's collection; maybe she should offer one of her soaps as a prize each week for the most creative "find." Lost in peaceful thoughts, she then noticed a group of boulders where the land curved toward Cape Poge. Another bundle of seaweed, much larger than the first, was twisted among the rocks.

Following Earl's instructions, Annie maneuvered her toes to separate the seaweed. But the dark-green mass was tough and slimy and too knotted to let loose. She looked around the beach. Her gaze landed on the driftwood by the dunes; she went over and retrieved a narrow but sturdy shard.

Poking at the mass again, she hooked a sizeable clump nearly the size of a soccer ball. She lifted it from between the rocks, and realized that the seaweed was wrapped around something hard . . . Another rock?

She dumped the whole thing on the sand and used the stick to peel away the weeds, and, sure enough, another rock was there—this one kind of whitish. She gave it a sharp poke . . . and punched through what might have been a hole. She wondered if it was a conch shell—a beautiful, smooth, white island one, not like the plastic ones in souvenir shops in beach towns or the huge pink ones transported by the thousands from the Caribbean.

"Well, jeez," Annie muttered, mimicking Lucy.

Then she tugged on the entire mess and lifted the stick. Some of the seaweed fell away, revealing a mass that looked almost like a bone; it curved the way a face curved along a jawline. That's when Annie realized that her stick was stuck in what might have been the socket of an eye.

She screamed. Jumped back. Dropped the stick. She slipped and fell hard on her butt onto the sand, her heart racing the way it hadn't raced since she'd thought someone or something had been trying to break into her cottage in the middle of the night in the dead of winter.

She put a hand up to her chest. "Lucy!" She must have shouted loudly enough for the long-dead Praying Indians in West Tisbury to hear.

But Lucy didn't answer; she probably was too far down the beach to be in range. Or she'd gone back to the Inn to flirt with Jonas.

Yanking her phone out of her pocket, her hands shaking, her lips quivering, and her eyes fixed on the bone, Annie tapped the link to Lucy's number.

"Call your father!" she shouted when Lucy answered. "There's a body on the beach!"

Chapter 5

Later, when the beach was clogged with EMTs, local and state police, and the Inn's construction crew of half a dozen, plus Earl and Kevin, too, Annie wondered why she hadn't called John instead of alerting Lucy first. She also wondered why she'd said it was a body when, in fact, it simply looked like a part of someone's head. Half a skull. White bone, bleached by seawater, yellowed in some places from being wrapped up in the seaweed and God only knew what else for God only knew how long.

She must have been in shock.

But now, because Annie had said it was a body, the entire cast of first-responder characters was there. They'd brought the rescue boat from the Chappy fire station because Annie had said the body was on the beach, but she hadn't specified whether or not it had been close to the water. Taylor was hanging out with the EMTs because she was one, too, though that day she was technically working at the Inn. As, of course, was her son, Jonas, who stood alone about a dozen feet behind Annie and Lucy, leaning against a dune.

The state police were there because the local ones (i.e.

John, et al) had notified them right away because it was an unattended death.

"Skeletal remains," John told Annie, who was barely listening, "are considered unattended. Then it's up to the Staties to work in conjunction with the district attorney's office on Cape Cod." He added something about Boston that Annie didn't follow, and then he wandered back to his fellow civil servants before she could ask him to repeat it.

All she knew for sure was that it seemed like a lot of manpower and falderal for a single piece of bone.

Ten or fifteen or who-knew-how-many minutes later, a state policeman walked over to her. He introduced himself as Detective Sergeant Lou Sloan. The brim of his hat shaded his face, except for his gray sideburns. He had questions for Annie: How much seaweed had been wrapped around the remains? Did she touch any of the actual "material"? Was it in the same spot where she'd found it or had she moved it? Then he told her that his team would be taking photos, collecting evidence, and trying to predetermine if it was human or animal.

Animal? Though Annie hated to think that anyone or anything had died, there was some relief in thinking that the bone might have belonged to a critter with four legs instead of two.

"Lots of bones are remarkably similar," the detective explained. "For instance, vertebrae that looks human can be from a whale. And did you ever see the paw of a seal once the flesh has been . . . well, once it's gone? It's a dead ringer—pardon the lousy pun—for the skeleton of a human hand."

With all the mysteries Annie had written and all the research she had done, she would have thought she'd have already known those things. Instead she stood, stupefied, her eyes fixed on the scene as Sloan's assistants gathered, tagged, and bagged. She felt like a gawking bystander, but could not pull her gaze away.

"That is so cool," Lucy said, giving Annie a nudge. "Especially about the seal."

"It's nature," the detective sergeant said with a shrug. Then he added, "Please don't leave Chappaquiddick. We might have more questions." And he went back to examining the area.

Over the years, Annie had been to plenty of crime scenes, studying law enforcement officers at work and taking copious notes (too copious, as the stacks of notebooks in her desk drawers attested). She'd spent countless hours firing questions at police, forensic specialists, psychological profilers, prosecutors, and district attorneys—whoever could offer real-life facts to help create her made-up mysteries. This time, it was different. It was in her backyard. Literally.

"I took a picture," Lucy whispered to Annie. A few minutes earlier, John had tried to get Lucy to go back to Annie's cottage, but the girl had planted her hands squarely on her slim hips and said, "Really, Dad? I'm not a baby anymore." He'd opened his mouth as if to argue; then he'd merely shaken his head and gotten to work.

"A picture of what?" Annie asked.

"The guy's head. I took it with my phone before my dad or anybody got here."

"Please tell me you're joking."

"Someone had to do it. I shot it when you went up to the driveway to ask the cops to turn off their sirens."

Annie had forgotten that she'd done that.

"I figured, what if something happened to the guy's head before anybody got here?"

Annie closed her eyes, then slowly opened them again. "First of all, it's not a head. It's part of a skull. And what could possibly have happened?"

Lucy pursed her lips. "Lot of things! A dog could have come along and carried it away. Or a coyote."

"We don't have coyotes here."

"Somebody saw one in Edgartown."

"And you think it swam across the harbor?"

"I doubt they would have let him on the *On Time*. Not unless he had a round-trip ticket."

Jibber-jabbering with Lucy should have provided some distraction, but it didn't. All the while, Annie wondered whom—or what—the skull might have belonged to, how long it had been in the seaweed and on the shore, and what the circumstance of death had been.

"Hey," Lucy added, "wouldn't it be creepy if you found out the guy was killed while you were sleeping in your new place that's a few short steps from the beach?"

Annie shoved her hands into the pockets of her jeans. "That's enough, Lucy. I'm going inside; my feet are cold. It's too early in the season to be shoeless in the sand." But as she turned to leave, Earl ambled over.

"This is a fine way to spend a spring afternoon," he said. "And not too great for business."

"At least we haven't opened yet," Annie said. She hoped she'd also asked the drivers of the "official vehicles" to shut off their flashing lights; North Neck Road had seen enough of those.

"It might take them that long to finish, though," he said.

Then Lucy stepped into the conversation—of course she did. "Will they put the guy's head in one of those big black bags like on *CSI*?" she asked. "Or do you think they have smaller bags for body parts?"

"Lucy," her grandfather said sternly, "be nice."

Annie noticed that Lucy had glanced over at Jonas as she'd spoken. Perhaps she'd hoped to garner some attention from Taylor's good-looking son.

"I heard the Statie say he'd notify the medical examiner

in Sandwich on the Cape," Earl said. "If he has to come over, it's going to take a while."

"Let's hope not," Annie said. She knew little about Cape Cod, other than it was the southernmost chunk of land in Massachusetts and was attached to the mainland by two bridges. It was also the last leg of the trip from Boston to Woods Hole to get the ferry to the Vineyard. In spite of all the times she'd driven the route, she hadn't paid much attention to the Cape other than to feel it seemed to take forever to get from the Bourne Bridge to the Steamship Authority terminal.

"Well," Earl was continuing, "on top of everything else, we can't get back to work until the ME figures something out."

Annie hoped she'd misunderstood. "What do you mean you 'can't get back to work'?"

"At the Inn. Per the directive of Detective Sergeant Sloan. We can't continue with the construction 'til we know what we're dealing with."

"It's an old skull!" Annie cried a little too loudly. "What's the big deal?"

Earl scratched his chin with his thumb and forefinger. "We'd better have a talk. Got any java in your place?"

Annie made coffee for Earl and poured iced tea for herself. Lucy had stayed down on the beach. She'd said she wanted to watch the process in case she became a cop someday.

"Chocolate chip cookie?" Annie asked. "Though I just learned that peanut butter are your favorites."

He chuckled. "I'll pass on a cookie. But for future information, chocolate chip are my favorites. Peanut butter cookies were the first things Lucy ever baked—she must have been seven or eight—and I guess I extolled their virtues too much. The truth is, they're too dry for my taste, but I still swill 'em down with milk, give her a big hug, and tell her they're the best cookies ever."

A terrific grandfather, through and through.

He waited until a steaming mug was in front of him before clearing his throat for what Annie suspected were details she might not want to hear.

"So . . ." He began slowly, as was his typical pace, the kind that tempted her to lean across the table, reach down his throat, and pull out his words. "We might have a problem."

She sipped her tea, waiting for the rest. She stared down at her feet and realized she'd forgotten to rinse off the sand.

"Here's how it works," he finally added. "If the ME concludes your skull is human, then the fun begins. He'll call in the state archeologist, and one of them has to determine if it's ancient. The archeologist might want to come out and do his own assessment of the area. My guess is one of them is going to look for other fragments, then the skull and any backup evidence will go to Boston to be studied, scanned, and God knows what else. I'm not exactly sure who does what, but I do know a lot of folks will be involved."

"Hold it," Annie interrupted. "What do you mean by ancient? Could this thing be thousands of years old? Like that Kennewick man they found in Washington State back in the nineties?"

"Doubtful. When it comes to bones, around here they call them 'ancient' instead of 'fresh' if they're not from a new death. Like if they didn't wash ashore because of something that happened a few days ago or even a month. If it's been around a while, it's considered old news. Ancient."

"Okay. So if it's fresh and not ancient, they'll have to investigate."

"Right. They'll need to figure out if it was an accident or . . . foul play." At least he hadn't said "murder."

"I don't know much," Annie said, "but it looks to me as

if, yes, that bone's been around a while. If they determine that it's ancient, why will that be a problem for us?"

Earl sighed. "Native people, dear girl. In addition to the ME and the archeologist, the state police have to notify the tribe about your find. On Chappy—or anywhere on the island—it would most likely be Wampanoag. In which case, the bone will be turned over to them. No matter how old it is or isn't."

Annie stirred her tea. "So . . . what am I missing? Why would that be a problem for us?"

"Well, for one thing, it's going to take time to determine who this guy was—assuming it's a guy."

"Detective Sloan said it could be from an animal."

Earl shook his head. "That's no animal, Annie. He might have told you that because he thought you'd be less upset. But nope. That's a human skull. Or I'd guess about half of one. But no matter what, right now, we'll have to stop construction."

Impatience began a slow burn inside her. "Why? *What does this have to do with the Inn?*" She wondered if her voice had been too loud.

Earl cleared his throat. Again. "Here's the short version: we might be sitting on sacred land, Annie. If your skull is Wampanoag, they have to make sure it didn't come from an old burial ground. Also, if it really is ancient, as in the 'old' kind of ancient like that Kennewick guy, our property might be declared a historic site. In either case, it means there's going to be a ream of red tape. And we need to be prepared for the worst."

"The 'worst' being?"

He took a long drink of coffee. "The worst will be we won't be allowed to have an Inn here at all."

About some things, Earl liked to exaggerate—the weather, the size of the blue fish someone caught during the derby, the fact that peanut butter cookies were the best ever. But Annie didn't think this was one of those times. Her slow burn of impatience settled into smoldering worry. If there was no Inn, Earl and Kevin would lose their investment. Though they— not even Kevin—had not detailed their personal finances, Annie didn't think that either man could afford to lose that much. She supposed that, like many older islanders, most of Earl's worth was tied up in his land. It reminded Annie of an elderly friend of Winnie's who lived on a meager Social Security check but couldn't bring herself to part with her valuable ten acres because it was where her life, her home were rooted. Island tradesmen and landscapers took turns taking care of the woman's place for free; their families made sure she was looked after. After all, her husband had been a fisherman who'd once fed most of them.

Kevin had an income from a few condos in Boston that he owned and rented, but Annie thought that was it. The money from the sale of his business had gone into a trust for his wife's medical care, which might continue for a long time.

And if there were no Inn, what about the tenants that they'd already signed up? Annie knew firsthand the struggle to find year-round housing on the island. Then she gulped as something else occurred to her. What about *her?* Annie couldn't afford to buy a place, not until her income caught up with the years that it had taken to pay off her ex-husband's debts.

She knew that neither John nor she were ready to make a lifelong commitment. But without one, what should she do? Should she move back to Boston where she'd lived most of her life? If Kevin went too, at least she'd have family there. And Donna! Why did Annie often forget about her birth mother? At the very least she needed to get ready for Donna's visit. If Annie's world was going to fall apart anyway, what was one more bit of drama over which she had positively no control?

Earl pushed back his chair and stood. "There's always a

chance none of this will come to anything. Maybe your skull isn't even real; maybe it's a leftover toy from a party last summer. Or maybe it's an old Halloween prank. Stranger things have happened out here on Chappy."

Annie wished he would stop calling it *her* skull. She stood and carried her glass and his mug to the sink. She couldn't see very far down the beach from her kitchen window. But if she opened the window, she might hear voices talking in low murmurs. It was hard to believe that one small, solitary part of someone or something might impact so many innocent people.

"As the kids today would say," she said, "this totally sucks."

"Yup," Earl replied. "In the old days, if somebody died and the family didn't have a plot, or if the poor dead soul didn't have a family, it wasn't uncommon for a neighbor or a friend or even an acquaintance to roll the body in a rug—or maybe in a tarp if he was a fisherman—and stuff him in the back of somebody's station wagon. Then they'd drive onto the boat and deliver him to a funeral home over on the Cape."

As he was telling his tale—"spinning his yarn," her dad would have called it—Annie felt her eyes grow wide. "That's a joke, right?"

Earl shook his head. "Nope. Even back then it took a whole lot of paperwork and a lot of dough to get a body off this goofball island. It was easier to use a station wagon. And it meant that the dead guy would have a decent burial. 'Course, if he or she was cremated, the ashes were picked up later and brought back to the Vineyard for distribution off the cliffs or somewhere on his or her property. Back in the fifties, I remember my dad telling me that one guy wanted his ashes spread on the sidewalk outside The Ritz in OB." He chuckled. "More than once, I've wondered if that was another island legend or if it really happened."

If there was an appropriate comment, Annie couldn't think of it.

"Anyway," he continued, "we have a funeral home here now that takes care of everything. And, as for us, until I get the official word on what is or what isn't going to happen, I'm going back to the main house. I can finish up painting the front bedroom. Nobody but us will know the difference. Besides, I'm better off being productive than standing around, staring at a bunch of sand and seaweed, playing armchair detective."

Chapter 6

"I need to tell Mom not to come," Kevin said.

Annie had known she was too distracted to sit at her laptop and get any halfway decent writing done, so she'd walked back to the beach, retrieved her sneakers, then gone to where Kevin stood—on the outside of the area that was now squared off by yellow police tape, the kind that sent chills down the spines of most passersby, not that anyone would be passing by a private beach on Chappaquiddick, especially in April. John, two other Edgartown officers, and the state police remained. Annie noticed that Lucy was still there, too, though she'd moved over to the dunes and was talking to Jonas. Taylor was gone, which was fine with Annie, though she felt somewhat guilty about that.

"I sent the crew home until further notice," Kevin said.

"There's still six weeks to finish," Annie said.

"Five weeks, three days."

"But who's counting, right?"

"All the more reason I can't deal with Mom right now. I love her dearly, but sometimes she can be—what's the word?—formidable?"

He'd smiled as he said it, but Annie got the point. She

also wondered if that was why she hadn't yet been able to fully connect with Donna. But for both her sake and Kevin's, she wanted to sound optimistic. "Maybe by Saturday they'll know where the skull came from and it can fade into one more piece of short-lived Vineyard gossip."

"Seriously? Do you know how long things can take when you're dealing with the government? Especially in Boston. It takes forever to get a building permit. And God forbid someone claims to have seen a new species of a creepy spider or a minuscule shard of what they think might be old pottery, because it can shut down major construction of a high-rise for months."

So Earl's predictions hadn't been exaggerations.

"Well, I'm sure Donna will be disappointed. But she'll probably understand."

He laughed. "No, she won't. She'll want to come anyway. Then she'll drive everyone crazy—including me—which won't be helpful. She means well. She really does. But she doesn't want to see me—or now you, too—not get what we want. All I need to do is figure out how to tell her not to come. Then let her know I mean it."

Annie wondered why he was so insistent. Maybe *he* was the only one who Donna would drive crazy.

"Kevin?" she asked gently. "What's wrong? You've told me about a few things Donna did when you were young that were upsetting at the time, but wasn't that just typical kids-versus-parents stuff? Has something else happened?"

He looked out to the water. "No. It isn't really about her."

"What then? I mean, right now I could do without company as much as you, even our mother. But you seem kind of angry."

"Not angry. Distressed."

"About the Inn?"

"Partly."

Only partly? "What else?"

He folded his arms. "John suggested that the skull could be partial skeletal remains from a body that had fallen off, or been tossed off a ship. Or a boat. Buried at sea, intentionally or not."

"That would be good for us, though, wouldn't it? Wouldn't that mean our property wasn't sacred ground?"

"Yeah, but it could mean that your little treasure is something worse."

"Like what?"

"Like it could be from the body of Taylor's old boyfriend. Remember the story about him? Jonas's father?"

Of course Annie remembered. Taylor had had a boyfriend over twenty years ago, a son of wealthy seasonal Vineyard residents (who later became Annie's landlords). Taylor had been an island girl; her father, a fisherman. It had seemed like one of those too-predictable summer scenarios: rich boy meets poor girl, boy's family disapproves, boy goes back to prep school in September. But that boy—whose name Annie couldn't remember—had an unfortunate accident, or so it was recorded, on his small sailboat that he and Taylor had taken out one day. He had fallen overboard; Taylor claimed she'd tried, but hadn't been able to find him in the water, it had happened so fast. What few people knew at the time was that Taylor was pregnant. The baby's grandparents—the Flanagans—had insisted on raising Jonas; they'd told everyone that his mother was a Boston girl who'd wanted money but not the baby. The truth, however, was that Taylor hadn't felt she'd had a choice. She had no way and no means with which to raise a baby, while her boyfriend's parents could well afford to give him a good life. The money they gave Taylor paid for her college education, got her parents out of debt, and enabled her mother to stay in their home after Taylor's father died. But Taylor and the Flanagan boy had truly been in love—and

Jonas had found letters that proved it. It wasn't until the previous summer that mother and son had been reunited; since then the two of them had become "thick as thieves," as Earl would have said with a lighthearted chuckle.

It had been a sad love story with a surprisingly decent ending.

Until now.

Annie touched Kevin's arm. "But if it is . . . What was his name?"

"Derek."

"Right. Derek Flanagan. But if it's . . . him . . ." Her words didn't gel.

"Yeah, well," Kevin continued, "I guess the good news would be that because Derek wasn't a Wampanoag our property won't be labeled 'sacred land.'"

Yes, that was one thought. Then Annie had another. "And because Derek's death was years ago . . . because the remains wouldn't be what Earl told me would be considered 'fresh' . . . it shouldn't delay construction, should it? Wasn't Derek's case closed?"

Kevin unfolded his arms and swung them at his sides as if he were preparing to do the broad jump at a junior high track meet. "Technically, I guess it was. But things might change if this is new evidence."

So Kevin's concern about their mother's visit had less to do with Donna, and more to do with the added stress he now was under, wondering how supportive he could—or should—be for Taylor. It also had to do with his need to know if Taylor had, in truth, murdered her boyfriend. None of which would have mattered if Taylor weren't still Kevin's girlfriend. So that answered Annie's curiosity about that.

"I'll call Donna," Annie said. "I'll ask her to postpone her visit for a week or two. I'll make up a good story. That's what I do for a living, isn't it?"

Just then the state police walked past them; one carried a thick black plastic bag that was not much bigger than a gallon Ziploc. By the distinct shape of the bulge, Annie knew what was inside.

Annie waited until evening to call Donna; there was no response, so she left a message asking her to call her back. There was no need to offer details.

Then Annie went to bed.

And tried to sleep.

And tried not see what she had seen.

Or worry about what it might mean.

But it was not until the sky started to wake up that she finally found sleep.

She didn't rouse until after eight, didn't shower and pull herself together until nine. If she tried to think about the Inn's décor, she'd only dwell on the events of yesterday and the "red tape" that Earl had cautioned her might lie ahead. So instead, Annie sat at her small corner desk, staring out the open window, trying to focus on her manuscript. But the sunshine and the warm breeze—promises of summer—were not helping. She kept her phone at her elbow in case Donna returned her call.

"Focus, focus, focus," Annie admonished herself. But it was hard to separate the yellow police DO NOT CROSS tape on her beach from the murder in her manuscript.

Annie's mystery series revolved around two main characters who once had been college pals but now were very different: studious Emma was a hardworking career girl struggling to climb the ladder at a Boston art museum; fun-loving Maggie was a trophy wife who volunteered at the museum in order to do something "civic-minded" that would look good to members of the other boards on which she (or her husband) served, and that someday would read well in her obituary. Annie had not crafted the characters after Murphy and herself; if she had, the book would have been easier to write.

She pulled her gaze back to the screen that read "Chapter 4" at the top. The rest of the page was blank. At the end of chapter three, a museum guard had found a corpse in the Monet Room. She shifted her gaze from the screen to the keyboard; she wondered if she were the only bestselling author who had never mastered typing without using the two-fingers-of-each-hand system, as if technology had surpassed her basic abilities.

And now a different kind of technology would determine the identity, or at least the ancestral origin, of the remains that might change her future.

She limbered her four typing fingers over the keyboard. "Focus," she whispered. "Please, focus."

She thought about the Monet Room in her fictitious museum, which led her to remember the Monet gallery in Paris where she'd been not once but half a dozen times when she was with Mark, though she'd rather not think about him, any more than she wanted to think about the skull she'd found. So she forced her mind to wander to the Paris gallery and Monet's painting of buttercups that featured a beautiful woman in a white dress and white hat and carrying a white parasol; it was a bright summer day; the woman was resting in a field among the yellow flowers. The title of the painting was *In the Meadow*, and it had inspired Annie to include, in the landscaping plan around The Vineyard Inn, a large tract for a meadow that would be filled with buttercups.

The idea, Annie knew, had formed because of her mother—not Donna, but Ellen Sutton.

Every year in late spring, the Suttons had gone to the Vineyard for a weekend, ostensibly to pick out the cottage where they'd stay on their August vacation. (It took a long time before Annie figured out that those weekends had been an excuse for an early visit to the island, because they always wound up renting the same cottage in Edgartown.) One of those spring trips had been extra special. She knew that she'd been eight, because the following year her mother had left them for a while, and Annie had never fully trusted her again. Maybe that was why her memories of the weekend were so vivid. And good.

That Sunday morning, her dad had wanted to sit on the porch—the *piazza*, he'd always called it—of the old hotel where they were staying to smoke his pipe and read the *Boston Globe*. In an uncharacteristic move, her mother had suggested that the two "girls" go for a drive up island to Alley's General Store in search of clever kitchen gadgets to bring back to the city. They had waved good-bye to Annie's dad and climbed into the family's Rambler, her mother pushing the push button that read "Drive," and tooting the horn as they headed off toward West Tisbury.

Somewhere along the way, they had spotted a meadow. Her mother had stopped the car. "Buttercups!" she cried as she jumped out. Annie followed. They ducked under a split-rail fence and stood in tall, verdant grasses that were topped with bright yellow blossoms stretching "as far as the eye can see," her mother said. In the distance, two brown horses and one white one strolled through the grass and seemed as happy to be there as Annie was. Then her mother plucked one of the flowers.

"Raise your head," she said to Annie. So Annie did. Then her mother held the yellow cup under her chin. "This proves it! You like butter!"

Then Annie took the flower and held it under her mother's chin. When she saw the golden reflection on her mother's skin, she giggled. "You like butter, too, Mommy!" It wasn't as exciting as doing the he-loves-me-he-loves-me-not with daisies or making a wish before blowing on a dandelion puff, but having her mother play a little game with her was worth all the he-loves-me's and wishes coming true in the world.

Her mother then hugged her and ruffled her hair, and they picked a whole bunch of buttercups to bring back to Daddy.

When Annie had seen the painting at the Monet gallery, it had reminded her of that day. The memory had not only inspired her to design a meadow at the Inn, it was also why she'd inserted a "Monet Room" in the museum of her book.

She smiled a small smile. And then she blinked. Still staring at the keyboard, she suddenly realized that several more minutes had passed, and she still hadn't typed a single word.

Don't make it a corpse. Murphy's voice suddenly floated into the open window on the breeze.

"What?" Annie sat up straight.

Don't make it a corpse, her old friend repeated.

And then Murphy was gone, as quickly as she—or rather, her presence—had arrived.

But Annie laughed. Loudly. Because Murphy had offered the key that Annie needed. Instead of the corpse she'd hidden in the Monet Room the last time she'd done any worthwhile writing, she would make this one a skull. Or part of a skull. God knows, she now knew what one looked like. Besides, she reasoned, one would tuck nicely into the room without drawing attention from the buttercups.

Her fingers came alive, thanks to her old pal, who had helped Annie redirect many literary jams. Her four fingers—two on the left, two on the right—had churned out a couple of scenes when her phone rang.

Damn!

She considered not answering, but what if it was John with more information? Or what if Kevin had a new crisis?

With a loud groan, Annie turned from her desk and recovered her phone from the bookcase next to her. But Caller ID reported that it was neither John nor Kevin; it was Donna.

Aunt Elizabeth left Donna a little money when she died. "It's not enough for you to have the kind of happiness that you deserve," Elizabeth had penned in a note that she'd tucked into an envelope along with six thousand dollars in one hundred dollar bills, "but it might come in handy if, like me, you never find a rich man to marry you." Elizabeth's attorney had handed Donna the envelope; it had been in the safety deposit box next to Elizabeth's last will and testament. Though Donna had known her aunt had longed for exquisite, expensive things, she'd never had any of her own. She'd been a spinster all her life; it was amazing that she'd been able to save that much. Donna's parents never had; they'd scrimped their whole lives and, in the end, they each only had a five thousand dollar life insurance policy. It had cost that much to pay their final medical bills and to bury them.

Donna would have loved to buy the Louis Vuitton with part of her windfall from Elizabeth. But the woman hadn't died until six months after the trunk had vanished from the shop on Newbury Street.

So instead she used the money to go to business school at night. If she had no man, she figured she'd need an education to support young Kevin and herself. Or she would risk ending up like her parents and Elizabeth, leaving her dreams behind.

Chapter 7

"All the more reason for me to be there," Donna said after Annie told her about the pressure mounting toward opening the Inn. Annie saw no reason to tell her about the skull and its potential ramifications—not until they knew more about what would happen.

"But some of our construction crew has left," Annie said, "and it looks like we won't be able to replace them for a week or two. So Kevin and Earl are really busy." She was, of course, stretching the truth, as her father would have called it. "Wouldn't you rather be here when we can have fun? I was hoping you'd help me make soap for the artisan festivals . . . or give me a hand with some last-minute decorating."

"No," Donna interrupted. "A week or two has a way of turning into a month or more. I don't want to wait that long to see my children. And you won't have time to come up here. Not now, or once the Inn has opened."

She was right, of course. And Annie didn't know how to dissuade her. "Kevin and I want to see you, too. But this week, well, to be honest, everyone's nerves are frayed. I'm sure you understand. Can you at least wait until next week?"

"No," Donna repeated.

A lump returned to Annie's throat. "Oh." She wondered if she sounded as close to tears as she suddenly felt.

Silence.

Then Donna said, "I'm sorry, Annie. But I need to see you." Her voice had dropped an octave or two, as if this were serious.

"Is something wrong?"

After another pause, Donna said, "When I was on the cruise last year I took a class in estate planning. I've since received the final payment for my business, and it's all going into a trust. I need to review it with you and Kevin first."

"But surely a few days . . . ?" Annie held her fingers to her throat as if the gesture would dissolve the lump.

"No," Donna said again. "My attorney is going out of the country for a while. I want to button this up before he goes. I'm sure you understand. So I'll be on the noon boat on Saturday as planned. If no one can pick me up, I'll take a taxi. Or the bus. You still have busses there, don't you?"

So Annie told her someone would meet her at the boat, because what else could she say? After they rang off, she realized that Kevin had used the perfect word—*formidable*—to describe their mother. With a sigh of resignation, Annie sat for a moment, then looked back at her computer. But the inspiration was gone. Instead, she needed to find Kevin and tell him the news. There would always be tomorrow—or the next day—to get back to her manuscript. At least Murphy was around in case of writer's block.

The Inn was quiet, except for the crinkle of paint-splattered tarps under Annie's feet. She paused in the kitchen and surveyed the transformation; the only thing left to do was install the white porcelain tiles on the floor. Otherwise it looked complete: the lustrous counters, the stainless steel ten-burner gas stove, the Sub-Zero refrigerators (two). The cabinets were also in place, their gleaming white blending with the white marble countertops. The windows framed a perfect contrast of the thick green lawn, the whispery beige sand, the shimmering aqua water. The scene was breathtaking. If only it didn't become an abandoned masterpiece.

Pushing down negative thoughts, she went into the great room. Though the floor-to-ceiling windows had been installed, the room hadn't yet been painted. The blue slate fireplace was not complete; the wood floor wasn't in place; there was so much left to do. And with the crew having been sent home until the state police gave them the all-clear, it was up to Earl and Kevin to race against the clock. And sneakily, at that.

"Earl!" she called as she circled into the two-story foyer. "Kevin!" Neither responded. She paused and listened. But there were no sounds. Opposite the staircase, she peeked into the cozy reading room that abutted a large powder room, then walked past a storage closet to the media room. That side of the house was finished; each room sat ready, its walls and floors and fabulous furnishings emitting fine scents of newness. But Earl and Kevin weren't there, either.

She returned to the foyer and quickly climbed the stairs, wondering if they'd been told they couldn't work there, either, that no one was allowed on the grounds until the mystery was solved. Then Annie had two thoughts: Why the heck had she ever gone searching for decorative items on the beach? . . . And if no one was allowed on the grounds, did that mean her, too? If so, where would she go—what would she do until this was resolved? The cottage was her home now, wasn't it?

At the top of the stairs, she made a quick right into the front bedroom that Kevin had said she could use.

But though Earl had said he'd be painting, the work wasn't yet done. Maybe she and Kevin should book a hotel room for Donna after all. Or one for Annie, if Donna preferred the cottage. It was only April, so hotel rooms would be available—though, like restaurants, few places were open year-round. And even at off-season prices, the costs would add up quickly.

More expenses would only heighten their problems. If Annie could write faster, the income from her next book would come in sooner, but, she knew, not soon enough. Besides, if she spent every day hard at work at the computer, the best she could expect would be to finish the manuscript in six months, maybe seven.

"Earl! Kevin!"

But there were no sounds, not of paint being swished across a wall . . . or of footsteps . . . or of anything.

She needed to call Kevin. But when she reached into her pocket, she realized she'd left her phone at home.

Trying not to give in to utter frustration, she spun around and retraced her tracks down the stairs, through the great room, the kitchen, then into the mudroom by the back door. Which was where she bumped smack into Kevin.

"There you are," they said simultaneously.

"You're looking for me?" he asked without cracking a grin, which was out of character for him.

"Yes. But go ahead. You first."

He rubbed the back of his neck, which was not a good sign. Annie's stomach tightened. Was it bad news from the ME's office or the state police?

"It's about John's daughter."

Her whole body tensed. She sucked in a short breath and grabbed a sleeve of his denim shirt. "Lucy? What?"

"She's fine. Or she will be until her grandfather gets ahold of her."

Annie released her grip. "What happened?"

"That sweet girl who's become your sidekick took a picture of the skull."

"I know. She said she was afraid something would come along and take the thing before her father got there."

"Well, she posted the picture on the internet this morning. The damn thing went viral. Over twelve thousand viewers already. Probably more, because I haven't checked in the last five minutes."

Annie was stunned.

"That's not the worst," he added. "The headline reads: 'Skull found on Chappaquiddick, Martha's Vineyard. And it's *def* not from a shark.'"

"Dear God," she finally managed to say. "Does John know?"

Kevin shrugged. "He worked last night, according to Earl. He's probably sleeping. Earl's going to tell him after he picks Lucy up at school."

Annie rubbed her arms. She moved back into the kitchen; Kevin followed.

"I thought she was smarter than that," Annie said. "If I ever thought she'd . . ."

"What? You would have taken away her phone? It's a new world, Annie. Oh, and there's more. She hashtagged Martha's Vineyard. Chappaquiddick." He paused. "And The Vineyard Inn."

Annie went back to the windows over the sink. The beautiful view that moments earlier had looked so serene now seemed dulled, its magic tainted. "Anything else?"

"She added a picture of Jonas standing in front of the yellow tape. I can't imagine why."

Of course, Annie could. It was clear that Lucy had been trying to impress the guy. "Oh, God, Kevin. Someone needs to make her take those pictures down. And fast."

"It's the first thing Earl's going to tell her when she gets into his truck. But I'm afraid it isn't going to help much. Once something's gone viral . . . well . . . From what we can figure, it's already hit the news feeds. So it's out there. Everywhere."

"Who told you about it?"

"A friend of Earl's called him from the chamber of commerce. They saw it online; they check all the Martha's Vineyard tags. We were here, working on the upstairs room. I was going to tell you first, but when I walked down to the cottage I saw you through the window. You were sitting at your desk, deep in concentration, and I knew this would be a major distraction."

Deep in concentration? Hardly. She'd only been reminiscing until Murphy had jarred her out of it. "We'd better go to John's. This will take a few clear heads to sort out. I'll just run down to my place and get my purse . . ."

"Sorry," he said as she brushed past him. "But you'll have to go alone. Taylor wants me to talk to Jonas. About being 'careful' around Lucy."

Annie didn't have to ask what he meant by "careful." She agreed it was a good idea. Jonas, after all, had never had a father who might have taught him about setting boundaries around young teenage girls. Annie left the Inn, but halfway down the hill, she remembered she'd forgotten to tell Kevin that Donna was still coming on Saturday. She supposed that it could wait. There was only so much bad news a person could handle in one day.

John was furious. Earl was grumpy. Lucy was defensive.

By the time Annie arrived, the three Lyons family members were sitting in John's living room—John in his recliner, Earl in a wing chair, Lucy on one end of the love seat, her legs curled under her, her spine tipped slightly forward. All of them had their arms folded—the men, no doubt to block their anger; Lucy, as if she were trying to avoid an old-fashioned flogging. By the startled look on her face, Earl might have mentioned that if this were fifty years ago, that would have been a possibility.

"So," Annie said as she stepped farther into the room, "what are we going to do about this little problem?"

"I took it down," Lucy said.

"And as I told you," John groused, "it was too late. For starters, you tagged Jonas, so all his friends saw it. It might even have been one of them who alerted the news feeds. Or someone who saw the 'Vineyard' tag and thought it was hilarious. I swear, everyone under twenty-five these days is too technology-smart and too common-sense-stupid."

Annie sat in the wing chair opposite Earl. "I've never been good at deception," she said, "but on the way over here, I tried to think of something we could post to deflect the spotlight—a way to shift the narrative." It was a technique she'd often seen her ex-husband use, though she'd hidden her distress each time he'd boasted about it. The three generations now looked at her intently.

"I'm a cop, Annie," John said. "It can't be illegal."

She shook her head. "Just a playful distraction." She didn't think that lying had become illegal, unless you were in court. She glanced at Earl. "I got the idea from something you said yesterday about the skull's maybe being from an old Halloween prank. Or a kid's toy, leftover from a party. So I thought, why not put those things together and come up with another post?"

The generations were silent for all of five seconds. Then Lucy asked, "Like what?"

"Like what if we posted a picture of a pumpkin carved up like a jack-o'-lantern and wrote: 'Pranksters play early Halloween hoax on Martha's Vineyard.' Or something like that? Even though Halloween's a long way off, I bet people would buy into the drama and believe it."

"People will believe anything these days," Lucy said, once again sounding way beyond her years. She unfurled her body, opening up to the idea. "We could make the type bold and black for added attention."

"Or set it all against a black background, reverse the type so it's white, and paste the glowing jack-o'-lantern next to it," Annie added.

The men offered no comments.

"It could work," Annie said. "At least, it should help diffuse the fallout."

"If we do it fast," Lucy said.

"Where's your laptop?" Annie asked, just as the doorbell rang.

The four of them sat, frozen in place. It rang again.

With a guttural hiss, John stood up and went to the door. On the other side, stood a large, pale woman. She had jet-black hair and substantial gray roots; she wore a dark blue blazer, khaki pants, and a tight-lipped, crimson grin. She had a notebook in her hand.

"Hello, Marilyn," John said. "How are things over at the newspaper?"

Chapter 8

Annie supposed that telling lies on the internet was one thing, but telling a reporter the same made-up story might ride an edge of being unethical, especially when one knew the reporter—which, in John's case was more than true because it turned out that Marilyn Sunderland had been his sixth grade teacher. Small island, Annie thought.

"The rest of them are headed for Chappy," Marilyn said.

The rest of whom? Annie wanted to ask. But seeing as how there were only two newspapers doing business on the island, she feared she knew the answer. Boston, probably. Maybe Providence. Surely the story wasn't big enough for the networks or cable outlets. Was it? And what about the plethora of online "news" magazines?

Marilyn fidgeted with her pen, clicking it on and off. Her cheeks were flushed. "We haven't had this much excitement at the paper since Michelle Obama showed up unexpectedly at the Edgartown Library."

The former first lady's visit had been a fabulous surprise; Annie knew that her discovery was hardly in the same category.

"But I'm not here for gossip. I would, however, like an exclusive, John. Seeing as how I taught you how to read and write."

John actually laughed. "I hate to burst your bubble, Ms. Sunderland, but I knew how to read and write fairly well by the time I was in sixth grade."

She waved the notebook in his face as if swatting a fly. "I'm serious, John. Right now, the *Globe*, the *Cape Cod Times*, and a bunch of online rags are queued up at the ferry trying to get over to the scene. I also heard that CNN is on its way and plans to do a feature that's somehow tied to *Jaws*. It sounds farfetched, but who knows? In any event, we islanders want the best for the Inn. It's a fine piece of property, and we know Earl will do it justice." She peeked around John's shoulder and waved to Earl, who nodded in half-hearted response. "But this kind of publicity could put a quick kibosh on it. Give me an exclusive, and we'll get the real story out. It's the only way to ward off gossipmongers."

John stood in the doorway staring at Marilyn Sunderland. Annie didn't feel it was her place to say anything, and Lucy had returned to cowering.

Earl stood and hoisted the waistband of his workpants. "Let her in, son," he said.

Lucy offered everyone a cold drink; John told her this was not a social event.

Marilyn sat on the love seat next to Lucy. "How are you, honey?" she asked as she tapped Lucy's knee. "That must have been a dreadful experience, finding that skull. I remember when I was about your age, Ronnie Slovich was walking to school one morning and he found a dead body on West Tisbury Road. Remember that, Earl?"

Earl shrugged. For as long as Annie had known him, she didn't think she'd seen him that mute for that long.

"So," Marilyn went on, "do you want to tell me about it, honey?" She clicked her pen and looked at Lucy.

"I didn't find it," Lucy said. "Annie did."

All gazes skulked over to Annie.

"I did," Annie said. "And I need to tell you up front, Marilyn, that it might be a hoax." She said it with a straight face and a clear voice, and, for once, she didn't stumble over a lie. Perhaps because so much was at stake.

"A *hoax*?"

Toying with the hem of her T-shirt—good grief, Annie realized, she was wearing an old T-shirt and yoga pants, her work-at-home wardrobe, not her go-to-Edgartown attire. She wondered if she'd put on any makeup in the morning, then recalled that, no, she hadn't. On top of that, she'd looped her hair into a quasi ponytail—quasi because her hair was too short for a real one, but so long that it hung in her face when she was bent over her keyboard, studying the letters, waiting for words to find a way out to her four typing fingertips. She sat up straight and squared her shoulders, hoping that good posture would help neutralize her god-awful appearance.

"It's possible that the item is an old Halloween toy, perhaps a decoration once used at a party. It was hard to tell because when I pulled it from between the rocks, it was covered with seaweed."

"A *toy*?" The woman's jawline sagged.

"We won't know for certain until the state police get back to us. But, of course, we had to go through the proper protocol just in case." Annie looked at John, who was standing behind the wing chair where Earl sat, his arms still folded. "Right, John?"

It took a few seconds for John to answer, then he said, "The Staties are in charge. But I'm sure you know that, Marilyn."

Marilyn exhaled a breathy sigh through her large nostrils. "A toy?" she repeated, then quickly turned back to Lucy.

"I hope this wasn't your idea. Because planting a toy on the beach, pretending it's a human skull in order to get attention, not only wastes a massive amount of police work and law enforcement time, but I believe it would be akin to pulling a fire alarm at the school." Marilyn whipped around, back to John. "Am I right about that, Sergeant Lyons?"

He squared his shoulders the way that Annie had, though his were broad and strong and much more assertive, despite the fact that he had on the scrub pants with the drawstring that she knew he wore to bed. She wondered if Marilyn felt intimidated, or if the woman still saw John as a twelve-year-old who was, as Winnie had said, always off in a million directions.

"Lucy knows better than to do something like that. And I'd appreciate it if you would not insult or interrogate my daughter." His thoughtful, pearl-gray eyes turned dark and penetrating.

Marilyn stood. "I assure you, I meant nothing by it. But she is the one who posted the photos, isn't she? Which are bound to have the other members of the media conclude that your daughter does not, as you call it, *know better* than to do something like that." She headed for the door, stopped, then rotated back around. "No matter what the investigation reveals, I do hope you'll consider giving me the exclusive. I'm probably the only one who truly doesn't want negative publicity about our island." She attempted a small smile, said that she'd let herself out, and, sure enough, she did.

They were silent for a moment. Then Annie said, "I'm surprised you had nothing to add, Earl."

"Me? Hell, no. I dated that woman about a hundred years ago before I met Claire, but, believe me, Marilyn never let me forget it. At least she didn't wink at me this time. She usually does that when Claire's around, to see if she can get my goat. Or Claire's. Behind closed doors Claire and I laugh about it, but the truth is, Marilyn Sunderland gives me the creeps."

"Dad? Are you kidding? You dated my sixth-grade teacher?"

"She was not your teacher at the time, as you hadn't yet been born. I think we were still in high school. Yeah. We must have been. All I really know is that it wasn't pretty when, oh, I guess you could say, I dumped her for your lovely mother, who, unlike Marilyn, did not scare the hell out of me." He chuckled.

"Well," Annie said. "We didn't give her what she wanted. Do you think she'll somehow use it against us?"

"Dunno," Earl replied. "I never did understand what made her so crotchety."

"In that case, I guess we'd better take care of this right now. Lucy, is your laptop downstairs?"

She shook her head. "It's in my room."

"Why don't you girls go upstairs and work on that," John said. "I'll go back to Chappy with Gramps. I'm awake now anyway, so I might as well take care of a few things over there."

Lucy's room was papered in posters of her favorite musicians, none of whom Annie recognized. She was familiar, however, with the theme of the décor; when she'd been a teen, her bedroom walls had been plastered with images of Springsteen, David Bowie, Queen. And Madonna, though her mother had not approved.

Grabbing the laptop from her desk, Lucy sank onto her bed. Annie went to a small wooden chair that was painted pink. Before sitting down, she noticed that LUCY was spelled out in pink, glittery crystals on the back.

"My dad made that," Lucy said. "He made one for Abigail, too. I was seven, and she was ten. I thought mine was the most beautiful thing I'd ever seen. Abigail scrunched up her face and asked him why he thought she was still a little girl."

Annie's heart melted like a snowman on South Beach in August. Sometimes she forgot that Lucy had a sister—John's older daughter—who lived with their mother on the mainland and decried all things "Martha's Vineyard." Lucy hadn't seen Abigail since Christmas. Annie pulled the chair closer to the bed and sat. "Do you miss your sister?"

"No." Her head was bent; her long hair was unbraided, spilling down her cheeks. Her eyes were focused on the screen while her fingers—all of them—hopped over the keyboard like stones skipping across the water.

Then Annie asked, "Lucy? Why did you post a picture of Jonas standing on the beach?"

Lucy didn't answer right away, then said, "He was there, you know?"

"I do know, yes. And I know he's really cute. Do you agree?"

"Sure. Yeah. I guess." She kept typing, though only God and the internet knew what she was writing.

"Lucy? You do know he is quite a bit older than you are, don't you?"

"Duh, yeah."

"He's in his twenties."

She kept typing.

"It's just that I wouldn't want you to . . ."

Lucy stopped typing, looked up at Annie, and tucked her hair behind both ears. "Look, Annie, I know what you're trying to say, but forget it. I'm fourteen. I might not be starting high school until September. But I'm not naïve."

Annie wasn't sure if that meant Lucy knew that Jonas was too old for her or that she thought she was mature enough to make those decisions for herself. Which maybe she was. What did Annie know about raising a teenager?

"I know. I just don't want you . . ."

"What? To get hurt?"

"For one thing, yes."

"Don't worry. Besides, Jonas would be the last one to hurt me. That guy knows what hurt feels like. Do you know he only met his mother—officially—last summer, and that he never got to know his father?"

"I know, honey," Annie said. "I also know that might make him vulnerable." She remembered when Jonas had showed up at her door not even a year ago, when he'd apologized that his grandfather had booted her from her rental. Jonas had been kind. And sensitive.

Lucy laughed. "He's hardly vulnerable. He graduated from college last year. He's an artist. And he's really good. He's even been asked to show his paintings at the Sculpin Gallery and Featherstone this year. A ton of people have friended him online, but he never posts anything. I thought that if we showed his face doing something exciting, it might get him some visibility. Help make him more famous, you know?"

"So you were only trying to help him?"

"Duh, yeah," Lucy repeated.

Annie realized it was just as well that she'd never raised a child. She clearly had no idea how a young mind worked, perhaps had never even known how hers had. Otherwise, her life might have been very different.

After cutting and pasting an image of a jack-o'-lantern and announcing the hoax, Annie left John's house. She did a few errands in town, then made it back to Chappy around dinnertime. Neither John nor Kevin had mentioned mealtime plans; maybe it was just as well—she needed time alone.

Best of all, when she arrived no media had been lurking at the *On Time* or seemed to have made it across the channel to the property. When John had said he had a few things to take care of and had left for Chappy with Earl, he must have taken care of the reporters. In his peaceful, coply way.

Digging through her refrigerator, she came up with various bits and tossed them into a salad—greens, tomatoes, some vegetable lo mein, and leftover chicken. Thankfully, it tasted better than it looked. She sat by the window while she ate, not turning on either the television or the radio for the false company of voices. She did not check her phone for texts or her laptop for mail; she simply sat and pondered. Mostly, she tried to steer her pondering to Donna's impending visit.

Kevin would be upset that their mother was still coming. Maybe he should have been the one to call her—he knew Donna so much better than Annie ever could.

Annie could not imagine what it would have been like if she'd been Kevin, if she'd been raised by a mother but no father, a working mother, which still had not been common in the seventies when Kevin was growing up. For Annie, it might have been fun to be around all of Donna's beautiful antiques, to have been surrounded by her friends who probably had creative minds and knew about history and art and all kinds of interesting things.

Bob and Ellen Sutton had provided a much different kind of home. But it had been a nice home. Where Annie had felt loved.

Tears began to well. She missed the mom and dad who'd raised her: the caretaking predictability of her mom, the unpretentious, nonjudgmental steadiness of her dad. Pushing away her salad now, Annie stood, went to her bookcase, and removed a large blue binder—the photo album she hadn't looked at in a long time. She sat down in her rocking chair, slowly turned the pages, and remembered.

As a toddler, she'd always looked bewildered, her mass of black curls so different from the fair hair of her parents. By elementary school, her curls were gone, her hair then long and straight, parted down the middle because she'd wanted to be Cher. At her high school graduation, when Annie was named class valedictorian, Bob and Ellen Sutton looked so proud standing beside her on the dais. She traced her finger, first around her mother's smile that had softened with the years, then around her dad's receding hairline, that he'd often joked displayed his age the way the rings of an old tree trunk showed off theirs.

Throughout the album, the photos showed the years of their Vineyard vacations, those treasured, annual weeks. Her dad began to save for the next year as soon as they got home; instead of a Christmas Club at the local bank, they had a Vacation Club.

There weren't as many photos of Annie once she'd gone to college, except . . . She turned the page and saw what she knew was glued on there: a photo that her dad had snapped of Annie and Murphy, laughing over something that no doubt was ridiculous. Their hairdos—Annie's ebony, Murphy's carrot-red—were very big and held together by tons of spray; their sweaters had shoulder pads that made them look like linemen on the football team. They'd met the first day of college in the hallway of their dorm and wound up being best friends for more than three decades.

"That's us," she said, hoping Murphy would hear.

Then Annie drew in a small breath and turned another page to the pictures of her wedding to Brian. Young, sweet love, so tender, so innocent. The boy who'd loved her when she'd been young.

Which made her think of Jonas, and how life seemed to give everyone some sorrow. In some way. At some time. Still, she wondered if there might be a way that she could help Taylor's boy.

But right then, her thoughts were blurred by reminiscing. So Annie closed the album and returned it to the shelf.

Chapter 9

Thursday morning, Annie woke up late, not wanting the memories she'd evoked last night to disappear again, to be folded back into the faded pages of the old photo album. It was after ten before she shook off her hangover of memories, pulled herself together, and pretended she might get some work done.

She was on her third cup of coffee when a quick knock on the door saved her from her self-pitying self.

"Well," Kevin said, "you look like hell today."

Annie laughed. "Thanks for the confidence boost, brother. I'm glad you're here. Sit. We have to talk."

"Coffee?"

"Help yourself. Then sit. Please."

He did as he was told. He was a terrific brother. *Half-*brother, she remembered.

She sighed. "I did my best, but she's still coming."

"Crap."

"Sorry. She wants to talk to us about the trust fund she set up. She said she needs to go over it with us."

"Can't it wait?"

"Apparently not. Something about her attorney leaving the country for a while."

"Did you tell her what's going on here?"

"Not about the skull. I thought we should wait until we knew what was going to happen. But I mentioned that a few of your crew have left, so you and Earl are really busy. I told her nerves are frayed. But I'm not sure she listened."

He swigged the coffee. "She didn't want to hear it. Mom never handles it well when someone tries to change her plans."

"I didn't know that. Maybe I shouldn't have been the one to call her."

He cupped the mug in his palms. "It wouldn't have mattered. She's set on coming; nothing will change her mind."

"I'll keep her occupied," Annie said. "You keep doing what you need to do. Will you have a room ready for me?"

"If you don't mind sleeping in a place where the floor isn't finished. Or where only two walls have paint. Or where the blinds aren't in place. Or . . ."

"As long as there's a bed, I'll make do."

"Good. I hope our guests will feel the same when they start arriving."

"If the law lets us have an occupancy permit."

"Right. There's that, too." Everything about Kevin looked tired—his expressionless face, his droopy posture, even his clothes that sagged.

"How did it go with Jonas yesterday?" Annie asked.

"Pretty much as I expected. He denied having any 'special feelings' for Lucy. Other than that he said she's a good kid, with the emphasis on 'kid.' I guess he has over a thousand online friends, mostly artists or fans of artists. He was happy that Lucy suggested posting his picture so, as he said, 'people will know I'm still alive.'"

"An odd choice of words, under the circumstances."

"No kidding." Kevin shook his head briskly as if he were a dog shaking out his jowls. "There's too much going on around here! What happened to the peace and quiet of the Vineyard?"

Annie laughed. "Life happened. Life *happens*. Everywhere, anywhere. Whether we like it or not."

"Ah, yes. My wiser, older sister." Then Kevin's phone pinged. He took it out and stared at the screen. "Crap."

"Crap what?"

"Crap. It's John." His eyes quickly skimmed the screen.

"*My* John?" As soon as Annie said it, she felt ridiculous for referring to John as hers.

"Yup." Kevin's eyes shot from his phone to her. "The preliminary report is in. The bone is from a human skull. Not an animal. Crap."

She waited patiently—well, sort of patiently—while Kevin read the text. Then she couldn't stand it anymore. "So what now?"

"We wait," Kevin replied, his eyes fixed on the phone, still reading. "The archeologist has the fragment." He looked back at Annie. "They're calling it a fragment now. At least that sounds . . . kinder? Tidier?" He scanned the screen again. "They're going to test it for heritage. It will take a while." He set down the phone. The news, apparently, was done.

Annie sighed. "I don't suppose it's the first time this has happened on Cape Cod or the Islands."

"Small consolation."

"At least we have local law enforcement on our side. Maybe they can help hurry things along."

"Not sure how tight the Vineyard cops—or even the state police here—are with the guys in Boston."

"With all the construction you did up there, you never ran into a situation like this?"

"Bones? Nope. We found a turtle once. A rare little thing. Everything had to stop until they could determine that it wasn't a nesting ground."

"Was it?"

"Nope. We lucked out. They figured that Mr. Turtle's

GPS had taken him in the wrong direction. But I don't re-member how long it took them to reach that conclusion. It was a while back." He sighed and took another sip of coffee. "Earl and I just have to keep working. Our crew won't be able to wait. They'll have to go to work for someone else so they can get a paycheck, but we can't risk having violations slapped on us—or the bad press that's sure to follow—if we blatantly ignore the stop order."

Annie stood and went to the only window that didn't look out to the harbor but up to the main house instead. The new cedar shingles that covered the exterior were tan now, but they would turn an iconic silver-gray in less than a year, whether or not the Inn was ever allowed to open. It was hard to believe that all the planning, all the time—all the money spent—was now in jeopardy, thanks to something that had washed ashore the way so many islanders had. The year-round tenants and the three winter renters would have to return to fruitlessly searching, searching, *begging* for a place to live, as Annie had tried to do last summer. Not to mention that Kevin and Earl's investment might never be recouped. The value of the property would be moot if it was labeled ancient Native American ground. On the other hand, maybe the Chappaquiddick Wampanoags would have somewhere to call home again.

"I feel so torn," she said. "If it ends up that the land be-longs to a Chappy Wampanoag, I'll be happy for them. I re-spect their culture—and them—and I'd be glad that it would be theirs again. But I'd be lying if I said I'd be happy for us."

"I don't know much about the history, but I get what you're saying. Meghan would have said 'we can't win for losing.'"

It took a few seconds for Annie to remember that Meghan was Kevin's wife. Annie turned back to him; he sat, wide-

eyed and motionless, as if he, too, were surprised that he'd
mentioned her name.

"As long as we're talking about sad situations," Annie said,
"any word on Meghan?"

He shook his head. Meghan was in a long-term care facility in Stockbridge, where she'd been for several years following a serious fall from scaffolding while she'd been working
for Kevin's construction company in Boston. She'd suffered
a traumatic brain injury and was not expected to get better.
The last time Kevin had seen her, which as far as Annie knew
was nearly two years earlier, Meghan had not known who he
was. Kevin had told Annie that after that, the thought alone
of making the trip had been too painful; a year ago, he'd
contacted an attorney about getting a divorce, about trying to
find a way to have a life again.

"I'm so sorry, Kevin."

"My lawyer said it's going to take time." He shrugged.
"Which is fine. It's not as if I want to run off and get married.
Again."

"Tell me if I'm prying, but how does Taylor feel about
that?"

He snorted. "We're not at that stage, Annie."

"Okay then, let's try to be more cheerful. Maybe it's good
that Donna's coming. If nothing else, she's bound to keep us
occupied."

Kevin dropped his chin to his chest. "She will do that."
Then he drained his mug, walked it to the sink, and rinsed
it out. "I'd better get back to work so you'll have a halfway
decent room."

"And I should think about giving this place a good cleaning before Donna arrives." Then Annie gave Kevin a big
hug. Because she knew that no matter what happened, what,
when, or how, she wanted him in her life.

She watched as he left the cottage, walked up the slope, and disappeared into the house. Then she exhaled and looked around the room.

"Time to clean!" she commanded herself. Her gaze landed on the braided rug that her adoptive grandmother—Bob Sutton's mother—had made as a wedding gift for Annie and Brian. She wondered if she should tell Donna its history, rather than have her think Annie was out of step with home-decorating trends. Then she looked to the old blue photo album in the bookcase. Would Donna like to see the pictures of Annie growing up? Or should she avoid that can of emotional worms?

She had no idea. Rather than dwelling on it, she went to the closet and pulled out the vacuum cleaner.

One interesting part about living on Chappaquiddick was that getting Wi-Fi could be a challenge. Cell phone service, too—two bars, one bar, none. The glitches typically occurred in winter when the island breezes were stirred up like mistrals, those unrelenting winds that whirled and swirled in the South of France where Annie had gone several times with her ex-husband, con man Mark. On Chappy, as in France, one became accustomed to blustery interference. On Chappy, the interruption of services was sometimes a relief. Back to the good old days of peace and quiet and nothing else.

Which was why, later that sunny day, with her cleaning binge completed, Annie checked all plugs and portals, found them up and running, then turned off the alerts on her laptop and her phone and descended into the blissful silence of no distractions in order to write.

The trouble with silence, however, was the shock when it was broken. After nearly five hours had elapsed and seven new pages had magically now appeared on the screen of her laptop, a loud banging on her door jarred her back to the real world.

She hauled her body from the chair in her peaceful writing room and went into the living room. Through the screen door she saw two men and a woman, in their twenties or thirties, standing on the small porch. They were dressed in jeans and lightweight hooded jackets that did not look new. The men looked vaguely familiar.

"May I help you?" Annie asked through the screen. She wondered if they might be reporters of online media who hadn't yet heard that there was no viable story there.

"Greg Collins," the taller man said. He had black hair and brown eyes and round, cheerful cheeks. "We're here about the Inn."

If one's heart were really capable of sinking, Annie's did. She smiled at the group, trying to mask her dismay.

"Marty Amanti," the woman then said, and pointed at the other man. "And my husband, Luke."

Then the names rang a few bells. Three, to be exact. Greg Collins and Marty and Luke Amanti were soon-to-be tenants who had signed two of the three year-round leases for rooms at The Vineyard Inn.

"Of course," Annie said, shifting on one foot. "How are you all today?"

"We heard about the bones," Greg said. "We need to know what's going on."

"It was on the internet," Marty added. "We watched the video on YouTube."

The *video?* As far as Annie knew, Lucy had only taken a photograph. Two, counting the one with Jonas. Had someone turned them into a video?

Marty's husband stepped forward. "Has construction shut down? Is there going to be an Inn or do we have to spend the winter camping again?"

Annie raised both hands. "Please. One at a time. First of all, I'm the one who found the bone." She couldn't bring

herself to say "the skull." "And, yes, there are some legal pro-
tocols that have to be observed before we can finish up construction. But things are moving along, and we don't see this
as a problem. We still plan to open Memorial Day weekend."

"The guy on the video says the thing is human."

What *guy*? What *video*? Annie shifted again. She tucked
her hair behind her ears. "It's true. And it looks as if it's ancient, but they're testing it to be sure. Chances are, it's from an
old shipwreck." She had no idea where that last idea had come
from, but she thought it sounded plausible.

"Unless it's the guy's father," Marty said. "Like he said it
might be."

The guy's *father*? Was he talking about *Jonas's* father—
Derek Flanagan? Good Lord, Annie thought. Had Jonas shot
a video? Was he as concerned as Kevin was that the skull
might have been from that sailboat accident over twenty years
ago? Cautiously, Annie said, "I haven't heard that bit of ugly
gossip. But there's no basis for it. None at all." She stopped
herself from adding that she sometimes hated the internet and
its opportunities to mislead while hiding under an umbrella
of dispensing information.

"What if it's one of my people?" Greg, the dark-haired
one asked.

Wampanoag, Annie thought, and her stomach clenched.
"We'll know its history soon enough. And, please, be assured
that every necessary step will be taken. If the archeologist de-
termines that the bone is Native American, it will be turned
over to the tribe."

"What if there are more?"

"Believe me, the local and state police have scoured the
area. To our knowledge, they haven't found any more . . .
fragments."

Marty set her eyes squarely on Annie's. "How long until
you have the results?"

"Not long. But we're prepared."

"They might determine this is sacred ground," Greg said. "Are you prepared for that?"

She wanted to be honest and say no, they were not at all prepared for that. They hadn't even been prepared for this much to have happened. She supposed she could invite the new tenants in and show them the Excel spreadsheets that held detailed facts and figures about how far the Inn was in debt, so they would know how desperate she, Kevin, and Earl were for the Inn to open, too. She wanted to tell them they weren't the only ones whose quality of life was at stake. But, of course, Annie couldn't do any of those things, so she simply smiled and said, "Look. I know this is hard for you. Believe it or not, I know what it's like to live on the island and find yourself without a home. I don't know if any of you know Earl Lyons. Or his son, John, who's an Edgartown cop. The Lyons family has been here for a dozen generations. This Inn was Earl's idea, and he'll do everything in his power to make it happen. He takes care of people here. So please, don't worry. As it stands, before this happened we'd made considerable progress on the interior so, in any event, we're almost done." She didn't know if she should have said that last part because, in truth, they weren't "almost done."

"Can we see the rooms?" Marty asked.

Annie hadn't expected that. She smiled again, hoping to kill a few seconds while she dreamed up a believable reply. "I'm so sorry, but I can't let you in yet. Until we have an occupancy permit, the town doesn't want people walking through the construction site." Hopefully, none of them knew more than she did about the inner workings of town regulations. Still, there was no way she wanted them to see the extensive amount of work that was still needed upstairs. "Nothing's stopping you from peeking in the downstairs windows, though!" she added with forced exuberance. "You can see the kitchen through the wall of glass along the back. It's really spectacular. And if you walk around front, you can see into the great room—it isn't quite finished, but the reading room and media room are. Feel free to explore from the outside. But, please, don't go in. We could get into trouble, and that might hold things up even longer." She wondered if in her next life she could become a hawker of miracle potions or swampland in Florida. What had happened to innocent Annie Sutton who'd never been able to tell a lie?

By some unexplained mystery of nature, the group seemed appeased. Greg thanked her, the others nodded, and they began to walk up toward the house.

"Stop back any time!" Annie called after them, though she hoped to God that they would not. Not until the mess had been sorted out.

Too rattled to accomplish any more work, she knew that she needed to regain her emotional balance. So she retrieved her phone and texted John: ANY BIG PLANS FOR TONIGHT? A ROCK CONCERT? A SOX GAME? WANT TO SPEND TIME WITH ME?

He replied quickly: I WAS GOING TO ASK YOU THE SAME.

Chapter 10

By the time Annie walked off the *On Time* ferry and onto Dock Street, the clouds had turned the sky a dull shade of gray. She wondered if later there would be fog, that pea-soup kind of stuff known to blanket both the land and the sea and deliver a bout of claustrophobia to the heartiest of islanders.

She went up Main Street and crossed over South Water, eager to see John. She knew she had to tell him about Jonas and the video. She knew she had to tell him and yet . . .

When he opened the door, he was wearing his at-home scrubs and an enticing grin. As soon as she stepped inside, he wrapped her in his strong, comforting arms. Then he kissed her. Long and sweet. When he was done, she pulled away and laughed.

"Wow. If I'd known I'd get such a welcome on a school night, I'd come by more often." Surely her latest news could wait a little while. At least until they'd had time for pleasure.

He took her hand and kissed her fingertips. "I have good news. I made pasta. Again. And Lucy's gone to her friend Maggie's, so it's just the two of us."

Annie laughed. She traced the outline of his chin. It was

smooth and clean; he had shaved recently. "She's doing home-work?"

"Doubtful. But she's staying overnight. She brought Rest-less with her for protection. Maggie's parents went off island for the day and got stuck on the Cape. They didn't want Mag-gie to be alone all night."

"Are the boats canceled?"

He shook his head and toyed with her hair. "One did. Another broke down. Even if the late ones go, there isn't enough room for more vehicles." He leaned down and kissed her cheeks, her eyes, her forehead.

"How much did you pay the captains to cancel the trips?"

He stood back and took her hands in his. "Not a penny less than was required."

"I hope it was worth it."

He shrugged. "Why not judge that for yourself?" He let go of her hand and guided her into the foyer, up the stairs, and into his bedroom. And Annie felt a special warmth begin to rise in her—the same warmth that arose whenever John stepped into her breathing space.

Pushing away the comforter, he then removed his T-shirt and his scrubs. She relished the thought of what awaited. He lay down, and then gestured for her to join him. She slipped out of her jacket and her jeans.

In the dim light from the hall, she watched his eyes watch her—every part of her—as she undressed. She'd worn her pale pink sweater, the one she'd come to love because he'd once told her she looked beautiful in it. "It makes your face glow," he'd said. She started to remove it just as John's phone rang. Sharp. Loud. Incessant.

He groaned as it kept ringing. "I would shout out every single swear word I know, but it wouldn't change the fact that I have to answer it."

"Right," Annie replied. Being in a relationship with a police officer had both perks and pitfalls.

He rolled to one side and freed the phone from its charger. "Sergeant Lyons," he said while Annie climbed onto the bed and nestled beside him. "She is."

Then Annie sensed his body grow rigid. He sat up. "They're at your house." He paused. "Aren't they?" Another pause. "Where are you? Aren't you on the Cape? I thought the boats were canceled." He paused again. Then he stood up, his jaw set firmly, one hand on one hip, his libido wilted. "Are you fuc . . . Are you kidding me?" He darted to a corner of the room and grabbed his jeans from the back of a chair. He yanked them on with one hand.

Annie snapped on the bedside lamp. Something was wrong. Lucy . . .

"I'll be right there," he said, then hung up and quickly called another number. He waited . . . and waited . . . as lines of frustration deepened on his face. "It's Dad," he hissed into the phone. "Where are you? Call me. *Now.*" He disconnected the call and shoved the phone into his pocket. "Damn her," he grumbled. "What the hell is she up to?"

Annie quickly started to dress. "Is she okay?"

"Good question. My daughter seems to have disappeared. For that matter, so has Maggie." He pulled on his shirt.

"I take it that Maggie's mother isn't on the Cape?"

"She came back on the two thirty. So Lucy lied."

Annie bit her lip.

Wiping his hands across his face, he said, "I don't know what to do."

"You're a cop," she said, as she straightened her pink sweater. "You do know what to do. Try to imagine that she's someone else's kid." Then she brushed back her hair and followed him down the stairs.

"Come with me?" he asked.

"Of course." She stopped him at the door, put a hand on his arm. "John, she'll be all right. She's a teenager."

"I know that all too well."

"What did your daughter say?" John grilled Maggie's mother.

Annie didn't know her name; they had not been introduced.

"Your daughter made her go."

They stood in a mudroom on one side of a small ranch; a number of rubber slickers hung from coat pegs along one wall; the space held the pungent aroma of the sea. The woman remained in the inner doorway; she was dressed in sweatpants and a flannel shirt. With sandy brown hair that showed signs of gray, she looked around John's age—late forties. Her eyes were large and dark, perhaps magnified by fear. Or anger.

John's chest inflated. His stance stiffened.

Annie rested her hand on his back, hoping it might help diffuse his anger.

He exhaled only a little. "What did she say?"

"She left a note. They took off from school after lunch. They stopped here, then went on their way. Wherever that was. She said she'd be back by six. It's now eight thirty."

"Have you tried calling her?"

"Maggie does not have a phone. She's only fourteen. She'll get one at sixteen, not a minute sooner."

Annie tried not to show surprise. Then she remembered that this was an island, where the crime rate was low and year-round people often knew one another. Everyone—kids included—was part of a larger community where people looked out for one another: the good, the bad, the in-between.

John didn't mention that he'd tried calling Lucy but she hadn't answered.

"Do you still have the note?"

"No." She did not explain why or where she'd disposed of it. She only glared at him.

"Did she say anything else?"

"Only that she'd gone with Lucy to help one of Lucy's friends. No offense, John, but your daughter is a bad influence on mine. Maggie was saving her babysitting money for school clothes. Lucy got her to use it for some ridiculous DNA test kit. As if my daughter doesn't already know who her parents are. She *lives* with us." Maggie's mother's large eyes narrowed, reducing to slits. "My husband might be a fisherman, and maybe he's away too much. But make no mistake. We are a two-parent family. One of us always knows where our daughter is. Except tonight. Because she's with Lucy Lyons. Who seems to have the run of the island. Because her father is a big-time cop."

Annie flinched.

John rocked back on his heels, but his eyes remained steady on the woman. He lowered his voice and said, "I'm going to be the adult here and chalk up your rudeness to panic. Now, please. Did Maggie say anything else? Any clue about where they might have gone?"

The woman turned her head so she no longer faced him but was looking straight at Annie. Her thin, over-arched eyebrows shot up, as if she'd only noticed then that John wasn't alone. "She said something about learning how to make a movie. Something for YouTube. For all I know, your daughter talked Maggie into doing something horrific. Like filming porn."

Annie suspected that John would be reacting differently if he were talking to Maggie's father not her mother. "Well, Bernice, if that's what they're doing, you can damn well be sure the idea would not have been Lucy's."

The woman slammed the inner door; a sharp click of the deadbolt pierced the air.

"Well," Annie said, once they were back in John's pickup, "I don't think Bernice likes you very much."

He grunted. "I lost my virginity to her when I was sixteen. She dared me. She's been embarrassed around me since then."

Annie blinked a couple of times. She was reminded once again that growing up on an island was not always idyllic, that there truly was nowhere to run to if you made a mistake, nowhere to be anonymous. Then her thoughts wandered to Earl and Marilyn Sunderland, the sixth-grade-teacher-turned–journalist—*Stop!* she shouted to herself before Murphy did. Still, though Annie knew that, sooner or later, almost everyone lost his or her virginity to someone, it was hard to imagine John with Bernice, even though it had been decades ago and had nothing to do with what was happening now. She closed her eyes and tried to think. And then the answer came to her. She almost felt ridiculous that she hadn't realized it sooner.

"I know where they are," she said as John backed out of the driveway, "and what they've been doing. And it is not making porn." She told him about the visit from the new tenants and the video they'd seen that apparently was of Jonas pleading for information about his long-dead father.

They reached the Chappy ferry in record time.

"Take it down. *Now.*" John's eyes drilled into his daughter's. He didn't even seem to notice Restless, who was dancing around his feet. "Why did you do such a stupid thing, Lucy? Didn't you learn anything after you posted the pictures? Now you made a *movie?*"

They stood in the small apartment over Taylor's garage, the same place Annie had almost rented when she'd been on the brink of homelessness. Jonas had removed the heavy brocade draperies, had covered the beige-flocked wallpaper with a few nice abstracts of island scenery, and replaced the stiff Victorian furniture with futons and a wide-screen TV. The place looked like a livable bachelor pad instead of the old-fashioned dollhouse that Taylor had once created for her mother who had died in February. But now, with the five of them and the dog, the space was far too crowded.

Lucy and Maggie sat on the floor, a laptop open in front of them. Jonas stood in front of John, looking despondent, as if he, too, were a teenager instead of twenty-two. "I thought it might be a chance to solve my father's death."

John sighed. "Jonas, none of what happened to you was fair. And I'm sorry for that. But the bone Annie found could be from one of hundreds of people—or more—from hundreds of miles—or more—away. Bones get caught up in the current. And they usually don't last more than a few years in the ocean."

"But Dad," Lucy interrupted as if John had been talking to her, "if the seaweed wrapped itself around it, couldn't that have protected it from deteriorating once it got stuck in the rocks?"

"Doubtful."

Annie didn't know if that were true.

"But why do we have to take it down? We didn't show the bone again . . . or mention the Inn."

Jonas stuffed his hands in his pockets. "Never mind, Lucy. Your dad's right. It was stupid. We'll take it down, sir. And we won't do a GoFundMe page. We thought I could raise enough money to hire an off-island detective. Someone who wouldn't know the history about my family."

John let out a loud groan. "Believe me, Jonas, a lot of manpower went into trying to find your dad's body back when it happened. I was a rookie then, but I remember. And your grandparents spent a ton of cash on private investigators. All it did was piss off the local police. And nothing came of it."

Jonas lowered his head, his red-gold hair falling onto his forehead.

"But they had no evidence back then," Lucy said. "Maybe they do now."

John tipped his head toward his daughter. Annie had a sense that he would have liked to tell her to stop the nonsense and go to her room.

Then Lucy jumped up. "Maybe it's not Jonas's father but one of our ancestors! Or a Chappy Wampanoag. That would be so cool! There weren't many of them . . ."

"Lucy? Stop. Take the dog and get in my truck. Now. And by the way, Maggie, your mother is furious."

Maggie lowered her eyes. She was a timid girl, clearly shy in their presence. Annie wondered if she should say that one of the main characters in her books was named Maggie, too. Perhaps it might elicit a smile. But Lucy scampered to her feet, deflecting any chance Annie had to try to make Maggie feel better.

"Or . . ." Lucy prattled, "maybe the skull came from a shipwreck! Like the *City of Columbus* . . . remember? The one that ran aground on Devil's Bridge during the blizzard of 1884? One of the dead sailors could have been carried to Chappy by the currents. Or"—her pearl-gray eyes lit up as if they held a secret—"maybe it was the lady from that ship . . . the one they found with her kid's shoes frozen to her dress right where she'd been holding him . . ."

"Lucy!" John said. "Move." He waited until the girls and Restless crossed the room, then he ducked and clomped down the narrow stairs behind them.

Annie followed him, thinking that, aside from Lucy's imaginings, the girl might have been right about one thing: once the bone got onto the shore, it might have been preserved by the salt and seaweed once it became lodged in the rocks. Climbing back into the truck, she then wondered if Lucy, too, had the makings of a mystery writer. And, if so, how well John would cope with two novelists in his life. Then she realized she was thinking about him as if they'd be a long-term couple, and she, a stepmother, the three of them entwined like seaweed, bonded by the tides.

Friday passed in a blur of comings and goings and trying to get things done. Annie moved a few things into the bedroom at the Inn, then made a quick run into Edgartown for food and wine. Thankfully, the media, indeed, had backed off; there were no other comments on social media or YouTube about The Vineyard Inn or its unusual guest.

Late that afternoon, Kevin stopped by. They hadn't bumped into each other all day; he looked haggard, stressed, forlorn. What had happened to her happy brother? She offered him a beer, but he said he had to get to Vineyard Haven to pick up slabs of glacial rock before Cottle's closed. "Earl thinks the hearth should be vintage," he added.

Annie thought it was a good idea, but not a reason for Kevin to look distraught. "Great," she said. "What else is up?" She wondered if he'd heard about the video.

"I need a favor. Can you get Mom tomorrow?"

"You have too much to do?"

"Well, seeing as how Earl and I are trying to do the work of six men and one woman now, and do it undercover, yeah. You might say that."

Annie bit her lip. "In some ways, maybe it's for the best that no one else in your crew is here. This way, none of them can get wrapped up in our added drama."

He plunked down on the rocker and rubbed his weary face. "Jonas told me about the video."

That answered that. "I think we nipped it in the bud.

The media seem to have given up. And John says it's been scrubbed from the internet. And at least the kids didn't post a GoFundMe page." She paused. "Did they?"

"Not that I know of. But this whole thing got me thinking. Jonas has a point. Even if this bone isn't from his dad, shouldn't he try to find out what really happened?"

"But what about Taylor? I thought they were getting along really well. I thought he was happy to be with her."

"I asked her. All I got was crickets. Then she walked out of the house. I'm not sure if she's pissed or guilty."

Annie sat on the sofa across from him. She couldn't imagine how Kevin felt. He was, without a doubt, in a relationship with Taylor. Who might have murdered someone she'd supposedly loved.

"But Kevin," Annie said, searching for words to cheer him up, "Jonas has letters that prove that Taylor and his father were in love. Weren't they going to elope to Hawaii?"

"Someone convinced Jonas that the letters might be fake . . . that Taylor might have written them to take the heat off her."

"Good grief. But who would have suggested that to Jonas? And why?"

Kevin didn't respond, but studied his fingernails one at a time, first the right hand, then the left, with careful deliberateness.

And that's when Annie knew. "Did Lucy tell him?"

Kevin folded his hands. "Jonas didn't say. But I think it must have been her. I know that she did say he should get his DNA done. In case his father wasn't really Derek Flanagan but another boy—maybe an islander and not a preppie who came from tons of money. She said the guy might still be alive and have other kids."

The day had turned warm for late April; the late afternoon light slanted through the windows of Annie's cottage, turning

tiny dust motes into golden flecks. "Kevin?" she asked quietly. "Why would Lucy do that?"

"I was hoping you'd tell me."

"Well, she's fourteen. And she can be pretty naïve. Sometimes she gets excited about something and doesn't use common sense. Like, I don't think it ever occurred to her that
posting the picture of the bone would have such a negative
impact on all of us. But this? This is so much worse. I know
she loves the genealogy stuff, but . . ."

"But this could have longer-lasting effects. You need to
speak with John, Annie. Tell him what I think she's done."

"Agreed." She stood and went over to the window. She
wondered how much patience John could possibly still have.

"I don't think Taylor killed the guy," Kevin continued.
"And I think the chance of the skull belonging to him is about
one in a triple-trillion. But she and Jonas have to work this
out without my being around to open my big yap and offer
my opinion."

Her brother was a good man. But if Taylor had intentionally killed one boyfriend . . . would she do it to another?
Annie looked away, so Kevin wouldn't see the fear settling in
her eyes. "I'll talk to John tonight. And tomorrow, I'll pick
up . . . Mom." She was pretty sure that was the first time she'd
used that word for Donna. It had stuck a little in her throat,
but Earl would have been pleased.

Kevin got up and gave her a hug. "Thanks. You're a pal.
And by the way, the fact that I'm so busy—even though I
am—isn't why I asked you to pick her up. I just need some
time to breathe before she gets here."

Chapter 11

Annie knew it was her fault. If she'd never moved to the Vineyard, if she'd never rented the place from Roger Flanagan, if she'd never found herself almost homeless on the island, Kevin and Earl would never have invested all their money in a dream. Though Kevin had been a contractor in Boston, and Earl a caretaker on the island practically his entire life, neither of them knew anything about running an inn, so if it hadn't been for her, it probably would not have been on their bucket lists. And if Annie had not allowed it in the first place, she would never have searched for shells and sea glass on the beach, never have found the bone, never have opened such a Pandora's box and triggered so many upsetting events. Yet there she was, stuck in the middle now, because the bottom line was that it was her fault.

And now she'd have to deal with Donna. And try not to speculate as to why Kevin felt he needed time to breathe before he saw her.

Annie poked around the cottage, straightening things that did not need straightening, killing time until John would be awake after he'd worked midnight-to-eight. At five o'clock, she called him.

"I've been up for hours," he said. "I slept three and a half."

"Any special reason?"

"Yeah. My daughter." He went on to tell Annie that Taylor had banged on his door just after noon, shaking the whole damn house and rousting him out of bed. "She found out about the video. I swear, my daughter is going to be the death of me."

Annie knew that if she ever wrote that line in her manuscript, Trish, her editor, would mark it heavily with blue pencil and write *cliché* in the margin. Then she blinked and wondered why she was thinking about her editor when John was waiting for a response.

"Lucy's a curious kid with a vivid imagination, but she still has some growing up to do. She's only fourteen; she's not going to get everything right."

He sighed. "Maybe I should have left her with her mother."

That was a statement Annie didn't want to touch. "She's happy here, John."

"Maybe for the wrong reasons. I don't give her as much supervision as her mother did."

After the mess that Lucy had been in last year, Annie hadn't seen a single sign that John's ex-wife was a parental guru with all the answers. At least no more than John—or any parent—could be in the world today. "Kids today don't have it easy . . ."

"Lucy's not just anybody's kid. She's mine. I'm responsible for her. I thought she got the message about not posting stuff that might hurt other people. I thought she was smarter than that. Now I can't stop worrying about what's going to happen next. And why the hell is she hanging out with a twenty-two-year-old boy, anyway? Even worse, why is he hanging out with her? Never mind. Please don't answer those questions."

Annie forced a small laugh and said, "I don't think it's ever smart to try to think like a teenager. Mostly because you'll probably fail. Besides, she and Jonas weren't alone, John. Maggie was with them."

"Right. Another fourteen-year-old. And don't forget the dog."

Annie knew not to argue. She also knew it wasn't the right time to share Kevin's supposition that Lucy had told Jonas that the old, handwritten letters—the only proof he had that his mother probably had not killed his father—might have been faked. By Taylor.

"Can I see you in the morning?" John interrupted her thoughts. "Breakfast at the diner or something?"

"Sorry, but I have to pick up Donna. Kevin can't take the time off work. My great archeological dig has left them stranded for help, but the Inn still needs to be finished. In case it's allowed to open."

"I didn't hear that," John said. "I'm sworn to uphold the law, remember? Which includes the part about stopping construction on the property. Which refers to *all* construction. By anyone. My father and your brother included."

"Right! How silly of me. Kevin is not working on the Inn at all. Neither is Earl. I must be mistaken."

"You're a terrible liar."

"It's part of my charm."

They talked a few more minutes, and Annie tried to sound upbeat. She was, however, grateful that John hadn't asked what boat Donna was coming in on. The noon boat would arrive in Vineyard Haven at twelve forty-five. Which meant there would be plenty of time for Annie to see John before she had to leave to get her. Maybe Kevin wasn't the only one who needed time to breathe.

Saturday morning it was raining. Not just a few drops, not even a steady shower, but a relentless downpour. Annie's short trip on the *On Time* from one side of the harbor to the other was like being stuck in a car wash. Visibility was awful, and the wind was picking up, so she hoped the big boats would be running. High wind was typically the first thing that caused ferry service to be canceled on the eight-mile voyage between Woods Hole and the island.

Craving more time alone before picking up Donna, Annie took the beach road instead of the shorter, faster, less scenic route that cut across the island, east to west. But as soon as she went right at the infamous Edgartown Triangle and crawled toward State Beach, she knew it had been a mistake; mixed with all the rain, the high-tide surf had blown onto the road, leaving puddles the size of salt-water ponds.

For the umpteenth time, she was grateful that she'd traded her Lexus for a Jeep. She hoped Donna didn't mind the less luxurious ride.

Crawling past the jumping bridge—the site of a million photos of kids jumping into the channel that connected the ocean with Sengekontacket Pond, which had provided a scene in *Jaws* that even today induced audience gasps—Annie tried to stay focused on her driving while thinking about Donna. Though Annie had stayed on the Vineyard over Christmas instead of going to Boston with Kevin, she hadn't regretted it.

The truth was, Annie had preferred staying on the island to spending the holiday with Donna. Lucy had gone to Plymouth to be with her mother and sister, so John—and Earl and Claire—would have been alone. Besides, Annie knew all of them better.

Life is like that sometimes, Murphy suddenly whispered from the empty passenger seat. *If you recall, I once knew you better than I knew my own husband.*

Annie winced. Yes, she remembered. Murphy and Stan had been a love match envied by many in the early nineties, the fun-loving, talented, family behaviorist and the brilliant Boston neurosurgeon. They'd wanted badly to have a family;

they'd tried very hard, followed all the biological "rules," but nothing happened. Then they went in vitro. Several times. Suddenly, Murphy was pregnant. They were elated. Even more elated when they learned that twin boys were heading their way. Stan doted on her every move, her every mood. The love match continued until . . . until the boys were born prematurely. Maternal twins—identical. Rare with in vitro fertilization. The day they found out Stan laughed nervously and asked, "Are you sure they're mine?"

Needless to say, the bubble of joy burst.

In a postpartum frenzy, Murphy metaphorically kicked him out of the house. It was weeks before they got back together, before Stan admitted he had always been jealous because Murphy was, after all, the most beautiful woman in the whole freaking world, and he had no idea why she'd bothered to marry old, nerdy him.

While Stan was gone, Annie spent hours with Murphy every day in the neonatal unit at Brigham and Women's Hospital . . . every day for the nearly twenty days until both twins were pronounced "out of the woods" and released. Murphy would not cry; only once did she reveal self-pity by saying, "I thought I knew my husband. Even worse, I thought he knew me."

Annie wondered how sure Kevin really was—really could be—that Taylor hadn't killed her boyfriend. Maybe, after the trauma with his wife, Kevin didn't want to deal with reality again. Maybe he thought La-La Land was a better place to live.

As for Annie, she knew she'd never get close enough to Taylor to voice an educated guess.

Maneuvering the Jeep into Oak Bluffs now, more than halfway to the harbor, Annie wondered if Donna had needed to believe in fairy tales when she'd learned that she was pregnant with Annie. Maybe she'd given Annie up for adoption because she'd convinced herself that Annie's birth father didn't want her (or Donna didn't want him), and that Annie would go to a wonderful home with two wonderful parents who would be able to raise her in a wonderful world—much more wonderful than Donna could have given her back then.

Then Annie realized maybe it was time to ask: about her birth father; about the grandparents she'd never known; about how it happened that she'd been born and then adopted. It might be nice to know something other than that her birth mother had been in the antiques business and that Annie had a half-brother. Maybe, if she knew a little more about her background, she'd ask Lucy to do her genealogy.

Rounding the curve, driving up and over the drawbridge, Annie headed toward the pier, deciding that, yes, while Donna was there, they would have that conversation. Perhaps when they were hunting for sea glass on a beach—any beach, other than the one on the shoreline of the Inn.

With her plan in place, Annie felt relieved until she reached the last leg of the road, where five spokes of four streets merged tenuously together—and were flooded.

A U-turn. Back to Oak Bluffs. Cutting through back roads of which she was unsure. Noting the time that rapidly ticked toward the arrival of the *Island Home* if it had not been canceled. Why hadn't she checked before she'd set out? Too late now, Annie thought. She didn't want to waste time pulling over to call the Steamship Authority. And the number she had for Donna was a Boston landline.

When she finally reached the roundabout, she turned onto Edgartown-Vineyard Haven Road as the rain pummeled her windshield. She passed the alpaca farm, the campgrounds, and the unofficial wild turkey crossing. Once on State Road, she slowly headed down the hill toward the boat, avoiding those infamous five corners by turning onto Main Street and then cutting down Union. She was glad it was still April so few cars were on the road; after all, even tropical storms did not deter tourists from visiting in season—not even Annie's dad. Her dad, Bob Sutton. Not the dad she knew nothing about.

Surprisingly, she made it on time.

Zipping across the street to the terminal lot, she parked just as vehicles began to slither from the mouth of the giant white boat that now was safely in its berth, its passengers huddled in an assortment of drenched slickers as they shuffled down the ramp.

Annie grabbed her umbrella, got out of the Jeep, and gingerly crossed to the covered portico that faced the boat. She scanned the soggy crowd, but did not see Donna. Then a woman moved slowly toward her. She was stooped and thin; she carried a black-and-white polka dot umbrella; she wore a long raincoat, red rain boots, and a small grin. She was wheeling a large suitcase and a carry-on that was almost as big. Perhaps she was planning on a lengthy visit, or maybe she lived on the island and was coming home. Annie grinned back and continued to scan the crowd.

"Annie!" the woman called from beneath the polka dots. Her voice barely rose above the splats of unrelenting rain, the cries of puddle-jumping people, and the stop-and-go insistence of cars and trucks and slapping windshield-wiper blades. Annie tipped her umbrella, allowing a better view. The woman's face was thin—no, *gaunt*. But it was Donna.

"Oh! Here you are!" Annie was both startled and embarrassed that she hadn't recognized her. Years ago she'd read that the first few seconds when connecting with someone set the emotional tone for the entire meeting. She hoped it was one of those common internet lies. "I'm so sorry. With the rain and all the umbrellas . . ." Awkwardly, she stepped aside so Donna could squeeze under the covered entrance.

"I'm sure you're not accustomed to seeing me in red boots.

Neither am I!" Donna gazed around at the confusion. Her
hazel eyes seemed as glazed as the horizon, making her appear
strangely befuddled. She had aged over the winter.

"Follow me," Annie said. "I'm parked in the lot." She
took the suitcases without asking. Then she wondered if she
also should reach for Donna's arm to steady her.

No. Murphy's voice slipped through the raindrops. *Give
her space.* Annie heeded the advice; Murphy had never steered
her wrong.

When they reached the Jeep, Donna said, "How about
stopping somewhere for a cup of hot tea? And getting the hell
out of this rain?"

Annie laughed. And finally began to relax.

*She had started keeping secrets in 1956, when she was seven
years old and pretended that she was a princess who lived in a castle on
the Mediterranean Sea instead of a nobody who lived in a triple-decker
in the heart of the Neponset area of Dorchester. It wasn't Boston's finest neighborhood, but with three bedrooms, one bathroom, a kitchen,
and a living room, the apartment was big enough for her parents and
her and her brother, Donald, who was five years older than she was.
At least she had her own room; some of her friends did not.*

*Then, right before Grace Kelly married Prince Rainier and was
destined to live happily ever after, Donald was horsing around with
some of his friends on their way home from school, and he tripped
over a rail and fell into the path of a streetcar. He had just finished
presenting his sixth grade science fair project that he'd titled "Building
America's First Subway," because Boston held the honor of having
developed it and gotten it up and running in a heralded engineering
feat. Donna's father said it was ironic that Donald's life had been
snuffed out by public transportation after he had studied it. It was nice,
though, that the judges awarded Donald first prize, "posthumously,"
her mother said and wept. Donna had to look the word up in their
big dictionary.*

Her parents never talked about her brother after that. One night, Donna saw her father take the science project and dump it in the metal trash can in the alley. After everyone had gone to bed, she'd crept outside, lifted the clanging lid, retrieved the blue ribbon, and sneaked back into the house. She brushed it off and hid it in the small metal chest that Aunt Elizabeth had given her for her birthday and was designed to hold doll clothes.

She soon added another treasure to the chest—a picture that she'd torn out of her grandmother's Life *magazine of Princess Grace in her wedding gown. Over time, Donna had had to remove things that once had belonged there—her doll's pink dress, then her blue one, a pair of high-heel shoes, a gold vinyl purse. But Donna had needed to make room for the newspaper clippings when a man named Alan Shepard was the first American to go up into space; the dance card and dried corsage from her junior prom; the back page of a Howard Johnson's menu where her first boyfriend, Joe, had scribbled:* Love you always.

In 1982, when Donna saw the Louis Vuitton in the window of the antiques shop on Newbury Street, she supposed it was only natural that she wanted it—it was the perfect place to hide her grown-up, special things. She wondered if it was ironic that Princess Grace had been killed the week before. And that the fairy tale of each of their lives had ended.

Chapter 12

Wedging the suitcases into the back of the Jeep, Annie suggested going to the Black Dog because it was close by. The walk would require sloshing through some puddles, but Donna said her red boots would protect her. Annie led the way as they traversed the twists and turns of the clamshell walkways, until they finally made it inside the low-ceilinged building that was flying its black Labrador flag despite the rain.

"May we please sit by the fireplace?" Donna asked the young hostess. "I've seen enough water views to last me for a while." Then she marched across the room with the confidence of a city woman who always seemed to know where she was going.

"Well," Donna said, once they sat at the table and had removed their outerwear, "that was certainly a memorable journey." She smiled a small smile that did little to reveal her actual thoughts. Dressed in a navy cashmere sweater and gray jeans that once might have been skinny but now hung rather loosely, Donna was rail thin. She also was pale; even the finest Lauder makeup couldn't mask the marks of time. Perhaps they would have been less noticeable if her hair hadn't been cut shorter than Annie remembered seeing it.

"Was it rough going?"

"Not as bad as a typhoon in the South China Sea, but it was fairly rocky. And it's always unnerving to be on a boat, a plane, or a train, whenever passengers fall silent, when they stop scolding their children or commiserating with their traveling companion and, instead, sit very still and white-knuckle their seats. I find that more disturbing than rowdy laughter, babies squealing, and on these ferries, dogs barking. Don't you?" While she spoke, she fussed with the napkin—first on the table, then in her lap—then straightened the knife, the fork, the spoon, the salt and pepper, never losing her small smile.

It was a sardonic smile, Annie realized. A knowing smile. She recognized the look, because she suspected that she, too, wore that expression when there was something she did not want to talk about. She wondered if it was a trait she'd received from Donna through Lucy's favorite topic, DNA.

"I'm so sorry," Annie said. "But it's good that you didn't bring your car over. The driving is awful. I take it you figured out where to get the shuttle in the lot?"

Donna shook her head. "I took the bus from South Station right down to the pier. It was far easier. And less costly."

Annie didn't want to ask if that meant Donna planned to stay a while. She'd leave that up to Kevin to address.

Their server arrived, and both women asked for tea and a crock of quahog chowder.

Then Donna drove the small talk about how much she was enjoying retirement ("It is delicious, like fresh herbs plucked from a dew-dropped garden in the French countryside, served with cheese drizzled with olive oil"); how wonderful it was that Kevin had adapted so readily to island life ("He'd never even been here before!"); and how well Annie's next book must be coming along ("My goodness, I don't know how you do it!"). She sounded more energetic than her frail appearance suggested. "And the Inn!" she added as their tea and chowder arrived. "How are the men doing on their own? What a shame that some of their crew abandoned them."

Annie nodded and savored a spoonful of chowder, then decided to tackle the elephant in the Black Dog. "Everyone's making do," she said, then rested her elbows on the armrests of the captain's chair and quietly added, "Donna? Are you all right?"

Her birth mother blinked, added a few granules of sugar to her tea, and slowly stirred. Annie wasn't sure if she'd heard her.

Finally setting down her spoon, Donna sipped her tea, then set the mug down, too. Without looking at Annie, she said, "I was quite ill this winter." Her announcement was followed by a soft thump of silence.

"I'm so sorry, Donna. Kevin didn't tell me," Annie said. And while illness—a cold? The flu? Pneumonia?—could explain the weight loss and the gauntness, it certainly had done an awful number on Donna.

Donna tasted the chowder. "Kevin didn't tell you because he doesn't know. I didn't look this bad when I saw him at Christmas."

"You should have called. Either one of us would have gone up there . . ."

The older woman shook her head. "I did not want to crowd you. You'll never know how thrilled I am that you two are friends. But you and your brother have each been through a lot. So, yes, I did not want to crowd you. You're both working hard; you didn't need your mother interrupting that."

Annie winced at the reference to "mother." There was definitely a fine line between Donna MacNeish and Ellen Sutton that Annie did not want to cross. Maybe things would have been different if Annie had responded years ago when Donna first reached out to her.

That was then and this is now, Murphy whispered.

Taking another spoonful of chowder, Annie was aware that Donna was barely eating. "You would not have invaded our space," she finally said. "Do you want to tell me what was wrong?"

"No."

The ferry whistle blew; Annie turned her attention to the harbor where the big *Island Home*—the lifeline to the island—was pulling out of the dock, making its way back to Woods Hole.

Donna sighed. "I don't want to tell you, but I will. It's really the reason I've come."

The same instinct Annie had had the night that Mark hadn't come home—had never come home again—rose in Annie's stomach. This time, it churned the chowder.

"I've had a bout with cancer," Donna continued. "Ovarian. Not the best kind—as if there is a best kind."

Raising one hand to her temple, Annie reached across the table and rested her other hand on Donna's. "Oh, Donna. I'm so sorry. Are you having treatment?"

"I was. They're done. It wasn't pleasant, but now it's time for me to recuperate."

More than anything, Annie wanted to find the right words—if there were any right ones. She didn't have the courage to ask—what was the term? If they'd "gotten it all"? In her peripheral vision, she was aware of the white behemoth inching out toward Vineyard Sound, its back-and-forth mission similar to life: some crossings were smoother than others. "Kevin doesn't know?" she asked, though Donna had already said he did not.

Donna shook her head and sipped her tea again. "I hope you'll be there when I tell him. He and I have always been so close . . . after his father left . . . You know, Kevin was only four." She shifted her eyes down to the table and stared at

Annie's hand that rested on hers. "I'm afraid he'll be upset. And he'll ask a thousand questions that I don't really want to answer. I only want to recuperate so I can get back to my life."

Annie knew that sometimes a conversation between two people was more about the words that were left unspoken. But all she could think about was Murphy. She supposed it was only natural that once anyone had lost a loved one to the disease, whenever they heard the word, they jumped to the conclusion: *terminal*. Still, Annie knew that ovarian cancer could be tough to cure. And that, no matter what, Kevin would take the news far harder than she would. Or could. Donna had been the one who had raised him, nurtured him, loved him, picked him up when he fell down, nursed his outer and inner wounds. Donna had done those things for Kevin— Ellen Sutton hadn't. And now, in that moment, Annie became more concerned about Kevin than about Donna.

Neither mother nor daughter finished their chowder or tea.

It wasn't until they were in the Jeep, the wipers swiping the windshield with rhythmic gusto, that Annie suddenly understood why Donna's luggage was so large.

"Mom?" Kevin called out from the living room. "You're here?"

Annie and Donna were in the bedroom; Annie had been showing her a couple of empty drawers she could use.

"Jesus," he said now as he stood in the doorway, "you've lost weight. Are you on one of those stupid diets again?"

Donna laughed. "You know me, Kev. If I gain two pounds, I have to lose five to compensate." She went over and kissed his cheek. "But look at you. You're looking fitter than ever. Manual labor agrees with you."

"Yup. And I'm hoping it lasts. Did Annie tell you what happened?"

She turned back to Annie, who was watching the mother-son reunion with a hint of envy. "I did not," Annie replied. "I wanted you to have the pleasure."

"Very funny," Kevin replied.

Donna looked from one of her children to the other. "Perhaps we should go into the living room and talk?"

"Good idea," Annie said.

So that's what they did. Annie sat on the sofa, Donna went to the rocker, and Kevin whipped around a kitchen chair and sat backward on it, facing them.

"It's Annie's fault," Kevin said wryly. He began with Annie's idea to decorate the Inn with "Vineyard natural" accents, then told Donna about the skull and all that had happened since, ending by saying that the skull was in Boston being examined. At the onset, Donna's eyes had grown large; they stayed that way throughout the tale.

"And then, thanks to Annie's boyfriend's daughter," he added, "the whole story went viral. Photos included." He began to clarify the term "going viral," until Donna reminded him that she wasn't a Luddite, and knew full well what it meant.

"So now what?" Donna asked Annie.

"Now we wait. And we pray that the remains aren't Native American, because if this is determined to be sacred ground, we can't have the Inn. I don't know what will happen to the house. Or to Kevin and Earl's investment."

The three of them stopped talking. Annie wished she'd made tea, if only to give them something to do. Sip. Stir. Sip. Be productive in their silence.

"It's quite a story," Donna finally said. "When will you know the outcome?"

"Obviously, we hope it's in time for us to finish what needs finishing so we can open Memorial Day weekend. Mostly because we're already booked."

"Five weeks," Donna said.

"Four weeks and six days," Kevin corrected. "The first reservation is for Friday of that weekend."

"And our year-round renters will be moving in then, too. They don't have to pay rent until June first, but we gave them extra days because that's when they have to be out of their winter rentals."

"Which means," Kevin said, as he stood up and moved the chair back to the table, "I need to get back to work. Earl and I are calling ourselves the 'skeleton crew,' pun intended."

"Wait," Annie said as she, too, stood up. "Donna . . . Mom . . . has some news, too."

Kevin glanced at his watch. "Can it wait 'til later? Dinner, maybe? I've got to help Earl finish painting now that it's stopped raining."

That's when Annie noticed the sun peeking into the cottage. And that the Vineyard was looking like a happy place again.

"Of course," Donna said. "Go back to work. It's nothing important, anyway."

"You're not getting married or anything, are you?"

"No, dear. I am not getting married. We'll talk later. Shall we go to the Newes? I like it there. My treat."

Kevin said, "Absolutely," and that he'd be back at six o'clock to pick them up.

And Annie was left standing, wondering what to do with Donna until then, since it was apparent that the woman was in no shape for beachcombing, and had been too nervous to tell her son what was really going on.

Chapter 13

Entertaining Donna hadn't turned out to be a problem. After Annie helped her unpack and find places for almost everything, Donna said she needed a nap. Annie told her to make herself at home, that she'd be back later. "There's plenty of food in the refrigerator if you get hungry. Please, help yourself."

All Annie needed then was to find something to do. She could not go to the main house; she didn't want to see Kevin, for fear she'd give away Donna's secret. Even with the positive cancer outcome, it was up to Donna to tell him, especially since he'd be upset that he hadn't found out sooner.

Annie thought about driving up island to see Winnie, but trekking up and back, and having a good visit, would simply take too long.

She didn't want to go to Earl and Claire's, because Claire had a way of reading people's minds. If she asked Annie outright if everything with Donna was okay, Annie might spill what she knew. Then there'd be no telling whom Claire might tell. She was a wonderful, caring woman, but sometimes it was hard for her to hold her tongue. And if she told Taylor . . . Well, the news was sure to be dispersed across the island faster than skunk spray in breeding season.

Before spending more time ruminating, Annie realized there was only one place other than Winnie's where she could go and feel safe sharing Donna's news. So she boarded the *On Time* and went to John's.

"He's still sleeping," Lucy said when she greeted Annie at the door. "But go upstairs and wake him. He won't care if it's you."

Annie hesitated. After all, the bedroom was off-limits when Lucy was around.

"Oh, for God's sake," Lucy said. "Go upstairs. I'm not stupid. And I'm not five years old. If it makes you feel better, I'll walk over to the library."

Annie smiled. "Yes, that would make me feel better."

Lucy rolled her eyes, grabbed her backpack, and meandered out the door, texting as she walked away.

The heavy drapes in John's room blocked out every ray of daylight that might have tried to sneak in. Which was why when Annie opened the door, stepped inside, and was accosted by something small and furry, she let out a shriek. She wasn't yet accustomed to Restless being there.

"Hey," John mumbled from under the covers. "Whoever is entering this room better have a good reason."

"It's me," Annie whispered, as if whispering would make her interruption less startling. She bent down and scratched Restless behind his ears, which only resulted in him running in circles, yipping for more attention. "I'm sorry. I forgot about the dog." Her vision started to adjust to the lack of light.

"Restless," John said in a hushed, barely audible tone, "c'mere."

The dog leapt onto the bed, wiggling and whimpering, amazing Annie with both his acute hearing and his astute instinct to obey John's soft command.

"He loves you," Annie said. She sat down on the edge of the bed. "So do I."

John rolled onto his side, pulled her down, and kissed her. Then Restless jumped between them, his little tongue joining in the kisses while he panted his sweet puppy breath.

"No," John said, laughing. "Lie down. Sit. Go somewhere else."

"Are you talking to the dog or to me?"

"Get in your crate!" he continued with halfhearted authority, laughing again.

"I don't have a crate," Annie replied, just as Restless jumped off the bed, scuttled through the little door of the dog crate in the corner of the room, and plunked down on the blue plaid doggie cushion that John had bought online from L.L.Bean. "He's very good, isn't he?"

"He's getting spoiled. Like me." John kissed her again and ran his hands through her hair. "Speaking of which, to what do I owe the pleasure of being awakened from a dead sleep?"

She wished he hadn't said the word *dead*. It made her think of cancer and of Murphy and of the prognosis that Donna had just dodged. Annie sighed and sat up. "Lucy went to the library. She had the impression I wanted to be alone with you."

John propped himself up on one elbow. "Suddenly, I have a feeling this isn't a bootie call."

Smoothing the navy-striped comforter, she remembered when she'd gone over to the Cape with him to pick out all new bedding: the comforter, sheets, blankets, pillows, the works. It had been early in their relationship, that stage when everything was magical. "You don't have to try to impress me," she'd said. "I'll slide under your covers no matter how old they are." They'd been on the boat, loaded down with Bed, Bath & Beyond coupons, whispering like newlyweds, though no commitment had been involved. He'd shaken his head. "I will not have you burrowing under the same blankets that I've taken camping for over thirty years. Nor will I have you sniffing the questionable sanitation of my bachelorhood." That, of course, was before his daughter had moved back home and he'd cleaned up his act. Now, his bedding carried an aroma of his woodsy deodorant, fabric softener, and a bit of dog.

"I have a problem," Annie said.

He frowned. His brow furrowed, his eyebrows crinkled. He reached up and snapped on the lamp. "What's wrong?"

"Donna."

"You picked her up?" He fell silent then, waiting for Annie to go on.

"I did. She told me she had cancer."

He pulled himself up and put his arm around her. "Had, not has?"

She shrugged. "Had. But it feels strange that I didn't know."

"How does Kevin feel about it?"

"He doesn't know yet. And there's more. She says she came here to recuperate."

"And . . . ?"

"I have no idea how long it's going to take. Her suitcase is enormous. In fact, she has two."

"Maybe she brought you something special. Wasn't she into antiques? Maybe the suitcases are full of cash. Bills. Money she laundered through her business and wants to give you for the Inn."

Annie knew he was trying to lift her spirits. "Or maybe they contain all her worldly possessions," she said. "Like maybe she's planning to move here permanently."

His face turned serious. "How would you feel about that?"

"How would I know? I barely know her, remember?"

"Right. Well, I guess if she moved here that would change."

Annie sighed. "She's going to tell Kevin about the cancer at the Newes tonight. It should be a fun dinner, right?"

"I think I'll pass."

"All I know is that if Kevin wants her to stay, I can't very well say no. He's my brother, and I feel like we've gotten pretty close. Not to mention that if he left, your father wouldn't speak to me again. He says Kevin's the 'best goddamned assistant' he's ever had." She tried to sound like Earl, but the words came out sounding gruff, not at all like the man who might have wanted to sound crotchety but always wound up sounding kind of sweet.

"You might want to leave my nutso father out of this." John sat beside her on the edge of the bed, their legs touching each other's. Annie felt a surge of love for this man who seemed to really care about her feelings. "Okay," he said. "Let's get serious. You need to think about what you're prepared to do. I won't sugarcoat this, Annie. But Kevin is a guy. You're a girl. And you and I both know that, despite all the changes in the world, when it comes right down to it, females are usually the ones who wind up being the caregivers."

"But she's not sick anymore."

"Look. It sounds like she's been through a lot. Recuperating will probably take time. And patience."

"And I'll end up being her nurse."

"In a sense, sure. And, Annie . . ."

She had a feeling she knew what he was going to say next.

"What if the cancer comes back? Not that it will, and I hope it doesn't. But it's good to be prepared."

She sighed again. "I don't know. . . . I've never had to be a nurse before." Now wasn't the time to think about all the loves she'd lost and how. Her mother had been hospitalized throughout her brief illness and death, and her dad and Brian were both gone so fast she never even had a chance to say good-bye, let alone take care of either of them. All she'd done for Murphy was help her with her hair and nails and bring her cups of tea. Murphy's physician husband, Stan, had done the rest; he'd taken family leave for that.

"I can't—and won't—tell you what I think you should do," John said. "Besides, it sounds as if she's on the mend. But whatever happens, I'll be here for you." He took Annie's hand. "And Restless will be here, too."

She leaned against his shoulder. "You, Mr. Lyons, are the best kind of boyfriend a girl could ever have."

He did not disagree.

Annie arrived early and chose a table far from the bar that might get noisy on a Saturday night, despite that the season was a long way off. Four weeks and six days, she reminded herself. Perhaps not so long, after all.

She wrung her hands and looked nervously around the pub, grateful that only a few people were there at the early hour. She'd texted Kevin from John's, said she was in Edgartown and would meet them at the Newes. She suggested he bring his truck across because, though the restaurant was close to the *On Time*, Donna had been tired and might not want to walk that far. Hopefully, her brother didn't think there was anything odd about that—though Annie had always been terrible at lying.

Spring break, Murphy elected right then to whisper. She didn't need to say more.

Annie bit her lip, suppressing a wide grin, which she knew was absolutely *not* appropriate given the reason for the dinner. But spring break their sophomore year of college had been hilarious, one of many times with Murphy when all hadn't gone according to their plan.

"We're going to Daytona Beach," Annie had told her parents. "Murphy and I."

That part had been true. She and Murphy were going to

Daytona Beach. The lie was the omission that they'd booked two rooms: one for Murphy and Stan, the medical student she was engaged to (who wound up the father of their twins and taking care of Murphy at the end); the other for Annie and Brian (the same Brian who, a few years later, became her husband).

After three days spent inside their rooms instead of on the beach, Brian had suggested that, rather than ordering burgers from room service again, he'd go out and bring back pizza. Though Annie hated to see him go, she knew it would be a good time to take a long, luxurious shower, to wash her hair and shave her legs, and do those things that, at nineteen, still seemed too intimate to do around him, even though by then they'd been having sex for quite a while.

She was in the shower when he returned; she hadn't heard the phone ring; she hadn't heard him say "Hello" to the person who was calling who turned out not to be Stan or Murphy, as he'd presumed. The caller had been Ellen Sutton.

Annie's mother had been neither amused nor tolerant. "I knew it!" she'd bellowed. "I knew by the way Annie looked at the floor when she told us that she was going; I knew then she was not telling the truth." Then she pontificated about how Annie had been raised to know better than to have boys in her room, and that, if she planned to remain living under their roof and continue to have her college education paid for, she would be on the next flight back to Boston.

Thankfully, Delta had one leaving at six thirty, with one seat still available.

No, Annie had never been a convincing liar. The exceptions being the recent, bizarre altercation with Marilyn Sunderland. And, hopefully, the way she'd danced around the questions the new tenants had asked.

But Annie knew that fibbing wasn't a strong suit for her,

which was why, when Donna and Kevin walked into the Newes, she stood up and forced herself not to look at the floor. "I'm over here," she said with a small wave. She tried to hold a smile as Donna moved toward the table. Her navy pants were full in places where they should have been fitted; her jacket looked like she'd plucked it from a coat rack by mistake, as if it belonged to a much larger woman. Her makeup seemed out of place as well, including the coral lipstick that looked as if it were painted on a dowager lady who'd once been grand but now was not.

They ordered wine and talked about the weather and how nice it was that the sun was finally out.

They perused the menu as if Kevin and Annie had never been there.

They unfolded their napkins and placed them in their respective laps.

Once the wine arrived and they ordered their meals—fish and chips all around—Annie said, "So, Donna, have you told Kevin why you're here?" She knew that her abruptness might not be appreciated, but as bad a liar as Annie always had been, she was worse at keeping secrets.

Mother and son blinked in unison.

Then Kevin said, "Annie said you need to go over something with us, Mom, about the estate planning? I thought you'd already taken care of that."

Donna looked at Annie, not with anger, but with sorrow. Annie instantly regretted that she'd been so direct. God, she thought, I don't know how to do this. I don't know how to be part of a family. Not when it comes to this.

"I was sick," Donna said, her voice so low that Annie had a hard time making out the words.

"What?" Kevin asked.

Donna raised her chin, reached out, and took his hand. "I

was sick, honey," she said more clearly. "I had ovarian cancer. I came to the island to be near my children while I recuperate."

Kevin studied her a moment, their hazel eyes mirroring each other's. He did not say a word; instead, he turned to Annie.

"I didn't know, either," Annie said. "Until today."

"She told you?"

"She thought you were going to pick her up." Annie looked at Donna with what she hoped was understanding. "And you needed to tell one of us, didn't you?" Please, Annie thought, don't make me feel guilty that you told me before Kevin.

"I did," Donna replied, and patted Kevin's hand. "I'm sorry, honey. It's been bottled up inside me for so long. One of those ugly secrets you need to tell someone but can't. I needed to wait until the crisis had been averted."

"You've had plenty of practice."

"Which didn't always turn out bad."

"Like when you started your antiques business before you told me you were going to, because even I knew you didn't know a damn thing about antiques?"

"I knew I had to make a better living for us than I could by greeting people at a radio station. So I denied the odds and I won."

"And now you've waited for the crisis to pass again." He took a big swig of wine. "When did you get it?"

"Over a year ago. It's why I sold the business. It's why I took the cruise, which really wasn't the 'worldwide cruise' I led you to believe. It was a boat trip across the Atlantic, then a long train ride to a hospital in Switzerland where I had an experimental treatment for two months." Her gaze fell to her lap. "It took forever to get there, but my Boston doctor said I really shouldn't fly."

"He wanted you to go?"

"She. Dr. Geraldine Lang. And, yes. She wanted me to go. She recommended it."

Kevin rubbed his chin as if pondering what Donna had said. Then he asked, "So your boyfriend never left you?"

Donna raised her chin and let out a sharp laugh. "Hell, no. I gave him the heave-ho because he couldn't handle it when I told him the truth. He was afraid I wouldn't get better."

The three of them sat quietly. Annie felt like an intruder, as if the conversation should have been between mother and son.

"Mom?" Kevin asked. "You're sure you're okay? That it's okay for you to be out here on the Vineyard? Away from your doctor?"

"Absolutely. I've been chemo-ed and radiated to near-death, and now I want to recuperate around the two of you, as long as you can stand me." She smiled. "But just in case— and it's a long shot—anything unforeseen might happen, I've made both of you my health care proxies. And, Kevin, I've given you power of attorney over my financial affairs." She looked at Annie. "I didn't do that because I feel a man is more capable at numbers than a woman. But Kevin already knows everything about my finances. He's been helping me handle them since he was thirteen."

Annie smiled and said, "Of course." She felt a large pull in her abdomen, or maybe it was higher up, in her heart. A reminder that she was not, could never be, Donna's daughter. They had missed too many things that only come from sharing time together. Time, responsibilities, life—the good parts and the not so good.

Plates of food were set in front of them. "Enjoy your meal," the perky waitress said.

Annie said, "Thank you," because the others didn't seem to want to speak.

Then Kevin took Donna's hand in both of his. "How can I help? I don't want you to be sick."

He was being brave, Annie thought. Braver than she'd thought that he would be.

"I don't want to be sick again, either," Donna said. "But here's one thing you can do. Take me back to the Inn. I want to go to bed, and I want you two to talk about me. The truth is, I don't know how long this recuperation thing will take. And as badly as I want to be here, I don't want to disrupt your lives. Well, I suppose part of me does, or I wouldn't be here now, would I?" She pulled her hand from Kevin's and patted his again. "Now, let's get the check and have them wrap this food. It looks delicious, but I don't have much of an appetite tonight."

Kevin's eyes had filled with tears; his lower lip started to quiver.

Without expecting it, Annie, too, began to cry.

Chapter 14

It was no surprise that, over the years, from time to time, she visited her memories that were safe in the Vuitton. The place where she could remember her most important secrets.

More than once, Donna had wondered how it had happened that she had grown to be someone who had carved out a small, but successful, corner of the world, how she had learned to become strong and competent and in control of many things, a woman she often didn't recognize, especially when she peeked inside the trunk and was reminded of the things she supposed she should forget about but never could. Not even a little.

It had taken a long time for her to find it; she'd started by buying and selling antiques out of what had been her parents' bedroom in the triple-decker where she and Kevin had moved after her parents had both died. When she finally was able to buy the shop on Newbury Street, she insisted that their records be part of the sale. Which was how she was reunited with the Louis Vuitton. By then it belonged to the son of the woman who had plucked it from the shop window many years earlier, but she had since died. The son didn't want it. He didn't even know its true value.

So finally Donna had the only material thing that she'd ever longed for. The only place that was worthy of holding her greatest treasures.

★ ★ ★

"Jesus Christ," Kevin muttered as he flicked the top off a can of beer and swept a hand across his face—his cheek, his mouth, his chin, his other cheek. His eyes remained glazed, perched on the edge of tears.

Annie sat across from him on the canvas drop cloths that were spread across half of the great room floor where new hardwood had been partially installed by the workers who'd been told to leave.

"I can't believe she didn't tell me," he said into the air. "All this time, she never told me. What was she waiting for?"

"Maybe until she felt sure she was cured."

"Huh." He slugged the beer.

It had been a long day. Annie was exhausted, and wanted only to go to bed. "Look, Kevin. We don't have to figure out what to do this minute. We can sleep on it. Let it settle in, you know?" If Murphy had been there—the professional Murphy, in her role as a therapist—Annie expected she would have advised Kevin to take time to process the news.

"Mom's always been a master at keeping secrets. But this one? Jesus. It's even worse than the fact that she never told me about you until after she'd met you."

Annie hadn't known that. She wanted to reach over, grab his beer, and chug it. "She must have been trying to protect you."

"Or you. Or her."

"I guess."

Dusk was quickly turning into night; Annie snapped on the LED lantern that she'd snatched from the kitchen counter. It seemed like the best place to talk since God knew no one was around, and they couldn't go to Earl and Claire's where they'd be within earshot of John's parents. It was too soon for anyone else to know about Donna's illness—not until Kevin and Annie had decided what to do. Not that there was anything to do. True, they were Donna's health care proxies. And Kevin had her power of attorney. But those things didn't really matter now. Not yet. Hopefully not for a long, long time.

The only decision, then, was should she stay or should she go.

"She never talked about my dad, either," Kevin said. "I have a few vague memories of him. One is when he took me to a Red Sox game. He bought me a hot dog and a soda. I thought I'd died and gone to heaven. I think he was a good dad while he was with us, but he was gone before I could remember his face. Or his voice. When I was in junior high school I started going to Red Sox games whenever I could save up enough cash. By then Mom was working, so she didn't know. I took the T to Fenway and spent all nine innings walking around the crowd, searching for my dad, hoping he'd find me there. Hoping he'd recognize me. If he was there, he never did." Kevin took another drink. "Of course, he could have been living in California by then, or London, or Timbuktu. I told myself he must live far away, or he would have seen me."

Annie had never felt abandoned. When she'd been old enough to understand the true meaning of having been adopted, her dad had explained that her birth mother had known that the Suttons would be better able to take care of Annie and protect her and give her a good home. He'd said that her birth mother must have loved Annie an awful lot to have the courage to give her to them.

Kevin set down the empty can. "I know that Lucy's an enthusiastic kid, but I'll admit that more than once I've wondered if she's right—I should have my DNA tested. Maybe I do have other half-siblings somewhere in the world. And maybe I could find my dad."

Wow, Annie thought, trying not to gasp. "If that's what

you want, then go for it. But I don't think I have to warn you that if you think it will be perfect, you might want to think again."

He cocked an eyebrow. In the harsh, blue light of the LED he looked a little comical. "Speaking from experience?"

She laughed. "No. Honestly? I was never interested in finding Donna. When she first contacted me, I'd recently lost the people I'd known as Mom and Dad. I thought that if I met Donna I'd be turning my back on them. It was too soon."

"Is that your polite way of telling me that Mom having had cancer isn't a good reason for me to rush to find my dad?"

"Yes. No. I don't know." Where the heck was Murphy when Annie needed her?

"Anyway, she'll be okay, so I don't have to think about that. Right?"

"If only we could control the ways our brains behave."

He let out a not-so-subtle grumble. "What the hell are we supposed to do? With her? With our stupid Inn? With our lives?"

"Sorry, brother, I have no answers. But let's start by giving it time. Let her stay in the cottage. I'll sleep here, upstairs. For a week or two? By then maybe she'll have her strength back and be feeling better. Then we'll know what to do—and so will she. As for our stupid Inn, I kick myself a thousand times a day for finding that damn skull. But I have no control over that, any more than I know how long it's going to take Donna to recuperate. And while I'm at it, I confess I have no idea what to do with our lives. Just live them, I guess."

Kevin grew quiet. "I'm doing the best I can."

"I know." They sat in silence for a few seconds, then Annie said, "Like most of us, you're probably doing better than you think. But right now, how about dinner? The fish and chips won't taste nearly as good tomorrow."

They spread the take-out containers on the canvas car-pet and dined by the blue light of the lantern. Then Kevin wrapped the trash, said good night and headed off to Earl's. Annie took the lantern and went upstairs, weighted by fatigue and swathed in a layer of sadness—for Kevin and for Donna. And though Annie didn't want to know if ovarian cancer tended to be genetic, she also felt a little sad for herself that even in the best of times, life had a way of leaking in.

Annie woke up to the sounds of hammering downstairs. It was a moment before she realized that she wasn't in her own bed in the cottage, but in a guest room at The Vineyard Inn. Or what there was of the Inn. Reaching to the nightstand, she checked her phone and saw that it was only 7:00 a.m. No wonder the soft pink light of dawn had barely crept into the room.

She pulled herself together, dressed, and made her way downstairs, in the direction of the hammering. And there was Kevin, on his hands and knees in the great room, install-ing hardwood planks as if his sanity depended on it, which, perhaps, it did.

"Hey!" she shouted above the noise. "It's Sunday morn-ing!"

He set down the hammer and removed a few nails that had been sticking straight out of his mouth. "Sorry. I wanted to get an early start."

"I didn't know you could install a floor."

"Me either. But somebody has to finish it. If we can't have a professional on the payroll, I figured I might as well teach myself."

"So," she said as gently as possible, "I don't know if there's a regulation on Chappy that stipulates the hours for excessive noise, but seven in the morning seems a little . . . early."

He picked up the hammer again. "I no longer give a crap about rules and regulations." He stuck the nails back in his mouth, except for one that he hammered into the floor.

While Annie had heard about the stages of grief (she never could remember what they all were), she didn't know if they applied when a loved one was recuperating. If so, Kevin might be in depression, if that was one.

"Did something happen?" she asked. "You seemed okay when you left last night but now . . ."

He ignored her for a few seconds, then said, "I'm tired, that's all. I didn't get much sleep. I'm not trying to sound selfish, but I really didn't need one more thing on my mind."

"Kevin, she'll be all right."

"Sure. And Taylor didn't push her lover overboard twenty-something years ago, and the Inn will open right on time, and all the bills will magically be paid. But I'm sorry if my sleep deprivation woke you up."

Annie stared at him a moment; she'd never seen him so distraught. But the fact was, he was not the only one doing the best he could. "Well," she said, not hiding her annoyance, "I'm going for a walk. In case you give a crap about that." She headed toward the back door, took his hooded sweatshirt off a hook, and slipped into it. It was too early to wake up Donna by going to the cottage to get a jacket. Besides, it didn't seem as if Kevin would be going anywhere—not until he'd hammered out the last of his frustration.

She didn't slam the door on her way out.

She walked. Not down to the beach because she didn't need to be reminded of that clump of seaweed stuck between the rocks. Instead, she headed up the driveway, past the scrub oaks and pines, past the places where clusters of green shrubbery were dewy and expectant, not yet ready to reveal their buds.

Reaching the dirt road, Annie took a right. She didn't know where she was going, but she stayed on the main road rather than going toward Cape Poge Bay; the only things out there were osprey nests. As much as she loved living on Chappy, parts of it were still too isolated for her comfort.

She walked fifteen or twenty minutes, then fifteen or twenty more. She supposed it was not surprising that, subconsciously, she was headed to Earl and Claire's. Nor was it surprising when she saw Earl's pickup heading toward her.

He stopped; he rolled down his window. "Out for a stroll?"

"Very funny. But no. I'm fretting about my brother."

"Yeah, I noticed he was up and out kind of early. His bed looked hardly slept in. I figured I ought to try to track him down."

"I'll save you the trouble. He's at the Inn. Hammering down hardwood floor."

"I didn't know he knew how to do that."

"He doesn't. He's upset. Sleep deprived, he claims. He's taking out his troubles on a bunch of nails and wooden planks."

Earl scratched his chin, the way Kevin now did sometimes. Maybe Kevin wished that he'd had Earl as a father.

"He mad at someone?"

She shook her head. "Nope. Not even at Donna. Well, not at her exactly. But he found out last night that she had cancer. And that she didn't tell him." She hadn't intended to tell Earl so soon, and certainly not while he was in his pickup and she was standing on the roadside at seven in the morning where little could be heard above the engine of the truck other than the incessant chirping of a few birds.

"She's terminal?" he asked.

"No. She's actually recuperating. But she hasn't used the

word 'cure,' or even 'remission.' So that's where we're at."
Until that moment, Annie hadn't realized she'd been worried
about the possibility that Donna might not "recuperate."

"Well, God, that's unsettling."

She didn't tell Earl that she didn't know what God had to
do with it. Having faith in anything had waxed and waned
for her over the years.

Then Earl said, "Get in." He raised a thumb and gestured
toward the passenger side of the cab. "I can't have you trun-
dling all over this island in the wee hours of the morning. You
might run into Bigfoot or a gator."

She could not stop a smile. "There's no such thing as Bigfoot, at least not on Chappaquiddick. And I don't believe that
we have gators, either."

"You never know," he said. "Stranger things have happened here."

Annie didn't need to be reminded of that, either.

They went straight to the Inn where Kevin was still on his
hands and knees doing penance with the lumber and the steel.

"Coffee time," Earl said above the din.

Annie looked around. "Unless you have a few thermoses
in the truck, we don't have coffee here, do we?"

Neither man said, "No," because they no doubt knew
they didn't.

"Doesn't matter," Earl said. "We'll go down to the cottage."

"We can't," Kevin said. "Donna's there, remember?"

Earl nodded. "Yup. But she called the landline at the house
half an hour ago. She was looking for you, Kevin. She said an
awful lot of hammering was coming from the Inn, and she
was worried about vandals. She wanted you to find out what
the heck was going on. She also said she called your cell, but
you didn't answer."

Kevin pulled the nail heads from his mouth again and said something that sounded a lot like, "Shit."

"I suggested that she put the coffee on." Earl turned to Annie. "You have cinnamon rolls?"

"In the freezer," she replied, and the three of them journeyed down the short slope to the little cottage where who knew what awaited.

Chapter 15

"This isn't my business, so I shouldn't be here," Earl said once the four of them were seated at Annie's kitchen table. "But I figure I'll hear about it sooner or later, so I might as well save everyone the trouble." He looked at Donna. "I'm sorry for your situation, Donna. What can we do to help?" They'd seen each other twice before when Donna had come to the island. Annie had been pleased that they'd seemed to get along.

Donna smiled. "I'm not sure I should have come, now that I've heard about the alarming new problem here."

At least she hadn't referred to it as Annie's skull.

"Yup, well, it's a wait-and-see game. As much as I hate to say it, we're at the mercy of the folks in Boston now. But what about you? Are you going to stay here with us?"

"That's up to the kids."

The kids, of course, were fifty-two-year-old Annie and forty-three-year-old Kevin.

Annie cleared her throat. "Kevin and I think it's best if none of us makes a decision for a week or two. We want you to settle in, Donna. See how you feel then. Who knows? Maybe you'll hate recuperating here. But you're the one who matters now. Not us." There, she thought. Done. No further discussion needed.

"Sounds sensible," Earl said.

"Sounds wonderful," Donna said. "Thank you. Mostly I'm worn out from the treatments. But I'll feel better soon. You'll see." She picked up half of a now-thawed cinnamon roll. "Now what are we going to do about your situation?"

"The 'alarming' one?" Kevin asked. At least his sense of humor had returned, albeit through sarcasm. "Like Earl said, it's up in Boston. Out of the island's jurisdiction. Or so the state cops told us."

"You mentioned that yesterday. Which got me to thinking . . ."

Kevin turned to Annie. "She can't resist a challenge. Or a good argument."

"Stop," Donna said with a giggle. "It's apparent you need to do whatever it takes to move the investigation along. Right now, too much is in limbo. And forget about the tourists, what about the people who are planning to live here year-round? It isn't fair to keep them on hold. As I recall from Annie's situation last summer, housing is a problem here."

Annie nodded.

Earl agreed.

And Kevin rubbed the back of his neck.

"But never mind all that," Donna added, "I thought of something that might help."

"Listen to your mother," Earl said, and Kevin groaned.

"All the years I was in Boston, I never needed to get to know any law enforcement folks. On the other hand . . . Kevin? Remember Gina, honey? What was her last name? Medina? Molina? Something Italian, right?"

Annie had no way of knowing what Kevin was thinking, but by the way his face paled and his jaw contorted, she had a feeling that it wasn't good.

"Gina Fiorina, Mom. And no, I'm not going to contact her."

"But isn't she a doctor? If I recall correctly, she works with the Boston police."

Kevin stood up and held his hands in front of his face, palms out, creating the illusion of a barrier. "Forget it, Mom. Let it be." He brought his mug to the sink and dumped the contents down the drain. "I'm heading back up the hill to finish what I was doing. This thing will blow over before we know it, and I don't want to have to rush and do a half-ass job. See y'all later." He went out the door without looking back.

Earl stood, too. "Seems you touched a nerve," he said to Donna. "There are lots of nerves around these parts right now. Don't take it personally."

Donna nodded and said something, but Annie didn't hear—like Kevin, she had plummeted into her own paralyzing thought: she, too, knew someone who worked with law enforcement in the city. And though she had no idea why Kevin was averse to calling Gina Fiorina, Annie knew very well why she would not—would never—contact Larry Hendricks. No matter how much was at stake.

After Earl pocketed the last roll and said he'd best get a move on or Claire would think he'd run away, Annie cleaned up the dishes, then told Donna that she wanted to shower and get ready for the day. She asked if Donna needed any help before she went back to the Inn.

Donna shook her head. "I'm fine, dear. I didn't mean to upset Kevin. It seems like that's all I've done since I arrived."

"I'm not sure," Annie said with a smile, "but I think that's a mother's prerogative."

"I'll try not to misbehave again. But though I understand his hesitation, I do think Gina might be able to help. Or she might have connections to someone who could."

As tempting as it might have been to ask what Donna meant about Kevin's hesitation, Annie didn't. For all she knew, Gina was an old flame that he didn't want to cross paths with again. So she merely said, "I guess we'll have to wait and see," which seemed to be the new mantra for them.

But on her way up the hill, Annie knew that Donna had a point. Feeling homeless was still fresh in Annie's mind. And with the season coming fast upon them, Greg Collins, Marty and Luke Amanti, and Harlin Pierce (who'd rented the third room) might need to be back in the market for somewhere to live. Greg was a carpenter who had been commuting from Falmouth on the Cape; the Amantis were elementary school teachers in Edgartown whose landlord had sold the house they'd been renting, forcing them to move in with friends; Harlin was on the waitstaff at an upscale restaurant, had a marimba band, and currently lived with six guys and a whole lot of percussion instruments in a cramped two-bedroom apartment—Annie had asked if his band would play at the Inn's grand opening. The new tenants were all hardworking young people at the start of their careers who needed the kind of break that the Inn was intended to provide. The winter rentals would accommodate three more islanders come October; eleven people were already on the waiting list. Earl, Kevin, and Annie had gone into the project knowing they could not single-handedly solve the housing problem on the island, but they'd wanted to help in this small way.

Like the hummingbird, she heard Murphy whisper.

Annie stopped and looked out to the water, remembering the tale from the indigenous people of South America about a hummingbird. When a forest fire raged through his homeland, the hummingbird carried water in its tiny beak—one drop at a time—back and forth from a stream, attempting to put out the fire. The other forest animals huddled in fear; one asked the bird why it was bothering to try to do the impossible. The hummingbird said while he knew he could not douse the entire fire, he at least could do his part.

One of Murphy's twins had learned about the story—and its meaning had resonated when Murphy received her grim cancer prognosis, and as each person who loved her stepped up to do his or her part. Together, though they couldn't change the outcome, they'd made a bit of difference every day.

Annie turned back and looked up at what had been becoming their beautiful Inn. She knew if there was anything that could be done to accelerate the resolution and get them all out of limbo, she needed to do her part. With Larry Hendricks out of the question, maybe she could reason with Kevin.

"No," Kevin said when Annie found him, his teeth gritted, his biceps beating nails into the floorboards as if he were tenderizing them.

"What if I contact her instead?"

The hammering stopped. His body froze. He did not look up at her.

"No," he said again.

So she told him the hummingbird story.

When she was done, he sighed and put down his hammer. Then he sat on the floor. "I can't," he said. "This is not a drop of water, Annie. Will you please leave it alone?"

She hung her head and picked at the threads of her old sweater. "What if she doesn't know that we're connected? I could approach her as an author . . . ask her questions as research for my new book. Who knows, she might even be one of my fans. Or I could take a more honest approach and tell her I'm involved with the Inn on Chappy and that my business partners and I would appreciate a possible timeline for a reply so we can alert our tenants if they need to look for other housing."

Kevin stared at her, his hazel eyes unflinching.

So Annie continued. "It might be worth a try, Kevin. I won't mention your name unless you want me to. If she's an old girlfriend . . ." It was the most plausible reason Annie could come up with as to why he wouldn't want to make contact with Gina. It wasn't as if he could have the same kind of history with her that Annie had with Hendricks.

Kevin rubbed his forehead with the back of his hand. "She's not an old girlfriend, Annie. But stay the hell out of it. Please."

Oh, God, Annie thought, and sat down across from him. Like Earl had said to Donna, Annie had touched a nerve. "Well," she said quietly, "I'm sorry for whatever happened. It must have been something big . . . but you don't have to tell me. If you don't want to." She hoped he'd laugh, but he did not.

"Her full name is Doctor Gina Fiorina. She was the ER doctor who treated Meghan right after the accident."

Annie winced. Meghan. Kevin's wife. Annie reached out, touched his hand. "Oh, Kevin, I am so sorry."

"Yeah, well, she testified at my civil trial."

Annie gulped. "Your *trial*?" It was news to her that there had been one.

After a slow nod, Kevin continued. "When the extent of Meghan's injuries—and the conjecture about her future, or rather, her lack of a future—became apparent, her parents filed a civil suit against me. They said I had something to do with the accident, that the scaffolding broke because of negligence—*my* negligence."

"Seriously?" Annie couldn't hide her surprise. "Why would they do that?"

He shrugged. "At first I thought they needed to direct their anger at someone. I was the most likely target, though God knows why. We didn't have enough life insurance on either one of us for that to be a motive. Every dime we made either went back into the business or into investment property. That's how we bought the condos I still own."

Not to mention the one or two he'd either sold or borrowed against to pool with Earl's retirement money in order to buy the property for the Inn, Annie thought, but didn't say.

"If her parents knew there was no life insurance, why did they think you would have done that?"

"It was simple. Workers' comp took care of Meghan's medical bills. But because I'd made sure she was in a pricey, private facility, her parents were afraid they'd somehow get stuck paying for Meghan's long-term care."

Closing her eyes, Annie could almost feel his pain. "Wow. Had they always been so . . . cold?"

"Not her dad. Her stepmother was behind it. Meghan's mom died when she was a teenager, and her dad remarried fast. From day one, the stepmother let it be known that his daughter wouldn't interfere with their way of life."

"Yikes."

"Yeah. When they came to the hospital the night of the accident, all she said to me was, 'This is your fault, Kevin.' The police didn't agree; after all was said and done, they couldn't find a reason to arrest me. The civil suit came later."

"How did Gina enter the picture?"

"She testified for the defense; she described the condition I was in when I arrived in the ambulance with Meghan. Which backed up the testimony of the officers who were first on the scene." Kevin's voice cracked on those last words. He turned back to his work. "It's hard to talk about."

Weighing her words carefully, Annie said, "But it sounds like Gina was on your side, so couldn't she be an ally now?" Her words hung like fog on a dank, misty morning. Moshup's blanket, as Winnie had said, trying to bring comfort to his people.

"The day Meghan was hurt was the worst day of my life, Annie. The day I had to go to court like I was a fucking criminal was the second worst. So no, I don't want to reconnect with Dr. Fiorina. Bad memories, you know?" He hammered another floorboard.

Annie certainly knew about bad memories. "I'm sorry, Kevin."

"No problem. You didn't know."

"Does Mom know the details?"

He nodded again. "She was there. In court. She wanted me to ask Gina out for a drink. Or dinner. Or probably to marry me."

Annie stifled a laugh. "Are you kidding?"

"Nope. Mom doesn't want me to be alone. You're lucky you have John or she'd be trying to hook you up with someone, too. So I'm sorry, but I can't be your hummingbird. My little drop of whatever won't be coming to Chappy."

"Well, maybe the real birds are overrated. They're cute and fun to watch, but they eat bugs and rotten bananas. Terrible diet, if you ask me." Annie stood up. "Now, I have to take a shower. You are free to return to laboring." She bent down and planted a kiss on the top of his head. Then she went upstairs, her heart swollen with sorrow.

Chapter 16

Standing under the pelting hot shower, Annie mulled over Kevin's history with Gina. She was glad he had explained it; she understood why he didn't want to get in touch with her. There simply were some memories that no one needed to revisit. Did Larry Hendricks fit into that category?

How she wished Murphy were really there to share a bottle of wine and a long conversation. Among so many things, Annie missed how they'd had each other's backs, how she'd always felt safe telling Murphy everything. Murphy would have helped her decide if she should call Larry. Annie supposed she could have talked to Kevin, but there were some things a woman could only talk about with another woman, a best friend.

Winnie. The name popped into Annie's head as if Murphy had dropped it there. If Annie could talk to Winnie, maybe she could unburden her angst about the skull and its far-reaching consequences, about Donna's situation, and maybe, just maybe, about her reluctance to contact Larry Hendricks when Annie knew damn well he could help. Not that he would.

She quickly finished her shower, then dried and dressed. It was after ten-thirty when she left her room; it had already been a long morning, but Annie knew she needed to keep moving.

Half-hopping down the stairs she called out to Kevin, "Stop hammering!"

He stopped. Because though he was trying his damnedest to sort out his demons, he still was a good brother.

She ran around the corner into the great room. "I'm heading up to Winnie's. I'll be back later this afternoon, but you're in charge of Mom until then. Okay?"

He hesitated, then said, "Sure."

"Thanks. And by the way, you're doing a terrific job on the floor."

He managed a limp smile. "Yeah. Don't mind if I say so."

She swatted him on the shoulder, and then, feeling a little lighter, she darted through the kitchen and out the back door to her Jeep.

For the full two minutes it took to drive to the *On Time*, it seemed to Annie that things might work out after all. Her assumption was based on nothing in particular beyond a hoped-for talk with Winnie, but she wanted so badly to believe it that she refused to think otherwise—not even when she realized that Jonas was ahead of her in the ferry line. She might not have given it much thought, but she couldn't help but notice that the back of his small SUV was packed with duffle bags, art canvases, and a large, folded-up easel. Jonas was going somewhere.

She wondered if it had to do with Lucy planting that silly idea in his head about Taylor having faked the letters from his dad. It was a ridiculous assumption. If the woman had wanted to knock him off the sailboat, grab the family's fortune, and then write the letters to make people think she'd loved him and could never have done such a thing . . . well, why would she have hidden the letters for years? Still, Annie did not know how she might have felt if she were Jonas.

Three vehicles were ahead of him. A month ago there would have been no one on a Sunday; no doubt people had come from the mainland for the weekend to get their houses prepped for summer.

Staring at the back of Jonas's SUV, Annie sat perfectly still, aware that she shouldn't get involved, yet feeling that she was, thanks to Lucy.

The *On Time* scuttled toward its berth. There wasn't much time if Annie wanted to stop him.

She opened her door. "Hey!" she cried, scurrying toward his vehicle. "Jonas!"

He opened the driver's window and stuck his head out.

"Where are you off to on such a beautiful day?" She tried to sound nonchalant, but wasn't sure if it was working.

"I'm going to Boston. To see a friend. Then I'm going home. You won't see me again."

A tiny knot formed in her throat for the boy who'd been manipulated most of his life. "The last I heard, this was your home."

He shook his head. "New York's my home. I don't know what made me think I could live on the island. It's just too weird here for me."

The *On Time* arrived, and three vehicles exited.

"Don't," Annie heard herself say. "Please don't go. Not yet." Even if she discounted the role Lucy had played, Annie knew that if she hadn't found the skull, Jonas wouldn't have had his life turned upside down. Again.

He shrugged. "I have to. I can't live with my mother."

The vehicles in front of his motored onto the ferry and turned off their engines; the captain hitched the safety strap, and the ferry glided away. Jonas stepped on the gas so he'd be first in line for the next trip.

Annie knew she had about one hundred and eighty seconds to get him to change his mind. She dashed back to her Jeep, jumped in, and pulled up behind him. She got out again and ran up to his car door. Luckily, his window was still down.

"Let's talk," she said. "Please? I'll buy breakfast? Or an early lunch? At the diner?"

He seemed to think about that for five, ten, maybe twelve seconds. In her peripheral vision she saw that the ferry was close to reaching the Edgartown side.

"Jonas, please. I don't want you to do anything you'll regret."

He did not respond.

"Please," she repeated. "Lunch?"

Across the way the *On Time* was docking. It would only take a few seconds for it to unload, then load up again. Her time was running short. But maybe it would be enough for her to extend a drop of water to him.

"I don't blame you for the video," she said. "In fact, I don't blame you for anything. You've been a victim most of your life, thanks in no small part to your grandparents. For what it's worth, I admire not only how you've handled yourself, but also how you've seemed to thrive. Now that you're here, now that you've been reunited with your mother, please don't let old gossip push you away. And don't let it mess up your relationship with Taylor. I know it must he hard, but she's your mother, Jonas. And she loves you. She always has." Annie's voice fluttered, as if she'd been talking about Donna.

The *On Time* was reloaded and heading back to Chappy. Annie didn't know if anything she'd said had gotten through to Jonas, any more than she had a clue as to why she was defending Taylor. She wondered how much of that had to do with Donna. After all, Donna and Taylor had both been mothers whose children were taken from them. As for Jonas, if Annie had learned anything over the years, it was that running away hurt other people. Not to mention that it often wrecked the life of the person who'd done the running. Or so she'd fantasized after Mark had run from her.

In the few seconds she had left, Annie figured she had one more chance. "And we're coming into season," she said brightly. "It would be a shame if you missed this chance to get your career started. With all the summer people flocking to this 'weird' place, it's a perfect time to sell your paintings and get your work known. Lucy told me that the Sculpin Gallery wants your work. And that it's going to be at Featherstone. Most artists I know would trip over one another to try to get into either of those venues, let alone both. You're in the right place, Jonas. The buying power here comes from all over the country; it's radical in the summer."

The *On Time* docked; Jonas's eyes filled with tears.

"The diner?" Annie asked softly.

He nodded.

"She killed him," Jonas said, after Esther—the sweet, soft-spoken waitress—delivered a burger and a Coke to him, and a mug of tea to Annie.

Annie gripped the handle of the mug. "What?" She wasn't sure she wanted details; she hoped he wasn't going to tell her something she'd have to tell John, and have him think that she'd been meddling in police business—again.

"My mother killed my father."

Though Annie didn't ordinarily use sweetener, she took a packet from a small silver bowl; she needed time to consider her reply. She wanted to sound reasonable. But she wanted to be empathetic. She stirred the tea, reviewing what she knew: Jonas's life had been challenging. He'd been raised by a fi-

nancial wizard of a grandfather and a social-climbing grandmother, both of whom had only wanted him in order to hold
on to the memory of their son. At some point Jonas had found
letters between his birth parents that revealed they'd been in
love, and that his grandparents had tried to get between them.
And though Jonas then knew who his birth mother was, he'd
been afraid to tell anyone. Later, he'd learned that his grandparents were not the upstanding citizens that they'd portrayed.
So he'd been living with Taylor for several months, apparently
having reconciled himself with the fact that she, too, had been
manipulated by his grandparents. But now, for whatever reason, he was convinced his mother was a murderer.

Annie really, really hoped it was not because of Lucy.

"Jonas," Annie said, "are you sure it isn't gossip?"

He set down his burger, but kept his eyes fixed on his
plate. "I really think she did it."

Annie stirred her tea again, then sipped. The liquid was
hot and bitter. "Can you tell me what happened?"

Lifting his eyes, he looked out the window. "It started
with Lucy."

Oh, Annie thought, a small thud landing in her stomach.

"She's a sweet kid," he continued. "Smart."

Annie wanted to say that, in reality, that wasn't always
true. Instead, she said, "Lucy is sweet. And very smart. But
with smarts comes curiosity. Which sometimes gets her into
trouble."

"Like with the photos."

"And the video."

He closed his eyes. "I never should have done that. It was
my fault, not hers."

Annie paused. "What's going on now, Jonas? I'm on your
side, you know." She wished she knew how to make him
believe that.

"Taking everything off the internet was an easy fix. Other

parts aren't so easy." Abruptly, he slid out of the booth and stood. "I need to use the men's room." Before Annie could respond, he went to the cash register, grabbed the key, and ducked out the doorway to the restrooms.

She toyed with her napkin, then with her spoon, then with the handle of the mug—not unlike the way that Donna had fidgeted when they'd gone to the Black Dog. Also like Donna, Annie hadn't been born yesterday, nor—as Earl liked to say—had she been born the day before that. Jonas's manner, his hesitation, and the way he'd averted his eyes had given her a clear message: he hadn't told her everything. And whatever he'd left out, was no doubt why he'd packed up his car and was running away.

Picturing his vehicle loaded to the brim, Annie knew it looked like he was serious about leaving: first to Boston, then New York. As far as Annie knew, he'd mainly lived in New York City, on the Vineyard in summers, and, of course, in Chicago, where he'd gone to art school. Why was he going to Boston?

She stood up and looked outside to the parking lot. A pickup blocked her view. Then, suddenly, a burst of intuition rushed at her. Grabbing her purse, she tossed a few bills on the table and raced out of the restaurant. She wove between the cars and trucks until she reached her Jeep, which she'd parked next to Jonas's Subaru. But his vehicle, like him, was gone.

Annie climbed into her Jeep, dropped her purse and jacket onto the passenger seat, and rested her forehead on the steering wheel. Damn, she thought. She checked her watch: eleven-fifteen. Probably too late to drive up island to see Winnie; by the time she'd arrive, Winnie and her family would be well into their Sunday activities. Annie could go to John's, but he'd no doubt be sleeping. Which meant, if she were going to be able to resolve anything at all that day, her best chance would be to find Lucy—maybe she knew what had happened with Jonas. The good news was it hadn't seemed as if she'd run off with him.

Pulling her phone from her purse, Annie quickly sent a text. U AROUND? I'M AT E'TOWN DINER. She sat back and waited. It would be nice if Lucy was out with friends, doing something fun like learning crocheting or bonsai tree care at the library; taking lessons on the clarinet or flute; or shopping in Vineyard Haven at Rainy Day or at Basics in Oak Bluffs. But Lucy did not seem to enjoy doing ordinary girl things.

Annie rested her head against the seat back and wished she could stop brooding. About Lucy. About Donna. About Kevin's wounds. And, of course, about the skull. Added to those problems now, Jonas had taken off.

She sighed. She knew she had to leave Lucy's behavior up to John; Lucy was his daughter, not Annie's. As for Donna, there might be ways Annie could help with her recovery; Winnie might have some ideas about that, too, or Winnie's sister-in-law who was a nurse. And Kevin . . . Well, Annie supposed he'd have to resolve his angst about Donna, his guilt about Meghan, and his relationship with Taylor on his own. Because Annie had no idea how to help him. As for the skull, she could not ask John for help—he'd only get aggravated with her and insist that they follow procedures. John was a great guy, but not much use when it came to circumventing the law.

She checked her phone; Lucy hadn't replied. Digging into her purse again, Annie took out a Tums and tossed it into her mouth. She started the Jeep, figuring she might as well go back to Chappy, just as someone pounded on the passenger window. Annie jumped nearly a foot.

The culprit was Lucy, her face pressed to the glass. She was sticking out her tongue and waving like a five-year-old.

Chapter 17

Annie dropped her head again and pushed the button that put the window down. "You must be great at fright night."

Laughing, Lucy said, "I got your text. I was at the bookstore looking for something about the island cemeteries. They're going to order a book for me."

Well, Annie thought, at least Lucy seemed happy. "Where are you headed?"

"Restless and I were thinking about visiting my grandparents. You going back to Chappy?"

Annie popped the door lock and lobbed her purse into the back.

Lucy lifted the furry dog into the back seat, unhooked his leash, then climbed into the front. She had on jeans with tears across the knees and one of her dad's fishing jackets. Her hair was pulled back into a ponytail that made her look more like eleven or twelve. "Did you have lunch at the diner?" she asked.

Once again that day, Annie didn't know what to say. She wasn't sure if she should tell the truth, but if she didn't there was always a chance Lucy would find out, thanks to their living on an island. In any event, Lucy was smart enough to know that, if Annie was stalling, she was trying to hide something. So she said, "I ran into Jonas. We grabbed a bite."

"Jonas? Like, my friend Jonas?"

Annie nodded. "We talked about art. I told you I'm thinking about using paintings from local artists to decorate the Inn." She praised herself for landing upright on her verbal feet.

"I didn't know you wanted to use Jonas's. That'd be cool."

Annie put the Jeep into reverse and backed out of the space. Until that moment, she hadn't known it, either. But, why not? Because he was too young? Or because he was Taylor's son and Annie still hadn't completely warmed up to the woman? "Well, I haven't seen any of his pieces up close, but I'd like to give it a try." Even if his work wasn't to her taste, surely she could find somewhere to hang a canvas or two. It might be worth it solely to be a good neighbor. And a friend to someone who seemed to need a few. "But I think he's leaving the island. Have you talked to him lately?"

Scowling, Lucy said, "I texted him this morning. I asked if he wanted to grab a few beers today."

Annie paused. She did not want to seem shocked. She tried to summon a calm demeanor, the one she'd learned to use whenever her third graders had tried to test her. "Really?" she asked quietly. As much as she didn't want to pursue the topic, she was glad John wasn't there. "A few beers?"

Lucy laughed. "It's a joke. Slang, you know? Like 'you wanna' hang?' It's a joke because I'm too young to drink. And, anyway, he doesn't."

Annie wished they'd never started this conversation. She cut through the parking lot behind the courthouse and took a right onto Church Street. "I take it he didn't want to . . . hang?"

"He couldn't. He said he had somewhere to go. He didn't mention going off island, though." She shrugged her narrow shoulders in an offhanded way that made it tough to tell whether she was ambivalent or distressed.

The only thing Annie concluded was that she was grateful she no longer was a teenager.

"He's pretty messed up right now," Lucy added.

"I suppose that's understandable."

"Yeah, too bad, huh? I mean, my parents never got along real well, but I don't think either one of them would ever kill the other one."

"You don't know that's what happened, Lucy. Back then, the police said that it didn't."

"Yeah, I know. But Jonas isn't sure. Did I tell you that a few weeks ago his girlfriend dumped him? He really loved her, you know? She told him she'd never live on Chappy, even though he said it's the only place he's ever felt like he belonged."

And that was another surprise. Annie hadn't known that Jonas had a girlfriend. But even more curious was that, if Chappy was the only place he felt that he belonged, why had he left—and in such a hurry? Had he left because, as she'd suspected, he was vulnerable and then Lucy had come along and . . . Yes, Annie believed there was way more to this story than she'd been told. And as much as she hated revisiting the subject, she felt an inexplicable need to play a kind of stepmother, after all. "Lucy?" she asked. "Are you sure Jonas doesn't have a crush on you?"

She laughed. "Seriously? He's way too old for me. And I'm way too young for him. Jeez, we can't even stand the same music. We're good buddies. That's it. Case closed. Yuck."

Annie's nerves quieted. She hadn't realized how much she'd been worrying about that. "Sorry."

"And not that it matters, but I told you I've been trying to help him. He's a good guy, you know? Long before his girlfriend split, he was wicked lonely. His grandparents practically stole him from his mother, but he hardly saw them except on Chappy in the summers. He had a nanny until he was six—then they shipped him off to boarding school. And every time they gave him money or clothes or paid his tuition, his grandmother reminded him he was lucky that they'd taken him." She pulled out her phone and started to text. "I can't believe he'd leave without telling me. Unless . . ."

"Unless what?" Annie was now more concerned about Jonas than she was about Lucy.

"Unless he answered that woman's email."

"What woman?"

Lucy shook her head. "The one who saw the video and said she knew the truth about his father. She said Taylor only got pregnant so she could get the Flanagans' money. When Jonas said he had letters his father wrote, the woman said Taylor must have faked them. And then killed him. You say it didn't happen, but the cops never asked this woman. She's somebody who lives in Boston."

So it had been a stranger—not Lucy—who'd come up with the idea that Taylor had written the letters. And Kevin had thought Lucy had dreamed that up. Annie made it onto the *On Time* while trying to figure out what to say next. Then, as she set the brake, Lucy's phone dinged.

Lucy stared at the screen. "Well, that sucks."

Annie handed the captain the ticket from her coupon book at the same time that Restless vaulted over the seat and plopped onto her lap, wagging at the captain as if bidding him hello. "Lucy, get the dog . . ."

As Lucy absently reached out and scooped up the dog, her eyes did not leave her phone.

"What happened?" Annie asked. She presumed that the texter had been Jonas.

"He told her. He told Taylor he knew. He says he's on his way to Boston to get proof. After that, he'll be in New York."

Lucy's lower lip stuck out, her forehead scrunched. "Crap. He isn't coming back."

As Annie drove the Jeep off the ferry on the other side, she felt another twinge of sadness, this one for Lucy who was losing her friend—her *friend* and, thank goodness, nothing more. Feeling more than exhausted from the drama of the day, Annie wished she could go home and nap, which, of course, she couldn't, because Donna was in her bed. And the noise level at the Inn wasn't conducive to rest.

Instead of dropping Lucy off, Annie went into the house to visit Claire. Earl's pickup was not in the driveway; he no doubt was enabling Kevin's wishful thinking that the Inn would soon be open.

They stepped up on the deck where several flats of yellow and purple pansies were lined up along the railing. Lucy unhooked the leash and let Restless roam the yard; there was no traffic to worry about, and he liked being with people too much to wander very far.

"What the heck is Grandma going to do with all those?" Lucy said, pointing at the flowers as she knocked on the door. "She can't stoop over and dig in the ground. Not since her stroke."

The door opened. Lucy gestured toward the pansies without saying hello.

"Who's gonna plant those, Gram?"

Claire smiled. Her white, flyaway hair was living up to its description, but her forty-year-old jogging suit looked as clean and bright as the day she'd no doubt found it off island on a J.C. Penney rack. "I was hoping one of my granddaughters would come along and offer to plant them for me. Your grandfather doesn't have much time these days."

"Of course I will, Gram. Why didn't you text me?" Then

Lucy rolled her eyes. "Right. Grandmas don't text. Grandmas use the telephone."

Claire wriggled a bent, arthritic finger at Lucy. "And don't you forget it." They laughed. Annie smiled, feeling as if she'd stepped onto a stage again, where she was merely an observer of life. "Well, come on in first, the both of you. Have a cuppa something."

"Tea would be wonderful," Annie said.

"I'll have a beer," Lucy said, and Claire laughed. Clearly, she'd heard it before.

Restless did not reply. He was preoccupied sniffing the turf.

Five minutes later, after Lucy had guzzled ginger ale and the tea finally had steeped, Lucy grabbed the gardening gloves and went outside, leaving Annie and Claire alone.

"I hardly see you these days," Claire said. "I hardly see anyone. You wouldn't even know I had two men living in the house."

Annie agreed. "Earl and Kevin are so busy trying to finish the Inn. And now that they've had to let the crew go . . ."

Claire nodded. She must have heard all of that, too. "And your mother's here?"

Would it always take a heartbeat or two for Annie to remember that sometimes people would refer to Donna as her mother? Would her brain always need to reboot for her to realize they weren't speaking about Ellen Sutton?

"Donna's here, yes. We don't know for how long." Annie hadn't meant to sound as if she were implying that Donna was going to die.

"The doctors said she's cured?" Perhaps Kevin had told her; perhaps Earl.

"Well, she says she's come to Chappy to recuperate, so that's a good sign. But we don't know how long she'll be here."

"And she's staying with you."

"She's in the cottage. I'm in an unfinished room at the Inn. I thought it would be nicer for her to have privacy." Suddenly, Annie's thoughts collided again as if they were attempting to jockey for priority. Donna? The Inn? Lucy? Jonas? And what about her manuscript? Would Annie ever be able to get back to it in peace? She looked around the cozy kitchen, with the farmhouse sink, the café curtains at the window, the bead-board cabinets that were painted white. She remembered the first night she'd been there, Christmas Eve a year and a half earlier, the night she'd met John. Earl and Claire's house had felt like home from the beginning. It held a sense of warmth within its walls. "I don't know, Claire," Annie said, her voice dropping to a whisper. "I don't know if I'm capable of helping her."

"What would you do if she were your other mother? The one who adopted you?"

"I'd know what to do." Wow. Annie couldn't believe that she'd said that so quickly.

To Claire's credit, she made no further comment. Instead, she nibbled on home-baked shortbread. Then she said, "Earl says Donna had an idea on how to hurry things up in Boston. With the skull."

Annie sighed. "She suggested that Kevin reach out to an old friend. But he's not keen on it."

"Have you asked John?"

"No. I think that would cross the line for him."

"Probably." Claire sighed. "That boy is too darned honest. But, Annie, you're from the city. You were born there and grew up there. Isn't there someone you know . . . ?"

Claire had a way of getting to the heart of a matter without breaking stride. And it often felt as if she knew the answer to her question before she'd even asked it. "*Claire-voyant*," Earl had called her more than once.

Then, the trials of the past few days (or weeks, or months) bubbled to the surface and threatened to erupt. Annie pressed her hands against her head and said, "Larry. Larry Hendricks."

Claire leaned toward her. "Who?"

Annie breathed a moment longer—slowly in, slowly out—before raising her head and repeating: "Larry Hendricks. An assistant district attorney. I'm sure he knows the coroner or the archeologist. He might even go out drinking with them." She waited for relief from having told something she never thought she would. Especially not on the island. Not in her new home. That part of her life was long gone and far away. In another galaxy. Or was it?

"An old lover?" Claire asked.

"No," Annie said flatly, the same way Kevin had denied that Gina was one of his. "Actually, it's worse. He was my former husband's best friend. He was out with him the night Mark trotted from the bar onto Commonwealth Avenue and disappeared into the night. Like he was in an old British spy movie. Larry swore he didn't know Mark had planned to take off, or where he'd gone. He also said he had no clue if Mark had been unhappy or depressed . . . or that he was in the humongous debt that he so kindly left me."

"Did you believe him?"

"Not a chance." It was only then Annie realized that her fists were clenched, her fingernails embedded in her palms. "Murphy, my old friend, always thought Larry was pond scum—her term—and so was Mark." And then, a warm flush rose in her cheeks. Her shoulders started to tremble. And as Claire reached out to take her hand, Annie fell apart.

Chapter 18

It had been years since she'd allowed herself to "let it out," as her dad had instructed her the night Brian had been killed, years since so many tears had spilled down her face, since her insides had felt as if they were doing battle with each other. She rocked back and forth and back and forth.

At some point, Claire left her chair and went to Annie, encircling her arms around Annie's trembling shoulders and gently saying, "It's okay, Annie. You're going to be all right now."

It was a while before she was depleted, her heart and her soul dissolved into a tidal pool the size of Poucha Pond. Her posture remained slumped, but her breathing finally quieted, her tremors eased. The numbness of crying had provided needed relief.

Then Claire smoothed Annie's hair. "Tell Kevin," she said. "And tell your mother. Earl and I are your island family, but they should know, too."

Annie had seen the tender side of Claire when baby Bella had landed on the Vineyard. It had taken Annie aback; before then, she'd been intimidated by the untamed hair and the wild look Claire could get in her eyes if she felt she or her family were being wronged.

Pausing, Annie waited to gather herself. Then she said, "I shared the basics with them, but that's all."

"If they only wanted the basics they could read the bio on your book jackets."

"I don't have the patent on misery, Claire."

Claire returned to her chair, her pearl-gray eyes looking softer now, her mouth turned up in a small grin. "Oh, my. Sometimes life is shit, isn't it?"

The gravity of the moment fell away, and Annie laughed. Cussing—as Earl called it—was not commonplace for Claire. "That it is."

"What do you want, Annie? What are you hoping will happen next?"

"I want it all to go away. I want Donna to be fine, and I want to find out tomorrow that the skull belonged to a British sailor who went down with his ship in the eighteenth century and we are therefore free to rehire our crew and finish construction so we can pay our bills, get our occupancy permit, open the Inn, and provide a home to the people we're already committed to. Of course, even if that all happens, we won't have Jonas back." As soon as she'd said those last words, Annie wished she hadn't.

"Where's Jonas?" Claire's penchant for being a busybody quickly resurfaced.

"I heard he left the island. I guess he went back to New York, to show his paintings." It seemed kinder than sharing the rest. Besides, the day had already been emotional enough.

"I don't expect Taylor's happy about that. Is Lucy upset that he's gone?"

Annie had had no idea that Claire knew he and Lucy had spent time together. "Yes, they're friends. I'm sure she's sad to see him go."

Claire laughed. "Friends? Well, it's just as well he's gone. The age difference between them isn't good. Especially since Lucy's still a child." She sighed.

"You have the wrong idea," Annie said. "Lucy's been supportive, but that's all. Unlike me, she seems to be a natural caregiver. Jonas has been having a tough time. On top of all the drama going on here, his girlfriend broke up with him. He wanted her to move to Chappy, but she wouldn't. Maybe he left to be with her."

"Uh-huh. Well, enough of that then. Besides, we were talking about you. If you want my advice, if you can get the nuisance of that skull cleared up and get back to the business of the Inn, you'll be able to think better about how to help Donna."

Annie was glad that Claire had called her birth mother by name. "And I have a manuscript to write."

Claire waved a hand as if that were inconsequential. Trish had once said that today people often had the misconception that book writing was as easy as composing an email or a text. "But I have a question," Claire continued. "If this guy, Larry, really is a mucky-muck in Boston politics—and I think an assistant district attorney is a political appointment—he can probably pull a few strings. Am I right about that?"

"Probably." Annie didn't add that she'd thought of that a million times.

"Why not ask him? Years have passed, Annie. If he's any kind of a decent man, he might feel bad about what Mark did to you. He might even feel guilty because maybe he didn't tell you everything he knew. Call me crazy, but it seems like you have nothing to lose. Not even pride. Because you've really made something of yourself." Claire paused, then said, "It's hard to believe you married someone like that guy Mark."

"It wasn't my finest moment. Or ten years of moments."

"I've always believed there's a bit of a dark side in all of us. It's called being human."

"Thanks, Claire. I can't tell you how often—before and after he left—I wondered why I'd married him, too. But it isn't pride that's stopping me from contacting Larry. The truth is, I don't want him to know anything about me. Not where I live. Not what I'm doing. And not what my life's been like since Mark left. I just don't. Because it's not his business."

Claire laughed again. "You might have thought of those things before you wrote best sellers under your real name. And I believe your picture is right there with that book jacket bio. Not to mention what's on the internet."

"I wasn't a best-selling author when I started writing."

"Touché. But what are you afraid of? That he's still in touch with Mark?"

Annie shifted in the chair. "Probably. Yes."

"Well, no matter what, there's a strong possibility they both already know damn well where you live and what you do. But if you can get the Inn going as soon as possible, well, sometimes it's worth taking a risk to achieve a greater good."

Annie nodded, but was done discussing it. She thanked Claire for her advice and for being kind. Then she said she needed to go and check on Donna. "I'll think about our talk," she said as she stood up. "Thanks again, Claire. I don't know what I would have done on this island without you and Earl." She didn't add that Mark was the last person she wanted to risk seeing again. Ever. And despite Claire's comment that he might already know everything about her, Annie knew the odds were long that he wanted to see her, either. Still, she couldn't take that chance. Because part of her worried that if she saw him, her common sense would implode and she'd be sucked in by his charm again. "It's called being human," as Claire had said.

Lucy wanted to keep her grandmother company until Earl got home because she said Earl loved playing ball with Restless. (The truth was, so did Lucy, who still lingered in that great divide between being a tomboy and a grown-up woman.)

Claire sent Annie off with a container of freshly made fish chowder—Charlie Beebe had dropped off a striper that he'd hooked that morning off Menemsha—and a Ziploc of oyster crackers. "Comfort food for Donna," she'd announced. And though Annie thought Donna would appreciate the gesture, she wasn't sure if food would be much "comfort" to Donna until she had fully recuperated.

But when Annie got home, Donna was asleep. She dashed off a note, put the chowder in the refrigerator, then got back in the Jeep and headed toward a place where she knew she could think, Wasque Point, facing the Atlantic. She followed the familiar strip of paved street until it gave way to a rutty dirt road. With the four-wheel drive confidently bouncing along, Annie knew she felt better. Claire had helped; it was nice to grow closer to John's mother.

John, she thought as she reached the southern curve of the 200-acre preserve that skimmed Chappy's eastern shoreline. Would he be upset if she contacted Larry? That she'd attempted to interfere with legalities, and, even worse, had done so through her ex-husband's friend?

Parking the Jeep, she grabbed her phone, got out, and headed down the long path toward the water. The sun was starting to set; a vibrant orange ribbon stretched across the horizon where the ocean met the sky. The air had grown cooler—the chill reminded her that it still was April. She was glad she'd put on an old cable-knit cardigan.

She walked along the path that led out to the sandy beach; on either side, clusters of low-growing vegetation were already green; some of them would soon produce blossoms of delicate bluets. Later in summer other shrubs would yield sweet, juicy blackberries; by autumn, still others would be resplendent with deep red-orange bearberries. She and John often walked there; in their early days together, he'd pointed out the scrub oaks and pitch pines that flourished in the barren soil, and the ocean birds that made Wasque home: terns, piping plovers, American oystercatchers with their long, tangerine bills. It was a haven of nature, a perfect place to be alone to think.

She reached the beach; she sat down and inhaled a slow, pensive breath. She waited for the silence to bring her an answer to the big question about Larry Hendricks. It also would be nice if Murphy chimed in with a tip or two.

Murphy hadn't trusted Mark from the beginning. She'd understood when Annie had tried to explain what she saw in him—the magnetic smile, the copious (they thought) riches, the terrific sex. And Murphy knew that a piece of Annie's heart had been permanently broken when Brian was killed. She knew that her friend was lonely. Still, she'd cautioned her to take her time before saying "I do." It was one of the few times Annie hadn't followed Murphy's advice. But when Mark disappeared, Murphy never once said she'd told her so.

"If you were here right now," Annie said into the breeze off the water, "I promise I'd do whatever you say. I don't want to lose the Inn before we even start; and I sure don't want to lose John if I call Larry. And I'm doubly sure I don't want Mark to learn one sliver about me—especially that I reached out to Larry."

She waited.

She listened.

To nothing.

Then an oystercatcher appeared next to her, poking his long bill into the sand. He stopped. He looked at Annie—he *looked* at her; he really did. He emitted a rat-ta-tat peeping sound, then stepped closer, his bill aimed at the pocket of her cardigan.

"Shoo!" Annie cried, then felt guilty because she was the interloper, not him.

She stood and closed her sweater—which was when she

realized that her phone was in the pocket where the bird had aimed its rat-ta-tatting.

Retrieving the phone, she stared at it a few seconds. Then she turned back to the oystercatcher. But he was gone.

Murphy didn't typically send a winged creature to do her bidding or carry her messages. And yet . . .

She glanced at the screen again, and laughed. What the hell, she thought. I might as well see if Larry still exists.

Opening the Google app, she typed his name, then added *District Attorney's Office, Boston.* The search prompted a quick response—complete with a photograph of Larry Hendricks, Assistant District Attorney for the Commonwealth of Massachusetts.

Annie's heart started to race; her breathing turned to rapid staccato, in, out, in, out, in, out. She flung her phone on the sand as if the mere fact that she'd Googled Larry would set off alarms from Chappy to Boston then to wherever pond-scum Mark was hiding.

She said a few of the words that, when she'd been seven or eight, had resulted in her mother threatening to wash Annie's mouth out with soap.

Her eyes ticked back to the horizon where night was quickly setting in. She knew she should leave before it would be too difficult to navigate the path back to the Jeep. Unless she used her flashlight app.

Stuffing her hands into her pockets, she stood, rocking in the sand, not unlike the way she'd rocked when she'd melted down in front of Claire.

She understood why Kevin didn't want to contact Gina. If Annie never told him about Larry Hendricks, he'd blame himself if time ran out for opening the Inn. But now that Annie had told Claire about Larry, would Claire tell Earl? Would Earl tell Kevin? Had Annie dug her own self-centered grave?

"It seems like you have nothing to lose," Claire had said.

But Annie did. She could lose her peace of mind. And John.

Even if she did do it, they could lose the Inn anyway. Earl and Kevin would have squandered a lot of money and wind up with a mountain of undeserved debt. Annie knew what that felt like. But she also knew that the sooner they found out, the sooner they could all stop wondering and worrying, and begin to deal with the reality, whatever it might be. As Annie's dad once said, "It's the what-ifs that will kill you long before the knowing-for-sures."

And then she heard the echo of Claire's words: ". . . sometimes it's worth taking a risk to achieve a greater good."

With those thoughts in mind, Annie reached down, picked up her phone, blew off the sand. And called the number listed for Larry Hendricks.

Losing the trunk had been the best thing that could have happened to her. The day Donna had seen it, she'd known it had to be hers. Its image had stuck in her mind the way Kevin's image of his dad had stuck in his.

She'd never told Kevin his dad had divorced her in order to marry a nice Catholic girl who hadn't been spoiled. She never told Kevin that his dad had wound up living in Burlington, Vermont, and that he and his next wife had seven children that Donna knew of, one right after the other including a set of twins. She'd wondered who in their right mind had seven children anymore, what with the cost of living and the state of the world.

Once, Donna had driven there. Only once, after she'd tracked down the town where he lived from the postmark on one of the last meager child support checks that he sent. She'd borrowed a friend's old Toyota Corolla, spread a map out on the passenger seat, and headed to Route 93. Somewhere in New Hampshire the road changed to Route 89. It took a total of four hours to get to Burlington; she spent another two hours at the town hall, where she found his street address and learned his family's vital statistics. By then her mom had died; she'd told her dad she had to go out of town for work and asked if Kevin could stay overnight. He was twelve or thirteen at the time, old enough that, if he'd gone with her, he would have figured out what she was doing.

The house was on a narrow country road; part of her feared her ex-husband would see her and try to have her arrested, though she didn't know for what. Another part of her didn't care. She stopped right there on the side of the road and stared at the crumbling farmhouse that needed a few windows replaced, a layer of paint, and a porch that didn't list like the Titanic. *A child's swing set was in the yard not far from a small barn. A couple of black-and-white cows stood, staring at her. Donna supposed they didn't often have company.*

She left without going to the door; the place gave her the heebie-jeebies, as Aunt Elizabeth would have called it. But the visit had strengthened her resolve to make something of herself, to show Kevin they were fine without his father. That was when she started saving to start her business. Two years later, when her dad was dead, too, she did. All that time, the image of the trunk had stuck in her mind; it wasn't long before it finally was hers.

She never told Kevin that she'd found out where his dad was, or that he had all those kids. She supposed she should have told Kevin he had a flock of half-siblings—then again, he didn't know about the baby girl she'd given up for adoption, either. But Kevin was a nice boy—kind and sensitive—and she knew those things would upset him terribly. In any event, she was grateful that he looked like her, so she wasn't constantly seeing the image of the man who she'd once married.

Together, Donna and Kevin had a good enough life. She did, however, feel guilty about not telling him where his dad had gone, especially when he snuck off to Red Sox games, as if she didn't know, as if she hadn't figured out that he was trying to find his father. She'd found a ticket stub once, in Kevin's jacket pocket. Another time she found a list of the lineup when the Sox were playing the Yankees. Kevin must have been convinced that his dad wouldn't have missed that one.

Both Donna and her son had a similar reason for their very different goals: for Donna, the trunk represented a secret to a better life; for Kevin, finding his dad meant the same thing. Donna knew they had about the same odds—none—of reaching their goals. But she refused to let that stop her. And though she was sad for Kevin that he never saw his dad again, she was elated when she found the Vuitton.

The first thing she did the day she brought it home was tuck the ticket stub and the Sox/Yankees lineup in a pocket inside the lid, along with a handful of photos of Kevin with his dad that he did not know existed. Then Donna locked the trunk—to be opened at some time in the future. Like the tiny case for doll clothes, the Vuitton would keep her secrets safe.

Chapter 19

Monday morning, Annie worked for a couple of hours then walked down to her cottage from the Inn. After having left a voice mail message for Larry the night before, she'd gone back to her temporary room in the half-finished Inn, then tossed and turned all night. She hadn't even talked to John when he'd called to say good night; she chose, instead, to have him think she was asleep.

Mindful of the fact that it was a new day and that her birth mother no doubt was waiting for her, she forced herself to smile and think about what she could do to help. Maybe Donna would feel up to visiting two or three of the artists Annie wanted to approach about showing their paintings on the walls at the Inn. Maybe Kevin was right to act as if it was still going to open. Crossing the lawn, Annie held on to her phone; she'd put it in silent mode, but had turned vibrate on. In her message to Larry she'd said she was doing research for a book and had a legal question. "I need clarification on a state law," she'd added with a smile as if he could see her. Right after hanging up, she'd chastised herself for not having told him it was urgent.

As she neared the cottage, she glanced at the screen again:

no activity. It was already after ten o'clock. If he bothered to call back, he might wait until his lunch break, or maybe once his workday was done, which would conflict with dinner plans that she hadn't even yet thought about . . . *Stop!* she shouted silently. *Stop fast-forwarding!*

It felt silly to knock on her own front door, but Annie did.

Kevin greeted her. "Enter," he said. And while he didn't sound jovial, neither did he sound morose.

Stepping inside, she was treated to an aroma of sandalwood.

"Incense," he said. "Mom's in the bedroom meditating. She says it helps her gear up for the day."

Annie felt the tug on her heart again. She needed to remember to show Donna the kind of empathy that Claire had shown her.

"Shall I make coffee?" she asked.

"Done. Feel free to pour yourself a snootful."

As she moved toward the kitchen, she thought she felt a small vibration. Shifting her shoulder so Kevin couldn't see what she was doing, she checked her phone: false alarm.

"I took a few more cinnamon rolls out of the freezer," he said.

"Making coffee, serving brunch. Wow. You're the best brother ever."

"It's not like I had anything else to do. I wasn't about to meditate with Mom. If I sat cross-legged, I'd never get up again."

She poured coffee, then went to the table, mug in one hand, phone in the other. "You're too young for that."

"Too many years of manual labor."

"I thought that when you were in Boston you hired people to do the manual labor while you worked in the office." She sat down and balanced the phone on her thigh.

"Yeah, but I get more pity if people think I did the heavy lifting."

She gestured toward the plate of rolls. "Have one."

He frowned. "I've already had three."

Taking one for herself, she realized she should probably make more. Maybe she could find a recipe for something healthier, something made from whole grains and blueberries. Donna might appreciate that.

She glanced down at the phone again: still nothing.

"Expecting a call?" Kevin asked.

"Oh," she said. "No. Well, yes. Kind of. But it's not important. Book stuff. You know?" Why had she suddenly become such a liar? Especially when she was so awful at it?

Then the bedroom door opened, and Donna stepped into the room. She wore a pale blue silk robe; her short hair was neat, her eyes bright. She looked better—healthier—than she had the day before.

"Good morning," Annie said. "Kevin made coffee."

"I'll pass. I've had your brother's coffee before."

"Mom," he said without a smile, "since living on the Vineyard, I've turned over a new leaf. Earl says anyone who lives on Chappy needs to know how to use a percolator and a wood stove."

Donna laughed, poured herself half a cup, then joined them at the table. "So what's on everyone's agenda today?" she asked cheerfully.

Annie outlined her idea about the artists. "If you feel up to it, I'd love to have you join me and give me your opinion of their work. None of them know my plan yet, so we'd be cold-calling."

Donna said she liked the idea, adding that it would be best not to make promises until they'd seen everyone's work. "Otherwise you might end up with pieces that clash and too few walls to spread them out on."

They chatted amiably, as if they were planning an outing to a museum of masterpieces in Chicago or LA. Kevin interrupted with a few witty suggestions, including that they might want to go incognito and take magnifying glasses. Either his mood had lifted, or he was trying very hard to make her think it had.

The conversation was easier than Annie had expected, as if a bond were growing between them. Until her phone vibrated on her thigh.

The screen read UNKNOWN, but the area code was 617. Boston metro. She picked it up. It vibrated again. She touched the circle that read DECLINE. It wasn't the right time for Larry Hendricks. Her palms suddenly grew sweaty, as if they agreed.

"Take the call if you want," Donna said.

Annie shook her head. "It's not important." She put the phone into her pocket so it was out of sight. Specifically, out of *her* sight.

Then Kevin cleared his throat. "Getting back to our conversation, I've come up with another option for you, Mom."

Annie wrestled her thoughts back to the moment. She wondered when the last time was that her brain had needed to sort out so much multitasking.

"Other than going with Annie to check out a few artists?"

"Yes," he said. "I think you should stay here for a few days. But then I want you to go back to Boston. And I'm going with you."

Annie was stunned. Had his mood only improved because, like Jonas, he wanted to run away? "I thought we were going to wait to make a decision."

He shook his head. "I changed my mind. I'm taking Mom back to Boston. I'll look after her there."

Annie wished she had a pin to drop on the wood plank floor to see how loud it would sound. She couldn't imagine how Donna must feel.

"See, here's the thing," Kevin said as he stood and began to pace the room. "It's time to get realistic. Getting out from under this mess with the skull might take a very long time. We need to accept the fact that, more than likely, we'll never make our deadline. And I think we need to cut our losses before we pour any more money into a losing proposition."

It was clear he was not going to listen, but Annie had to try. "So this is about the Inn? Not about . . . Mom?"

"Well, partly. It's been fun being on the Vineyard," he went on, "but let's face it, Annie. You have a life here; I really don't. I'm still an interloper. In fact, both Mom and I dropped into your life so fast you probably wonder sometimes what the heck happened. You have books to write, you have soap to make, and you have a relationship that looks like it could go somewhere more than where it's at today if you could give it a little more attention. But I'm afraid that having this Inn isn't going to fix that. And I'd hate for you to lose John."

"Kevin . . ." Annie began, but he held a hand up to shush her.

"No. I've made up my mind. You have the cottage now. I don't think anyone will say you can't live here for now. That's why we started this in the first place, isn't it? As it stands now, that might be the best reason for us not to try to pull strings in a lame attempt to push Boston to come to a conclusion."

"I don't care about . . ."

He shushed her again. He paced some more. "Please, Annie. I've thought this out. The most important thing is that Mom will probably get better faster in her own home in Boston. Not to mention that, with summer coming, there'll be a whole lot of commotion around here. Hardly conducive to recuperating."

"I might not last until the summer." Donna's words were calm and matter-of-fact, suspended in the air as if waiting for someone to contradict them.

Kevin blinked.

Annie's stomach dropped the way it had when Murphy had said her days were growing shorter, and that before she "croaked"—her word, not Annie's—she needed to know that Annie had moved to the island and had followed her dream.

After a moment, Kevin said, "What the hell does that mean? That you might not last until the summer?"

"I've been very sick, Kevin. I came here to recuperate. I do not want to go back to Boston where I don't have fresh air, sandy beaches, and nature all around me—things I'm told are good for recuperation. More important, in the city I don't have my children, who aren't exactly children, but they're all I have. If you force me to go back, as much as you might want to disagree, I believe my recuperation will be short-lived."

Kevin turned his back again. Maybe he feared that if he tried to speak, he'd cry.

"That said," Donna continued, "to be perfectly honest, I plan to stay here until my recuperation is complete. Or until you throw me out. Whichever comes first. Now, Annie, if you'll give me half an hour, I'll be ready for what sounds like a fun day. I am quite alive this morning, and I intend to stay that way." She excused herself and went back into the bedroom, closing the door behind her.

"I guess that's that," Kevin said flatly as he and Annie walked up to the Inn. "Mom says she's staying, so trust me, that's what will happen."

"It will be fine, Kevin. We'll all be fine. Right now, I'm more concerned about you. What was that all about? Why on earth did you want to take her back to Boston?"

He shrugged. "It was just a thought."

"Really? I didn't think you could walk away so . . . easily. You've been working so hard. . . ."

He shoved his hands into the pockets of his jeans. "It wouldn't have been easy. I would have missed you. And everyone."

"What about Taylor? I thought you were trying to be supportive. Especially with the nonsense about her going on."

Shaking his head, he said, "I've done my best. And I know I see another—a better—side of Taylor that other people don't. But, honestly, for all I know, she killed Jonas's father."

Annie sighed. "Is that why you came up with that cockamamie plan? Because you saw a chance to use Mom as an excuse to leave?"

"It isn't about Taylor, Annie, and it isn't about Mom. It's about me. And how just hearing the name 'Gina Fiorina' reminds me about Meghan and how much I loved her. How much I miss her. And how I can't make any woman fit into my heart right now."

"All the more reason for you to stay right here where you now belong because so many people have grown to care about you a whole lot and want you to be happy whether you know it or not." She briefly wondered if she were talking to Kevin or to Jonas.

"I'm no writer, sister, but I'd say that was a run-on sentence."

She laughed as they went inside. "You drive me crazy, brother. Now get back to work. While Mom is getting ready, I have to call someone back. And I need to do it alone." As she climbed the stairs up to her room, Annie wondered how many times that morning she'd referred to Donna as Mom. It was, she realized, getting easier to do.

That time, Larry Hendricks answered.

She might not have recognized his voice if she hadn't known whom she was calling. She cleared her throat and wished that she could clear her mind as easily. "Larry? It's Annie. Sutton."

"Okay," he said instead of something friendly like, "Hi, Annie. How are you?"

A long pause followed, as if they both were actors who'd forgotten their lines. Annie looked around the room—a reminder that the Inn was important, more important than the drivel of the past. Besides, whatever anxiety she might have about Larry was nothing compared with what Kevin understandably had felt when hearing Gina's name.

"How are you?" she asked.

"Fine. But I don't expect that's why you called."

She squeezed her eyes shut, glad he wasn't there to watch her body language. "No," she said. "Not really." She sucked in a small breath. "I live on the Vineyard now."

"Oh?"

Maybe he didn't read the best-seller list. Or maybe he was playing an attorney's game of cat and mouse. "Yes," she replied. "And you? Are you . . ." She almost mentioned his wife, Suzanne, whom Annie had been friendly with in a trophy-wife kind of way, but she had no idea if they were still together. ". . . Are you still in Brookline?"

He laughed. "Yes. And my boys are both at Phillips." He said it with arrogance, purposefully, she knew, omitting the word "Academy" because people who traveled in his lifestyle circle would know what he'd meant. "But I hardly think that's why you called, either. What's up?"

His attitude reminded her of Mark, whose penchant for being haughty always escalated after he'd been with Larry. Already regretting having called him, Annie inhaled another long breath, knowing if she didn't dive right in, she'd hang up instead. Her eyes moved to the new stone terrace that spanned the full width of the Inn and promised congenial gatherings. Then she closed her eyes.

"I'm part of a new venture here. An Inn on Chappaquiddick."

"Chappaquiddick? As in Chappaquiddick Island?"

She ignored his smugness. "Yes. We're in the process of

restoring a beautiful old waterfront property. But we've run into a small snag. A bone—actually, part of a human skull—was found on the beach. It was tangled in seaweed and stuck between some rocks right at the tide line. Apparently it had been there a long time."

That time, the silence only lasted two or three brief seconds. "Go on."

She was careful not to interpret his prompt response as one of interest. Or as a way of saying he'd help. "You probably know that protocol requires that the state police hand it over to the coroner, which they did," she said. "The coroner determined it was human, not animal. Then it went to the medical examiner and the archeologist in Boston who will tell us whether or not it's Native American. If I have the details straight."

"Close enough," Larry said, then paused again. In the old days, he might have been puffing on a pipe in contemplation. "The forensic anthropologist must determine the date range. The North American Graves Protection and Repatriation Act of 1990 assumes that any remains dating before 1492 are Native American. And, of course, there's DNA, which they might or might not be able to extract."

That part was new to her.

"If Native American affiliation can be determined," he went on, "the government must turn the remains over to the local tribe." He was on a roll now. "If they were found on land and surfaced due to erosion, they originally might have been buried. Which means, if they are indigenous, you might be talking sacred ground."

Annie swallowed. Though she'd already been told that, part of her hadn't wanted to believe it. "I think it had spent more time in the water than on land."

"Well, that's not up to you. Did you have any other questions?"

Questions? She hadn't expected he'd have had any of those answers. She'd only been trying to get them moved to the head of the archeologist's line. "It's about our restoration," she said with trepidation, "of the . . . building. The Inn. We've had to stop construction."

"That goes without saying. Until they have definitive answers."

She chewed a thumbnail, something she only did in times of intense stress. "We're trying to learn if there's a typical timeline . . . To be honest, we're scheduled to open on Memorial Day weekend, and now we're . . ."

He laughed.

He *laughed?* A flame of anger flared her cheeks.

"And you called to ask me to pull some strings? Really, Annie?"

She could have denied it, but Larry Hendricks was a smart man. Too smart. So she simply said, "Yes. The livelihoods, the investments, and the homes of several people I care about are at stake. Believe me, if I didn't feel this were a crisis, I would not have bothered you." If Murphy had been there, she would have congratulated Annie for standing up to him.

"Unfortunately, like most of us, they're overworked in that department."

She closed her eyes again. "Please, Larry," she said, her voice softening, a gesture that was real. "It's important."

He paused again. He was definitely playing an attorney's game of waiting for a reaction from a witness, hoping she would leap into the dead air space and reveal the truth.

"I don't work directly with the archeologists," he said. "My staff takes care of that."

She guessed it was a lie. If he didn't work with them, he probably wouldn't have known that they were overworked. And, more than likely, he would not have known the details of a federal act that was three decades old and included directives for remains of people who lived five hundred years ago. Half a damn millennium. She wanted to say, "Thanks anyway," and hang up. But just as she opened her mouth to speak, Larry beat her to it.

"No promises, of course, but I'll make a couple of calls." His voice dropped to a less-intimidating octave. "If only to prove I'm not really an insufferable jerk."

It wasn't until after he'd said he'd be in touch in a few days and she'd thanked him and they'd hung up that Annie realized that neither of them had mentioned Mark.

Chapter 20

"Before we head out, would you like a quick tour of the Inn?" Annie asked when she returned to pick up Donna. "Then you'll be able to visualize someone's work in a specific place."

Donna smiled. "I was going to ask for that." In a pale aqua cashmere sweater, light gray pants, and short leather boots, she almost looked as if she were going to meet her lady friends for lunch in Chestnut Hill. And though Annie had on black jeans and sneakers, she'd put on a new white sweater. They both wore makeup, though it looked like Donna had applied an extra layer.

Annie had brought her iPad and the list of artists so Donna could see the type of work each artist painted, then suggest a given style that she thought would be a match for a specific location. As they walked through the Inn, Donna nodded and emitted many "uh-huh"s, which might have been a throwback to her antiques-buying days when showing no reaction was a technique for negotiation. After they'd gone through every room and hall, they stopped to say good-bye to Kevin.

"You'll be glad to hear I have good news," Annie said. "I contacted an old friend-of-a-friend in Boston who might be able to help speed up the process with the archeologist."

"Seriously?" Kevin asked, setting down the hammer.

"Seriously. And, believe me, if anyone can make something happen, it's this guy. So fingers crossed, okay?"

He smiled a little, enough for Annie to know he appreciated that she'd taken the heat off him for not having contacted Gina. Then he went back to work, and the women went outside and got into the Jeep.

"You made his day," Donna said.

"Having him around often makes *my* day."

Donna nodded, most likely because she already knew that. Then she said, "As for the Inn, it's going to be lovely."

Annie felt like a child who'd been praised by her mother. "Thank you. It's been a collaborative effort, right down to the color of the paint. From the start, we agreed that everyone's opinion matters. We all want the same thing—a place that looks natural and cozy and is beautiful, too."

"It shows. Your guests will feel lucky to be there."

Annie grinned, started the Jeep, and headed toward the *On Time.*

"And by the way," Donna added, and, for a moment, Annie braced herself for a dose of motherly criticism, "you can tell me who your 'friend-of-a-friend' is. I won't tell Kevin, if you don't want me to."

Annie hadn't expected that. "Like I said," she replied with half a laugh, "he's just that. Nothing more." After her meltdown with Claire, Annie had decided that, no, she would not share the story of Larry Hendricks with either Donna or Kevin. Not then. Hopefully, not ever. They both had too much to deal with at the moment; they didn't need to be dragged into the drama of Annie's past.

"You don't have to tell me," Donna said. "But I think he must be more than that. You're holding your head the same stiff way I do when I'm trying to hide the truth."

Annie made no comment.

"If you're trying to protect me from hearing something ugly, please don't," Donna continued. "If nothing else, I could use a juicy story to help take my mind off my own." Then she turned on the iPad, bent her head, and immersed herself in the eclectic images of the artists' work.

Driving onto the little ferry, Annie pondered Donna's comments. When they reached the other side, she headed up island to Elliott Stimson's studio. Elliott created lovely watercolors of island flowers—beach roses, hydrangea, day lilies—that might be soothing in the guest rooms. She didn't want to sway Donna's impressions of his work, so she simply kept her eyes fixed on the road as if she were in downtown Boston during rush hour and not on the rural Edgartown-West Tisbury Road, which was deserted except for a lone pickup that turned into the dump. The *transfer station*, she remembered she'd been corrected when she'd first moved there.

The Stimson property was easy to find. Like many West Tisbury settings, it included a gray-shingled house that looked a century or two old and was bordered on the three visible sides by lichen-covered stone walls. The studio was a small, restored barn—it stood off to one side in a quiet meadow flanked by gnarly white oaks whose branches dipped and curved and reached out in welcome. Annie turned into the dirt-packed driveway and drove directly to the studio. A sign on the door read: HONK FOR ATTENTION. So Annie honked.

While they waited, Annie simply said, "No."

Donna asked, "No?"

"No. Sometimes the past is best left to history. I'd rather not get into details about my contact at the DA's office."

Donna nodded. "I'll be willing to listen if you change your mind."

Then a white-bearded, large man who Annie recognized from the artisan festivals emerged from the house and sauntered over toward the barn. Like the trees, he offered a pleasant greeting.

After visiting four artists—one whose work was too ultra-modern for the Inn; two who showed pieces that were strong contenders; and a fourth who was nearing retirement and said she was only participating in the fairs to deplete her inventory—they made it back to Chappaquiddick shortly before five thirty. Donna looked exhausted. Annie asked if their outing had been too much for her.

"Not at all," Donna replied. "It was worth every minute. Elliott Stimson's work will work well in the great room."

Which, of course, hadn't been what Annie had planned, but she said, "You're right. That's a great idea."

When they reached the cottage, they found a note from Kevin.

Gone to VH for supplies, it read. *Earl invited you and Mom for dinner tomorrow night. Six o'clock. Bring cookies.*

"Looks like I'll be baking tomorrow," Annie said.

"And I'm afraid I'll be napping. Starting right now."

They went inside, and Donna headed for the bedroom.

"Will you want dinner?" Annie called after her.

"Doubtful," came the reply. "I shall feed off my artistic dreams!"

Annie marveled at Donna's positive attitude; she wished she had inherited some of it.

Because John was at work and Kevin was in Vineyard Haven, Annie took advantage of a rare evening alone. She ran to Edgartown, did some research at the library, picked up a sandwich to go, then went back to the Inn and texted Kevin, asking if he'd check in on Donna when he was back on Chappy. Then she climbed into her fleece pajamas, and, because—hooray—the internet was working, she streamed a movie. Then another. She fell asleep while marveling at how wonderful it felt to be completely unproductive.

In the morning, her energy returned. She called Lottie, the manager of the community center, to ask if it would be okay for her to make cookies there, but Lottie's voice mail message said she was off island. Next, Annie went down to the cottage, where Kevin was sleeping—apparently had been sleeping—all night on the small sofa. She looked in on Donna, who was awake, sitting in bed and drinking tea, nibbling on a piece of toast, and reading a book from Annie's shelf. Annie told her where she'd be and asked her to have Kevin tell Earl. Then, grabbing a frozen muffin and a bottle of water, she gathered a stash of baking supplies—while Kevin snored through the clatter—and juggled them into the Jeep where she'd already stashed her laptop. She knew it was possible that the community center would be locked and no one would be around, or that the space already was booked, but she wanted to bring fresh cookies to Earl and Claire's that night, and she needed to work at the same time. Writing, after all, was the best way Annie knew to keep her life reined in. Under control. Balanced. And it wouldn't be feasible to try and make cookies and write while Donna read, nibbled, or napped in the next room. Or while Kevin snored.

When Annie arrived at the center and pulled into the dirt driveway, she noticed a black pickup parked between two scrub oaks. Earl had a black pickup, but she thought his was newer. At least there was only one truck and not several, so there must not be a meeting; whoever it belonged to was more than likely inside, which meant the door would be open.

That's a start, she thought, then turned off the Jeep, got out, and walked toward the building while preparing her plea: a mother at home who was recuperating, a dinner party that night, and chaos all around on account of that skull, which she figured everyone on Chappy, the Vineyard, and probably the entire internet nation knew about by then.

She turned the handle and opened the door. Perfect. She stepped into the commodious gathering room, with its wood-beamed, cathedral ceiling, and walls that sported photos and memorabilia that embodied Chappy over the years. No one was there.

An enormous stone fireplace stood at one end of the room; a long, narrow office was behind the fireplace wall. Annie walked toward the office and peeked into the doorway, but no one was there, either.

She turned back to the main room, her footsteps echoing in the emptiness. She wondered if the driver of the pickup was outside cleaning up the yard for summer. But as she reached the back door, a voice shouted:

"Annie?"

She blanched. She snapped around. And there was Taylor, who apparently had been in the small kitchen at the opposite end of the main room. Or she'd been in the restroom that was there, too. Or she'd been in a closet. Hiding from the world. In any event, Taylor was one of the last people Annie felt up to seeing. Pretty much ever.

"Earl told me you were coming. Lottie's off this week, so I have her key."

"Oh." She didn't add: "That was fast."

"I thought you'd appreciate it if I came over and unlocked the door for you."

"I do. Yes. Thanks." Annie didn't know why, after all this time, Taylor still had a way of unnerving her.

"There's no meeting today, so it's all yours. How long will you be?"

"I don't know. A few hours? I need to make cookies and do some writing."

Taylor nodded, her auburn mane marching in time to her nod. "Too bad about your mother. Is she doing okay?"

As much as islanders left one another alone, it always

amazed Annie that everyone seemed to know his or her neighbor's business. "She is. Yes. Thanks."

Taylor nodded again. "I hardly got along with mine, but I miss her."

Annie did not respond because she saw no need to get into a discussion about Taylor's recently dead mother or about Donna.

"Jonas is gone."

"I heard that. I'm sorry, Taylor."

They kept their distance, standing a good thirty feet apart, as if getting closer would imply, well, getting closer.

"I didn't do it, you know. I didn't kill his father. I hope that's his skull. Maybe it will prove I didn't push him overboard."

Annie felt her body stiffen. "We might not hear anything for a while," she said. "Believe me, we all want this resolved as quickly as possible."

Rubbing her hands on her hips, Taylor said, "Kevin's going to leave next. He'll say it's because of your mother, but it's really because of me. I don't think he believes me, either." She managed a half-grin. "Who wants to be with someone they think already killed a man?"

Annie did not want to be having any of this conversation. Nor did she like standing there with Taylor when no one else seemed to be around. "I don't think Kevin thinks that," she said.

The auburn mane stilled. "Do me a favor? Tell Kevin I'll understand if he leaves. I can't say what I'd do if the tables were turned." Then she snorted. "Of course, in a sense they are, aren't they? I mean, I never doubted that he had nothing to do with his wife's accident." She made a huffing sound. "That's how things go sometimes, don't they? Sometimes the people you trust turn out to be the ones you shouldn't have."

By then Annie's legs were weak. All the other chaos in her life seemed far less threatening. Then Taylor walked toward the front door.

"You'll lock up when you leave?"

Annie uttered a mouse-like "Yes."

And the woman was gone as quickly as she'd appeared.

Annie didn't move until she heard the tires of the pickup rumble over the dirt and accelerate out onto the road. She realized she'd been holding her breath, but wasn't sure for how long.

"Yikes!" she said aloud. "That was bizarre."

It certainly was, Murphy replied from somewhere in the rafters.

And Annie smiled, less agitated now, thanks to her friend who had been with her in spirit. She went outside, retrieved her essentials from the Jeep, and got to work.

Donna claimed she'd eaten half a sandwich earlier that day, and Annie didn't dispute her. Donna seemed at ease in the Lyons's home that evening. Earl was entertaining, Claire was gracious, and John couldn't do enough for her. Lucy, too, seemed on her best behavior, refilling Donna's ice water when the glass was only half full and trying to keep Restless from jumping into Donna's lap despite her cheerful protestations that she loved dogs.

Kevin didn't say much, and he sneezed a few times, though he said he didn't have a cold. He seemed to have to work at smiling.

"I think the ladies should retire to the living room," Claire said once the fish and wild rice and green beans had been consumed. Annie would have bet that Claire had prepared the light meal with Donna in mind. "My favorite part of having friends for dinner is when I leave the men to clean up."

Lucy said she'd take the dog outside to chase birds, then she'd make tea to go with Annie's cookies. In addition to the usual chocolate chip, Annie had baked a batch of lemon wafers dusted with confectioners sugar, which she thought

Donna might enjoy. Though she'd done a lot of baking at the center, Annie hadn't written a damn word. It wasn't only because she'd been unnerved by Taylor—she also recognized an undercurrent of Mark, as if he'd slid back into her life on Larry Hendricks's slimy heels.

Settling into the rocking chair by the fireplace, she chose to let the others do the talking. As a writer, she preferred listening, anyway.

"Your granddaughter is charming," Donna said after she and Claire were seated, and Lucy had gone outside.

"She has her moments," Claire responded, winking at Annie. "She's a good girl, but I worry that she's like her father. Spunky sometimes to her detriment."

"And she has a sister?"

"Abigail, yes. We hardly see her anymore; like her mother, she never enjoyed living on the island. The girls are polar opposites." Then Claire offered a sly smile and added, "Lucy is the smart one. She knows how to get her way."

Donna laughed. "Then she's bound to succeed at whatever she does in life."

If she can learn to control her enthusiasm, Annie thought, absently shaking her head.

"Annie?" Claire asked. "You disagree that Lucy will be successful?"

"Oh, no. Not at all. I was just marveling at her energy. I don't think I came close to having that much at her age."

"None of us did, dear," Claire replied, a look of bewilderment crossing her face. "I've often wondered how John turned out as well as he did. If I only could get back the days—and years—that I spent worrying . . ."

"We always worry about our children, don't we?" Donna said. "Even before I met Annie, I worried about her." Then she turned to her. "You didn't know that, did you?"

"Well, no." Annie had no idea how else to answer.

Donna looked back at Claire. "When I learned she was on the Vineyard, I was so pleased. I loved it here when I was young."

At first Annie thought she must have misheard.

Then Claire asked, "Oh? Family vacations?"

Donna shook her head. "No. I worked here one summer after I graduated from high school. I was a waitress at a restaurant—the Blue Lagoon in Vineyard Haven. Do you remember it? It was a small place; it's probably long gone."

Annie was too shocked to speak.

"I remember the name," Claire said. "But years ago, except for once or twice a year when we went off island to buy clothes and supplies that we couldn't get here, we only went to Vineyard Haven to get the boat, not to eat out. There weren't many restaurants then."

"They mostly made fried clams. Not strips, mind you. Whole bellies. *Only* whole bellies."

Annie froze. That was how Murphy had liked her clams. Whole bellies, never just strips.

Claire laughed. "So you were here only that one summer?"

"And for spring break just before it," Donna replied. "When I came down to apply for the job."

And then a disturbing thought crept into Annie's mind: One summer after Donna graduated from high school. Could that have been when she'd gotten pregnant? With *her?* Annie froze. Had she been conceived right there on Martha's Vineyard?

But before she had a chance to think it through, Restless bounced into the room, vaulted onto Donna's lap, and shifted the conversation to what a wonderful comfort dogs could be.

Chapter 21

"Well, that was fun," Kevin said.

After Annie and Donna had left Earl and Claire's and were tucked into their separate spaces, Annie had known that sleep would elude her. So she'd texted her brother and asked him to come to the Inn. They sat in her "temporary" room now, each in one of the wing chairs that faced the bow window that still had no blinds.

"They were nice to Donna," Annie replied. "All of them." She hated that John had had to bring Lucy back to Edgartown then get ready for his midnight shift. She had wanted him to come home with her. She knew that was how it needed to be and yet . . . and yet she was glad that at least she had Kevin to talk to. "You didn't say much, though."

"Did you hear Mom ask Lucy to visit anytime and to bring the damn dog? She never let me have a dog when I was a kid, and now she can't get enough of that one. What's its name again?"

"Restless. So you were a boy without a dog?"

She was about to feel sorry for him until he replied, "Yeah. Well, I'm allergic."

"And that's why you were sneezing." She threw a toss pillow at him. "You are such a pain."

He picked it up and tossed it back. "I am, aren't I?"

"Well, I hope Lucy follows through. Lots of nursing homes now have programs where they bring pets in to visit. Apparently the patients love them."

"Is that why you wanted me to come over? Do you think we should get Mom a dog?" He almost looked as if he were serious.

Annie remained often amazed at his seeming innocence. "No. I wanted to ask you if . . . Mom . . . well, if she ever told you she'd been to the Vineyard before."

He thought for a moment, then shook his head. "No. Not that I remember." He frowned a little. "Well, she came here when she first met you. Is that what you mean?"

"No. Earlier. Like when she was young."

"No. Oh, wait. Before she came to meet you she asked me if I knew if the boats still came into Oak Bluffs or Vineyard Haven. I think I said something stupid like, 'How would I know? I've never been there.' Anyway, for a second I thought it was kind of weird that she knew the names of the towns where the ferry docked. A couple of times she'd gone to Nantucket on business, but I don't think she ever mentioned the Vineyard. Not to me, anyway." He crossed his legs. "Why?"

"She told Claire that after she graduated from high school she was a waitress one summer at a clam place in Vineyard Haven. It was news to me."

Kevin shrugged. "I suppose it was no big deal or she would have mentioned it sooner, don't you think?"

"Unless it was a big deal, Kevin."

"I don't follow."

Annie fell silent.

Then Kevin said, "Holy crap. Are you thinking . . . ?"

"That she met my birth father here and got pregnant with me? Yes, that's what I'm thinking."

"Wow. And she's never given you a clue about who he was?"

"No. Other than to say he was 'just a boy.' "

Kevin let out a whistle.

"Did you ever see any pictures of her when she was young?"

He pondered. "Nope. Real young, maybe. Like when she was a little kid. But no others I can think of. If she had any, maybe she threw them out."

"Well, she was on the island that one summer. That's all I know. And it might not be connected. But now I'm wondering if Lucy has a point. That I have a right to know who my birth father is."

The next morning, Annie woke up feeling better than she'd felt in a while. Less stressed. Clearheaded. Almost happy. Which made no sense with her future looking more tenuous, with more questions than answers. Not to mention that her relationship had begun to feel like a long-distance one, as if Chappy and Edgartown were a few time zones away. She wondered if it was nature's way of slowing down the fire so she'd be better able to handle big changes ahead.

Yes, she thought, it was ridiculous that she was in such a good mood.

Maybe her spirits had improved because she'd come out of emotional hiding: she'd talked to Larry Hendricks; she'd told him what she needed. Surprisingly, it hadn't brought on a panic attack. And she'd decided to talk to Donna about her birth father. Which wouldn't kill her. As she jumped into the beautiful, new, marble walk-in shower, she supposed that facing her demons was a good reason to be clearheaded.

By the time she finished dressing, it was after nine o'clock. She went downstairs and waved at Kevin, who was on his hands and knees again, this time laying down the porcelain tiles in the kitchen now that the great room was complete. Four weeks and two days, she thought, then made a mental note to meet with Kevin and Earl to see what was left to finish, if there was any point in finishing. Or if there were any funds left to buy the rest of the materials. Then she remembered that the three soon-to-be year-round tenants had already ponied up their first, last, and security deposits—almost ten thousand dollars that might have to be refunded.

She gulped. And opened the back door before anxiety had a chance to sink in.

Outside, the morning sky was a shade of misty pewter, and it was drizzling. Pulling up the hood of her pale green zip-up sweatshirt from Menemsha Blues (which, in tandem with her Black Dog one, were the warmest, longest-lasting clothes she'd yet to find), Annie headed to the cottage, hoping that Donna would feel up to meeting a few more artists. Once the artwork task was checked off Annie's to-do list, she'd only need to figure out the situation with the tchotchkes, though she was no longer enthusiastic about beachcombing for small treasures.

As she reached the cottage, she noticed that overnight the daffodils had begun to bloom; their little yellow heads were open and drinking in the mist. Claire had showed her how to plant the bulbs last fall—Annie, the city girl, knew she could have watched a YouTube video, but that was not in the spirit of the community, not the island way. Maybe by Memorial Day, the hydrangea that they'd put in all around the terrace would begin to show their vibrant lavenders and blues. And maybe the buttercups would have blossomed in the meadow.

Hoping Donna was awake, Annie tapped on the front door.

"Come in!" she heard her birth mother's voice call out. It sounded pleasant and strong. Perhaps this was due to the Vineyard air, drizzly or not.

Once inside, Annie saw Donna in the rocker. And surprisingly, a woman Annie didn't recognize was sitting on the sofa. She was older than Annie, but not as old as Donna. Her hair was short and silver-gray; her blue eyes were bright and friendly. Her parchment-like skin and tiny threads of age lines reminded Annie of someone she couldn't quite place.

"Good morning," Annie said. "I'm sorry, I didn't know you had company. I can come back. . . ." She half-turned toward the door.

"No, no," Donna said. "I was going to call you in a few minutes. This is Ms. Nelson. Georgia Nelson."

Ms. Nelson stood and neatened her pink-flowered shirt into the elastic waistband of her denim skirt. She might be an old friend of Donna's, but she dressed more like an islander than someone from the mainland.

"Call me Georgia, please," the woman said, extending her hand to Annie.

"And this is my daughter," Donna added. "Annie Sutton."

"The mystery writer," Georgia stated. "Your mother has been telling me about you. She didn't have to, though. I've read all your books."

"Oh," Annie replied. "Well, thank you." She was never sure how to respond to that.

"And I love them!" Georgia added. "When's the next one coming out?"

"Late September." Annie wished someone would explain why Georgia was with Annie's mother, in Annie's house. "So," she asked as she put on her best smile, "are you a friend of my . . . mother's?"

Donna laughed. "We hope to become friends, don't we, Georgia? No, dear, Georgia is a home companion. I used my

phone to search for someone local, and here she is! Forgive me
for not telling you sooner, but I wanted to outline some spe-
cifics first. She's going to help with my day-to-day personal
things so you and Kevin won't have to bother. As long as I'm
going to stay, I thought it would be best."

Annie felt the edges of her good mood begin to fray, the
way the shoreline did after a storm. "What kinds of things?"
she asked. Hadn't she already said she'd do whatever Donna
needed? Did her *mother* think she wasn't capable? She stood
for a moment, until Donna told them both to sit. Then
Annie removed her sweatshirt. She took a notebook from the
kitchen out of habit, brought a chair over from the table, and
formed a conversation triangle. Then, because she had no idea
what was going on, she began to make notes as if she were
researching a book. It was, apparently, the only thing that
Annie could do well.

Georgia explained that she would stop by every morning.
Later, they could figure out if she'd be needed in the evening,
too. Luckily, she lived right there on Chappy with her sister,
Lottie, who managed the community center. "I bet you know
her!" Georgia added, as if the cottage were a hair salon and
they were chatting about the neighbors.

Annie smiled patiently, or at least with what she hoped
would be perceived as patience. At least she now knew why the
woman looked familiar—she resembled Lottie, though Annie
didn't recall if she'd ever heard Lottie's last name. Annie had
met the woman on a number of occasions when she'd gone to
the center. Not the day before, of course, because, as Taylor
had noted, Lottie was "off" for the week, an abbreviated way
of saying someone was off island.

Several minutes passed before Donna got to the point.
"Georgia will keep the cottage tidy. She'll also do my laundry, and she'll go with me into town when I feel I need a

break from lovely Chappaquiddick. Once or twice a week perhaps. Whenever I need to see more people than the ones I've already met."

Georgia smiled empathetically. "You must know that feeling, Annie. Your mother tells me you came here from the city. I expect that up there, seeing strangers all day, every day, is part of life. But here there aren't many unfamiliar faces, except, of course, in the summer. I suppose that can be tedious at first." As she spoke, Annie noticed that Georgia's front teeth protruded slightly as if her parents hadn't been able to afford orthodontic work when she had been young.

No, Annie thought, she didn't feel that seeing familiar faces on the island had grown tedious. Nor did she know what had triggered Donna's sudden need for a "home companion." Just because she planned to stay? Didn't she think Kevin and Annie were capable of "tidying" and doing laundry and taking her off "lovely Chappaquiddick" when she needed a break? Annie wanted to ask, but not with Georgia in the room. So instead, she made a few more haphazard notes. She was glad that Kevin wasn't there; he would have had trouble sitting still.

Then Georgia took what looked like a checkbook from her bag; its plastic cover was splayed with happy daisies. Annie could see that there was a title on the front—perhaps a slogan, like "Have a Sunny Day" or "A Smile is the Greatest Gift that You Can Give." Georgia opened it; it was not a checkbook but a calendar. She announced that she could start Donna's "program" effective Monday. "If you need anything beforehand, please give me a call." She handed a laminated business card to Donna and another one to Annie. Annie glanced at it; within a border of pink roses, Georgia's name was set in a flourishing script with her phone number beneath it. Annie shoved it in her pocket.

Finally, they were finished. Donna thanked her, and Annie led her to the door. They said good-bye, and as Annie watched her leave, her only thought was "Good riddance."

Donna said she'd like to rest, so Annie went back to what was going to be her room for the foreseeable future. It was one of three bedrooms reserved for summer guests; she wondered how much income would be lost if Donna was still there once the season started. If they opened the Inn. Maybe Annie would need to stay at Earl and Claire's after all. Or with John . . . and Lucy?

She sat down in a wing chair and put her face into her hands, trying to slow her brain. Again. She hated that her thoughts often ran on—much like the sentence that dearest Kevin had pointed out.

What she needed was to work.

But she didn't want to go back to the community center.

Raising her head, she looked out the window. "With our good wishes and the best of luck for your new venture," the previous owners of the house had written on a card that had been attached to a beautiful hand-carved wooden bowl that was made right there on Chappy from Edgartown sycamore maple. Annie thought back to how it had all come to pass, how she'd lived next door in the place that had belonged to Jonas's grandparents until . . . Well, she didn't like thinking about all that. It had been the first rental she'd lived in since right after college, the first place she'd lived outside of the city, and the very first location where she'd been able to totally relax and work. She'd written *Renaissance Heist: A Museum Girls Mystery* there; her editor expected that it would soar to the top of the best-seller list when it was released. To put it mildly, the muses in that little rental had been wonderful to her. Could she bring her laptop over there now, sneak in, and recapture some of the magic?

Did she dare?

She glanced in that direction. Squinting through the trees, she saw no vehicles and no activity. The property had been purchased by seasonal residents; over the winter, there hadn't been a single sign of residents in either the main house or in the tiny place where she'd been. Annie doubted that the rental would be locked; there probably was little left inside to steal or trash.

Of course, she would be trespassing. John would hate that. But how would he know?

Then again, there would be no lights. Or heat. And it was a fairly chilly day.

But her laptop had a nicely lit screen, and she could bring a thermos of hot tea. She could put on her thick socks and old fleece shirt and the matching pants that she'd been sleeping in because the Inn did not have heat, either. Not yet, anyway. Besides, who would care what she was wearing? It was not as if she'd see anyone.

No one would have to know.

And she'd be nearby and would have her phone with her in case of emergency.

She did not allow herself another second to think about it. In less than ten minutes, she pulled together what she needed, tossed on the tattered clothes, told Kevin she'd be back later, then hurried out the door and across the side lawn where the landscapers had yet to plant thickets of beach roses and wild berries that would create a bounty of natural, old Vineyard flora. Last week, Earl had put the landscapers on hold. Even if they had the funds to pay them, they might not be needed. If The Vineyard Inn was on sacred Native American ground, the Wampanoags might prefer to leave it as it should be, as it was.

The path was overgrown, yet recognizable, a jumble of scrub oaks dividing one property from the other. Annie ducked and made her way through, trying not to think about the many times she'd done that when there had been more than one scary situation that she'd felt she should resolve.

Reaching her cozy refuge, she drew in a long breath. In addition to having been a wonderful creative space, the tiny, gray-shingled place with its creaks and cracks and quirks had been where her dream of moving to the island had come true, where she'd learned that life could start again. It held fond memories of finding baby Bella, of meeting Earl, and, of course, of spending many nights with John, learning to love again. Maybe one day her new cottage would hold fond memories, too. Unless Donna chose to stay there forever.

Tiptoeing onto the porch, Annie didn't see a stack of wood—reassurance that no one was there. Though the calendar was quickly turning to May, anyone who lived there would still need the woodstove.

She slipped her laptop and thermos under one arm and turned the door handle. It was locked.

"Damn," she whispered. She jiggled it, then tried again. Still locked. Closing her eyes, she tried to let her wiles override frustration. One night, Francine had figured out how to bypass the lock; surely Annie could. Maybe there was a YouTube video to show her how. She reached into her pocket and pulled out her phone. Stuck to the back was Georgia's laminated business card. Annie smiled.

You're welcome, Murphy said.

Annie zipped the card between the door and doorjamb as if she were scanning her debit card at Cronig's Market before they'd installed the chip readers. A soft "pop" heralded success, and she wondered if the charge of trespassing had now escalated to breaking and entering. Somehow, it didn't matter.

As expected, the interior was chilly. It was also dusty and cobwebby, and she was pretty sure the small dark particles around the edges of the floor had been left by a family of winter's mice. But the table and two chairs still stood in the kitchen area—the same table where she and Earl had shared countless mugs of steamy morning coffee and batches of homemade cinnamon rolls, and where she and John had savored scores of newly caught fish, island-grown veggies, and fresh-baked bread, but then had skipped dessert, choosing to make love instead. Next to the woodstove, she'd once set her rocking chair, where she'd sat for hours rocking Bella to sleep. It was also where she'd been living when she'd met Donna the first time, before Donna had been sick, or at least before Annie and Kevin had known that she was.

Annie teared up with nostalgia.

Then suddenly, from the rafters, came Murphy's voice again: *All this blubbering isn't going to get* Body in the Blue Room *written.*

Annie laughed. "We have to change the title," she said. "You suggested that they only find a skull, remember?"

You're the writer, not me.

"Some friend you turned out to be."

But Murphy didn't reply, and Annie knew she was gone. Again.

With a lingering sigh, she sat at the table, set down the thermos, opened her laptop, and got to work.

At first, the writing was slow and labored, her thoughts bouncing from Donna and the sudden way she'd decided she needed a "home companion"; to the skull and its pending peril for them all; to Kevin, Lucy, Jonas, John. Even Taylor. No matter how hard Annie tried to focus on her novel, she couldn't unwind. She growled. She snarled. Then suddenly, a title flashed into her mind: *Bedlam in the Blue Room.*

Perfect, she thought she heard Murphy agree.

Annie went back to page one and inserted the new words that were so simple, it was annoying she hadn't thought of them sooner. Then she returned to the page where she'd left off and moved fluidly into the writing zone, her fingers skating over the keys as if they were as lightning-quick as Lucy's, and as if she'd known all along what the next chapter would reveal.

Several hours passed until late afternoon started to turn to dusk, and the chill inside the cottage began to permeate her bones. Annie finally snapped out of her daydream and realized it was past time to check on Donna. Glancing one last time at the screen, she saw that she'd typed fifteen pages while hardly paying attention. On rare days when a miracle like that occurred, she was reassured that leaving her third grade students had been the right thing to do.

But reality was calling. She checked her phone: no calls, though surely someone must have wondered where she'd gone. Especially since her Jeep still stood in the driveway next door, which, unlike her, was where it belonged.

Chapter 22

"It's open," Earl's voice unexpectedly responded when Annie knocked on the cottage door.

Stepping inside, she was greeted by Restless, his tail wagging so fiercely that his rear end jerked back and forth. She bent down and patted his head, scratched his ears, and said, "I didn't expect to see you here." She slipped out of her sneakers, revealing her old socks.

"Lucy brought him for a visit," Donna said from the rocking chair, as Lucy emerged from the bathroom.

"And I stopped by to get this young lady home in time to do her homework," Earl added as he leaned, arms folded, against the refrigerator.

Annie glanced back at Donna, who looked rested. Her cheeks had a nice pink color as if she'd never been ill. Restless scooted over and settled at Donna's feet as if that was where he'd been stationed when Annie had opened the door. It made for a sweet tableau.

"Did you have a nice visit?" she asked Donna.

"We did. Lucy brought us homemade date nut bread. And this little guy's a gem." She leaned down and ran a hand gently across the dog. "I love dogs. We never had one, though. Kevin is allergic."

Annie refrained from mentioning that he'd told her that. "You're really a good kid, aren't you?" she asked Lucy, who responded by sticking her tongue out at Annie, a gesture that Annie had learned to consider a term of endearment.

Then Lucy laughed and said, "Nice outfit, Annie. Has my dad seen you in that?"

Earl let out a chuckle.

Annie looked down at her attire. She looked pathetic, right down to her socks. "I'm saving it for a special date. Like maybe if he takes me to the symphony. Or the opera."

"Good luck with that," Lucy said. "But you might at least make an appointment with Patti Linn for a cut and color. If she fixes your hair maybe the rest of you won't be so . . . noticeable."

Annie smoothed her hair behind her ears; she knew it had grown long and wasn't short and neat, like Donna's. *Scruffy*, her mother Ellen would have called it. "I'll do that. And I'll take good care of my outfit so you can wear it to the prom." The ladies giggled.

Earl shook his head and stood up straight. "Time to leave. Get yourself together, granddaughter." He turned to Donna. "It's been a pleasure to see you again, Ms. Donna. I'll stop by tomorrow after I run down to the boat."

Though Annie had no idea what he was referring to, she didn't ask. Donna must have asked Earl to pick up something in town, and, coupled with having enlisted Georgia whatever-her-last-name-was as a home companion, Donna certainly was entitled to manage her own life. As for Earl, God knew, he'd comply. Without his penchant to help others, Annie wasn't sure how she would have navigated her first year on the island.

Then, as Earl zipped his jacket, he abruptly asked Annie, "How are things over at the Flanagan place? Was it unlocked or did you have to break in?"

Stupefied, Annie said, "I wasn't in the main house."

"Well, I didn't figure you would be."

"But how . . ."

Lucy laughed. "Your car was here, your keys were in it, so Grandpa said you couldn't be far. It took him two seconds to find the path again. Then he saw your footprints on the ground."

"Fresh prints," Earl added. "It rained pretty hard last night, but you probably slept through it. If someone had left 'em earlier, they'd have washed away. I figured not many people either know about or would bother with that path. No reason to. Since no one's around. Bet you never knew that my son gets his investigative skills from me." He donned his baseball cap and tipped it toward Donna. "Have a pleasant evening." Then he waddled out the door and into the waning sunset, with Lucy and the dog behind him, the teenager mimicking his gait, and Restless continuing to wriggle his backside.

"You broke into your old rental space so you could write?" Donna asked after they were out of sight.

Annie snapped on the light over the table and sat across from her birth mother, knowing she must look sheepish. She toyed with the buttons on her fleece. "I loved that little place. I wrote one of my novels there. It has nice memories."

"Earl thought you were hiding from us."

The laugh Annie emitted sounded more like a sputter. "Earl likes to spin an incident into a tale. The longer you know him, the more you'll get to hear. But if he drives you crazy, let me know. The whole first fall and winter I was here, he stopped by every day. He usually pretended he had something to do, like bring me wood or fix the door. After a couple of months I realized he was keeping a watchful eye out for me. In case anything happened, you know? Anyway, let me know if he gets to be a pest."

"There could be worse pests to have around. And Lucy is delightful."

Annie nodded. "That she is." There was no need to fill Donna in on Lucy's not-so-delightful antics. "So how was your afternoon? Did you get any rest before your visitors arrived?"

"I did. Georgia wore me out. She's very nice but . . . perky. Perky people can be exhausting. Don't you think?"

"You have plenty of hands around here who are willing and eager to help; you don't have to hire more. Especially if they exhaust you."

"No. It's important to me that I take the burden off of you."

"You're not a burden, Donna."

She laughed. "Maybe I haven't been here long enough."

"If push comes to shove, I'll send Earl over more often. He never tires of being a do-gooder."

"Let the dog come, too. I really like the dog."

Annie smiled, stood up, and went to the kitchen to fill the kettle for tea. The day had been rather pleasant; despite the uncertainties in life right now, the good mood she'd had first thing that morning had been justified after all.

She stayed in the cottage for a while, fixing the leftover chowder for dinner; she and Donna ate it with Lucy's date nut bread, because Donna said she had an appetite. They chatted about nothing and everything as the night grew darker and the clock ticked toward bedtime. And though Annie had elected not to bring up the issue of her birth father—yet—after she'd cleared the table and fixed tea, she introduced a prelude of sorts.

"Can you tell me about my grandparents, Donna? Your mother and father? Only if you want to. But I have been curious." She'd once asked Kevin, but he'd said he didn't remember much about them, except that they were nice to him.

Donna smiled. "I never wanted to force that on you. I thought that telling you might be presumptuous."

"Presumptuous? Why?"

"That it might make you sad. For not having known them."

"It won't. At least I don't think it will. And I'd really like to know. Were they originally from Boston? You grew up there, right?"

"Yes. In Dorchester," she said. "My dad was a laborer; my mother, a homemaker. They were older than most parents of my friends. I was raised in a three-bedroom, triple-decker. I had a brother, but he was killed in a streetcar accident when he was twelve. His name was Donald."

"Oh, my gosh. I am so sorry. How awful for all of you."

Donna stirred her tea. "I cried for a while, but then, because I was a child, I moved on to other things. It wasn't until after you were born that I was able to feel the sadness. That's when I began to understand how hard it is to lose someone you love."

"How did your parents handle it when you told them you were pregnant with me?"

A thin smile crossed Donna's mouth. "It was difficult. As I said, they were older, nearly in their sixties by then. Their generation was much different from mine; they didn't know what they'd done wrong to have raised a nineteen-year-old daughter who was going to have a baby, but didn't have a husband."

It was the perfect opening for Annie to ask about her birth father. But the words stuck in her throat and, she supposed, in her heart.

"They sent me to a home for unwed mothers right in Boston. I could have run away, but that wouldn't have been right for you. So I made it work. The home was run by nuns, and, though my parents weren't Catholic, they were God-fearing Anglicans. Scottish descent, you know?"

When Annie was a teenager, she'd daydreamed that Donna's parents had comforted her and tried to talk her out of giving up her baby for adoption, that maybe they'd even considered trying to raise Annie as their own. She had been, of course, still naïve then.

"The 'home' must have cost a lot of money," Annie said. "As a laborer, it must have been a hardship for your father." She wanted to ask if her birth father had ponied up some of the cash, but hoped Donna would offer the information.

"No," Donna replied. "The nuns were nurses—it was actually a nursing home. They only had two rooms allotted for 'their girls,' so they only took in four of us at a time. We worked for our room and board; we did the laundry and kept track of their patients. We took care of housekeeping duties too. It was a big old Victorian right in Back Bay. Not far from where I later opened my antiques store. And you . . . you were born there."

So, Annie had been born in a big old Victorian in Back Bay. She wondered how many times she'd walked past it over the years, never having known its history or its connection. For the first time since they'd met, her defenses began to melt away. Donna was no longer the mysterious birth mother who hadn't wanted her, but a young woman who'd been trying to do the right thing for her baby.

"Were you . . . scared?" Annie asked, barely above a whisper.

Donna let out a laugh. "Every minute of every day. I was scared and I was afraid—for you. I had no idea . . ." Then she started to cry. She hadn't cried when talking about Kevin's dad who'd left them, or when telling Kevin and Annie about the cancer. Nothing Annie had witnessed so far had stirred such feelings in her mother.

Annie stood up to go to her when suddenly, an insistent knock—one-two—rattled the cottage door.

It might have been Earl. Or John. Kevin would have walked right in, though Annie wasn't sure if he could have handled the emotion in the room.

Donna wiped her tears. "You'd better get that."

"They'll leave."

"They'll know we're here. The light is on. Whoever it is will worry."

Annie smoothed her hair. "Okay. I'll tell them to come back tomorrow." With an aching heart, she toddled across the hardwood in her old socks. She turned the lock and opened the door. And came face-to-face with her ex-husband, Mark.

Annie stared.

He stared back.

It was dark outside, but the light from the living room spilled across his face. And the glow from headlights up on the hill beamed down at them, framing the frame that she remembered well. She grasped the door to stop from falling over.

"Annie?" he asked.

Panic surged.

Panic.

Fear.

Rage.

She slammed the door and bolted it.

She stood in place a few more seconds, trying to get her bearings. Trying to breathe.

Adrenaline kicked in. She raced from window to window, checking the locks, pulling the curtains. She flicked off the lights, as if that would fool him into thinking no one was home.

"Annie?" Donna called, but Annie couldn't answer.

She grabbed her phone. She hadn't realized until then that her hands were shaking. No, they were more than shaking. They had spasmed into tremors. She gripped the phone. She scrolled to the Chappy emergency alert and fumbled to touch the link. For added measure, she punched in 911. She said some words, but did not remember them. She didn't even care if the first responder turned out to be Taylor.

She groped in the darkness for the chair, then flopped into it. She thought: What if he has a gun? What if he'd come to shoot her? "I'll make a couple of calls," Larry Hendricks had said. "If only to prove I'm not really an insufferable jerk."

She pressed a hand to her chest.

Then she remembered Donna.

"It's okay," Annie whimpered. "John will be here soon."

Donna didn't answer.

Perhaps she'd guessed that Annie didn't know if John would show up because she couldn't remember if he was on duty.

Had her panicked message to the emergency line made any sense? If not, would the dispatcher have recognized her number and accelerated the alert? Annie didn't know if GPS was working or if, that night, the signal was too weak. Was it foggy out? Wasn't the signal worse when it was foggy?

What if they thought Annie had said she'd found another body—or the remains of one—and that her imagination had spun out of control? What if they thought that nothing—once again—was urgent? Like the boy who'd cried wolf?

Her thoughts zoomed around the room like a cloud of bats soaring, dipping, banging into walls, knowing they were trapped.

And then the knocking came again.

It was far too soon for John.

Besides, it was Mark's knock. One-two.

"Help!" Annie wanted to cry out, but she could not. She didn't want to scare Donna more than she already must have.

Suddenly, she heard sounds inside the cottage. Footsteps in the bedroom. Moving into the living room. She sat, frozen. Her heart thump-thumped again.

Then the front door flew open.

A shot rang out.

"Now get the hell out of here!" a woman's voice shrieked. Donna's voice. "Next time I won't miss."

Chapter 23

By the time the red and blue lights splashed across the lawn and the Inn and the sky, Annie had stopped shaking. She was still sitting in the chair; Donna sat nearby, holding Annie's hand.

John blew into the cottage with more ferocity than a nor'easter in February. "What the . . . ? Annie? Are you okay?" Donna let go of her hand as John crouched down.

Annie reached for him. "I'm okay now. I am."

"Dispatch said a trespasser broke in."

That must have been what she'd said whcn she had called. "He didn't really break in, but . . ."

John shifted on his haunches. "But what?"

"It was my ex-husband. It was Mark."

John gripped her arm. "The jerk? The one who disappeared and screwed you over?"

Annie nodded. It was tough to hear those words being said out loud. Tough. Embarrassing. Humiliating.

"He won't be back," Donna said. "I let him know he was not welcome here."

Annie noticed that the gun had vanished. Perhaps she shouldn't mention to John that her mother had one.

"I can't believe he found you," John said, his voice quieter, but his anger, Annie knew, was not far under his skin. "How the hell did he find you?"

"It's my own fault. I called a friend of his at the Boston DA's office. I thought he might . . . help out. With the skull, you know?"

John dropped his chin. "Jesus, Annie. I thought by now you knew not to get involved."

"But so much is at stake . . ."

He let go of her arm. "Where'd he go?"

"I have no idea."

"What's his last name?"

"Lewiston."

"Do you have a picture of him?"

She frowned. Did John really think she'd saved a photo of the man? There was no need to tell him about the bonfire she and Murphy had ignited in the dumpster at Annie's condo building that quickly had destroyed the photos, clothes, and every single thing that Mark had liked or touched or even breathed on; or how the fire department had showed up and lambasted them. "I got rid of all his photos," was what she said now.

"What kind of vehicle was he driving?"

"I don't know. I only saw the headlights."

"Was he alone?"

"I have no idea."

"What was the guy's name at the DA's office?"

"Larry Hendricks." She realized she was breathing more easily, that she was worn-out, that she was thirsty. "Donna?" she asked. "Could you please put the kettle on while John interrogates me?" Her anger about Mark had turned into irritation at John.

"Jesus, Annie. I'm trying to help here."

She lowered her head. "There's nothing to do, John. He's

probably off Chappy by now. And he probably took the late boat off the island."

"It's almost nine thirty. Unless the guy went airborne, he couldn't have made it off Chappy and to Vineyard Haven in time." John was standing then, though Annie didn't remember that he'd gotten up. His stance was rigid, his gaze penetrating, as if he were awaiting a response. Yes, Annie thought, he was angry that she'd contacted Larry, that she'd tried to circumvent the authorities. *His* authority.

She shrugged. "I have no idea if he knows anyone here he could stay with. Or which hotels are open before Memorial Day." The reminder of the holiday made her stomach roil. She had a fleeting thought that their tenants might try to sue them for breach of their leases if the Inn wasn't finished. "John," she said, "please forget about it. He didn't hurt me or threaten me. It was a shock, for sure. But I'm all right. And, like Donna said, he won't be back."

"I'll post someone outside tonight."

"There's no need to. Honestly."

He turned away. "Let's go," he said. "There's nothing to see here."

That's when Annie noticed two other policemen—one was coming from the bedroom, the other was inside the front door.

"If this jerk's still on the island," John added, "we'll find him. It's not as if we have a ton of work to do right now." He looked back at her, then turned around again and followed his fellow officers out into the night.

Donna set a mug of steaming tea in front of her, and Annie closed her eyes.

"I didn't know you had a gun," she said.

"Don't worry. I have a permit. When I had the business, I dealt with a lot of cash. It made sense to carry one."

Annie remembered that Kevin had had one, too, locked in the glove box of his truck. She'd never asked if he'd gotten rid of it. "Good thing we're on Chappy and that it's still April. Otherwise, you'd probably be arrested for 'improper discharge of a firearm' or something."

"John would arrest me?"

She laughed. "He'd arrest *me* if he thought I'd broken the law."

Donna sat again. "In that case, if I have another chance to shoot your ex-husband, I might as well aim for his heart. As long as I'll be arrested anyway, I should make it worth my while. But first, if you're okay, I think I'll go to bed."

"Please," Annie replied. "Please do. And thank you. You saved my sanity. And maybe my life."

"My pleasure," Donna said. "Now go back to the Inn. And sleep."

After Donna closed the bedroom door, Annie didn't feel like drinking tea. She started to carry the mug over to the sink when, halfway across the room, she noticed a small white paper on the floor inside the door. She moved closer to it and stopped. Then she picked it up. It was a business card: MARK LEWISTON, COMMERCIAL PROPERTY CONSULTANT. His phone number was on the bottom.

Before Annie could freeze again, she finished walking to the sink, then flung the card into the trash.

She'd done as she'd been told and gone back to the Inn. She'd been unafraid to meet Mark in the dark, on the lawn, because she'd suspected he was long gone. Still, Annie couldn't sleep. She'd called Kevin, told him what had happened, and then asked if he'd come over and crash on the sofa in the cottage—just in case. Mark wouldn't know that Annie wasn't still there, and she didn't want to risk that he'd barge in on

Donna. Though Annie knew she could have gone back, she felt Donna would be safer with Kevin there. And there wasn't enough space for the three of them.

More than anything, Annie wanted to call Larry Hendricks and blast him. She'd trusted that he wouldn't have told Mark that they'd talked. Or where she was. Why had she been such a fool?

"Don't answer that," she said aloud, in case Murphy was listening.

Then Annie thought about Donna. Wow. That had been some performance, the mama bear defending her cub. Annie would not have believed that Donna could be so . . . tough. Was that the word? Donna had had no idea who the intruder was. . . . She'd only known that Annie felt threatened. Annie thought about her mother—her other mother—Ellen Sutton. Ellen probably would have stood behind Annie, not in front of her, and there was no way she'd have had a gun. The poor woman had been afraid of most things.

"Duck!" Annie remembered her dad shouting one night when a bat had flown into the house. He had a broom in one hand, a bucket in the other. His command hadn't been to her, but to her mother who was in the corner, cowering, trembling, crying. Annie had been at the opposite end of the living room, a broom and bucket in her hands, too.

"Come on, kiddo, let's get this bugger!" He'd always called her kiddo when they were on a mission together, whether they were going to go out for ice cream or swatting bats out of the house. "Damn pine trees!" he said with every swat. "One of these days, we'll chop 'em down." They never did, of course. The bats lived in them, and her dad had secretly told her that every critter needed to live somewhere.

"Like me?" Annie had asked the first time he'd said it. She'd been around seven or eight, and they'd been walking past the pine trees en route to the ice cream shop. "Is that why you adopted me?"

"You bet, kiddo," he said, resting a hand on her shoulder. "You could have either lived in our house or up in the pine trees, and you know that your darn mother doesn't like you outside after dark."

His reasoning made little sense, but Annie had giggled and skipped alongside him because he'd always made her feel special. Protected. And, most of all, loved.

She didn't think he'd ever owned a gun.

Hauling herself from under the covers now, Annie guessed it might be easier to get to sleep if she paced for a while first. She pulled on her quilted robe and stepped into her slippers. Inside the room the night air was cold.

She looked out the window, up at the sky. It was ink-black, as was typical on Chappy. Also as usual, stars were bright and abundant, as if silver confetti had been tossed into the air. "Millions of stars!" her dad had whispered every summer when they were on the Vineyard. "Maybe more! Who knows?" He once said he whispered so he wouldn't wake up the stars because it was past dark, past Annie's bedtime, and no doubt, past the bedtime of the stars as well.

These days, her dad was on her mind. A lot. Perhaps because she needed to begin accepting that he was the only dad that she would ever know.

Sighing, she knotted the tie of her robe and headed from her room. If she went outside, she'd have a better view of the sky. Maybe she'd see the Milky Way; she never grew tired of that breathtaking sight. The light from the heavens would be illuminating, so there was no need for her lantern. Still, she'd bring it. "Always be prepared, kiddo," her dad had often said. He'd been talking about hurricanes and snowstorms and such, not predatory former jerk husbands. Not for the first time, Annie was glad that neither of her parents had lived long enough to have known Mark or to see the person she'd become when she'd been with him: shallow, materialistic, phony—all those things she'd been raised not to believe in.

Swinging the unlit lantern, she made her way down the tall, wide, winding staircase, counting each step—twenty-four—as she went. When she reached the bottom, she turned left and went through the great room, past the fireplace, where, suddenly, she heard a low, growling sound. She stopped. And froze.

A dog?

A raccoon?

A skunk? Did skunks even growl?

For the second time that night, Annie's heart began thumping. She wasn't sure which way to turn. But all she could see in the starlight shimmering through the windows was a pile of tarps that Kevin must have left by the doorway that led to the kitchen and the back door.

She wished she had a broom and a bucket. She wondered if she could shoo away whatever the growling intruder was with one swipe of the lantern.

Sucking in a quiet breath, she slinked toward the sound, "like a darn fool," her mother Ellen would have said. Annie listened. The sound stopped for a moment, then resumed.

She moved closer.

When she reached the tarps, she hit the on switch; the beam flared down from the lantern onto the floor. And there, curled in a ball, white hair spiking up, was Earl. Asleep. And snoring.

"Earl!" she squealed.

He shook his head, no doubt clearing cobwebs. He opened his eyes and saw her. "Hey! You scared the hell out of me!"

Exasperated, Annie plunked down beside him. "What are you doing here?"

He rubbed his eyes. "I'm on guard. My son ordered me to come. He might even have deputized me, though I'm not sure about that. He told me what happened. I told him Kevin was in the cottage with your mom. And John didn't want you up here alone."

John, she whispered to herself. So he wasn't angry with her after all. She smiled. John. Donna. Kevin. Earl. As much as Annie believed she could take care of herself, it was nice to have protectors all around her.

Sometimes it was hard to believe that she was there. In her daughter's home. In her daughter's bed.

It had not been an easy journey. It was not easy still. Donna had, after all, never been comfortable telling a lie. She tried hard not to, and yet . . .

She was glad she'd told the truth about taking the bus from South Station, even though she'd failed to mention that she'd done that because she'd sold her car. It was one less thing for anyone to have to worry about. Because times had changed, and, if nothing else, Donna MacNeish had learned early on the importance of rolling with the punches. If she hadn't, she never would have succeeded in business, small though it had been. She'd had a select group of loyal customers—clients, they'd preferred to be called—with perpetual lists of items they desperately needed: Tiffany lamps, Chippendale consoles, eighteenth-century Louis XVI bergeres. She never regretted having used her inheritance from Aunt Elizabeth for tuition at business school.

She'd loved her work, loved her clients. Loved being surrounded by beautiful things. Of course, she'd kept the Vuitton trunk safely at home. Not for public viewing. Not for sale. Ever. It had become symbolic of the good things that—against all odds—had come to her.

As awkward as it had first felt to be back on the Vineyard, it was beginning to feel like home. Donna knew that the picture would be complete once the Vuitton arrived.

Chapter 24

Kevin told Annie he'd buy her breakfast at Linda Jean's in Oak Bluffs. Donna said she needed to sleep in. Earl had disappeared sometime after dawn, having left a note saying he needed to go home before Claire had "a hissy fit."

Annie hadn't ridden in Kevin's pickup in a while; she stared at the glove box, but declined to ask if he still had the gun. The near miss the night before would remain a secret between Donna and her.

They sat in a booth by the window that looked out onto Circuit Avenue. The narrow one-way street was silent and still, an occasional vehicle inching past.

"Won't be long until this place is booming," Kevin said.

Annie laughed. "You're starting to sound like Earl."

He tossed his napkin at her. Though he was being playful, Annie suspected the real reason he'd taken her to breakfast was so they could be somewhere far from Chappaquiddick and their mother. Or far enough. Annie hoped he didn't want to talk about Mark—she'd had her fill of that conversation after the drama of last night.

"So," she began, in an effort to help Kevin start, "what's

on your mind? Not that I don't love having a meal with my brother, but . . ."

"She's still sick, isn't she?"

Their coffee arrived for which Annie was grateful. She smiled at the waitress, straightened the napkin in her lap, opened a container of cream, and added a little to her mug—all while considering how to answer Kevin's question.

She sipped. She swallowed. Then, unable to procrastinate any longer, she asked, "Mom?"

He glared at her. "Yes. Mom."

Annie sighed. "I only know what she told us, Kevin. That she had ovarian cancer, radiation, and chemo. But that she's 'all clear' now. Don't you believe her?"

"No." It was his turn to fiddle with the sugar and the cream while Annie waited for him to gather his words. "She's a terrible liar. She says she's exhausted from treatment, but she looks like shit. And I caught her sitting in a chair just before dawn, staring into space."

"Maybe she was enjoying the view. Sunrises here are amazing, though I haven't seen many of them. They always happen too early, you know?" Annie was trying to lighten the mood, though it did not seem to be working.

Ignoring her comment, he pushed his mug away. "She had a visitor yesterday. Earl told me he saw her."

"So did I. In fact, I met her. Her name is Georgia Nelson. She's a home companion. She's going to help Donna out around the cottage—cleaning, doing laundry, that kind of stuff—so we don't have to. Donna seems excited that she's, as she called it, 'taking the burden' off us."

He studied his coffee as if searching for tea leaves. "Georgia Nelson is a hospice nurse."

About to take a drink, Annie stopped, her hand, and the mug, paralyzed in midair. "What?"

"She's a hospice nurse. You probably know what that is?"

She set the mug down. "Of course. But really, Kevin? Are you sure?"

"Earl told me."

Earl. Of course he knew Georgia. Everyone knew pretty much everyone on the damn island. She lifted her mug again, then set it back down without taking a drink. "Maybe hospice nurses do double-duty here. Maybe they help people out wherever they're needed. Lots of people on the island have two jobs. Or three."

Kevin set his eyes on hers. "Do you really think that's what's going on? That Georgia showed up just to help wash out her undies? She's a hospice nurse, Annie. They help people when they're . . . dying." His voice cracked on the last word; Annie's throat tightened as he said it.

She reached across the table and rested her hand on his. "Kevin . . . what else? Did you ask Donna about it?"

Shaking his head, he started to speak when their orders arrived: scrambled eggs for Annie, an omelet for him. Annie thanked the waitress and said they didn't need more coffee. She didn't say it was doubtful that they'd touch their eggs.

"When I saw her staring out the window, I asked her if she couldn't sleep because of all the commotion when your ex showed up. She said probably. She also said it had been an adrenaline rush."

Annie pulled back her hand, picked up her fork, and pretended to get busy with her food. "Let's not talk about that, okay? I'd rather pretend it never happened."

"Do you think he left?"

"I have no idea. I don't care. I have no intention of seeing him. Ever. Again."

"Mom said he really scared you."

Annie looked back at him. "Kevin, please. I don't want to talk about it, okay?"

"Oh, sure. Is it easier to talk about Mom's cancer?"

She set down her fork. "We don't know for sure she still has it. We don't know that she's not doing exactly what she said: recuperating."

He chewed at a thumbnail. "Should we ask her?"

"I don't know." She thought for a moment, then said, "No. If it isn't true, can you imagine how much it would upset her? And if it is . . . we should let her keep her dignity. Let her decide when—if—she's ready to tell us."

Kevin looked at his plate. "I don't feel like eating."

"Me either."

He paid the check, and they left the restaurant. If they'd been in Edgartown, Annie would have walked back to the ferry. The exercise might have helped to clear her head. But it would be a long walk from Oak Bluffs. So they rode in Kevin's truck, sitting next to each other in rare silence, the latest news simply too big to absorb.

After checking on Donna, who was still asleep, Annie made another thermos of tea, and then grabbed her laptop and sneaked back through the scrub oaks on the path to the Flanagans' place. She needed distraction; she needed to work, to engage her mind with the made-up murder in the made-up museum and not have to think about the real world. Not about real-life cancer. Or Mark.

"She's still sick, isn't she?" Kevin had asked.

Annie didn't know. But if it were true, why didn't she? Why didn't Kevin? Why couldn't the child be able to tell if the parent was seriously ill? Wasn't there a sensor in the genetic code that made it obvious? Like when a parent intuitively knew when his or her child was sick?

And now the greater question was: Instead of having come to the Vineyard to recuperate, had Donna come there to . . . die?

Annie stared at the wall.

Then she wondered: What about Mark?

He wouldn't be stupid enough to try to find Annie again. Would he?

Doubtful, Murphy said. *He always was a weasel.* Then, as if she couldn't help herself, she added, *I never liked him, you know.*

"Yes, I know that," Annie replied. "Please don't rub it in. Not now."

So Murphy went mute, which Annie appreciated.

Opening her laptop, she assumed that she'd be able pick up where she'd left off the day before: the skull had been found in the Blue Room; the police had arrived; the evidence had been sent to the medical examiner, as the scene had played out on Chappy. Except in Annie's book, the remains hadn't washed ashore but had been found on the second floor of a museum, so the protocol needed to be different. And the story wouldn't involve ordinary people losing their life savings and several others being made homeless. But as she stared at the screen, she realized that, as in her life, Annie had no idea what should happen next. Unfortunately, neither did her characters.

She upcapped the thermos, poured a cup of tea, and zipped her fleece hoodie. Without wood on the porch, she couldn't start a fire in the stove, which she supposed she shouldn't do, anyway. No sense announcing that, once again, she'd broken-and-entered, though technically, that time she'd only entered, as she'd done the actual breaking part the day before.

She wondered if it were possible to type while wearing gloves. She might try that sometime, when she actually knew what to write, when her mind wasn't clogged with shadowy thoughts of Donna. And when her muses hadn't abandoned her the way that Mark had.

Should she or shouldn't she call Larry? It was clear he'd wasted no time contacting Mark—who had waited only two days before emerging from whatever rock he'd been hiding under.

Annie grimaced.

The truth was, though his appearance had shocked her, she had survived. There had been a time, during those first years after she'd moved into a four-hundred-and-fifty square-foot excuse for an apartment, when she'd still been teaching, had started writing, and had sunk most of her salary into making small dings, hardly dents, into the debt he'd left, that she hadn't believed she'd ever feel whole again. She had, however, been convinced that if she saw him she would drop dead on the spot. That was when she was still hurting, before the anger had set in. She didn't know if she'd ever find acceptance, if there would ever be a time when she'd feel sorry for him and everything he'd lost, including her. For now, she needed to be content with knowing that, when she'd opened the door and had seen his still handsome face (yes, that part was sad, but true), even though she'd panicked, she had not dropped dead.

With both hands on her cheeks and her eyes fixed on the lifeless keys on the keyboard, her thoughts moved back to Donna.

Was Kevin right?

Was Georgia a hospice nurse and nothing more? Her card only showed her name and phone number and those damn pink roses. It did not show a title that included the word "Hospice," but neither did it say "Home Companion." Simply Georgia Nelson. Nondescript.

A shudder rippled through Annie. She didn't know what to expect. When her mother Ellen had been ill, the nurses had taken care of her because she'd been in a hospital. She hadn't been in a tiny cottage on Chappaquiddick. And Annie's father had merely died of a massive heart attack—swift, clean, done.

She dropped her chin, her eyes now on the floor, her fingers clasped across the crown of her head. She didn't know how long she'd been in that position when the door to the Flanagans' cottage creaked open. She was too deep in thought to be afraid.

"Don't you know you don't live here anymore?" John filled the doorway, blocking the sunlight. Annie didn't have to ask how he knew where she would be; Earl, good old Earl, no doubt had told him.

"Sometimes it slips my mind. Especially because it's so peaceful here. And it's where I actually can write."

"Am I interrupting?"

She pulled herself up and went to him. She wrapped her arms around him and tipped her head onto his shoulder. "Never."

He kissed the top of her head, then rubbed her shoulders. "We found him," he said.

Annie jumped back. Stung.

John held her arms, steadying her. "He'd checked into the Harbor View. Used his real name. That was a surprise. He was with his friend Hendricks."

She shook off John's hands and began to pace. She hated that her heart was thumping again. "Did you make him leave the island? Please tell me you did."

"I can't do that, Annie. He didn't do anything but show up at your place."

There was no need to go into the rest. Years earlier, Annie's attorney had explained that because Mark had made sure her name was on all of their accounts, she'd been liable for the debt when he'd disappeared. It was not a crime. They had, after all, been husband and wife. Community property was community property, whether they were divorcing or the other party died. Or disappeared.

She slumped down in the chair again, wishing her rocker were still there.

"So he's still here."

"He's at the station. I wanted to hold him there until you knew where he was."

"Did you suggest that he stay away from me? Or isn't that protocol, either?"

"Annie . . ." John walked to the chair, squatted before her. "I'm sorry I can't arrest him. I'm sorry I can't deport him back to wherever the hell he's been all this time. Hell, I'm especially sorry I can't shoot him. But that does bring up a question. He told us that a woman in the cottage came after him with a gun. And that she fired it. At him."

The right corner of Annie's mouth twitched up a little. She knew she should try to stop it; she knew it would give the truth away. But she couldn't help it. She was just so damn proud that Donna had defended her before she'd even known who the shadow was. Donna. Her mother. Her possibly very sick mother.

Annie willed her mouth to straighten. "I don't know what he's talking about." If she didn't make eye contact, maybe John wouldn't know she was lying.

"You sure?"

"I don't own a gun, John. Guns make me nervous. You know that." She wasn't even comfortable whenever she saw John's weapon safely holstered at his side.

"What about your mother?"

"Donna? Why would she have a gun?"

"I have no idea. But I do know one is registered in her name. She's had a permit nearly forty years."

"Oh," Annie said with a shrug. "Well, you'd better ask her, if you must. But right now she's sleeping. She's been sick, you know. And she didn't shoot anyone last night." That part was true. Only because she'd intentionally missed.

John began nodding like a bobblehead doll. "Annie, Annie, whatever will I do with you?"

"Oh," she replied, "you'll think of something. But first,

I'll feel better when I'm sure Mark has left the island. And that his friend has gone with him."

John rubbed the back of his neck. "Larry Hendricks. Yes, that brings up another matter."

She stopped rocking. She leaned forward. "What?"

"He claims he's in tight with the assistant who's working with the archeologist. He said that the skull has been moved up to the next case on the list."

Of course, it was quite possible that Larry and Mark had concocted the story solely to pacify her. "Do you believe him?"

John offered a noncommittal shrug. "Apparently that's why they came here. Hendricks said he got in touch with Mark and told him what's been going on. Mark said he wanted to come with him so they could deliver the good news together. He said it might help you forgive him for, in his words, 'past mistakes.'"

Annie went to the kitchen window. The view had changed since she'd lived there; last fall, the new owners had old shrubberies removed; newer, smaller, flowering ones had been organized by a landscape architect and planted by a professional crew; the driveway had been updated from clamshells to neatly arranged pavers. And the weathered shingles on the house had been replaced by white clapboard. It now almost looked as if it were on North Water Street rather than on Chappy. She supposed that next they'd tear down the cottage and replace it with a stylized playhouse for small children. Like the children Mark had made sure that he and Annie never had. Intellectually, she knew she should be grateful for that now. But she was not.

She folded her arms and turned back to John. "Never," she said. "I will not forgive him. And I will not forgive myself for having believed his lies. Not in this lifetime, or in the next. Feel free to pass that on when you let him go. And, by the way, can you tell me when that might be?"

"Seriously? I have the guy who nearly destroyed the woman I love in an interrogation room, sweating his . . . well, sweating a lot, and you think I want to let him go? But I can't keep him there, Annie. I'm sorry, but, like I said, he didn't do anything illegal."

"Thanks for being sorry. I would have loved to stand beside you and watch him sweat, too. As for his claims about a woman trying to shoot him . . ."

"A woman?" John asked. "Trying to shoot him? What claim? I have no idea what you're talking about." He then went toward the window, kissed her briefly, and said he had to get back to the barn, which Annie had learned was cop slang for when they returned to the station, their second home.

"So that's the latest," Annie told Kevin after she'd packed up her laptop and returned to the Inn where she'd found her brother painting one of the upstairs bedrooms. "I'm not sure if it's true, but our so-called 'case' might have been moved to the head of the class."

"I think it has to be. I can't imagine why your ex would have come out of hiding after all this time if they'd made that up."

Annie hadn't considered that. "Maybe he thinks I have money now? Maybe he'd hoped to try for another stab at me?"

"If the Inn were in jeopardy, I'd expect he'd know that, even if you had money, you'd lose it if we didn't open."

"Good point. And I suppose it would seem pretty farfetched to think he could enlist Larry's help so he could fleece more out of me."

"Yup. Farfetched. For one thing, from what you told me, he never 'fleeced' you. More like he stuck you."

"Right. Never mind." She rubbed her arms. No matter what Mark Lewiston did or did not do, the thought of him still made her skin crawl. "But let's change the subject. Where's Earl, anyway? I thought the painting was his job?"

"He had to pick something up from the boat."

"The big boat?"

"Dunno. I guess."

"Okay. I'll check on Donna and let you get back to work."

Kevin picked up his paintbrush and wagged it at Annie. "Let me know what you think, okay? About her . . . condition?"

"You'll be the first," Annie said, her stomach suddenly knotting. She paused, took a deep breath, then went downstairs and outside, striding across the terrace with false confidence, heading down the sloping lawn. Which was when she saw Earl at the cottage, struggling to maneuver a large box up the front steps.

"Need a hand?" she called.

He looked up and smiled. "Or a forklift, if you have one."

She scooted down the hill; she saw that the box was actually a wooden crate, standing upright, strapped to a moving dolly.

They tipped it to one side, then the other, and managed it up to the door.

"What the heck is in here?" Annie asked.

"Your guess is as good as mine," he grunted.

That's when Annie saw a label with Donna's name and Annie's address. Below that were block letters stenciled in black: 15.4"h x 33.9"w x 15.7"d. L. VUITTON.

"Your mom asked me to pick it up at the boat. She said it's something she's going to need."

"But she didn't ask Kevin to get it."

"Nope. And she asked me not to tell either of you before I got it here. Don't ask me why. I learned from Claire that when a woman is doing the asking, it's usually better for me to just do what I'm told."

They angled the thing through the doorway and into the cottage. How curious, Annie thought. Then she took over, wheeling it to the sofa, unstrapping the crate, and sliding it off the dolly. She supposed it wouldn't be right to crack one of the slats and peek inside. Even though Donna wasn't in the room.

Which led Annie to wonder where the heck she was. Had she been sleeping since last night? It was nearly two o'clock—shouldn't she be awake?

Glancing into the bedroom, Annie saw that Donna was, indeed, in bed, nestled under the white comforter.

"Donna?" Annie whispered. When there was no reply, she said, "Mom? Are you awake?"

Still, no reply.

She tiptoed closer, not wanting to startle her, but convinced it was past time for her to rise and shine. Sleeping all day could not be good for her condition, whatever it was.

"Mom?" Annie said again as she touched Donna's shoulder.

There was no response.

Donna's face was warm, but her breathing was shallow. And she seemed to take a long time between breaths.

"Mom?" Annie repeated, louder.

Donna stirred, opened her eyes, and looked at Annie. But she held Annie's gaze for only a second, then seemed to pass out again.

Annie reached under the comforter and grabbed Donna's wrist. She barely felt a pulse.

"Earl!" Annie shouted. "Call 911! And hurry!"

Chapter 25

Earl fast-walked up to the Inn to get Kevin to make the call, because he'd left his phone in his truck and figured that getting to Kevin would be faster. Annie couldn't rebuke him for not using her phone, which sat on her laptop that she'd set down on the front steps when she'd helped him haul in the crate. Earl simply wasn't yet totally tuned in to using a cell phone—he was more comfortable doing things the old way, his way.

In less than a minute or two, they were all in the cottage. Waiting. Earl wandered around the living room, Kevin paced the bedroom, and Annie sat next to Donna, smoothing her hair and trying to soothe her. Then, without warning, Donna's dark tresses moved, sliding back on her head, revealing a pink scalp that was completely bald. Annie stifled a gasp; she quickly pulled the wig back into place before Kevin could notice.

She hadn't known that Donna had lost her hair, only that it was shorter. What else had her mother failed to mention?

The screech of tires on clamshells halted Annie's thoughts. She knew it was probably Taylor's truck. As an EMT, a first responder right there on Chappy, she usually arrived before the rest, then instantly connected to the on-call team in Edgartown.

"In the bedroom," Annie heard Earl say.

Taylor blew straight into the bedroom, her auburn hair flowing behind her, her emergency bag in hand. "What happened?" she barked. She wasted no time taking Donna's vitals.

Kevin started to talk, but his words sputtered out, scattered and indiscernible.

Annie took over. She explained what little she knew about Donna's cancer, including that she'd finished chemo a few weeks ago. She didn't remember how much of that Taylor already knew.

"How long has she been out?"

"She opened her eyes once. Then passed out again. Or fell asleep. Whatever she's doing. We saw her earlier. She said she was really tired." Annie wrung her hands. "She's been tired since she got here. I thought it was a normal consequence of chemo." Had that been less than a week ago? So much had been happening . . . so fast.

Taylor got busy on her phone, relaying Donna's vital numbers to the hospital and to the EMTs who by then were en route in the ambulance. Annie knew how the process worked—the efficient island emergency medical care would arrive on the scene faster than such care would have in Boston; even better, the island crew was tied into the big hospitals up there. Fast service; world-class connection.

The police arrived, followed by the ambulance. Someone told Annie that John was on another call, an accident out in Katama. She would have preferred if he were there, but knew that Donna would be safe and well cared for; they slid her onto a gurney and into the back of the vehicle with deft precision. During the process, Donna lifted her eyelids once or twice, looked around, then promptly closed them.

Kevin opted to ride in the back of the ambulance; Annie

said she'd drive behind them. Taylor offered to bring her
in the pickup. Earl said he'd go home and tell Claire what
had happened, then he'd swing by the hospital to see if they
needed anything.

Though it was broad daylight, Taylor put a portable, red-
flashing light on her dashboard, and they rumbled toward the
On Time in their small parade.

There was no waiting at the dock: the police car and the
ambulance drove right onto the ferry, bypassing a short queue
of other vehicles. Ninety seconds later, the police and the ambulance reached the other side and rolled off the *On Time*,
which then deadheaded back to Chappy so Taylor could cross
next.

Once they, too, reached Edgartown, Annie braced herself
as Taylor gunned the engine; they caught up with the ambulance before reaching the Triangle. Luckily, it wasn't summer
yet so the traffic was manageable. But the thought of tourist
season began to bear down on Annie: what it might or might
not bring. And, most of all, what would happen to Donna.

"Did your mother relapse?" Taylor said, and once again it
took a few seconds for Annie to realize that "mother" meant
Donna and not Ellen Sutton who'd been dead for years and
whom Taylor hadn't known, anyway.

"I don't know." She didn't tell her Kevin's suspicion.

"Kevin must be taking it hard."

"He will if something's gone wrong."

Taylor nodded. She did not pry further, which caused
Annie to feel more nervous about Donna's condition. Annie
knew practically nothing about any kind of cancer except the
leukemia that her mother Ellen had had, and, of course, Murphy's multiple myeloma. But ovarian cancer was a mystery to
her. Except she now knew that Donna had lost her hair.

She hoped the EMTs hadn't removed Donna's wig while
Kevin was there.

"I always believed that mothers and sons had a special bond," Taylor continued as they chased the ambulance across Edgartown-Vineyard Haven Road, past the numbered streets from Twenty-First to First on the north side, some of which had names instead of numbers, though Annie did not know why.

"Kevin and Donna do have a special bond," Annie replied.

"I wanted one with Jonas. But it didn't work out that way."

Annie tried to think of something kind to say, instead of asking Taylor to please be quiet so she could concentrate on what might be going on in the back of the vehicle ahead. Would Kevin text her if anything else happened?

She cleared her throat. "I'm sorry, Taylor. But have you heard from Jonas? Is he settled in . . . somewhere?"

"If he's settled anywhere, it would be at his grandparents' place in New York. He has no money of his own. But no, I haven't heard a word."

"I'm sorry, Taylor. I wish I could have helped."

The ambulance turned right, down County Road; Taylor steered the pickup behind it. "You could start by finding out who that bone belongs to. I think Jonas became obsessed with thinking it's his father. For some reason, he still thinks I might have killed the only man I ever loved. So, yeah. The sooner you find that out, the better. Though I don't expect that if it's him, they'll be able to tell from half a skull that I didn't push him."

Annie didn't respond. She certainly didn't want to tell Taylor what Lucy had said about the email Jonas had received from the woman up in Boston. Taylor had enough reasons to be angry at the world right then.

They passed Farm Neck Golf Club where former President Obama was known to play, then they slipped through the intersection where Barnes Road cut across to Wing Road toward the center of Oak Bluffs. Just as Annie knew the emergency protocol on Chappy, she also knew the route to the hospital.

Though it seemed like more than an hour, only minutes had elapsed when they pulled into the ER entrance at the hospital, where the EMTs were already rolling the gurney from the ambulance. Annie sucked in her breath and got out of Taylor's truck.

"No change?" Annie questioned Kevin once they were inside and Donna had been whisked down the hall to a private room. They'd been asked to take a seat in the waiting room until the doctor examined her.

They sat, pitched halfway off the chairs, ready to leap when they were told they could go in.

Kevin shook his head, then rubbed his hands together. "She came to—twice—in the ambulance, but went out again. Now I know she's sicker than we thought."

Sicker than she led us to believe, Annie wanted to say, but did not. She patted Kevin's hand. "Let's not jump to conclusions. For all we know, this is routine after chemo."

He nodded, but did not look convinced. After another minute he said, "She's wearing a wig. I didn't know that."

Annie bit her lip. "I'm not surprised. Hair loss is common, Kevin. The chemo. You know?"

"Well, she didn't tell me. I wonder what other secrets she is keeping."

Annie didn't answer because she did not know, either.

Taylor came into the waiting room after parking the truck. "Do you want me to go out back and find out what they're doing?" As an EMT, she must have had access.

"Yes," Kevin answered before Annie could say, "No, thanks." As badly as she'd tried to like Taylor, the claims from the email that Lucy had recalled came back to Annie's mind:

"Taylor only got pregnant so she could get the Flanagans' money. . . . And then she killed him."

Taylor disappeared, and they sat some more, Kevin rubbing his hands, Annie's gaze fixated on the walls.

"Things had been going pretty well, hadn't they?" Kevin asked after a time.

"They had," Annie replied.

"I really think I should get her back to Boston now. If she's this sick . . ."

"That's up to the two of you. But let's see what the doctor says."

"You'd be okay if we pulled out? If I bailed on the Inn? Would you come, too, or would you stay?"

Annie sighed. "I don't know, Kevin. Let's wait and see."

He nodded, but she knew that wasn't the answer he'd wanted.

They waited.

And waited.

Every few minutes, Kevin stood. And paced.

After about an hour, John was there. He held Annie for a couple of minutes and told her everything would be all right. Though she was not convinced, it was nice to hear him say it. Then he said he had to work until midnight, and that the next day he had to be on the Cape at a regional meeting at the courthouse in Barnstable. He asked her if she wanted him to cancel it.

Though she wanted to say yes, Annie said no. After all, Kevin was there. And Taylor. And Earl and Claire were just a phone call away.

So John went back to work. And Annie went to the lobby a few times for water.

"I thought Taylor would be back by now," Kevin said when she returned.

They went back to waiting.

Then Annie said, "It can't be much longer." In her mind, she feared that the delay couldn't result in anything good.

And, still, they waited.

Two hours and forty-five minutes from when they'd walked into the ER, Taylor reappeared. "Come on back. They've finished the tests." She guided them into a small, pale yellow room that had two straight-back chairs, a stool, and a computer desk.

A nondescript doctor introduced himself; Annie immediately forgot his name. Taylor backed out of the room and closed the door behind her.

"Your mother is slightly anemic," the doctor explained in a low voice. "But that wasn't reason enough for her to keep losing consciousness. She does, however, have fluid around her lungs. We're draining it so her breathing will be somewhat better, but we don't know how long it will be effective. We've spoken with her doctor in Boston and reviewed the results of her treatments. At this point there's nothing left to do except to keep her comfortable. I'm sorry. But, as she has probably told you, the cancer has metastasized to her liver."

After two, five, ten seconds, Annie put her hand on Kevin's back, hoping to keep him steady. She hadn't expected that she'd be the one to wobble, the one to get light-headed. She backed away and sat on one of the chairs.

The doctor resumed talking. He said they would keep Donna for a couple of nights and give her a transfusion to try to build up her red blood cells.

"Can we see her?" Annie asked.

"I think it would be best to let her rest. Perhaps wait until morning?"

Annie glanced at her watch: it was only five-thirty, though the day seemed to have gone on forever.

Then the doctor added, "I understand that Georgia Nelson has met with her? That's good. Georgia is excellent."

Kevin turned to Annie, who said, "She was planning to start coming by on Monday." So Kevin had been right. The plan had been for Georgia to do much more than "keep the cottage tidy" and do Donna's laundry.

"Many patients find that hospice workers are merciful angels."

Merciful angels. The description rolled around in Annie's mind, crisscrossing with Donna's words: "A bout with cancer," "I only want to recuperate," and then, "I might not last until the summer." Clearly, she had not wanted to tell them the rest. Perhaps she hadn't known how. "How long does she have?" Annie felt Kevin's eyes bore into her. She didn't dare look at him.

"Hard to say. If she'd been my patient all along, I'd have a better idea. Still, everyone is different, so we're never certain. Based on my conversation with the good folks in Boston, I'd guess a few months. Maybe less. She's staying in your home?"

"Yes." Annie still did not look at her brother.

The rest of the conversation was a blur. She asked a few questions that were probably unimportant, but she wasn't ready to get up, to walk out, to have to face the world. The doctor answered each query and apologized that his answers were vague. "There's no way to know for sure," he said. "I'm sorry."

Kevin said nothing the whole time, a robot devoid of feeling. But after they'd squeezed into Taylor's truck—together, yet alone in their solitary pain—they rode back to Edgartown and onto the *On Time*, and Kevin silently cried. Which, of course, made Annie cry, too. She held his hand, rested her head on his shoulder, and stayed that way until they reached the Inn and Taylor dropped them off.

She really wished that John was there. And that she'd asked him not to go to Barnstable tomorrow.

★ ★ ★

"What are we going to do?" Kevin finally spoke once he and Annie were in the cottage and she'd put on the kettle.

"Exactly what the doctor told us," Annie said. "We're going to make sure she's comfortable. And we're going to let Georgia Nelson be in charge, because the doctor was right; they are merciful angels." She remembered the hospice volunteers who had brought Murphy comfortably through her last days. Propping her elbows on the table and cupping her chin with her hands, Annie said, "We'll do this together, Kevin. Like Donna wanted. I really think it's why she came here."

He went to her refrigerator and popped a beer. "Tell me about your parents again. How they died. If you don't mind."

It occurred to her then that Kevin had not witnessed death. The closest he'd come had been with Meghan, whose tragedy would linger as long as she was technically alive. So Annie took a deep breath and began. First, she told him about Brian. Then about Murphy. "I might have more experience at this than you, but, it's not the same. My dad and my husband died suddenly. My mother was in the hospital for six weeks and died there in her sleep. Murphy had her family, and by the time she passed away I was down here on the Vineyard. So I've never taken care of anyone. Not like this."

He chugged his beer. "And now you have to do it for a woman you barely know. That sucks."

Annie got up and fixed her tea, a bundle of emotions twisting inside her. "She's my mother, Kevin."

"Right," he replied, peeling the label from the bottle with his thumb. "And your father was the guy you know nothing about."

Annie leaned against the counter next to him. "That's not important anymore."

He nodded several times. "So we'll do this together? You. Me. And Georgia whatever-her-name-is?"

With a small laugh, Annie said, "Nelson. Georgia Nelson.

And yes. I'm game if you are. But please . . . don't take Mom back to Boston."

He nodded again, this time with purpose, as if strength had returned to his heart. "I won't. That's a promise."

Annie hoped it was the right decision for them all.

Chapter 26

Earl stopped by with food for their dinner: chowder, green salad, and apple turnovers fresh out of Claire's oven—which was really nice, because by then it was nearly seven, and Annie hadn't yet thought about what they might eat. Earl said he was sorry he didn't make it to the hospital, but Claire had made it clear that Donna needed Annie and Kevin, not him, and she'd insisted he stay home. When Annie told him about Donna's prognosis, Earl rubbed his forehead and uttered a heartfelt grunt. When Annie added that Donna would be in the hospital until Saturday, he said he had to go to the hardware store in the morning, so he'd stop in and see her. "And I'll be sure to tell her that her crate has arrived."

Though it nearly dominated the room, Annie had forgotten about the wood-slatted delivery.

As soon as Earl left, Kevin gestured toward it. "Give me a dollar, and I'll tell you what's in it."

"I only know it weighs a ton."

Without further comment, he pulled out his key ring—a Swiss Army knife dangled from it. But after quick examination, he scratched his chin the way Earl often did. "I definitely need something stronger. Got a crowbar I can use to pry this thing apart?"

"Not in the kitchen drawer," she said.

He rolled his eyes, then went outside. In half a minute, he returned, a tire iron in one hand. "Good thing I know my way around tools." He proceeded to jimmy the slats, each cracking, splintering, then giving way. In a matter of seconds, the interior was visible, though a thick layer of packing was wrapped around whatever was inside. He tore off a corner of the padded paper. "Yup," he said, "exactly as I thought. The Louis Vuitton."

Annie had become exasperated with his cloak-and-dagger game when other things were much more pressing, like the need to discuss how they were going to manage Donna's care in conjunction with hospice. She might even have preferred to talk about the fact that Donna was dying. But at least the distraction of the crate had stopped Kevin from crying.

Slow down, Murphy interjected just then. *There is time.*

So Annie closed her eyes. And breathed.

"You know about this?" Kevin asked.

"No."

He went back to prying—first one side, then the other. Then he said, "Okay, let's hope it comes out right side up." He overturned the crate, removed the final slats and peeled off all the packing. "Ta da!" he said.

Sitting in the middle of the room was a rectangular trunk in shades of brown and gold, about the size of a small coffee table. What appeared to be a canvas covering featured rows of decorative symbols interspersed with *LV* logos; narrow strips of wood on the top and sides decorated the trunk; leather straps, brass corners and studs, brass handles and a brass lock finished it . . . perfectly.

"Wow," Annie said. "It's gorgeous."

"Antique. Authentic, of course. Vintage early twentieth century," Kevin said. "You might not know it, but good old Louis started his business in 1854, in Paris, of course, on the Rue Something-or-other. He made a fortune off his trunks that had flat tops like this because they were lightweight and could easily be stacked. Not like those round-topped steamer ones."

"Wow," Annie repeated. "I did not know any of that."

"If Mom was willing to sell it—which I highly doubt—it could be yours for about thirty grand, give or take a few thousand. I'm not sure what the market is now."

Annie took a step back. "Thirty thousand *dollars?* It's a trunk! Are there gold bricks inside?"

"That's what it's worth empty. It's handcrafted, you know? But don't ask me what's inside. I have no idea. I only know I've never been allowed to touch it. Mom kept it in her bedroom, in a 'special place,' as she called it. She got it right after she opened the shop on Newbury Street."

"And you really have no idea what's in it?"

"Nope. I've never even seen it open. Of course, the more I was told NEVER to open it—'under ANY circumstances'—the more I wanted to. There's nothing like temptation to drive a kid nuts. For years, I searched for the key. Never found it. Somewhere around age twenty-five, I gave up on the damn thing."

"But the trunk is full?"

"I guess. 'Cuz I don't think it weighs this much by itself."

"And Donna wanted it here."

"Looks like."

"Maybe she'll let you look inside now?"

He scratched his chin again. "Ha," he said. "I wouldn't dare ask." He stared at the trunk a few more seconds then said, "We might as well slide it into the bedroom. My bet is she'll want it there." But his eyes had grown misty again, and he didn't move.

Annie put her hand up on his back. "Come on," she said. "I'll help. We can do this together." She hoped he knew she wasn't only talking about moving the trunk.

They ate a little dinner, then Kevin said he wanted to get back to work because manual labor helped calm his nerves; he said he had plenty of LED lanterns to provide enough light. As soon as he left, Annie put a call in to Georgia Nelson, which went straight to voice mail. While waiting for a response, she surveyed the bedroom, hoping it would be big enough if they needed a hospital bed for Donna. Annie knew so little about caring for a sick person. When Claire had had her stroke, Annie had helped out around their house and had done a few personal things for her when she came home from rehab. This time, however, things were different: Donna would not be rehabbing. Instead, she'd be waiting for her body to do what it was going to do. And when.

Looking at the trunk again, Annie was pleased that it fit nicely between the window and the bureau. She hoped its presence would bring Donna comfort. No matter what was in it. Annie smoothed her hand across the top, but when she reached the brass lock, her fingers stopped. If the trunk held secrets, they were not her secrets to investigate. Donna's life, after all, was not a book, and Donna wasn't one of Annie's characters.

Knowing it would be impossible to accomplish any work, Annie wondered if, though it was late, she should go back to the hospital and sit with Donna whether or not she was still sleeping. As long as a patient or visitor did not have a communicable disease, the hospital had no restrictions about visiting hours. But before Annie had a chance to opt for going or staying put, Georgia called. Annie brought her up to date; she also said that she and Kevin now knew that Georgia was with hospice.

"I hope you understand your mother didn't want either of you to know," the woman said.

"I do," Annie replied. "And I appreciate that you kept her confidence."

Georgia agreed to come early the next morning and prepare the cottage for Donna's return. "And don't worry, dear. Our goal is to make the family as comfortable as the patient." She added that the best thing Annie probably could do that night would be to stay home and rest. She did not need to elaborate that the coming weeks might be difficult.

Having Georgia in their corner made Annie feel better . . . as much as that was possible. So when they got off the phone, Annie cleaned up the kitchen and lay down on her own bed in the cottage. She fell asleep quickly.

Friday morning Annie woke up at seven, surprised that she'd slept through the night, startled when she realized she still had on her clothes. By the time she cleaned up and tossed some things for Donna into a canvas bag, Georgia arrived. They spent a few minutes going through the cottage one room at a time, with Georgia offering suggestions such as removing scatter rugs so Donna wouldn't trip and buying a stock of personal items for a patient who might be confined to bed for long periods of time. She also reassured Annie that she'd see them Monday morning as scheduled, and that because of Donna's setback, she could extend her stay through most of the afternoon. However, if Annie needed her before then, she wasn't far away.

By the time Georgia had left and Annie reached the hospital, she was fairly sure that her frame of mind was suitably secure. Musing over how to open a conversation with Donna, she paused at the doorway to the room. That's when she heard Earl's voice.

Earl? Already in Oak Bluffs before ten o'clock?

It was good to know that Donna was awake. However, knowing that once Earl got to talking, he liked to go on and on, Annie knew she had to get him to leave so he wouldn't wear out the patient. But as Annie quickly whirled into the room, she abruptly stopped. Earl was sitting by the side of the bed where Donna was lying . . . and he was holding her hand.

Really? She cleared her throat, and he withdrew his hand as if it had been in his lap all along.

It was a bit confusing, but Annie reminded herself that Earl could be that way sometimes. Mr. Reliable. Mr. Friendly. The pseudo Mayor of Chappaquiddick. She pulled a chair up to the opposite side of the bed.

"How are you doing?" she asked Donna with what she hoped was a respectful smile.

"Better. Not as weak. Sorry I gave everyone such a fright."

"I'm just glad we came along when we did."

Earl stood up. He seemed to have more color in his face than usual. Almost as if he were . . . blushing?

"I'll leave you ladies alone," he said. "I've got a big order to pick up at the hardware store."

They said good-byes, and he left. Annie asked Donna if he'd woken her up and if he'd exhausted her.

She shook her head. "I've been awake since six. Earl is pleasant company. I don't have many friends my own age, so it's nice that he and Claire are here."

Sometimes Annie forgot that Donna was older than she made herself look. That morning, however, as she lay under the scratchy, over-bleached sheet, Donna looked her age. And frail. And ill. Her clear complexion was almost powdery; the color of her eyes seemed to have faded. Were those things possible in a few short hours? Annie looked around the room, trying to frame her next question without staring at the wig that now was back in place. "Are you feeling better today?"

Donna nodded. "A little. Yes."

Annie squirmed in her chair. "I brought you a few things. . . ." She opened the bag and took out toiletries, Donna's silk robe, some clean underthings, and pants and a sweater for when she was released the next day, Saturday. "I hope you don't mind that I raided your clothes."

"Not at all. You are a dear."

Lowering her eyes, Annie said, "I only wish you'd let us know sooner how sick you . . . are." She pulled out a book she'd thought Donna might enjoy and the latest issue of *Martha's Vineyard* magazine. She set them on the nightstand.

"The less I talked about it, the easier it was to deny it," Donna replied. "Can you understand that?"

"I think so. But maybe we could have . . ."

Donna held up a hand, a plastic IV tube snaking up along with it. "You couldn't have done a damn thing. The fact is, I was hoping I'd simply fall asleep, and we never would have had to have the 'talk.'"

"About hospice?"

"And the rest."

"By 'the rest' do you mean how I'm more than a little angry that my birth mother might be leaving me before I've really gotten to know her?"

"Yes. I suppose that's what I mean."

"Well, so you know, I *am* angry. And I'm sad. For you. For me. For Kevin."

Donna turned her head toward the window. "Now that you know what's really going on, are you still all right with having me stay in your place?"

"Of course I am. But we'll put a twin bed in the living room. Earl and Kevin can take care of that. I want to stay with you, not up in the Inn. I want to be there if you need me during the night. That's not negotiable."

When Donna looked back to Annie, tears were in her eyes. "Now look what you've done. You've made an old lady cry."

Annie stood up, leaned down, and kissed Donna on the forehead. "My dad always said tears are caused by angel's kisses."

Donna closed her eyes. "I have a feeling your father was right about a lot of things."

It was odd to have Donna mention Annie's adoptive father, but Annie supposed it was no weirder than seeing Earl holding Donna's hand. But Annie well knew that dying often shifted people's perspectives.

Annie sat back down, and she and Donna began an honest conversation about hospice and expectations. Then an aide appeared with a coffee and cranberry juice and a blueberry muffin, saying they'd noticed that Donna had not eaten her breakfast and thought she might be hungry now. After the aide left, Donna begged Annie to help her eat because everyone there was so nice, and she didn't want them to think she was ungrateful.

They both had a few nibbles, then spent more than two hours keeping the conversation real, not holding back, or at least, Annie didn't hold back. She couldn't, of course, be sure if Donna did, but there was no need for that to matter. When her emotions had been drained, and Donna seemed tired, Annie said, "The Louis Vuitton is incredible."

Happiness sparkled across Donna's face. "You've seen it?"

"Kevin tackled the crate with a tire iron."

Donna laughed. "That boy has been wanting to get in there since the day it came home. I'm afraid it doesn't hold any buried treasure, but I didn't want him to dig around and mess up what I've put in there. Besides, the trunk is worth a good deal of money, and a curious boy might have marred it somehow."

"Yes, I heard it's pretty valuable."

"It's priceless to me." Donna closed her eyes then, and softly said, "Annie, when I'm gone, almost everything in there is yours. Except in the pocket inside the lid. There you'll find my brother's blue ribbon from the science fair. Oh, yes, and Kevin's Red Sox memories; he'll be surprised I have those. And there's a photo album for him. But don't tell him ahead of time, okay?"

Annie knew what Donna meant by "don't tell him ahead of time"—there was no need to ask her to elaborate. Before Donna could make any further comment, the day became more surreal: Taylor walked into the room.

"I'm checking in on the patient," Taylor said. "Not in any official capacity, of course." Her hair was knotted up in a large bun at the nape of her neck. She was not as attractive as when her auburn tresses spilled over her face.

Annie explained to Donna that Taylor had been the first responder.

The three of them made small talk for a while, until it was clear to Annie that Donna was done talking. "I won't come back later today," Annie said as she stood up. "But Kevin will be here. And he'll pick you up tomorrow, so I'll see you at home." Home, Annie thought. For as long as it would be for any of them. She kissed Donna's forehead and told her to call her if she needed anything or wanted to talk more.

"I'll be fine," Donna said, her smile genuine.

Taylor followed Annie into the corridor.

"I'm glad I caught you," Taylor said as the pair walked down the hall. "Kevin said you were here. I need to talk to you, Annie. I need a woman's perspective, so it's either you or Claire. I picked you."

Annie winced, but hoped it didn't show. She didn't want
to have to deal with Taylor or with whatever was going on
with her now—she needed to make sure the cottage was
ready for Donna's homecoming. But for Kevin's sake . . . Annie blinked. "Shall we have coffee at Linda Jean's?"

"That would be good."

"I thought Jonas left the island because he hated me," Taylor told Annie after they'd both ordered coffee and Annie a
tuna on rye because she realized it was almost one o'clock
and all she'd eaten that day were three small bites of a muffin.
"For all I know, he does," Taylor went on. "But I had a very
brief, very tense phone call from him. He said he had a message from a woman in Boston who saw that stupid video. He
didn't go to New York like I thought he might. He went to
Boston to meet that woman—who claims she knew me when
I was pregnant. And says she knows details about his father's
accident."

Annie felt disinterested and detached; she wanted to tell
Taylor that she was sorry but she couldn't help, that she had
enough problems of her own right then. But Annie was still
Annie, so instead, she said, "Oh, Taylor, I'm so sorry."

"I need you to try to get him to listen to reason. He's
all I have, but even if he never comes back to the Vineyard,
I can't let him ruin his life." Taylor looked drawn, her skin
blotchy, almost gray. As if she should be in a hospital room
near Donna's.

"Jonas seems like a nice young man, Taylor, but I hardly
know him. . . ."

Her eyes penetrated Annie's. "It's Lucy's fault," she said.

Annie flinched.

Taylor waved her hand, dismissing contradiction. "He
didn't come right out and say it, but I think Lucy put ideas
into his head. She shouldn't have gotten involved. She egged

him on in the beginning, posting the pictures, getting him to do that video. And trying to get him to do that ridiculous thing with DNA . . ."

Apparently Taylor either didn't know or didn't believe that the video had been Jonas's idea. As much as Annie wanted to set the record straight, she could tell that Taylor was a woman on a mission, and was not going to back down. Besides, Annie only wanted to go to the pharmacy and pick up a few things that Georgia had suggested, then go home and get busy rearranging the cottage for Donna. Again.

"As if Lucy hasn't done enough damage," Taylor continued to prattle, "now she's put together a website for him. Have you seen it? It doesn't mention the skull or his father, but it puts Jonas 'out there.' On the damn internet. With his artwork, like he's some kind of Picasso." Taylor's hand was trembling as she drank her coffee.

Annie had no idea where the relationship stood now between Kevin and Taylor, but if, after everything was over, they wound up being together, Annie supposed at least she should be able to feel that she'd tried to be Taylor's friend. And though Lucy had only been trying to be nice to Jonas because he was lonely, it did appear that she'd been a catalyst. Annie tried to summon some mental energy. "What would you like me to do?" she asked before she had time to change her mind.

"Call my son. Go find him, if you can. Tell him the woman is trying to scam him. He wouldn't tell me her name, but my gut tells me I know her. And I think she saw that video online and figured she could make some fast cash. Jonas is such an innocent."

"Exactly what did she tell him?" Once Annie heard the details, she might get more involved than she would have wanted, but she could not walk away. Not with John's daughter in the mix. *Lucy, Lucy,* she whispered to herself.

"The woman told him that even if the skull isn't Derek's—that was his father's name—she had information on who his birth father really is. She said it was a guy who lived on the Vineyard. And that I told her so."

Annie swallowed hard. "Did you?"

Taylor gripped her mug so hard her knuckles started to turn white. "No! For one thing, it isn't true! Derek is his father, not 'a guy' from the Vineyard! She claims she lived in the same building where the Flanagans sequestered me until Jonas was born. If it's who I think it is, she was nosy and always on the take. She slept with every guy she met—always married ones—then bribed them to keep her mouth shut."

"But if she made up a lot of details, I don't know how I can convince Jonas. . . ."

By then, Taylor's top teeth had sunk into her lower lip.

". . . but I'll try," Annie added, wishing someone was kicking her under the table. Where the heck was Murphy when she needed her? "I'll give him a call. But I can't go and try to find him. I'm going to be a little tied up with my mother." She reasoned with herself that it would only be one phone call. Then she could get back to worrying about Donna's situation. And the Inn, though the Inn might not matter anymore.

"Use Lucy's phone. If he thinks she's calling him, he'll probably answer." Then Taylor stood up. "I have to go now." She paid her share of the bill and marched out of the restaurant without saying good-bye.

Well, you've done it now, haven't you?

"Thanks a lot," Annie whispered. "But you're a little late."

She could have sworn she heard Murphy chuckle.

Chapter 27

Before heading back to Chappy, Annie texted John and asked him to call when he got home. Or sooner if he could. She said it wasn't urgent; she just wanted to hear his voice. There was no way she was going to report Donna's prognosis in a text.

Then she stopped at Basics in Oak Bluffs and picked out a pretty nightgown and a new pair of slippers for Donna, along with a warmer robe than the silk one. She went to the pharmacy and checked items off her list, then to Stop and Shop where she picked up ingredients for several meals so she wouldn't have to bother anyone to run errands at least for the first few days that Donna would be back. By the time she was finished she knew that school would be out, so she went directly to John's. She saw Lucy through the window; she was in the living room, engrossed in something on her iPad.

"Dad's at a meeting on the Cape," Lucy said when she opened the door. Restless greeted Annie with wet kisses.

"I know."

"He should be back on the seven thirty."

"Well, I'm not here to see him. I came to talk to you."

"What have I done now?"

"You sound guilty."

"You sound like a teacher."

"I was a teacher."

"I know." Lucy laughed, then invited Annie inside.

They sat down, and Annie gave Lucy a quick rundown of Taylor's plight. "I told her I'd help. Not only because she feels this is your fault, but also because she's been dating my brother, and I don't want to mess that up for him if he'd rather I didn't."

"She's weird."

"Sometimes."

"Do you really think Jonas is being scammed?"

"It sounds that way, yes."

Lucy seemed to think about that. "Yeah, you're probably right. He's vulnerable."

"He is."

She fidgeted with the iPad. "Did you see his website? It came out really cool." She passed the iPad over to Annie.

Annie didn't want to waste time looking at the site, but wanted to reassure Lucy about her work in having created the site—that she'd done a good job.

"Click on the menu bar to see the pages. . . ."

With a small smile, Annie said, "I know about navigation."

"Oh, sorry."

In a matter of seconds, Annie became surprisingly fascinated by what was on the screen. Page after page, image after image revealed outstanding art. Exceptional, simplistic landscapes, magnificent blends of colors and light, painted with textures created not only from brushes but also palette knives—and all were venues on Chappaquiddick. Picasso, indeed.

"Lucy? Are these really his?"

"Duh. Yeah. He's been working on his portfolio for years. Every summer that he's been here with his grandparents."

Annie was astonished. "These are incredible. Not to mention that they'd look amazing at the Inn. We could showcase his work throughout the common rooms where the most people would see them. What do you think? Would he like that?"

"Um, I think you should talk to him first, don't you? I'm not exactly his agent. Besides, I'm not even sure he wants to think about this place right now, let alone come back."

"Does he have the paintings with him?"

"The ones on his site are in storage in New York. Some place near where his grandparents live. I used his photos of them to create the gallery page."

Suddenly, Annie had another reason for wanting Jonas to return. It was a selfish one, but added to Taylor's relationship with Jonas and Kevin's relationship with Taylor and Jonas's future and maybe even Lucy's opportunity to have a good friend who she might help save from being lonely, the motivation had piled up. Calling the young artist now felt necessary. And a nice distraction from the sad things going on.

"May I use your phone?"

Lucy handed it over.

And Jonas picked up on the first ring.

Annie was tired, but she was happy about Jonas. Also, she was glad she'd asked the waitress at Linda Jean's to wrap up the rest of her sandwich—she wolfed it down on the quick ferry ride back to Chappy.

Even though he hadn't sounded terribly thrilled, Jonas had agreed to have two or three of his paintings shipped for her to hang in the Inn. "I'll do it for Lucy," he'd said, "for building my website."

But when Annie had broached the subject of the woman in Boston, he'd shut down. All he'd said was, "It's about my mother. And about who my father might or might not have been."

Which had turned Annie's thoughts to two things: first, how to stop Jonas from being scammed; second, who her own birth father was, and if she'd have the chance—or the courage—to ask Donna before it was too late.

She realized then that she was not only exhilarated, but also depressed as hell. Yin and yang. Or yang and yin. However that went.

When she pulled into the driveway at the Inn, she wondered when she should stop thinking about it as an Inn and start to face reality. It was Friday—four weeks to the day before their guests were due to arrive. Before their account would have money coming in instead of going out, or, as was the case now, before it would come in instead of inching closer to maxing out Earl and Kevin's American Express accounts. They didn't need to share the numbers with her for Annie to know that disaster was imminent.

As she parked the Jeep, she decided to sleep at the cottage again that night, before Donna came back. But first she would do the laundry and give the whole place a good scrubbing, which would be nice for Donna, not to mention that the activity might help boost Annie's mood.

With renewed purpose, Annie hauled the groceries and the other bags out of the back seat and made her way to the cottage. Just as she reached her front door, her phone rang. Juggling her purchases, she fished in her purse, pulled out her keys with one hand and the phone with the other, assuming that the caller would be John. So she didn't bother to check caller ID.

"Annie? Larry Hendricks."

She stopped. She squeezed her eyes shut. Next to Mark, Larry was the last person she wanted to talk to. Ever again.

She almost hit the END button, but then remembered the skull and all the people that the outcome would affect.

"What?" Her tone was angry; she could not seem to help it.

"First, I'm sorry Mark was with me. But whatever stupid thing he did to you, he's still my friend. He's often mentioned trying to find you, so . . ."

"Is that why you called, Larry? Because if so, I am not interested. Not even a little."

Silence hung in the late day air. Annie unlocked her door and snapped on the light. The place was tiny, but so homey. It was who she was now. She was no longer the person she had been when she'd been with Mark. Thank God.

"I'm also calling about the skull," he said. "It's a man. But *really* ancient. More than a century old."

Before her legs could give out, she dropped into the rocking chair, her bags sliding to the floor. A giant sigh escaped her lungs. "Jonas," she said.

"What?"

She shook her head. "Nothing. Thank you for the information. Do they know if it's Native American?"

"Not yet. I'll keep you posted. And again, I'm sorry about Mark." And then Larry hung up as quickly as he'd called.

All Annie could think was: more than a century old. So it wasn't Derek. Smiling a big smile, she slumped against the backrest. There were others she should call first: John, of course. And Kevin. Earl. Taylor. But instead of them, Annie scanned her phone numbers and dialed Jonas.

"It's not your father," she said when he answered. "The skull. It isn't him."

He was as silent as Larry had been when Annie said she wasn't interested in hearing his mea culpa about Mark. Then Jonas said, "So I still won't know what happened to him."

"No one will probably ever know for sure, Jonas. Maybe

it's time to trust your mother. Try to focus on the letters you have. The ones between your mother and your father. Believe in them. Because I do. I think your mother was a young girl caught in a terrible trap. I think they were very much in love and that they really did plan to elope to Hawaii. And raise you as their own."

With every word she spoke, Annie was thinking—and wondering— about Donna.

Jonas said nothing, so she added, "I'm sorry things didn't work out that way, Jonas. For all of you. But you do have lots of people here who care about you. Good people. People who believe in you and want to help. Instead of shipping me the paintings, won't you please come home? This is your home now. Chappaquiddick."

If they'd been in the same room, Annie thought she might have heard his heartbeat. Then he said, "I didn't mean to hurt my mom."

Annie laughed. "We always hurt the ones we love. Never mind, those were lyrics from an old song that you've probably never heard. Come home, Jonas. Your mother loves you. And so do we." The last line had popped out unexpectedly, but she realized it was how she felt about a lonely young man, with a solitary life, reeling from having been abandoned—again— that time by his girlfriend, seeking an answer where there simply was none.

But the best response was yet to come when Jonas simply said, "Okay."

In less than thirty minutes, Annie had gone from tired-but-happy to depressed to angry to peaceful. Her next call was to Taylor, because she deserved to know. Then she would call Kevin, because she was relieved for him, too.

John came to Chappy straight from the boat. Annie was asleep. "I wanted to return your text in person," he whispered as he crawled into bed beside her. "In case you were wondering, I love you. Very much."

In the morning, Earl didn't seem surprised to find them having coffee, sharing a cinnamon roll that he'd often said he thought she made only for him. He helped himself to coffee, took another roll—the last—out of the freezer, and stuck it in the microwave as if they were at his house instead of hers. Annie promised that she'd make more before Donna came home. Home. Yes, the cottage now was Donna's home, as well as Annie's.

She and John had talked most of the night; or rather, Annie had talked and he had listened. He'd held her close when she'd cried about Donna's situation; Annie had finally fallen asleep in his arms. It did not surprise her that she felt better now.

"What time is Kevin picking Donna up?" Earl asked.

"Around noon."

He nodded. "They must want her out of there before they have to serve her another meal. It's all about the insurance company's bottom line."

John laughed and stood up. "I'd better get home to my daughter."

"You tell her you had an emergency last night?"

John's face turned a little pink, the way Earl's had when Annie had walked into the hospital room and seen Earl holding Donna's hand. "She tell you that?"

Earl nodded. "She did. She also figured out it was not a police emergency. I'm only telling you that so you don't think your daughter's stupid."

"Believe me, I know full well that Lucy is anything but." John kissed Annie's cheek, fist-bumped his father, and went out the door.

"So," Earl said, "Kevin gave me the good news about your skull."

"It's not my skull," she corrected him for the thousandth time. "But, yes, as John said when I told him, 'at least it's one less hurdle.' The only obstacle left is the most important one."

"Yep. I also heard a rumor from my granddaughter that Jonas is coming back."

Annie wasn't surprised that Jonas had called Lucy. "Yes. I'm happy for Taylor."

"You did a good thing, Annie."

"I only told him the truth."

"Nonetheless, a good thing. Now, what about your mother?"

There was that word again, tossed at her from out of nowhere. By now she should be used it. Still, it made her feel a little bad for Ellen Sutton. "I was surprised to learn the truth about her yesterday."

"Go easy on her. She's dying, Annie."

Annie closed her eyes. "I know that, Earl. But it's hard to believe she wants me to be her daughter—to be with her until the end—when she didn't feel close enough to me to tell me what was really going on."

"Maybe she was afraid if she said the words out loud it might make it too real for her. Maybe it had nothing to do with you. Or with Kevin."

Tears welled; Annie brushed them away. "No more emotion right now, okay? I've had enough in the past two days to fill my quota for a year."

He laughed, grabbed the bun from the microwave, and took a hearty bite. "If Claire and I had ever been blessed with a daughter, I would have wished that she was just like you."

Annie's mouth tipped up in a smile. "Eat your breakfast, then please get out of here. I want to clean this place from top to bottom so Donna will be comfortable."

"Didn't you just do that a week ago?"

"Dear God, was that only a week ago? It feels more like a month."

Earl chewed, swallowed, and gave Annie a rare hug. Then he left the cottage, chuckling as he went. And Annie got to work. She began by stripping the sheets off the bed—sheets that still held the scent of the man who loved her. Life, she knew, could be better, but some parts could be much worse. She intended to always try to remember that.

By the time Kevin and Donna appeared, Annie had finished cleaning and clipped daffodils from the garden, arranging the flowers in a pretty vase that had belonged to her mother Ellen, and setting them in the center of the table. Then she'd made cinnamon rolls, followed by chicken sandwiches on warm wheat-berry bread from Orange Peel Bakery. She'd also made tomato and basil soup that simmered on the stove. The tomatoes had come from Chappy's own Slip Away Farm; Claire had showed Annie how to can last fall— a word that still befuddled Annie, as glass jars, not cans, were used. As for the basil, Annie had grown and dried it by herself. She hoped if Donna wasn't hungry, maybe the aroma in the cottage would feel welcoming.

Looking smaller, thinner, and tired, at least Donna was smiling as she stepped inside without Kevin's assistance. "My goodness," she said. "It looks lovely in here. And smells wonderful."

Annie returned the smile and hugged her. "Welcome home," she said. She hung up Donna's coat on a peg inside the closet door.

"Nice flowers," Kevin said. "You steal them from Earl's?"

"No. You must have been too busy to notice that ours have bloomed," she said with a note of pride. "I suppose you'll stay for lunch?"

"Me too?" came Earl's voice as he stepped in the doorway behind Kevin. "Then Kevin and I can go get your bed."

Except for the furniture in the room at the Inn where Annie had been sleeping, they'd told East Chop Sleep Shop in Vineyard Haven to hold the rest until the interior work was complete. The room that they were going to permanently reserve for Francine and Bella would have twin beds; Earl had arranged to pick one of those up that afternoon.

"Makes no sense to buy or rent one when we already bought one," Earl said. "We'll figure out something else, once we need it for the Inn." He not only spoke as if the Inn were going to open, but also as if Donna would still be there. In the nearly two years Annie had known him, she would not have thought that Earl would wind up being the optimist. No one, however, mentioned that, once they picked up the bed, the cost would show up on one of their credit cards. Unless the Louis Vuitton was filled with gold bricks after all.

Donna said she'd have a bowl of soup but would pass on the sandwich. Earl said he'd have the one that Annie had made for Donna. The four of them then squeezed around the cottage-sized table and shared a pleasant meal, the conversation brimming with hope.

"In case Annie's attorney friend is right, I made some housing inquiries," Earl said. "If the yahoos up in Boston can't give us an answer before Memorial Day, that doesn't have to mean our Canada goose is cooked. Hard as it might be to believe, I have a few friends here on the Vineyard. Even some on Chappaquiddick. And I've been asking around."

Kevin leaned back in his chair and folded his arms. "Asking around for what?"

Then Donna piped up, "Don't lean back in the chair that way, honey. You'll fall over and split your head wide open."

Annie and Earl laughed, but Kevin resumed a straight-up

position. "She's only saying it because I did it once. Well, I didn't exactly split my head wide open, but I did get a nice gash. Seven stitches."

"Eight," Donna corrected him. "Not to mention that it scared me half to death." No one acknowledged that she'd used the word "death."

Earl cleared his throat. "Anyway," he continued, "I've lined up a couple of places where our tenants can stay until we can officially open. They're only temporary, and they're not very special, but they're clean and, more important, they're available if we need them. I still need to find one more—I'd hoped Taylor would let us use Jonas's apartment, but now that he's coming back, that idea's out the window."

"But we're happy that he's coming back," Annie said firmly.

"Yup," Earl replied. "We're going to need his extra pair of hands once we get the go-ahead to finish."

"*If* we get the go-ahead," Kevin said.

"We will," Earl said, then winked at Donna. "Donna and I discussed it, and she insists we should stay positive, so that's what I'm doing. As soon as I did, then like that"—he snapped his fingers—"two solutions out of the three appeared under our noses. Or rather, under my nose, I suppose."

It was really sweet that he'd befriended Donna—for all his yakkety-yak tendencies, Earl was a good person. And Annie was pleased that his presence seemed to keep Donna's spirits up. Even so, she wasn't sure that Claire would have approved of her husband's winking at another woman, or holding her hand, whether she was sick or not.

Then Donna stood. She wobbled a little. Annie, Kevin, and Earl reacted quickly by reaching out, ready to steady her. Donna laughed. "Stop! I'm fine!" They pulled their arms back in unison. "And right now, despite the wonderful news about the rooms, I'm sorry, but I must break up the party because I need to rest." She turned to Annie. "Thank you for the delicious soup. I hope there will be enough left for dinner." She then smiled and wobbled into the bedroom, closing the door behind her.

"Okay," Earl said, standing, too. "Let's get to Vineyard Haven, Kevin. My truck or yours?"

They picked Kevin's truck because the back was bigger.

Annie sent them off with two baggies of chocolate chip cookies, as if they needed baggies, as if the cookies wouldn't be devoured before they made it to the *On Time*. It seemed strangely inappropriate to feel the energy of happiness, given the circumstances with Donna, but Donna had insisted that they all stay positive, so Annie was determined to try to do her part. If only one of Earl's comments wasn't niggling at her: "In case Annie's attorney friend is right . . ."

Enough! she thought. Then she knew that while so much that was happening was out of her control, there might be one thing she could put to rest.

Chapter 28

If she waited long enough, Annie knew she might change her mind.

So she went outside into the shed where the trash barrels were kept. She hadn't put on gloves because she didn't want to waste time trying to find some, and, besides, it was her trash, anyway.

Three barrels were full. She thanked God and the universe that Kevin had been so busy that he hadn't yet gone to the transfer station. She dragged out the first, unhooked the lid, hoisted the barrel, then dumped it upside down. The contents spilled onto the lawn, and Annie started to dig through them.

A couple of beer bottles that Kevin should have recycled; cleaning remnants from Annie's tear through the cottage before Donna's arrival; two old towels that she'd tossed; the ferry stub from Donna's passage. Things that had been thrown out earlier than what Annie was seeking. She stuffed it all back in and replaced the lid.

Barrel number two held the latest things: latex gloves and medical wrappers that had held who-knew-what and had been torn open when Donna was passed out; miscellaneous bits and pieces; padded packing paper from the Vuitton trunk. Again, not what Annie needed.

As soon as she upended the third barrel, she knew it was the right one: parchment paper and other remnants from the cookies that she'd made for dinner at Earl and Claire's (she'd been polite and brought her rubbish home from the community center); the random notes Annie had scribbled during Georgia Nelson's visit; the wrapper from Lucy's date nut bread that Annie and Donna had enjoyed . . . when? Yes! It was the same night that Mark had showed up at the door. She quickly rifled through the rest and, finally, there it was: the small white business card. MARK LEWISTON. COMMERCIAL PROPERTY CONSULTANT.

She shoved it in her pocket, stuffed the trash back into the barrel, and pushed all three barrels into the shed. Then she marched back to the cottage, willing her stomach to stop tumbling, forcing her brain to focus on Donna's mantra and stay positive.

Once inside the cottage, she took her phone out of her purse, then went back outside so her voice wouldn't disturb her mother. Her hand wasn't even trembling when she tapped in the number, but her throat closed up a little when she heard his voice.

"Mark Lewiston. How may I help you?"

Did she really want to do this? Did she really want to ask if he knew if Larry had told her the truth? Did she really want to pin her hopes—*their* hopes: hers, Kevin's, Earl's, and the rest—on a man who had once nearly destroyed her life?

"Hello?" his voice repeated.

Then Annie heard herself say, "Mark, it's Annie."

There was silence on the other end. Perhaps he'd hung up. But she thought she heard him breathing.

"Annie? Are you going to yell at me? 'Cuz if you are, please get it over with. I deserve everything you have to say."

She hadn't expected him to sound as if he'd been the one who'd phoned her, as if he'd been practicing those words and hadn't been caught off guard.

"I need help," she said, not acknowledging his question. "Did Larry tell you why I'd been in touch?"

"About that skull?"

"Yes. He said it's over a century old. I need to know if that's true or if he's screwing with me. I also need to know how much longer it will be before we know the rest—whether or not it's Native American."

Mark paused again. "First, I'm sure it's true, Annie. Larry has no reason to lie to you. Second, I know as many people as he does. You could have called me. It's in the archeologist's office, right? I'm always running into issues about historic sites we're trying to develop."

She hadn't figured out what her next words would be, so she was surprised when they came out sounding coherent. "Even if I had known where to find you, Mark, why on earth would I have called?" Before he could respond, she pictured her support team—Donna, Kevin, Earl, John—and went back to the topic. "But yes, the remains are at the archeologist's office. It might not seem like a big deal, but there's a lot at stake."

"I don't think I can reach anyone before Monday. But I'll let you know. I'll head up there as soon as I can get a boat."

"A boat?" The question jumped out on its own.

"I'm still on the Vineyard, Annie. Your friend, the cop, threatened me within an inch of my life, but I'd really hoped to see you. I thought if I hung around long enough we'd run into each other. It isn't crowded here right now, is it?"

She froze. She looked out toward the harbor, toward Edgartown. Was he staying over there? Was he right across the water at the Harbor View? Was he standing on the veranda, looking across to Chappy, hoping to catch a glimpse of her?

She ducked back into the cottage and lowered her voice. "I don't want to see you, Mark. I only want the information."

She counted: three, four, five, until he answered.

"Okay," he said. "I owe you that much."

Annie held off saying that he owed her so much more.

When she got off the phone, Annie realized that her heart was pounding, had probably been pounding from the time she had decided to call Mark. She shuddered now and pulled her sweater close around her. She had no way of knowing if she'd made a big mistake. For starters, John might never speak to her again. And there was no reason on the planet why Mark would have told her the truth. Even if he knew as many people in the archeology department as Larry did.

She knew she should tell John before he found out another way. Especially since Mark was still on the island. Maybe if John learned it from her, he'd be more inclined toward forgiveness. Wasn't that what people in a relationship did?

But as soon as she lifted her phone to call him, a familiar voice called out, "Hello?" followed by the sound of a barking dog. Apparently, Lucy and Restless had come to visit. Again. Shielding her eyes, Annie watched them trundle down the slope. They were followed by a large woman, silhouetted in the afternoon shadows. It took only seconds for Annie to realize it was Winnie.

They walked on the beach in the opposite direction of the spot where Annie had found the skull. Lucy and Restless raced ahead, Lucy tossing twigs of driftwood, Restless catching them, then dropping them onto the sand.

"I was on my way to see you when I spotted Lucy walking along Main Street, looking lonely and forlorn. I suggested that she and the dog hop into the van and come on over. I hope you don't mind."

"Not at all. I love it." Annie knew Winnie must be right, that Lucy was feeling lonely and forlorn, what with Jonas gone and Maggie's mother having forbid her daughter to see Lucy. "But what prompted you to drive way down here on a Saturday afternoon?"

"Claire called me this morning. She said you've been having a devil of a time. I needed to know why didn't you call or come up island to see me."

"I almost did one day. But I got sidetracked with another situation." Annie filled Winnie in on the saga about Jonas and Taylor and the role Lucy had played.

"And on top of this, I was told your birth mother is very sick."

Annie nodded. "And there's the skull."

"Yes," Winnie said. "After I talked to Claire I went to see our tribal council. The people in Boston had already alerted them. . . . The tribe is always notified when cases like this come up. The council chair knows the archeologist, so we're usually brought into the loop fairly quickly, which helps get the testing on the fast track. You've probably been told that if it's one of ours, we get to choose what to do with the remains; the state police take any necessary measures about the property. Which is why I came today. I figured that the Inn might be in jeopardy."

Annie nodded. "It is. Very much, I'm afraid. I should have thought to call you. I'm surprised Earl didn't. He never mentioned that the tribe might have a say in speeding up the process."

"I'm not sure he knows. It's especially tenuous if the property is in financial trouble, and the owners are trying to get out from under. We've actually had situations where fake artifacts were planted so the owners could pretend that the land belongs to us. It gets them off the hook while they maintain their dignity." Winnie paused and looked up at the colors that were softening on the horizon. "Our leaders have discovered that you're in debt."

Sinking down onto the beach, Annie sat back on her heels. She picked up a handful of sand and let it trickle through her fingers. "We are. Kevin underestimated the building costs. I've seen the books. I don't think he factored in enough for the added expense of shipping the materials over on the boats. Not to mention that a lot of boats were canceled over the winter. Some cancellations were weather-related; more were mechanical issues. No one could have predicted that. And Kevin hadn't known that when a boat doesn't run, we still have to pay for the truck and driver by the hour, even when they're simply sitting in Woods Hole, waiting to get across."

Winnie sat beside her. "It's happened before. Businesses can get stuck through no fault of their own."

"A hazard of island life?"

"One of them. Yes."

Annie let more sand sift through her fingers. "If it means anything, Winnie, I really doubt that either Kevin or Earl are behind this. Planting a skull? No. They wouldn't do that. Not for any reason."

Winnie nodded. "I know that. I told the tribal council. Still, we have to wait. None of this will matter if they determine that the remains are not Native American. But I wanted you to know what you're up against."

Annie watched Lucy playing with Restless. At fourteen, her innocence would probably not last much longer; Annie hoped it would never morph into stupidity the way hers once had done. Then she said, "I called my ex-husband, Winnie. I can't believe I did that."

"Isn't he missing?"

After Annie and Winnie had become fast friends, she'd shared the gruesome story of her marriage to Mark and its consequences. "He was missing. For more than ten years. But like a fool, I called his best friend, Larry, who's an assistant district attorney in Boston. I thought Larry might have contacts in the archeologist's office. Someone who could make our problem a priority. The next thing I knew, Mark showed up here. Donna tried to shoot him."

Winnie laughed. "I think you'd better start at the beginning, Annie. This sounds like one of your books."

"If I'd made it up, I would have invented a happy ending." Annie started with the day she and Lucy had walked the beach in search of tchotchkes, and ended with her conversation with Mark minutes ago. "And now I've opened a door I never should have. I should have just let whatever's going to happen, happen. I've been too worried about losing the Inn, when I should have focused on building a relationship with my birth mother who, it appears, is going to die soon."

Winnie put her arm around Annie's shoulder. "You were trying to help the ones you love. There's nothing wrong with that."

"If it's determined that this is sacred ground and we can't open the Inn, Kevin and Earl will lose a lot of money. And Kevin and I will lose our home. Not to mention that we were trying to make this a home for a few islanders who can't find one they can afford."

"My goodness," Winnie said. "It sounds like you feel responsible for a whole lot of people."

"Donna needs to come first. Why can't I focus on her? I should be happy that she wants to be with me for her last— I don't even know what they are—days? Weeks? Months? Of course, if I keep making myself busy doing other things, I won't have to confront her about the one thing I'd like to know: who my birth father is. I don't know if she'll tell me, but I do know that she's going to die, and then I'll never have the chance."

They sat quietly for a few more minutes, thinking private

thoughts, watching Lucy and Restless bound up and down the beach.

Then Winnie said, "One thing at a time. I'm glad you were able to help Jonas come back to the island. His mother is a native. And don't tell Lucy or she'll turn green with envy, but Taylor has some Wampanoag in her. Her paternal grandmother. So Jonas has our blood, too. As for the skull, I can put a word in to try to accelerate things even more quickly. When are you scheduled to open?"

"The Friday of Memorial Day weekend. Less than four weeks now."

Winnie nodded. "Okay. I'll see what we can do. But as for your ex, it sounds like you're still angry. You have the right to be. But even the best lives can't be lived to their full potential if anger lies beneath. Maybe this is your chance for closure."

"Are you kidding? If Mark comes snooping around again, never mind Donna, I don't know what John will do. It's going to be bad enough when I tell John that I called Mark."

Winnie nodded. "I guess you'll have to work through that. So why don't you sit here a spell and watch Lucy and Restless, which is the strangest name I've ever heard for a dog, but it seems to fit. Stay here on the beach, and I'll go up to the cottage. I only met Donna MacNeish once when she visited you last year, but I'd like to tell her what terrific kids she has."

Thirty minutes later, after having left word with Lucy that she'd be gone for a little while, Annie was sitting at one of the long picnic tables at Memorial Wharf, waiting for Mark. It hadn't taken long for her to realize that Winnie had been right; Annie needed closure for her life from hell, as she'd come to think of the years that had followed him. The years until she'd moved to the Vineyard and begun her new life.

Thankfully, he hadn't yet left the island; he couldn't get a boat until the eight thirty.

Annie sat facing the harbor, not wanting to see him approach from Dock Street behind her, not needing to see the swagger in his walk that had first attracted her, that bad-boy kind of walk that had once said, "Come and get it," and, stupid her, she had. He had swaggered into her life at a time when she'd been sad and scared. She was grateful she was no longer that young woman.

As she waited, she listened to the gulls and watched a few old fishing boats bobbing in the harbor that would soon be filled with sailboats and small, yet dazzling yachts. She began to realize that, in truth, her life had started to change long before she'd moved to the island; instead, it was when Murphy had encouraged her to take the writing course, when she'd helped Annie find the strength that was—had been—inside her all along. What was it that the good witch had said to Dorothy in *The Wizard of Oz*? That she'd always had the power, but she'd had to learn it for herself? Annie's third graders had loved that story; Annie hoped that someday they, too, would learn the truths beneath its words.

"Annie." Mark walked to the other side of the table and stood facing her. The years had hardly changed him. He still looked youthful and as handsome as he had the day they'd met. His hair was still golden-boy-blond, his body firm and sexy, his skin lightly touched with tan that looked real, not from a booth. Golfing, Annie thought. In Palm Springs. Or St. Kitts. But despite the way he looked, Annie no longer felt a shred of desire.

"Sit," she said, gesturing toward the bench.

"Do you have a gun?" he asked with a smile that revealed that his teeth were still straight and as white as if he were a model for sparkling toothpaste.

She smiled back because she knew it wouldn't hurt her. "No gun." And so he sat. She could have told him who the woman was who'd wielded the twenty-two. But that would have exposed her life to him again, and he did not deserve to know about the happiness she'd found. Yes, she thought, she did have happiness. Some sorrow, but more happiness.

"You look well," he said.

"Thank you," she replied. There was no need to return the compliment. Men—or women, she supposed—who had movie-star genes like Mark knew exactly how they looked. "My wardrobe has changed a little." That was when she realized she was in her comfort clothes—a flannel shirt, jeans, short boots. She'd pulled her hair into its casual, short ponytail, not caring if the silver streaks were more noticeable that way. She'd also foregone wearing makeup; she rarely wore it anymore.

"It suits you," he said. She almost thought he'd intended to be nice until he added, "Though I have to say I'm surprised you're living here. God, what do you do all day, day after day? Other than during July and August, does anything really happen on the Vineyard?"

"I write books," she answered. "And I make soap." She could have told him that she also now canned vegetables because she enjoyed spending time with Claire, or that sometimes she went fishing with John because it was fun, or that she loved being part of the artisan festivals and that she planned to get into gardening, having been inspired by helping with the Garden Tour the previous year. She could have told him that her calendar was packed with films and plays and lectures, and that she had wonderful, trustworthy friends. But Annie doubted that he'd care about any of it. More important, she did not care to tell him.

"Yeah, I heard you were a writer. You make any money at it?"

The wrath that had long simmered in Annie might have boiled up then. But time and circumstances finally enveloped her in healing kindness, and she simply said, "I didn't ask you to meet me to talk about money. I wanted to let you know I don't need you to get involved with anyone in Boston about the remains. It's been taken care of. But thank you, anyway."

For a second, Mark almost looked dejected. Then he squared his shoulders. "Really?"

"Really." She made sure to hold her head high. "And thanks for meeting me. But I have to get back to Chappy now." She unknotted her legs from beneath the picnic table bench and stood up. He stood, too, and went around the table, blocking her path toward the *On Time*.

"Annie," he said. "I've missed you."

She shook her head. "No, Mark. You might have missed the woman that you thought I was. But that wasn't me. The real me is here. The real me is happy. Go back to Boston. We were finished long ago."

He touched her arm. "I'm sorry. About all the bills I left."

It would have been a lie if later she told herself that she didn't feel a twinge of anger then, that she hadn't had to hold back from shouting that she'd paid his bloody bills, every last dollar, every last cent of them. It would have been a lie if she believed she hadn't wanted to spit straight in his face. Progress, she thought, isn't always easy.

But it also wouldn't have been honest if she had said, "No problem. I took care of it." So instead Annie told him, "I've decided that if we're lucky, we get to learn from our mistakes." She smiled again, then slipped from his touch, and headed back to the *On Time*, feeling lighter than she had in years, not caring if he watched her walk away.

Chapter 29

Winnie was stepping out of the cottage as Annie was return-
ing. Annie told her where she'd been and what she'd done;
Winnie responded with one of her loving hugs. But she was
quiet, unusually subdued.

"I've had a lovely visit with your Donna," Winnie said as
she led Annie from the cottage, up toward the Inn. They sat
along one of the newly built stone walls that framed the terrace. "Lucy's with her now. When I left them, the dog was on
the bed. I hope that's okay with you."

"If Donna likes him there, absolutely. Whatever she finds
comforting."

"I think what she finds most comforting is being here.
With Kevin and you."

"I hope the outcome of the archeological tests doesn't
boot us off the land before . . ."

"Before her time has come?" Winnie patted Annie's
hand. "Let's not worry about that. The tribal council knows
the value of family and the importance of living . . . and of
dying."

Annie nodded. Then she said, "At least I finally had closure with Mark."

"And how are you after seeing him?"

"He's the same. I'm the one who has changed."

"Life changes all of us when the time is right. Speaking of which, I suggest you have a talk with Donna. There are things she wants to tell you."

"Such as?"

Winnie smiled. "They're not for me to say. Just remember to be patient and listen carefully. And that though most of us do foolish things throughout our lives, we're all just flesh and blood. There's no getting around that." Then Winnie stood. "Now this old flesh and blood of mine needs to get on the road before the light of day totally fades. I called Earl; he'll pick up Lucy. She'll spend the night with them. The dog, too." She placed a finger on her chin. "I suppose that means John will be alone tonight."

Annie laughed. "Thanks for the thought, but I'll stay here with Donna. Especially since you've given me so much to think about."

"Ah, but that can wait another day. Your John matters, too. And I'll bet that Kevin would be happy to stay here to-night."

"He and Earl went to get another bed . . ."

"Earl told me. Which was when I came up with the idea for Kevin to sleep in the cottage." Then Winnie ambled toward her van, her long plait bouncing on her back. The van rumbled to life, and off it went into the gathering sunset.

By the time the men returned, it was dark. Still, using Kevin's truck headlights to guide them, they managed to unload the bed and haul it inside without scratching, nicking, or dropping anything. Annie put sheets and a warm blanket on the mattress for her brother; Restless promptly leaped on top and snuggled down.

"Out!" Annie cried, and everyone laughed, and Earl took

his granddaughter by the arm and his granddog by the leash, and they said good night. At the top of the hill, Earl reached inside Kevin's truck, turned off the headlights, and turned with a final wave.

"I'll be back in the morning," Annie then told her brother. "Will you be okay? There's lots to eat, and soup if Donna wants . . ."

"Out, yourself!" Donna called from the bedroom. "Kevin and I lived under the same roof for over twenty years. We'll be fine."

"And John is waiting," Kevin whispered to Annie. "Earl called him after he talked to Winnie."

And that's when Annie knew that love on Martha's Vineyard was often the result of a conspiracy.

As much as Annie had grown to love the little black-and-white, furry ball, she was grateful that he hadn't been in his house during the night, encroaching on her space in John's bed. Or in the morning, when John had pulled her close and they'd made love again. Each time they were together, it felt more and more right. She hadn't realized how wrong she and Mark had been together, how she'd never just felt free to be herself. She stared at the Vineyard light that slid through the blinds now and warmed her face. For so many years, she'd been convinced she'd never love again, yet here she was, wondrously in love with a man who loved her back.

John reached over to her again, and Annie laughed. "You are a crazy man!"

"A lovesick man," he mumbled into his pillow. And she moved onto him, finally believing that this really was happening, and that she could trust it.

"You're right, I was crazy," he said a short time later when he finally admitted that he was spent, "so I think it's time we got married."

Though she'd heard him perfectly fine, Annie whispered, "What?"

"I want to marry you, Ms. Sutton. If you'll have me."

She toyed with the dust flecks that danced on the sunlight. "John, I don't know. . . ."

"You don't know if you love me?"

"I do know that. I know that for certain. But so much is happening . . ."

"Don't you get it? 'So much' will always be happening. You'll have the Inn, or maybe not; we'll have Lucy to challenge the hell out of both of us; and God knows what else will come our way. I've been thinking more and more about this since I met your ex. Call me old-fashioned, but I want to protect you forever from that kind of guy."

She leaned over, pushed back a small lock of his hair, and kissed his forehead. "And I love you for that weird, old-fashioned thinking. But I married Mark because I'd lost Brian. I didn't love him; I couldn't risk loving anyone again. That's in the past. I know I love you. I know I want to be with you, but . . ."

"But what?"

"Well, first, there's my mother. Donna."

"If we tell her it might bring some happiness to her last days. Maybe she'll get on board with planning a wedding."

Annie couldn't argue with that. Then, without thinking, she said, "She did try to shoot him, you know."

John closed his eyes. "I did not hear that. But if it's any help, I'd already figured it out."

"And if we're cleared to open the Inn, where would you and I live? If I'm going to manage the place, don't you think I need to live there?"

"I've thought about that, too. If it all happens, maybe Kevin could take over the cottage. They still haven't built his apartment over the workshop, have they?"

"No. But Donna's still with us, remember?"

"Oh. Right."

"Well, then, you could move in here."

"Not while she's still alive. I need to be with her. And I need to be on site for the Inn."

"I don't suppose there will be extra rooms for Lucy and me? And the dog?"

She laughed. "Sorry. We're booked solid."

He pouted. "This is ridiculous."

"The thought of marrying me?"

"No. It was my idea, remember?"

"Well . . ." she said, tracing her fingers across his muscle-taut chest, "what if we get officially engaged? And worry about the marrying part once things have settled down?"

He thought for a moment, then he agreed.

By the time Annie got back to the Inn, Kevin and Earl were hard at work on the upstairs bedrooms. The downstairs was complete except for the furniture in the great room. But, as with the rest of the beds and bureaus, the deliveries had to wait until they figured out how to pay for them. Annie had already decided that the first half of the advance for *Bedlam in the Blue Room* would cover much of it, and she really wanted to chip in. In the meantime, as long as Kevin and Earl were determined to stay positive, she might as well get serious about collecting decorative pieces, including the art. With Jonas coming back, maybe he could help gather Vineyard natural pieces that would complement his paintings that Annie chose with Donna's help.

"Mom wants to see you," Kevin said.

"Is she okay?"

"About the same I think. But she said she was really tired this morning."

"Probably from the trip back from the hospital." Annie was looking forward to Georgia Nelson's starting the next day; in spite of the guidance Georgia had already provided, Annie feared that she'd do something wrong.

Kevin kept painting and didn't answer. His moods were still swinging these days—Annie didn't know if it was only because of Donna, or if part of it was due to Taylor, whom he no longer mentioned, and, as far as Annie could tell, he was no longer seeing. Maybe it was both those things plus the money issues. She would talk to him later. And she certainly wouldn't flaunt her engagement to John.

Her engagement!

Annie Sutton, on the dark side of fifty, engaged to be married for a third time. Murphy would have been excited; she would have been her maid of honor and made sure the day was perfect. And she, too, would have loved John.

With a small lump in her throat, Annie left the Inn and went down to the cottage. She had once thought she'd grown used to having people she loved leave forever, but now, with Donna's situation, sorrow had returned. "Every loss reminds you of every loss you've ever had," she'd once read, back when she'd been grieving over Brian, her parents, Murphy. . . . *Stop!* she ordered herself, as she'd had to do too often lately. Then she put on her game face and went into the cottage.

Donna was in the living room, sitting in the rocker, wrapped in Ellen Sutton's quilt. Ironic, Annie thought, then she heard Murphy whisper: *Or is it?*

Clearing her throat, Annie asked, "How are you this morning?"

Donna smiled back, tilting her head in an "Oh, you know" kind of way. "Did you have a nice night?"

Annie sat on the sofa. "Can you keep a secret? An absolute secret for a few days anyway?"

"I been known to keep secrets for years."

Annie knew that. "How about one that I think might make everyone happy?"

"Is it about the skull?" Donna's eyes grew hopeful.

"I wish. But it's something even better. At least it is to me."

"And it is . . . ?"

"John and I are engaged."

Donna sucked in a short breath. "To be married?"

"Well, yes."

"My goodness. That is a surprise."

"We're so right together, Donna. He's smart and kind, and he gives me space. . . ."

"But where will you live?"

Annie hadn't expected that question so quickly. She hoped Donna wouldn't think they'd ask her to leave the cottage. "We won't get married until we know what's going on with the Inn."

"And with me? Like if I'll be out of the way?"

The comment was a jolt to Annie's gut. "Please don't say that. We want you in our lives. In fact, we're counting on you to help plan the wedding."

"In that case, you'd better hurry." So much for Donna's pledge to stay positive.

"Please . . . don't . . ."

Donna shook her head. "I'm sorry I said that. I want only happiness for you, my dear girl. I would love to know that at least one of my children is stable and happy."

So she, too, was worried about Kevin. "I think Kevin is going through a bumpy time right now."

"He needs to do some serious thinking. Especially about that awful woman."

"Taylor? She's not awful. Not really. She's . . . different. She's had a difficult life. . . ."

"Giving her baby away and then trying to reclaim him?

At least I gave you the dignity of having your own life. And happiness to the people who adopted you."

And that's when Annie knew it was the perfect chance to ask about her birth father. Short of having her DNA done and praying that he—or one of his other children if he'd had any—had had his done as well, Annie knew the only way she'd find out would be to ask.

"You did give me that dignity, and for that I thank you. I'm sure Bob and Ellen Sutton would, too, if they were here."

Donna didn't reply. Perhaps she was feeling the loss. Or guilt. Or envy. Then she said, "Kevin also is upset because he wants me to tell you something."

The lump reappeared in Annie's throat. Had Kevin warned Donna that Annie was going to ask about her father? "Tell me what?"

Donna rubbed a corner of the quilt where a square of red tartan plaid was stitched, a remnant leftover from the skirt Ellen had made for Annie's first day of second grade. The skirt that she'd been wearing in the picture in the old blue photo album in the bookcase. "I gave them the money," Donna said.

Annie was confused. Money? What money? Did Donna give money to Annie's birth father? She'd told Annie she hadn't had any money back then. So why would she have given him any? Had it been some kind of payoff? Annie had used blackmail as a theme in two of her books, but only when it had involved murder.

"I gave Kevin the money," Donna added. "And Earl."

Kevin and Earl? What did they have to do with Annie's birth father?

"I don't understand," Annie said. "Why did you give them money?"

Donna sighed. "For the Inn. I gave them the money to buy the Littlefield property. The place where we're sitting right now."

Now Annie really was confused. "What?"

"Did you not hear me?"

"I assumed Kevin sold a couple of his condos. I thought Earl . . . Well, I don't know what I thought about where his share came from."

"As far as Kevin goes, his condos are tied up because they're in his business's name. His wife's still listed as an officer. Vice president, I think."

"But Meghan is . . . incapacitated."

"Well . . ." Donna sighed. "In any event, these things take time to unravel. And he has to be willing to do so."

"Wait. I thought he sold his business to pay for her long-term care?"

"He did. But he only sold his customer list. Not the corporation. Or the personal assets. It's complicated. Which I think is why he hasn't wanted to address it. And partly why he still isn't divorced. It's too damn painful for him."

Annie knew the kinds of things that emotional pain could do to an otherwise reasonably intelligent person.

"I put up Earl's share of the money, too," Donna continued. "That wonderful man has a house, some land, and a big heart, but he doesn't have squat in the bank."

"*What?*"

Donna shrugged, then huddled further down into the quilt. "You didn't have a place to live, Annie. Kevin wasn't faring much better. Oh, sure, he had condos. And an income from the rents. But he was depressed. Very depressed. So when he and Earl came to talk to me one day . . ."

"Wait. Earl and Kevin went to Boston?"

"Late last summer. Just for a day. I believe you were busy helping Claire. Anyway, their proposition made sense to me. So the money for the Inn wasn't Earl and Kevin's. It was mine."

Annie thought she must be dreaming. She must still be in

bed, lying next to John, and dreaming. Had he asked her to marry him?

She shook her head. "I'm sorry, Donna. This is all too much. . . ."

"There's nothing to worry about. I had the money from my business. I still have my apartment and the furnishings, but the trust that I mentioned to you earlier doesn't exist. The funds all went into this place. And I recently sold my car. Which was the real reason I took the bus down to the ferry. I never made a fortune, and I tended to spend more than I should have, but selling the shop gave me a tidy sum. The only part that makes me sad is that it was your inheritance. And Kevin's. Other than my apartment, I'm afraid nothing is left. But, like I said, Kevin still has his condos, so if he ever gets a move on with his divorce, and if everything else goes down with the ship—or should I say, the Inn—I'm sure he'll find a way to help you out."

Annie couldn't speak for a long moment. Then she said, "Thank you," because it seemed like the only thing to say. She could have told Donna that financially she was starting to do much better, now that she'd paid Mark's debts and her books were selling well. But it seemed important to Donna to think that her son would take care of her daughter, that her little family would be together.

Then Donna announced that she supposed this had all come as a shock to Annie, which was an understatement, so she should take time to digest it. As for Donna, she needed a nap.

And as for Annie, she grabbed her laptop and went outside to the porch, glad to be in the fresh air, her head and her heart abuzz, her stomach spinning like a waterspout in tornado season. After a while, she got to work, outlining the rest of her novel, distraction being her best method of coping.

Chapter 30

Late that afternoon, Jonas came back to the Vineyard. Annie found out when both she and Kevin had quit working for the day, and she'd coerced him into taking her seat on the porch in case Donna woke up. Then, without sharing that she knew about Donna's investment in the Inn, Annie had taken a quick trip off Chappy, over to Edgartown not to see John, not to go shopping, not to drive up to Aquinnah to visit Winnie, but to sit at a picnic table on Memorial Wharf again and gaze at the current churning in the harbor, and finally mull over her talk with Donna.

It hadn't been the right time for Annie to ask about her birth father. But would there be enough time left when other things were more pressing? Or was she destined to never know?

She viewed the *On Time* come and go; she listened to the gulls, watched an old man fishing dockside, and studied the boats bobbing at their moorings, water gently lapping at their hulls. Nearly an hour had passed when she supposed she should get back to Chappy. But as she stood up, she glanced toward the ferry queue on Daggett Street and saw Jonas's SUV waiting to drive on. Even from that distance, she knew the vehicle was his by the large canvases and the artist's easel stacked in the back.

She jogged over as he moved up the small ramp. Then she skipped on board the ferry and waited until he'd turned off the engine before going over to his open window.

"Jonas! I'm so glad to see you." For all the weighty things that she was trying to deal with, Jonas had a whole lot more—had always had a whole lot more.

"Hey, Annie. Hi. I went to New York. I got some of my paintings out of storage. For the Inn. If you want. They're mostly Chappy scenes. A few of them are on my website."

"Wonderful! I can't wait to see the real deal." The fact that he really had come back to the island might be an omen that life would be good again. For all of them. She hoped.

"You need a ride back to the Inn?"

"No thanks. My Jeep's in the lot. But can you come by tomorrow and bring the canvases? Maybe right after lunch?" Thanks to the added hours, she knew that Georgia would be with Donna then.

"Okay. And thanks, Annie. For giving me another chance."

She smiled and tapped the well of the window. "That's what friends are for."

They docked on the Chappy side, and Jonas drove off. Annie walked slowly to her Jeep, wondering how it happened that her spirits were always lifted not necessarily by someone energetic, but often by someone like Jonas who, despite having a heap of issues, was doing the best he could.

Like the hummingbird, she thought.

Once home, Annie sent Kevin away, still not ready to talk to him about the Inn. She defrosted some soup that she'd made late in the winter and thought it might entice Donna to enjoy a homemade Sunday night supper. When Donna finally roused and joined Annie in the kitchen, she extolled the aroma and flavors, though she merely sipped the broth and barely made a dent in the vegetables or the chicken. It seemed that since she'd been forced to face the seriousness of her illness—and have others know it, too—she'd taken a downhill slide. She looked more wan than she had before and only seemed interested in sleeping.

But Annie had come up with an idea that might help perk up the evening and open the door to asking about her birth father.

"I was wondering if you'd like to see some pictures of when I was growing up," she said. "Unless they might upset you."

Donna smiled. "I'd love to see them. Photographs are wonderful gifts. They lend a permanence to life."

It was the perfect answer.

After Annie cleaned up the kitchen and Donna had gone back to the rocker and the quilt, Annie retrieved the album, sat on the end of the sofa that was closest to her, and gingerly opened the cover.

First were Annie's baby pictures, which evoked bittersweet smiles. A tear. Or two.

Then the outside of the house where she'd been raised, followed by shots of Annie's first, second, third birthdays; others of her riding her little tricycle; trying to rake leaves; showing off the matching dresses her mother had made for her and her first American Girl doll. Annie had forgotten how much she'd loved those dolls; every year her dad had given her a new one on her birthday, and her mother had made extra clothes. When Annie and Donna reached the first-day-of-school photos, Annie pointed out the red tartan plaid skirt. Donna commented that her mother had been talented.

Moving ahead, they laughed at the images of the school Thanksgiving play when Annie had played a Wampanoag

(Annie said that Lucy would have loved it!), and of her junior high graduation when her hair was cut to look like Princess Diana's, even though it was black and not blonde. And then there were photos of their vacations on the Vineyard: beach scenes, lighthouses, the historic, up island sheep farm that had been in the same family since 1762. But missing from the collection were pictures of Bob and Ellen Sutton, which hadn't felt strange to Annie until then. But her father had always snapped the photos, and her mother had said she was "camera shy."

Donna seemed to enjoy looking through the album; several times she placed her fingers on Annie's image and made small sounds as if she were laughing. But when they reached the pictures of Annie and Brian's wedding, Annie realized that Donna had not been laughing; she'd been crying.

"Oh!" Annie said, quickly closing the album. "I'm so sorry. I thought you said . . ."

Donna waved her away, and said she needed to go back to bed, that she was just tired again. But she said she'd like to see more on another day.

Annie helped Donna into the bedroom, waited in the hallway while Donna used the bathroom, then walked beside her, assessing her balance, until she got into bed. As Annie reached to turn off the light, Donna grasped Annie's arm, pulled her toward her, and kissed her cheek. Then she closed her eyes and smiled. It was seven o'clock.

Back in the living room, Annie sat in the rocker, and wrapped herself in Ellen Sutton's quilt the way that Donna had. Annie thumbed through the pages of her past again, thought about the people she had lost and who, in a sense, had made way for the new ones she now had. Including John. The man she was going to marry.

After a while she climbed into the twin bed in the corner of the room, covered herself once again with the quilt, and wondered how it happened that life's joys and sorrows often came at the same time.

Monday morning, Annie woke up to the sound of rain and the knowledge that a rainy spring would make for lovely early summer greening, lush plants, and vibrant flowers. Exactly the kind of look that would enhance the beauty of their property.

With a small sigh, she turned her head toward the window; she could barely see the Inn through the fog. It was the kind of day that she relished for writing, its grayness offering permission to tune out the world and escape to her inner calm. To "make stuff up," as Kevin liked to joke. Sometimes Annie liked to walk on the beach in the rain, the break of the waves frothy and energetic, the thwacks and claps onto the shoreline muffled by the mist. But that morning she'd be drenched, even if she donned her yellow slicker.

She made tea and checked the time: six-forty-five. Georgia Nelson had said she'd arrive "mid-morning." Until then, Annie could work. So she set her laptop on the table.

But she couldn't write. She thought about John, about marriage, about where they would live. His townhouse didn't have a separate space she could use as a writing room. Could she live at John's, let Kevin take the cottage, then come over to work at the Inn every day—maybe use the space over the workshop to write when business at the Inn was slow?

"It would look good on paper," she said to herself, and was surprised that Murphy made no comment. Maybe she was sleeping late, as Donna no doubt would be.

But Annie knew she also needed freedom to sit down whenever the muses spoke, even if they arrived in the middle of the night. Would John be okay with that once they were living together?

After a while she gave up overthinking. And pretending

to work. She moved through the bedroom, into the shower, and dressed, all while being quiet so she wouldn't disturb Donna. Then she returned to the kitchen, sat down, and texted Kevin. But he didn't reply. Perhaps he was already up and hammering again. Or painting, because the hammering was finally done, wasn't it?

She wondered if she should wake Donna up before Georgia arrived. Then she decided to leave her be. Maybe added sleep would help her regain some strength, at least enough so she'd feel like eating. And maybe later, after Jonas had come and gone and Georgia had left, Annie and Donna could have the conversation about Annie's birth father.

As Annie's mind drifted again, she wondered if Donna had once hoped her birth father would marry her, cherish their family, and grow old with her. Then Annie wondered what it was going to be like to grow old with John. It will be nice, she thought, to have each other to lean on when their skin started to wrinkle and the rest of them began to fall apart. It would be nice not to have to go through the tricks of Father Time alone.

But knowing that her wandering mind would not accomplish a damn thing, she turned back to her laptop, emitted a soft groan, and finally got to work.

Three cups of tea and a bowl of Special K later, there was a knock on the door. Annie stirred from her made-up world, turned off her computer, and went to welcome Georgia, who was bulked up in a slicker, the top of its hood pulled down to her eyebrows.

"Hallo!" she called.

"Come in, come in," Annie said. "It looks awful out there."

Georgia unsnapped her jacket, shook the bulk of the water off over the sink, then hung it on the doorknob. "We know that rain is good in the spring, but sometimes it's a darned inconvenience." She set her purse and a large notebook that was wrapped in plastic on the floor.

"Donna's not awake yet. Would you care for tea?"

"Oh, yes, that would be delightful. I did get a bit chilled." Georgia sat at the table and looked at the laptop. "Have you been writing this morning?"

Annie smiled while she poured the tea. "A little. I'm starting a new book that should be taking shape faster than it is. Sometimes that happens. Like the rain, it's annoying."

Georgia laughed. She seemed like a nice woman, open and friendly. She asked Annie lots of questions about her writing; in turn, Annie asked how she'd become a hospice nurse. They talked for some time until Georgia looked at her watch. "Oh, my. It's nearly eleven. I should get your mother out of bed so she can start her day."

Not knowing whether or not she should offer to help, Annie settled on saying, "Let me know if you need me."

"Oh, we'll be fine, thanks. I'm an old pro at this." Georgia went into the bedroom, her soft-soled shoes padding across the floor.

Annie wondered if Georgia had ever married someone she'd once dreamed she'd grow old with. Which gave Annie an idea for her book—the couple browsing through the museum who find the skull could be gray-haired and retired; the man could be horrified, while the woman could be thrilled that a real-life murder mystery had brought excitement to their day.

Perfect, she thought. Turning on her computer again, she quickly started to type. Until she was suddenly aware that Georgia was standing, unmoving, in the bedroom doorway.

"She's gone," Georgia said.

Annie blinked. "What? Where? I've been right here. . . ."

Georgia crossed to where Annie sat and took her hand. "No, dear. I mean she's gone. Donna has passed. My best guess is that it occurred sometime during the night."

Annie sat as still as Georgia had been standing. A dull sensation squeezed her head tightly, as if her brain were doing something, though she didn't know what. Was it shifting from reality to . . . disbelief? Or was it the other way around? Winnie had once said that fog was Moshup's blanket, covering the earth and sea to give his people comfort. Was that why it was such a foggy day? And why hadn't Annie been paying attention? She'd tiptoed through the bedroom and back again? While her mother lay there—dead?

She sucked in a loud breath. Her exhale was a cry. For help. For Georgia to say that she'd made a mistake, that Donna was still alive, still breathing in Annie's bed.

"Would you like to see her?" Georgia asked.

Annie flinched.

"Usually, people are glad they did. Later."

Annie supposed it was the right thing to do. So she stood, startled that the muscles in her legs were as numb as her mind had become. She shook her legs, willing the feeling to return. Then she moved into the bedroom.

Donna—her mother, yet a stranger—looked as though she were sleeping. In fact, she looked exactly as she had after she'd kissed Annie's cheek the night before, then closed her eyes and smiled.

Annie sat beside her, took her hand; it was cool. She wanted to cry. But she could not. So she just sat there, staring at Donna, as if waiting for her to wake up.

Then Kevin was in the room. He sat on the other side of the bed and held Donna's other hand.

Annie and Kevin did not speak. They did not have to. The silence was their communication.

The ambulance arrived, though Annie didn't know how much time had elapsed. The faces were familiar; Taylor's wasn't among them. After all, it was far too late for the skills of an EMT.

Whoever the responders were, they strapped Donna to a gurney and took her away.

Later—that night or the next day—Annie remembered that John had been there, that he'd driven Annie and Kevin to his parents' house because Earl and Claire were their family now. At one point, Annie went outside, sat on the deck alone, and stared at the pansies Lucy had planted. She could not bear to be in the same room with Kevin's grief; she'd been too unsure if she was feeling her pain or his.

Then John was there again. Sitting next to her.

"I love you," he said.

And Annie cried, that time knowing that the ache and the tears were hers.

He put his arm around her, and she wept into his chest over so many losses that she remembered too well.

Chapter 31

Annie spent the next days wandering the beaches, collecting wampum, shells, and sea glass for the Inn, and helping Jonas hang several of his lovely paintings in the great room. She did everything quietly, by rote, in a kind of slow motion that got her through to the nights. Kevin had returned to hammering; by then he was attacking moldings in the bedrooms. He seemed to take more solace in doing aggressive work. Annie finally told him that Donna had told her that the money for the Inn had come from her; Kevin had nodded, but there was no need for discussion. Sometime in the future, Annie knew they'd share how much that meant to each of them.

Donna had left instructions that she wished to be cremated; at the end of the week, they held a memorial service at the tiny St. Andrew's Episcopal Church in Edgartown. She'd once commented on how wonderful it was that the sanctuary doors were wide open every day, welcoming all. Annie wondered if Donna might have hoped that she and Kevin could find some comfort there.

"She didn't want to stick around too long," Earl said after the service, when people had gathered in small groups in the compact parish hall and were eating bite-sized sandwiches and tea cakes and sipping coffee from paper cups. "She worried about being a burden on you and your brother."

"I know about the money," Annie said quietly. "She told me she put up the money for the Inn."

Earl sighed. "That she did. Every last bit until she had no more. I didn't contribute one thin dime. Not that I didn't want to. But Lord knows I don't have that kind of cash."

Annie didn't ask how many dimes or dollars it had taken. "You became friends with Donna, didn't you?"

"We did. Claire and I talked to her every week or two. We were her spies; we kept her in the loop on how—and what—you and Kevin were doing. I think we all got a kick out of it."

Annie planted her hands on her hips. "Are you serious?"

Earl chuckled his trademark chuckle. "Yup. It was especially tough keeping that little secret the night you and Donna came for dinner. She never told us about the cancer, though."

So when Annie had walked into Donna's hospital room and seen Earl holding her hand, he must have blushed out of fear that their friendship had been revealed. Not because he'd been flirting with her.

"Nice lady, your mother," he continued now. "She invested her life savings so you and Kevin could have a stable future. Now it's up to us to make it work."

"But we have no control over it. Not now."

"Maybe," Earl said, "maybe not. But we're staying positive, remember?"

Several Edgartown police officers attended the service, along with many of Earl and Claire's friends, kind faces of men and women who Annie recognized—artisans, farmers, tradespeople. Even Marilyn Sunderland, the newspaper reporter who had been John's sixth grade teacher and had been scorned by Earl when he'd fallen in love with Claire. It turned out that she—not John—had been the one to chase the media off Chappy when they had descended, and that by the time John had arrived they were all gone. "No one messes with our island family," Marilyn told Annie as she helped herself to another diminutive sandwich.

Taylor and Jonas were there, too, and they seemed at peace. And Winnie and her whole clan had driven from up island, except for her sister-in-law who was on duty at the hospital and her husband who made his living as a fisherman and sent his blessing: *Wunniook*, be well.

Annie was touched by the outpouring of support for Kevin and her, wash-ashores that many people there hardly knew, and by the respect they showed for a woman most of them had never met.

After a while the crowd began to disperse, back to reality, back to their lives; as Annie stood by the door with Kevin and Earl, saying good-bye, she knew she wanted to embrace the cushion of community forever.

Then Winnie joined them. Her face emitted its calming, copper glow; her deep brown, sassafras-root eyes brimmed with kindness.

"I bring news," she said.

They waited, mute.

Finally, Earl spoke. "Well, get on with it, woman."

"You may have your Inn."

The surrealness of the hour, the day, the week intensified.

"What?" Annie asked, because one of them needed to.

"The bone is Native American. It is very old—probably nineteenth century—but not Wampanoag. Most important, it was not buried on your land; the archeologist determined it had come in from the water, possibly from a drowning, and had become tightly wrapped in the seaweed, which, when combined with the salt in the ocean, helped preserve the bone once it lodged in the rocks."

Annie didn't mention that Lucy had suggested that in the beginning. Such a smart girl, with such a bright future.

"Of course, no one can tell for certain how long ago that happened," Winnie was continuing. "But our tribal council will arrange a proper burial. Most likely in the sacred ground overlooking Cape Poge Bay."

Annie let the news sink in for a few seconds, then she signaled to John. He joined them, as did Lucy.

With Annie's hands pressing her cheeks, she said, "It's over. The Inn is ours."

Winnie repeated the details.

"But he's one of ours, right?" Lucy asked.

It took a moment to recall that Lucy's DNA had showed that she was a sliver of Native American.

"He's not Wampanoag, but, yes, indigenous," Winnie said. "The tribe will treat him gently and with reverence. And the council won't stop the Inn from opening. They felt no need to pursue it after I explained your promise to help the island, by doing your small part."

"Well, okay then," Lucy said, and added, "I'm not surprised the thing is old on account of the water and the seaweed, but I had kind of hoped it was that lady from the *City of Columbus*."

Kevin and Earl exchanged eye rolls; Annie simply grinned, focusing instead on how pleased Donna would be that it looked as if her children now had a chance for a stable future.

The days that followed accelerated, as Earl and Kevin hurried to finish the rooms for the year-round tenants first.

"Once they're settled," Earl said, "we'll do our best to get the tourists comfortable. If we miss the first part of the season, so be it. The islanders are more important, right?"

Kevin and Annie agreed.

Jonas joined their efforts; Taylor did not. Maybe after things had quieted down, Annie would ask Kevin if he knew why.

They'd also managed to come up with much-needed money. Though Donna's cash coffers were depleted, Kevin secured a quick loan from the bank against the sale of her apartment. And Annie was able to get one against the advance for her new book, thanks to Mark and his outrageous debts. Who knew she'd ever say those words? But it turned out that having cleared up his debts had earned her a terrific credit score. Together, Annie and Kevin raised enough to settle up with the suppliers, to pay for the remaining materials, and to arrange to ship the rest of the furniture.

Before Annie knew it, it was the morning of another Friday—with only one week left until their tenants and first guests would arrive. They would be greeted by Harlin Pierce's energetic marimba band and more food, drink, and merriment than Chappaquiddick had seen since, well, perhaps since the Flanagan wedding last summer. Undoubtedly with a better outcome than that night had seen.

She stood in the great room now, gazing at the furnishings—graceful wing chairs upholstered in a soft color of sea glass; exquisitely handcrafted (right there on Chappy) wooden end tables and side tables; simple, yet perfect Vineyard-natural tchotchkes, as Earl called them. Most of all, Jonas's lovely paintings filled the room with the beauty of island life.

"Do you think people will like them?" Jonas asked.

Annie hadn't heard him come into the room. And when she turned to face him, she was surprised to see Taylor with him.

"They're beautiful," Annie said. "Don't you agree, Taylor?"

The auburn-haired woman nodded. "They belong here. So does my son."

"We have something to show you," Jonas said, then held a small box out to Annie.

She took it, opened it. Inside were two silver bands. They looked like wedding bands.

"My dad bought them," Jonas said. "They're engraved inside with the date when he and my mom were supposed to get married."

Taking out one of the rings, Annie held it to the light. She saw a date; next to that, it read "Hawaii." "It's beautiful," she said.

"Derek had already bought the rings and had them engraved before the accident," Taylor said. "I gave Jonas the rings, along with the receipt, so now he has solid proof. Derek really did want to marry me; we were supposed to be a family. And we really were going to move to Hawaii. Derek had inherited a small house from his grandfather on the big island. I'm going to go there now, at least for a while. Legally, the place is Jonas's, but I might eventually move there permanently, as long as it's all right with Jonas."

"Only if I can come and visit," Jonas said.

"And as long as you stay here and take care of the house." She looked back at Annie. "My place on Chappaquiddick is now his house as well."

Annie handed back the ring, trying to process everything. "So you two are okay?"

"Better than okay," Jonas said. "Mom not only had these rings, but she's also got a letter from my grandfather to her. He's the one who gave her money for college and for her mother and father. But he didn't send it to her until after they took me. In the letter, he said he hoped she'd accept the check as recognition for the love that she and my dad had for each other, and for their appreciation that she'd honored his memory by giving me to them. Which proves she didn't give me to them for the money."

"I thought that they'd give you a better life than I could have."

Annie thought about it. "But you never used these things to prove your innocence?"

"No," Taylor replied. "Because I knew I hadn't done anything wrong." She lowered her eyes. "Please tell Kevin that I've gone. I wish it could have been different for us, but things don't always work out the way we hope. He and I had fun, but I know he doesn't want me in his life. But I do want him to be happy." Then she checked her watch. "I've got to run; I'm on the two thirty to Boston. I'm flying out tonight. Good luck with the Inn. I admit I wasn't sure at first, but it's been nice having you around." She started to shake Annie's hand, but Annie stepped closer and gave Taylor a hug. She felt it was the least she could do.

An hour later, Kevin returned from a mission of tackling errands in Edgartown. He had a paper bag in one arm, a bunch of plump yellow tulips in the other.

"For you," he said, handing Annie the flowers. "Because you are my sister, and I love you, and I don't think I ever could have managed these past weeks without you."

Annie fought back tears. She took the flowers and said, "I'm not sure vases are in the budget."

"I ran into Claire on the boat. She said a canning jar will do the trick."

Annie laughed. "What's in the bag?"

He pressed his lips together. "Mom's ashes. I picked them up at the funeral home."

Annie's laughter faded; she didn't know what to say.

"If you're not too busy," Kevin continued, "maybe we could spread them this afternoon? Before this place opens and we get too crazy?"

Donna had wanted her ashes sprinkled in the water off

South Beach. It had seemed odd because, as far as Annie knew, Donna only had been there one morning with Annie when they'd been exploring the island together, back when they'd first met. Perhaps it had meant more to Donna than Annie realized.

She drew in a long breath. "Do you want to go now?"

"I was hoping you'd say that."

She followed her brother across the room, stopping to rearrange a group of wampum on a side table. She knew it wouldn't be the last time that she fussed with them; she hoped their guests would enjoy doing the same.

Before heading outside, Annie stopped in the kitchen, pulled a pitcher from a cabinet, set it on the gorgeous new counter, and arranged the flowers. Then, as she turned to leave, she stopped and plucked two yellow tulips—so each of them could toss one into the waves along with their mother's ashes.

The sand was cool beneath her bare feet as Annie and Kevin traversed the path that led to the dunes and onto South Beach. The light breeze and the sunshine created an Instagram-worthy morning; the tide was growing high, curling in toward shore, its ribbons of white rising from the water and kissing the earth; the pinkletinks had passed their singing duties on to the island birds, now that summer was nearly there.

As Annie stood on the beach, the sun warmed her face; the presence of her brother warmed her heart.

Best of all, they saw no one else, no lone fisherman, no teenagers who'd cut school, no black dogs scampering between the waves. It was only them, their tiny family, now minus one.

"Before we do this, I have a couple of things to tell you," Kevin said.

Whenever anyone led with that line, Annie braced herself. "Okay."

He nodded, shifting the bag that contained the box of ashes to his other arm. "Jonas texted me. He said Taylor's gone."

"I know."

"It's for the best. My heart was never really in it with her."

"I know that, too. It's fine, Kevin. She's fine."

He sighed. "Remember when I asked you to pick Mom up at the boat? Remember that I said I needed time to breathe before she got here?"

"I do." Annie couldn't imagine what was coming next; she hoped it wasn't something negative about Donna.

"It wasn't because of Mom," he said, as if reading Annie's mind. He hesitated, then looked out over the water. "And it had nothing to do with Taylor. It was about me. I'd just received a call from my attorney. He told me my divorce went through."

Annie bit her lip. "Oh, Kevin . . ."

He nodded again, keeping his eyes fixed on the horizon. "Yeah, it kind of sucks."

"Are you okay?"

He shrugged. "Sure. Sometimes. Most times. I've had a few distractions, y'know?"

"But you've kept it to yourself all this time?"

He shifted the box again. "Yeah. We had other priorities."

She looped her arm through his and followed his gaze. "Please don't let 'priorities' stop you from telling me anything again."

"I'll try not to. That's a promise." Then he reached into the bag. Instead of pulling out the box of ashes, he withdrew a white, letter-sized envelope. "Speaking of promises, this is for you. It's from Mom. She gave it to me when I brought her back from the hospital. The back is glued with sealing wax—

she must have done that when she was still in Boston. She told me it was so I'd keep my big nose out of it." He laughed as he handed it over. "She knew me so well."

Taking the envelope, Annie closed her eyes and pressed it to her chest. Donna must have written her a letter—another letter, like the one she'd sent so long ago. Annie stood very still for a moment, then she said, "I think I'll save this for a later day, okay? Like maybe after the Inn has opened and I can take my time to read it?" She still hadn't let Kevin and Earl remove the twin bed from her living room in the cottage; Annie continued to sleep there, wishing that Donna were asleep in the next room.

"Whenever you want," Kevin said. "I don't think it has a deadline."

Annie tucked the letter in her pocket. Then they took turns sprinkling small cupfuls of ashes, saying silent prayers. When the box was empty, they each tossed in a tulip and watched as the last flecks of silver ash and yellow petals dissolved into the surf.

Chapter 32

The Friday of Memorial Day weekend arrived quickly, and with it came last minute scurrying and a few close calls: Did anyone buy a toaster? (No. Hence, a quick trip to Granite, the store for almost everything.) Why were there seven bedrooms but only six sets of linens? (Oops. Back to Granite.) If it rained, where could they set up the marimba band? (Harlin, their multitalented tenant and the leader of the band, suggested that they could construct a canopy on the terrace, using the tarps Kevin and Earl had used for painting; the musicians could set up under that. Everyone agreed it would be fun, rain or shine.)

Finally, between Annie, Kevin, Earl, and Jonas (who had been eager to pitch in), they were ready. Which was good, as Claire had sent tons of invites (not "e" ones, but "real ones," she'd said) to islanders for the Grand Opening of The Vineyard Inn. She'd already set up a table in the front foyer where she planned to greet visitors and hand them one of the Inn's brochures that Annie had made at the last minute, thanks to her experience with the Garden Tour the previous summer.

At eleven thirty, the tourists who'd reserved rooms arrived (early). The party was scheduled to start at one o'clock, so everyone could enjoy the afternoon, which, thankfully, the weather folks predicted was going to be beautiful. And surprisingly warm.

Having settled the tourists and the year-round tenants into their rooms and shared smiles at their oohs and ahhs, Annie was in the kitchen, where the caterers were finding their way around. She knew she was in the way, but she was trying to avert her eyes from the backyard where Kevin and Jonas were now hauling the twin bed up from the cottage to put in the Inn where it belonged. She turned from the window; sleeping in her own bed that night would be a final sign that Donna was really gone. That, and the sealing-waxed envelope that Annie hadn't yet opened, had been her remaining ways of holding on to her birth mother. She'd decided to open the envelope the next morning, after the Grand Opening was done. She'd be alone; John had a midnight-to-noon shift, with long days and nights in the near future, because, as of that very day, another Vineyard summer had officially begun.

"Hey, Annie," Jonas said as the men jostled their way into the kitchen, raising the bed over their heads, "John and Lucy are here. And the dog. They're outside talking to a girl who wants to see you."

"Who?" Annie didn't want to be distracted.

Jonas shrugged and only said, "Don't know. But she looks cool."

Kevin laughed, and they paraded past the caterers, their bounty held high.

Annie marveled at how much Jonas had changed, how his shyness had abated now that he'd come to terms with his mother, now that he could look forward to summer and to getting his career off to a good start. Annie felt a little sad for Taylor, but glad for her that she'd moved on. Taylor had already sent a post card from Hawaii, but hadn't written "Wish you were here." As for Kevin, Annie could only hope that, in time, he would find happiness again.

She excused herself from the caterers and went out to the yard.

She saw John and Lucy talking to someone whose back was toward her. Restless, of course, was the first one to spot Annie. He bounced toward her and leaped onto her white jeans and red-and-white-striped jersey top.

"Stop!" Annie cried. "Please! I love you, but get down!"

John and Lucy simultaneously called off the dog; the person they'd been talking with turned around.

"Oh!" Annie cried. "You're here!" It was Francine—beautiful, and so grown-up—all the way from Minnesota. She was holding Bella, the dark-haired, dark-eyed child who was no longer a baby but a real little girl. Annie began to cry; so did Francine.

"I'm here to work for the summer," Francine said. "If you'll have me."

"Of course! Your room is almost ready. In fact, your bed just walked by." Annie knew it would give her comfort to know that the bed was for either Francine or Bella.

"John told me about your mom, Annie. I'm so sorry."

"So am I. But this is a day to celebrate. Not only the Inn, but especially now because you're home." They hugged and cried, and Restless danced at their feet until John said, "Hey, break it up, okay? I want to kiss my fiancée."

Francine's eyes darted from John back to Annie. "Did I hear him right?"

"You did. We don't know when yet, but you're invited. In fact, would you like to be a bridesmaid?"

"I'm going to be the maid of honor," Lucy interjected, in case anyone had forgotten she was there.

"Absolutely," Francine said, then added, "I'm so happy for you!" They hugged again, and Restless danced some more, but Bella grew, well, restless, and wanted to get down.

"Lucy?" John asked. "How about if you take the dog down to the beach? So these ladies can go inside and see Gramma."

The next hour passed so quickly Annie felt as if she were in a trance. And then the guests started to arrive. By two o'clock it seemed that half the Vineyard population was there, all of whom were thrilled with, as Earl described it, "what they've done with the old place."

Meandering around the lawn, Annie caught sight of the meadow that sprawled next to the Inn: it was filled with yellow buttercups that had blossomed just in time, as if a small part of Ellen Sutton had come to celebrate with them.

Filled with happiness and love, Annie wove around Earl, who was talking with a couple of John's police-officer friends; she smiled at Claire, who had given away all the brochures and now stood, socializing with people Annie recognized from the garden club; and she watched Marilyn Sunderland, who seemed to wink at Earl every chance she got. Harlin's marimba band was a huge hit as the musicians lit up the terrace, and some of the guests began to dance. Harlin had noticeably been checking out Francine; if he had his eye on her, Annie suspected he'd have to compete with Jonas.

Annie smiled as she thought about the days ahead; joy, after all, often was infectious.

She also knew that joy could be interrupted in a heartbeat, which was what happened when Lucy appeared again, back from the beach with Restless in tow and something firmly set between his teeth.

Annie saw them first. She rushed over at a decided clip, maneuvering around unsuspecting guests who were admiring the view of the harbor and the Edgartown Light. "Lucy!" she whispered, as the mallets of the marimba speeded up the tempo. "What are you doing? What's he got?"

Before Lucy could answer, John was behind her.

"I'm not sure!" Lucy cried. "Restless found it on the beach—is it another bone?"

Annie's whole body went rigid, her heart and lungs and everything inside her dropped like a schooner mast in a nor'easter.

Suddenly, Earl, too, appeared.

And Kevin.

And Claire.

John bent down and pulled the thing from the dog's mouth.

The crowd grew silent, then the band stopped playing.

John held the thing up for everyone to see. "It's a damn plastic bottle," he said.

Hearty cheers rose up from the lawn.

"Put it in the recycle bin," John said to his daughter. "And try to stay out of trouble."

Looking somewhat dejected, Lucy shuffled to the bins.

"Was it really plastic?" Annie asked as he whisked her away.

He shrugged. "Looked that way to me." Then he took her by the elbow, and they went back to the party.

Annie woke up in the morning to the sounds of island songbirds; saltmarsh sparrows, eastern towhees, and red-eyed vireos were no doubt among those who had arrived in nature's procession after the pinkletinks had quieted. She lay in her bed again, surprised that she'd had a wonderful night's sleep. The Grand Opening had been a big success; reporters from both island newspapers (not only Marilyn) and online Vineyard sites had been there, taking notes and looking pleased. Claire reported a head count of two hundred fifty-two, not counting the caterers or the band or the people who now lived there.

Taking a deep breath, Annie said aloud, "We did it." She hoped that Donna and Murphy were both listening.

Then she sat up, dangled her legs over the edge of the

bed, and opened the drawer of her nightstand. She took out the white envelope, then slowly peeled off its wax seal. She paused a moment, then reached inside and pulled out a single sheet of paper. A small gold key was attached.

My dearest Annie, the note read.

You are reading this because I'm gone. I am so sorry we could not have had more time, but please know that I cherished every moment we spent together. I am so proud of you, of the woman you are. I am even more proud that you had the courage to reach out to meet me at last. I hope you know that.

I'm attaching the key to the Louis Vuitton trunk. I will have already told you that the things in the pocket inside the lid are for Kevin; the rest is yours.

Some time ago, when you asked about your birth father, I was deliberately vague. He and I had made a promise to each other that as long as either of us was alive, we would keep our secret. He loved you; I loved you. More than you will ever know. I hope you'll understand that, and that you will take comfort from what you will find in the Vuitton.

My love forever,
Donna

Annie waited a moment, then drew in a long breath. She crouched to the floor in front of the trunk; her hands and her legs were trembling. Still, she found the strength to insert the small key into the brass lock and turn it once. *Click.*

Slowly, she raised the lid. And stared at two stacks of what looked like very large notebooks.

Before taking them out, she reached into the pocket of the inside lid; she pulled out a small blue ribbon: FIRST PLACE, DORCHESTER ELEMENTARY SCHOOL, 1956. Then she took out a brochure: RED SOX–YANKEES LINE-UP, MAY 17, 1990. Along with it was a ticket stub. And then there was a photo album. She opened it; the first page read: *Kevin Raymond MacNeish*. That's when Annie realized that Donna must have taken back her maiden name after her divorce and changed Kevin's name to hers. She'd been an amazing woman.

Then she saw the pictures. Of Kevin. And his dad. Playing catch. Riding horses on a carousel. Fishing in a small stream using poles that looked like they were made of branches from a tree.

Kevin and his dad. The man he barely remembered. Annie emitted a small cry. She knew that Kevin didn't know that these photos existed. Donna had protected him by helping him move on.

Happiness flooded through her; she knew how much the things would mean to her awesome brother.

After a few minutes, she put them back into the pocket of the trunk, knowing that her time had now come.

She held her breath and reached for the first notebook. It was heavy, filled with pages. But as soon as she turned back the cover, she realized it was not a notebook but a photo album, similar to Kevin's.

She was greeted by a picture of herself. As an infant. It was the same image that was in the blue album in her bookcase. *Annie*, someone had printed beneath it. *Three days old*. The nuns must have provided the picture to both the birth mother and the parents who'd adopted Annie. How nice of them, she thought. Next to the photo a tiny bracelet had been taped; it was strung with lettered beads that spelled out *Baby MacNeish*, followed by her birth date.

Annie bit her lip, found her courage, and turned the page. And there was a photo of her dad holding her. The caption read: *Bob and Annie, one week old*.

Annie was confused. Why would the nuns have given

Donna a picture of Annie with Bob Sutton, her dad? Wasn't it a closed adoption? Had Donna known who'd taken her?

The next page showed Annie in a highchair at the table in the kitchen where she'd grown up. *Annie, one year*, it read.

She skimmed through the albums. Photo after photo was of *her*, taken on her birthdays—one, two, three—and days in between: the first-day-of-school pictures, her prom, graduation. And more. Many that were already in Annie's blue album, but also many more that she'd never seen. Tucked between the pages were programs from school plays Annie had acted in, newspaper clippings from when she'd received Girl Scout merit badges, the announcement of when she'd been accepted into college.

It made no sense to her, no sense at all. And then, in the bottom of the trunk, were six boxes. She recognized the packaging: each held a different American Girl doll. Instinctively, she knew that they'd been hers; she remembered that they'd disappeared when she'd gone off to college. She picked one up; it held the doll that wore the red plaid dress Ellen had made that matched Annie's skirt and the swatch that was now in the quilt.

That's when Annie saw another note. It was attached to the bottom of the trunk. It was not in Donna's handwriting, but her dad's.

Annie, my wonderful Annie,

By the time you read this, both your birth mother and I will be gone. Please know that we thought it was best never to tell you while one of us was still alive; we did that for you, and for Ellen, the only mother that you knew.

Donna and I met one summer on Martha's Vineyard. She was a waitress at the Blue Lagoon Restaurant, and we fell in love at first sight. One

Vineyard morning, we had a picnic on South Beach—do
you remember where that is? How we loved it there. It
was quiet back then. And magical.

But I was much older than she was, and I was
married to Ellen. We had our share of problems, mostly
because we couldn't conceive a baby, and she was very
angry about that. When I met Donna, Ellen and I were
separated.

Donna and I loved each other very much, but I felt
awfully guilty. After that summer, we decided I should
go back to Ellen and see how she was doing. She was my
wife, after all. I felt I owed her that, and Donna agreed.
But we said we'd stay in touch.

Three months later, after I'd reconciled with Ellen,
I received a letter from Donna. She told me she was
pregnant.

Neither of us knew what to do. We were so conflicted;
we were moral, respectable people who'd fallen in love. So
we arranged for a private adoption; we agreed that Ellen
and I would raise you as our own. And that perhaps one
day Donna and I could be together. The memories of my
time with her on the Vineyard were deep—and why I
wanted to go back every year. I wanted to feel the kind of
happiness again that I'd felt with her. And I often did,
especially as you grew up, whenever I saw her in your eyes
and your hair and your beautiful face.

I never saw Donna again. We both carried so much
guilt, and we wanted to do what was best for you. At that
time, divorce was still a stigma, never mind what we had
done. Sometimes we wrote, and I sent her lots of pictures
and other news of you. Your American Girl dolls had all
been gifts from her. I pretended that I'd bought them.

After many years, she married, and staying in touch
became too difficult. When you went to college, I returned

the dolls to her so she'd have something that had been a nice part of your childhood.

Ellen never knew the truth about your birth. And if she's still alive when you read this, I trust that you won't share it with her.

I love you so much, Annie. You have been the greatest joy in my life. And while it's true that you were unexpected, you were never, ever, a mistake.

I hope, in time, you will forgive us. But Donna and I had agreed that at some point it would be only fair to you to let you know who your real father was. It was me. One and the same. I hope that's okay with you.

Because we had a pretty good life, didn't we, kiddo?

Much love,
Daddy

Annie stared, unmoving, at the letter. She wanted to tell Kevin that she now knew why Donna had wanted her ashes sprinkled off of South Beach. She wanted to tell John—and Lucy—she knew who her birth father was. She wanted to tell Earl and Claire and, especially, Winnie. Because in Winnie's words, now that Annie knew her past, she might be better able to guide her future.

But those things were to come. Right then, more than anything, Annie only wanted to sit a while longer, and reread the letter from her dad. And then read it again.

It's okay, my friend, she heard Murphy's voice. *I'm right here beside you. In fact, all of us are.*

Author's Note

Martha's Vineyard is a destination for summer magic: festivals and fairs; music, shops, and restaurants; sailing days and clambake nights. And, of course, sunbathing on beaches, beaches, beaches—it's an island, after all. But when my wonderful editor, Wendy McCurdy, suggested this new Vineyard series, we agreed I should go beyond the summer fun and delve into the year-round experience of true islanders.

From natives to wash-ashores, full-time residents are eclectic and diverse, a blend of cultures and customs, a cacophony of talents and ideas. Together they are the foundation of the island's vibrant spirit of community. And, when mingling with summer residents and visitors, interesting things can happen.

My main character, Annie Sutton, a bestselling mystery novelist, moved from Boston to the Vineyard to put her past behind her. But whoever penned the saying "Wherever you go, there you are" must have had Annie in mind. Since the series debut, *A Vineyard Christmas*, Annie has been faced with truths about herself and the ongoing challenges that they still pose in her wonderful but very real world.

I hope you're enjoying this series. Book number four, *A Vineyard Crossing*, will be published soon. It promises more choppy waters ahead—plus an unexpected bombshell or two. I'm rooting for Annie to navigate it all. But who knows?

—*Jean Stone*